THE DEVIL COMES TO BONN

Jennifer Harris

Matador
Unit E2 Airfield Business Park,
Harrison Road, Market Harborough,
Leicestershire. LE16 7UL
Tel: 0116 2792299
Email: books@troubador.co.uk
Web: www.troubador.co.uk/matador
Twitter: @matadorbooks

ISBN 978 1803137 629

British Library Cataloguing in Publication Data.
A catalogue record for this book is available from the British Library.

Typeset in 11pt Baskerville by Troubador Publishing Ltd, Leicester, UK

Matador is an imprint of Troubador Publishing Ltd

For Rufus
For Rory
For Joel

The devil can cite Scripture for his purpose
An evil soul, producing holy witness,
Is like a villain with a smiling cheek,
A goodly apple rotten at the heart.

William Shakespeare
The Merchant of Venice Act II scene III, 99–102

The devil can cite heritage for his purpose…

PROLOGUE

BONN 1941

A LOOK SO PRECIOUS it cut.

Wolfish and veiled, they were not quite Kurt's eyes. Almost recognisable. Maybe a trick of torch light in the dark, wartime street. Far, far too late for Hildegard to understand. Kurt sat wedged in the black army car between two officers, their shoulders like iron blocks, his gold hair shining.

Only minutes ago, he had refused to see his young wife as he turned from the cold ash in the grate and faced soldiers ransacking their tiny living room. Now from the car, he gave back that lost moment, but with a stranger's eyes. Not Kurt's. They flickered across her—cherished, embracing, but alien. She would remember that was the first moment that she saw those eyes and the last.

Hildegard limped over the cobbles, reaching out as the Mercedes-Benz slid away with darling Kurt, further and further into the night until she could not keep up. SS lightning bolts bordered the number plate, and hooded tail lights washed blood-red arcs across walls and doors in the medieval lane. The car rolled towards the basilica and vanished.

She stood in the middle of the road while overhead a portent of monumental change gathered strength. Tens of thousands of blackbirds trilled as they lifted into the autumn migration, a vast, deafening mass, black over the rooftops of Bonn, filling the whole sky, muffling the sounds of the city, blocking out the stars as they flew south.

Hildegard stumbled home and bolted the door. As she drew the curtain, a blackbird, adrift from the flock, landed on the outside ledge. A yellow-rimmed eye peered in.

ONE

BONN 2015

WARNING BLACK DECALS of birds dotted the glass walls of the old West German Bundeshaus in Bonn. Eagles shot up, wings folded over curved bodies, sleek like cannons. Others hurtled earthward, wings arced, piked beaks splitting. Perspiration coursed down Stella's back as she halted to squint at splayed razor talons, black and glossy against greenish glass walls. They took her back to school days and the startling, evolutionary link between dinosaurs and birds. Bored teenagers, suddenly engaged, seized on evidence in the skin of a bird's claw—thick, ancient, reptilian—as if wrapped in scabs and scars. Scabs protected the body, but if you picked at them, you bled.

Stella blotted her neck as she dodged historians, archaeologists, architects, politicians and journalists, all of them flapping fans on the hot driveway of the old Bundeshaus, now a glass-walled conference centre which reflected heat and glare—a stiff price for the architectural metaphor of post-war German transparency. Beyond the pang of melting bitumen, the River Rhine emitted that slightly mouldy smell of warm freshwater as it swirled into sedge and stone wall cracks, whipping up blotchy froth of mud and bird dung.

Inside the conference auditorium, video screens in the lower chamber lit up: *Welcome to the World Heritage Committee Meeting Bonn Germany 2015*. Chatter, laughter and loud phone conversations filled the air. Through the glass balustrading in front of her knees, Stella watched preparations in the lower chamber for the afternoon session. Delegates plodded back to their desks to vote on sites for admission to the World Heritage List.

Stella inspected her last scab, shrinking on her elbow, but pulled and puckered and late to heal. A throb strummed up from her wrist as she waited in the first seat of the first row of the Observers' Gallery, a U-shaped mezzanine. She rubbed her arm, willing away a tenacious ache. Her arm felt foreign after six weeks in plaster, weeks of pretence to university colleagues: 'Clumsy old me'. The left arm retained its spray of freckles, but the right had faded and withered. She danced her fingertips along the pale skin which Peter kissed when he saw it released from the cast. 'Welcome back,' he said, as if he had not broken his wife's arm.

She stopped rubbing. The only way to survive was to pretend that everything was ok. Surely, the last few weeks *had* been about survival with Peter, not complicity. Not quite. Same old story for every woman.

Hot and jet-lagged, Stella struggled to keep her eyes open at her fifth annual World Heritage Committee Meeting. The Bundeshaus air-conditioning laboured. A stench of sweat swelled steadily over the semi-circle rows of blue seats as observers returned to the mezzanine. A woman in a summery orange jacket blotted her face as she paused on the aisle steps to the right of Stella's seat. Stella pulled in her legs to let her pass as she drowsily numbered fourteen hand-written pages of notes from the morning World Heritage discussion on the River Jordan where John the Baptist baptised Jesus, a heritage site that she wanted to visit—one day. With Peter? Perhaps. She hoped so, but…

She flipped through her notes, enough for two academic papers on the politics of World Heritage if she sliced and diced the topic. Maybe even three if she diced to a mince. Better yet, she'd grind that mince and show everyone that she was not a new professor resting on her laurels. What a thrill it had been to order business cards and add 'Professor' to her name. She had two hundred crisp, new cards to give out.

Below, a garden door opened; the blazing July day sucked a fug of humidity off the Rhine and swirled it inside. Against the auditorium glass, the garden crushed, green and sticky, strident with insects. Claws flared in bird decals, ready to snatch and shred.

A thump on her back.

Her head bounced off the glass balustrading in front of her. Pen and note pad shot from her lap to the floor.

Stella flung herself back, forehead on fire from the bash on the glass. 'Hey!'

A man hovered, his plump, middle-aged face shining with sweat; his eyes hard, bored, glazed in detachment.

'Get out! This is my seat.'

She pressed a hand to her forehead. 'I don't understand.'

His grey and black moustache lifted in what seemed a habitual sneer with the skin under his nose permanently wrinkled.

'The seat's mine.'

'Excuse me, it's mine.'

She smoothed her polka-dot jacket. 'Excuse me?' Why be polite? He hit her! With his brief case? His hand? She lowered her eyes. Expensive, black, leather brogues menaced from the aisle steps on her right. The man loomed over her. Looming, she hated it. Her ears rang and the rows of seats became fuzzy-blue as the U-shaped gallery slipped out of focus.

Seats behind and to the side filled up with people from everywhere, but no one noticed what was happening to her? She twisted to face the three people in the row behind, but they were deep in a conversation in Chinese. In the background, at least two hundred observers chatted or stared into the middle distance, fanning themselves with glossy heritage magazines which snapped back and forth. She turned to the few people who shared with her the almost empty front row. A man sweated in a brown woollen suit, his jaw set, reading the cover of a Cyrillic script magazine. The woman in the orange jacket watched from four seats away. She raised her eyebrows and shrugged as if to say: 'Men, what can we do?'

In the chamber below, senior World Heritage Committee members took their places on the podium in front of the voting delegates. The session was about to start; a hush settled on the upper and lower floors but Stella was caught in an awkward exchange.

The man's brogues inched closer. 'Give me my seat.'

She would not be that type of woman who caused a rumpus. 'It's my seat. I'm here!' Stella cringed; her voice was too loud.

A tap on her shoulder. A Chinese woman put a finger on her lips. 'Shhh.'

Stella started to apologise, but the looming man arched further over her body.

'Move!'

The word had two syllables in his accented English. His head took up the whole right side of her vision with a breathtaking look of entitlement. Now everyone was watching; it was too embarrassing. 'Shhh…' hissed along the rows, even from the man who had been reading Cyrillic.

The bag strap on the looming man sliced across his stomach flab; he clamped his suit jacket under his arm and a runnel of sweat dribbled down his left forearm. Her neck and face scarlet, Stella stared into the lower chamber, counting: one, two, three. Breathe slowly. Routine. That would help, as it had in the past. She opened her notebook. Four, five…keep control. She needed someone to join her in asking him to take another seat, but the new professor in an unseemly altercation? She'd never live it down.

4

A seat, it might seem trivial. She was not heroic Rosa Parks in 1955, retaining her Alabama bus seat against a white man and brutal, racist oppression. She was not igniting sparks in the US civil rights movement, but it was her seat and yet another man demanded that a woman move. It seemed an outrageous comparison, but banal, everyday insults could explode into the monumental.

The man's threatening bulk blocked Stella's view. She heard cables slithering and camera cases bashing against seats. Journalists and camera operators must have been arriving on the right side of the gallery, but she could not see them.

The man knuckled hard into her shoulders. 'This is my place. I need it to observe my delegation.'

She struggled to keep her voice low. 'But you can see into the lower gallery from anywhere. Help yourself. And sir—'

He punched the back of her seat. Thug! Blotches of heat inflamed her face. She itched to scratch his throat, but no one became a university Vice-Chancellor after that disgraceful scene. She calculated taking a stand, thrusting his horrible head up and away, but the career loss yawned in front of her. Professorships could be stripped.

From the seat behind, 'shhh, shhh' filled her ears.

Below, a spokeswoman tapped a microphone. 'Testing, testing.'

Someone sneezed. A mobile phone rang. Instantly shut off. Chatter died. It should have been an exceptional professional afternoon, one that fascinated her and advanced her career. Instead, she found herself pointing to hundreds of identical blue seats.

'Behold, seats!' Too loud again.

'I want *this* seat.'

Ah…so it was 'want'. Tough luck, buddy, I was here first.

The man reading Cyrillic script whispered angrily. 'Quiet!'

The looming man's eyes narrowed and his garlicky breath settled on the right side of her neck, hot and greasy. He shifted his weight and gravity rammed his satchel into the side of her mouth.

5

'Ah!' A stabbing pain flared from her chin. 'Stop!'

Stella's voice rose, not by much, but more than she wanted. The blur in her head crisped into white-hot anger, crackling from her skull to the base of her spine. A broken arm, and now—a fractured jaw? More pretence coming up. Oafish me!

The man reading Cyrillic twisted sharply. 'Enough!'

The woman in orange turned and then looked away. Stella's lips swelled into a tractor tyre, but she wouldn't cause a fuss; she'd look hysterical. If she got up for ice, it would mean abandoning her seat. She'd look crazy if she then asked for it back. Victory to another bully. The politics of gendered behaviour were too complex.

She checked that the man's bag had not dislodged her new earrings, pink baroque pearls from Peter. Her anger at Peter and fury with the man fused, her visceral response sickeningly familiar—a tense stomach, confusion, sneaking self-doubt. But she wouldn't move. She wouldn't! A flush surged up her neck; ears burnt in the mess of her hair. Those explosive feelings again.

She tried to whisper. 'The chair announced free seating. Leave me alone or I'll call an usher.'

She looked up to his face hanging over her right side. Eyes wide, mouth tilting between a gape and a sardonic grin. Was he going to give in? She took a second to study his hair in transition to baldness, thick grey on the sides, but wispy on top. Most startling was a vestige of lime green hair dye.

Photographs of stony, Biblical streets transformed the giant screens in the lower chamber, but she found it difficult to concentrate on ancient Ephesus, the first site for discussion. The man hung even closer, not moving as the session began. A ripple of pleasure rose in murmurs of happy memories from the gallery behind. Many observers had visited the home of the famous words, 'love is patient, love is kind', from St Paul's *First Letter to the Corinthians*. Stella leaned forward to study the amphitheatre of Ephesus and, for the first time, spotted a business card taped to the glass balustrade. 'Professor Giovanni Costa, Cultural Heritage Services, Archaeologist, Via Nazionale, Roma, Italia.' The man had scrawled 'KEEP OUT! MY SEAT' across the top in a faltering red ballpoint pen. The card was barely visible against the patchwork of people below.

A tatty business card! Not enough authority to save a seat, not nearly enough. Why justify herself? She would not move, and taking notes would demonstrate it. She opened her writing pad to where, so recently, she had posed scholarly questions. She scribbled a spiral, glanced at his elegant shoes—she'd lost her train of thought.

Shock. Jacket buttons scratched her face. The man flung himself across Stella, from the aisle steps into the seat on her left when he could have selected from at least a dozen spare seats in the front row. Brute!

But she had kept her seat. A mortifying spectacle, but this woman had not moved.

Professor Giovanni Costa settled into the second seat by thrusting his shoulder hard against hers, forcing her own body to pinion her fragile right arm against the armrest. Pain zipped from wrist to neck.

With the incandescent truth of hindsight, Stella should have moved, nothing more than scooting along three plush blue seats—a passionless life blip—but she had not. Life should not veer off course because of a mere seat.

But it was *her* seat.

In abjection, Stella would look back. She had stayed put and over the next few days mutated into a rash, lying, heartless, violent criminal and, *ergo*, hell bent on destroying family and career.

A spurt of wrath unlike any other she had known. I know who you are, Giovanni Costa.

TWO

PROFESSOR GIOVANNI COSTA got up from the seat next to Stella at the end of the afternoon session, but did not look at her. He walked to the end of the almost empty row, bumping his bag over the legs of the woman in the orange jacket, who caught Stella's eye and shook her head in exasperation.

Stella stretched her arms. Costa had not let up pressure on her body for the first half hour, right through the presentation on Ephesus. His angry lean on the right side of his seat crushed her left shoulder. Creep! When Costa repositioned himself, Stella flowed across the shared armrest and claimed it, but still he leaned heavily, never letting up. She massaged her arms as Costa climbed the steps of the mezzanine, pushing his way through tired, noisy observers who also headed up the steps, into the glass-walled corridor and down the staircase into the foyer in search of drinks.

Stella peeled off the tape that stuck the business card to the glass balustrade. She ran an index finger around its grubby edges; he had not bothered to use a fresh card. The last formal event of the day ended five minutes ago, but she had not moved from the victor's seat. She was too flustered to face the people around her after that commotion.

Buzz. WhatsApp message from her friend Justine: 'Get together before the meeting? Beneath the linden tree on the far side of the garden? Now?'

Stella pushed Costa's business card into the inner pocket of her bag. A silly skirmish. Her anger had been disproportionate; it could have endangered her career.

🐦

'Professor Stel-lah! Stel-lah!' In an indigo linen sun dress, Justine waved a huge straw sunhat from the far side of the old Bundeshaus riverside garden. A demi-champagne and two flutes waited on a small white table, incongruously next to a garish bag of potato crisps. Most of the other tables were already occupied as delegates and observers rested for half an hour before the start of a multitude of events: side conferences, civil society talks, private dinners and cocktails.

'Hi!' Stella jogged across the garden.

Justine opened her arms wide. 'Professor Stella Robinson. Congratulations! It's been too long coming.'

Stella's history professorship was installed like a golden mantle, but it was not enough, a professorship was only one celebrated moment along the road to university Vice-Chancellor by her mid-fifties—a mere ten years—and the ultimate safety through power.

'I'm delighted to join you in the hallowed, professorial halls,' said Stella. 'Can't wait for our first Board meeting.'

Justine hugged Stella tightly, the brim of her straw hat sheltering them both. 'I wouldn't launch the journal without you. We've got some peppery tempers on the Board; I need you to keep everyone calm.' She sat down and poured two glasses. 'A toast to your professorship and our friendship.'

Stella lifted her glass; a trickle of champagne cooled her fingers. 'Two academic history papers with you and—'

Justine grinned. 'Correction, prize-winning papers.'

'And now we present to the world—da-dah!—a new history journal.'

Bubbles on Stella's tongue brought her back to the happy present as champagne blunted the stinging seat encounter. A floral perfume curled among the aromas of champagne, cheese and crisps. Laughter from other tables drifted on the hot air. Stella breathed deeply—such beauty in a summer garden on the Rhine. This was where she belonged; forget silly Costa.

Justine shook the crisps into a brown ceramic bowl. 'Thanks for agreeing to take the Board through the legal details of a journal; only you have the experience.' She rummaged in her tote bag. 'But first, a new mother's prerogative. Baby pics of Madeleine.'

Stella scrolled through one-year-old Madeleine on a swing, in the snow, in a pool. She thought of David at the same age, the light and delight of her life. Now, at fourteen, her son worked hard at being a teenager.

'They shoot up fast,' said Stella. 'I have to catch myself in confusing David's height for emotional maturity.' She returned the photos. 'I hope that I can visit again while Madeleine's a baby.'

'Your old room's waiting.'

'Thank you. How will she cope in your absence?'

Justine topped up Stella's flute. 'We'll speak every day. Between us, I'm grateful for a few days' break.'

Stella nodded; she understood the tug between a child and a mother's needs. 'Children are tough, but also fragile.'

Something soft brushed Stella's leg. She jumped. She peered under the table. A cat's tail swished in the shadow.

'Only a cat. A tom. I think he's hunting.'

Justine glanced around the garden. 'Oblivious of us.'

'But watch the ears, they're flat to his head, but twisted, and the head's outstretched, aggressive. The legs are low, as if he's slinking through ancient savannah grasses. Careless owners, there's no bell on that fancy, gold collar.'

Stella looked at her watch. 'Board meeting soon. The first face-to-face is always exciting.'

Justine poured the last of the champagne. The tomcat climbed stealthily up the linden.

'Oh, no! A nest.' Stella pointed. 'That dark cluster. That's where he's going. Listen—cheeping.'

She pushed back from the table; her chair crashed. 'I'll get a gardener. Watch the cat. Shout if you must. Unbearable if he attacks those baby birds.'

'Stella saved a nest of chicks from a ferocious tomcat.'

Claps and smiles flitted around the small Formica table in a windowless room in the basement of the conference centre.

Takura from Harare towered over her. 'Hi, Stella!'

She stretched up to him as they exchanged air kisses.

'How we move around!' he said. 'We first met in Lima? Five years ago?'

'Six,' said Stella. 'And don't forget the Tunis conference. It was good news when Justine said you'd be on the Board.'

Justine introduced Stella to the group of historians and archaeologists on the Board of the new history journal.

'You're the best people I know to think-tank the future for us. You're from all over the world. Li-jing and Dai send apologies; you'll meet them next year.'

Stella sat down and pulled out her legal notes. Justine explained that she and Stella were on-going Board members of another journal.

She smiled at Stella. 'Most of today will be devoted to Stella running through legal aspects of a journal, but first, who's bursting with ideas?'

'Identity and cultural restitution!' said Stella. 'Let's lead the argument.' That felt better; she was on familiar territory, far from bickering over a seat. Obliterate Costa and the humiliating encounter.

Michael from DC slapped the table. 'We're worn out by the shabby argument in favour of pulling apart world-class museums that have cared for centuries for African and Asian art and artefacts.'

Michael's formal, black jacket looked uncomfortably heavy to Stella. No wonder he was impatient.

'Ripping apart excellent museums has become a tiresome issue,' said Fatima from Bordeaux. She fiddled with a sapphire ring, smoothed her black hijab and leaned back.

Takura pushed up crisp shirt sleeves. 'It's not tiresome if we're speaking of stolen treasures.'

Stella observed the politics of the group laid bare in seconds. She revelled in the new Board, but her fury with Costa lingered, his louring head re-igniting long-ago nightmares.

A head in the garden. A bedroom door from her childhood slammed shut at the back of her mind, leaving her in hot, summer darkness with a killer outside, beyond the window and the Mickey Mouse curtains, and the tapping and scratching of branches. A serial killer roamed the streets for five years. Before that, her grandparents had always left their house key in the front door; anywhere else it could be lost. The killer's head, a giant, looming head. A blob jerking in the leaves. She, in her bed, inches away.

Stella pushed down childhood terrors. Get lost, Costa.

'Imagine if your society had been plundered and your most precious art had vanished,' said Stella. 'Even worse—tourists pay to see *your* art in foreign museums. Outrageous! Restitution of objects looted during wars or colonisation restores cultural identity and pride. This is exactly what the new journal should focus on.'

Justine sighed. 'Justice and identity versus state-of-the-art conservation in western museums. Then there's everyone's rights to World Heritage which for some people is local heritage...'

At the word 'rights', Stella made inverted commas in the air, insisting on its fraught nature, even as she struggled to banish Costa. It was horribly embarrassing that other professionals had asked her to be quiet. But she had not caused the fuss. *He* had!

The meeting table was too small, even for five. Twisting awkwardly, Takura held the gaze of each person in turn.

'Listen to Stella. Few Zimbabweans have the opportunity to visit the British Museum, but they are the heirs of the artists who made thousands of stolen objects. They live with cultural wounds. Even my great-grandfather's sculptures were looted.'

Michael coughed as if to make a polite interruption. 'Historical injustice will always exist. Let's work on interpretation philosophy.'

A stiff, graceless silence poisoned the table. Stella could feel a bruise on her shoulder where Costa had pushed so arrogantly against her.

'But restitution's red hot,' said Stella. 'Many Indigenous peoples do not hold their own art. That's a human rights' crime. I suggest—'

Michael butted in. 'Is the British Museum returning the Elgin Marbles to Athens? The Greeks have been asking for them for two hundred years.'

'Maybe, one day,' said Stella. 'Listen to Takura, he—'

Michael rolled his eyes. 'Are you proposing that the Louvre returns Napoleonic loot? Remove it from top conservation care in Paris? Give it a break, bleeding-heart Stella.'

'Bleeding-heart!' Working with Michael would be tough. He cut across her comments as Nigel had, a month ago, in the stuffy Humanities room of Great South Land University. Her professorship had been announced the day before, but the newest staff member smashed in and stole her point. Nigel was young, with his PhD newly conferred, and already throwing around his weight, while she had twenty-two years of lecturing experience in four universities and was a fully-fledged professor. A board room of thirty-five people pivoted as one, away from her and towards him. She scrambled to retrieve her point, but Nigel had made it his own. The Dean smirked. Before Nigel, there was Ron; before him, Laurence; before him, Brian and Ali together, and horrible Dimitri. It never ended.

Inside Stella, something already taut, stretched and strained, like a fragile, translucent membrane. After five minutes, she walked out of the university meeting. She looked back from the door, nursing her broken arm; no one had seen her leave.

In Bonn, an overhead globe flared, popped and went out in the airless meeting room, leaving Takura and Stella's end of the table in grey light. Michael clenched his jaw; Fatima's chair squeaked. Justine looked up at the popcorn, sound-deadening ceiling. Two people pushed open the door of the meeting room and stood inside, impatient, insistent, laden with folders, posters and pins. It was now their room.

Justine appeared relieved. 'We'll move to the garden for Stella's legal discussion; reconvene in fifteen minutes.'

Stella helped Justine gather up Board documents. Despite overbearing Michael, the Board was where she belonged.

The old friends wove through the foyer, noisy with dozens of languages and crammed with posters, books, bright African clothes, Middle Eastern robes, summer dresses and sombre suits.

Justine looked semi-apologetic. 'Michael's one of the reasons that I want you on the Board, as a counterforce. He's valuable but needs tempering.'

Stella juggled an armful of manila folders and glanced around for Costa. 'I'm fed up with rude men.'

Her words sounded bitter; she surprised herself and wished that she had not said them. She could cope with Michael.

Justine walked faster as they skirted tables overflowing with books and pamphlets. 'The journal needs you. You plunge with energy into discussion. I'm hoping that you'll come on as Deputy-Editor.' She grinned sheepishly. 'I plan to take leave in a year for another baby, then you might like to take over.'

A thrill tickled up Stella's back. Just what she needed, a Deputy-Editorship on top of a third editorial Board membership. The new prof would return to work with another prize. It all added up to safety through power, years of hard work paying off.

Two folders slipped from her grasp and slid under a table. She squatted to retrieve them among the legs of people examining piles of glossy, hardcover books. A heel scraped across the back of her hand. Ouch! First the brogues and now a stiletto... The battle with Costa dredged up her worst childhood memories, and the sensation that he was behind her now, pushing and pressing in the throng. Tremors raced into her throat. She felt his sausage-like fingers, stiff and relentless on the back of her jacket. Shapes shuffled in her childhood garden. In her good times and bad, the serial killer came back, but Stella remained composed.

She stood up. 'Count me in!'

'Great!' said Justine. 'You're the best person for the job. I like the way you deal honestly with people; you try to understand other positions.'

And sometimes I walk away, wounded and wordless, fretted Stella. She tightened her grip on the folders. She should have talked over Nigel, shouted him down, showed colleagues that she was the new prof, not Nigel.

She paused with Justine at a tourist information desk, stacked high with Beethoven brochures adorned with the composer's signature mane of hair.

'Beethoven's birthplace is tiny,' said Justine. 'But its presence dominates local Bonn memory, bigger than Allied bombing, bigger than World War Two.'

Centuries of Bonn history mounted up before the historian in Stella with the ancient Romans and layers of war competing with Beethoven in collective memory. World War II trucks trundled through Bonn's medieval lanes with their loads of human despair. Husbands ripped from wives. Neighbours turning away during the Jewish deportations.

From history nightmares to Costa. The emotional distance was not great. Costa, Michael and Nigel fused in a spurt of rage. An in-rush of breath. There he was, swaggering past in conversation with an older man. He rubbed his chin, miming *gravitas*.

Stella half-covered her face with the files. What was Justine saying? 'Beethoven? Hmm, yes.'

She tried to disguise her scan of the room. Where was Costa going?

Justine touched Stella's shoulder. 'You're pale. Too hot?'

Stella hesitated. Costa had probably not gone out to the hot, steamy garden, but to the cool riverside foyer behind the auditorium. She had ten minutes before the Board regrouped.

'Excuse me, I'll catch you up.'

THREE

PETER'S DISCREET PINK pearls belonged to the world of family and work, but a cocktail party demanded longer earrings, redder lips, higher heels. With her small grey backpack, Stella ducked behind a display board, pulled out her supplies and transformed herself. She headed to the rear of the conference centre where Beethoven's *Sonata in D Major* competed with conversation roar, and a chrome wall panel reflected her new self.

She squinted as she searched for Costa, skirting around the rear foyer with its panoramic view of the Rhine and glary yacht sails. A young family wearing swimsuits ambled along the shore. Waiters raced to relocate tables and drinks from the muggy garden to the narrow, air-conditioned foyer. Sweating men and women pushed inside. Each time the door opened, soupy heat swamped the dry, cool interior, mingling with aromas of cured meats and tangy cheeses. With its small windows and airless rooms, Bonn suffered in the bombshell heatwave that baked everywhere from Morocco to England.

Stella felt puzzled, uncertain about what she was doing, but she was so embarrassed that she had to do something. She had never in her whole life made a scene and disturbed others in a public venue. Memories of the hisses and frowns were humiliating. The Chinese woman had actually said 'Shhh' as if Stella were a fractious child.

The only way to fix things up was to extract a civil apology from Costa, as she should have tackled Nigel in the faculty meeting. Costa's apology would elegantly make up for her silence that time and provide good practice for keeping Nigel in check. She stood next to a black decal of a bird of prey, beak hooked, claws extended. She strained to hear the piano snatch the melody from the cello, but it made little headway against the cocktail din. In one of the apogees of Western civilisation, music was forced to compete with babble *about* civilisation. She liked the irony, Peter would too. She would email him the funny moments; a shared laugh was healing. But first, locate Costa.

A young waiter with a silver tray and champagne flutes manoeuvred through a sea of gesticulating arms. With a mouth like furred cardboard, Stella drank half a glass in one gulp and grabbed a second. The waiter raised her eyebrows.

Stella reddened. 'Not for me; for a friend.'

She dragged a chair from behind a pillar and climbed up, unsteady in eight-centimetre heels. Now she could survey the whole room and locate Costa's hair, but the room was full of wispy, grey hair and, in contrast, flamboyant African head ties in a clash of shapes and patterns.

A WhatsApp buzz from Justine. 'We're under the same linden where you and I met.'

Hold on, Justine, nearly with you. Stella supported herself with a hand on the wall. She would make extraction of apologies a firm habit.

The young waiter shook her head and pointed at the high heels gouging the brocade seat.

'Madam!'

Stella blushed again; at home she would never stand on upholstery in anything but socks. This was an aberration; she knew how to behave at a cocktail party. She nodded apologies and then spotted the faculty sneak. Georgette, another new professor from Great South Land University, eyed her coolly from across the foyer. Even standing on a chair for thirty seconds would snake its way back to the Dean. Stella mouthed to Georgette, 'Looking for someone'. She followed up with the most casual, friendly wave that she could force, but her arm shook. Georgette was a reminder that working hard might not be enough to advance her career further than a professorship. Sneaking, canoodling, backstabbing, all were more effective than hard work when the faculty spy was lurking.

Stella climbed down and looked around for two sofas; she would persuade the Board to meet inside—to keep cool—then she could watch for Costa. She pushed sweaty hair behind her ears while waiters dragged two pedestal fans to either end of the foyer. The whirr added to the din, spinning hair styles into dust devils.

Stella's furious, persistent response to Costa perplexed her. All this for an apology? Here she was, late for the Board meeting, keeping everyone waiting for her to outline the legal essentials while she shoved through a cocktail party and downed too much champagne. Justine buzzed again. Stella glanced at her watch. Twelve minutes late. Not good, but when had dutiful Stella ever been late? This was a first; everyone got waylaid at conferences. It was common knowledge that dutiful workers often lacked creativity because they sublimated it in the stress of being obedient. They reproduced work structures rather than contributing imaginatively. Creativity had been in short supply for Stella for too long. Three cheers for a break from duty!

The cello *adagio* struggled above the voices, then was lost. Heads milled in front of her in a cacophony of chatter over clattering glasses and the drone of fans. The jammed, narrow space was no match for the elegance of the garden, but it was preferable to humid heat. Champagne but no food. Dizzy. She was not herself. She ought to leave, run across the garden and apologise. Justine had given her a prestigious opportunity. Grab it, Stella.

Buzz. Justine, a third time. 'Are you ok? We're on the fence side of the linden. Can't start without you. URGENT!'

Through the glass wall to the garden, Stella spotted Costa. A rip through her body, flaring hot-white. Windows juddered, blinding yacht sails fragmented across the panes. A family jogged, headless, decapitated by the window frame. A shout from the shore. The cocktail noise dropped out; a thick hum glued her ears.

A white hydrangea with massive pendulous blossoms obscured Costa's paunch. He mocked a bow as he opened the door for a surprised, décolleté young woman. A student? Escaped school for the day? Stella breathed hard, thrill mixing with panic as she became again the child in bed, gaping at shadow blobs. It was not only her sense of justice that he had attacked; her body responded to his vileness at the endocrine level.

Sticky, garden heat gushed in with Costa and the young woman. Stella would know that half-bald head anywhere; she could see the lime-green tips of his hair from across the room. He greeted the throng with hand kissing, a flutter of fingers, majestic inclinations of his head. That arrogant face, with a name—and a thrill she had not expected, a curious, unidentifiable quiver. Her whole body was alive to his outrage. She would check him out, gauge his mood, how he interacted with peers, then confront him with rehearsed words: 'it is unacceptable to behave…' What a relief to extract an apology. At last, a win to Stella.

Costa manoeuvred through the narrow foyer, mopping his brow while a fan blew his green and grey wisps horizontally across his ears. The piano echoed the cello and voices competed in crescendo. He headed to an alcove at the rear, the venue for a semi-private cocktail party within the larger party. It had been decorated in tourism posters—Venice's Salute church at dawn, Mount Etna exploding into a starry night, Christmas shopping on the Corso in Rome. Oregano and pecorino wafted in front of the Grand Canal. Little bowls of risotto steamed next to glistening, green olives—fabulous, huge like plums—but Stella had no appetite. Costa tossed his bag under the buffet table. He crammed in a mini pizza and balanced two more on the flat of his hand, chewing as he perused the platters. He wiped his mouth with the back of his hand, leaving pastry flakes dotting his moustache.

Stella glanced at her watch. Eighteen minutes late. Da-dah! Creative Stella had arrived, breaching stultifying schedules. One more minute to get an insight into the cocky guy. A polite confrontation. An apology from him. The end of Costa!

A crystal glass chimed as a chic, elderly woman in a superbly tailored, grey linen shift tapped with a spoon. Talking continued. A young man and woman wound their arms around each other. The chinking insisted, until an exasperated voice called, '*Silenzio*'. Laughter.

Stella had a perfect view of Costa's arm darting towards the platters. He gorged while pushing across an elderly man. He grasped two tranches of grilled aubergine, the purple skin shiny with oil, and ate them quickly, then two more mini pizzas. The last time Stella saw frantic eating was at David's eighth birthday party when giggling boys and girls scoffed crisps, cup-cakes and chocolates.

'*Silenzio!*' Cheering. Tapping fingernails on glasses of prosecco. The elegant woman began to speak, slowly enough for Stella's undergraduate Italian.

'Welcome all. Good fortune to Italian historic sites.'

The group stumbled back from around Costa, who gave a small bow while he continued to chew. Stella missed the occasional word, but the gist was clear.

'We are indeed blessed to have our dear friend and esteemed colleague, Professor Giovanni Costa, among us tonight. I do not exaggerate to say that he is one of the greatest, if not the greatest archaeologist, historian and interpreter of Roman cultural heritage.'

The audience hurrahed and tapped fingernails on glasses. Several people took photographs of Costa with their phones, so Stella did too, then she took four more in close-up. She looked up from the lens. Costa was bowing again, clutching a fistful of olives. She snapped two more in extreme close-up.

'We know that Italy is the pre-eminent nation in World Heritage.' The woman smiled to calm the cheering. 'It will never be otherwise, even if China and France plot takeovers. You cannot give birth to the Romans, Medicis and Leonardo without being the world leader!'

Outside of her lens, Stella perused the high-fashion party-goers in their silks, linens, lavish but discreet jewellery and footwear from Milanese boutiques. This was the world of Costa. Despite all the riches of Italy, it had stolen North African antiquities. She and Takura were right; the new journal should focus on the return of artefacts.

Stella scrolled quickly through her six photographs. Small eyes in a chubby face. Mean eyes. Cruel eyes. Calculating eyes. Now what? Cruel eyes—sure—but what did a bunch of photos mean? She already knew that he looked sadistic. She was hardly going to upload them with 'Da-dah! Check out these peepers!'

She heard Costa masticating. How bizarre to photograph a stranger, her first time. She could pretend to stalk him, have fun, be the voyeur. Men watched women all the time; why not reverse it? Why not flex the muscle of the feminist gaze?

'And Botticelli, who makes a tourism fortune for Florence!'

More cheering. Stella watched the woman's slender hands bring order, a discreet band of diamonds sparkling over the assembly. Cascading into the sudden peace came the cello and the *allegro vivace*.

'The Italian nation has much to be grateful for in dear

Giovanni. He has contributed not only to research, but to tourism and the great wealth that it brings us. He is a mentor to post-graduates and a cultural ambassador for Italy. We toast him tonight to celebrate his thirty years in the field.'

Costa oozed into the microphone. He thanked everyone with his hot, beating, grateful Roman heart; the rest was too colloquial for Stella. From time to time, he swigged prosecco.

He lifted his glass, but found it empty. 'Fuck!'

Mock horror from the audience. Stella edged to the back of the room; any moment Costa would realise that she was standing close to him.

Something dragged her finger back to the camera button, but she needed no more photos. 'Needed'? Of course she needed none, but she clicked on: Costa bowing, waving his arms, slipping his arm around the waist of a tall woman in a low-cut silk dress. He slobbered on the woman's neck as she leaned away. A gigantic bouquet appeared; he waved yellow and white roses around his head like a lasso.

'Papal colours,' he laughed. 'I'm infallible!'

A rose tumbled free. An admirer scooped it up mid-air and tucked it behind Costa's ear. Someone started singing the Italian national anthem. A few people giggled; then most joined in, wobbling through the words.

Stella stumbled in an upside-down world where the disreputable were feted. The babble of the room receded as dizziness fluttered around her head. Smiles stretched to grimaces, teeth were bared, voices screeched over Beethoven. The fraud, Costa. She alone saw the truth.

When the prosecco was finished and the platters nearly empty, the beautiful people dispersed and Costa scooped up cheese, the last of the olives and a handful of mini cannoli before leaving the alcove. Stella felt as if she had been in the wings of a stage. Unbelievable, Costa was a heritage rock star.

He blew a kiss to three young women and turned into the glass corridor that bordered the garden. Stella followed, leaving a couple of people between them, but slowed when she saw a shaft of fierce light catch the hem of Justine's indigo dress. Stella's new Board colleagues pressed close around a white table under the linden, their shoulders hunched into a tight circle, the dense purple-green shade, protective and defining the group. Stella faltered and glanced at Costa waddling near the end of the passage. She remembered previous conferences where she had joined groups for dinner and enjoyed debates that blossomed into writing collaborations. Maybe a further paper with Justine. Perhaps one with Takura.

Go back to the Board and apologise? She lingered. Costa would soon be out of sight.

A buzz from Justine. 'Sorry we missed you. You didn't look well earlier. Please let me know that you're ok.'

Stella could still join them; it was not too late. She would get away with missing half a Board meeting. Justine had praised her energy in the first half. She'd built credit, had a little wriggle room. Near the end of the corridor, Costa steadied his bag with one hand; the other he held flat, a fleshy tray for olives, cheese and *dolce*. She should turn away; there was nothing more to learn. Costa did what he did; barbaric behaviour was his norm. She should open the door to the garden immediately and join the group. She should.

The distance to Costa lengthened. With all her heart she wanted to go back and discuss the new journal, but she had become the female gaze in action, yanked by feminist duty to skewer with her eyes. An unknown feeling. Cutting. Urgent.

He turned the corner. She followed.

FOUR

STELLA TRACKED INTO the pungent trail of Costa's melting cheese as she followed him to the train station. What astonishing strength there was in looking, in even pretending to look with her secret photographs. For once in gender history, let a man squirm. She imagined herself stroking the forehead of the terrified child she had once been, soothing, comforting and empowering her to stand her ground. Adult Stella felt taller, her eyes drilling.

A Swedish colleague waved from the opposite side of Heussallee, the tree-lined avenue leading from the conference centre to the local railway station. Her blonde hair glinted in relentless, early evening sunlight as she shouted, 'Got time for an icy drink?'

Stella waved. 'Sorry. Catch you tomorrow.'

Everyone else would have to wait; confronting Costa was the priority. She walked a few paces behind him, but close to the trees because it was possible that he could turn. Delegates dawdled on either side of the road, while she walked alone in the dusty heat, unthinking of the day's heritage sites, adrift from the conference pulse. She had let down Justine; she knew that. She was a new professor with duties and a career, but she could not stop herself chasing Costa to the Heussallee Station and straight onto the jammed Line 16 platform from suburban Bad Godesberg to central Bonn. Elegant Bad Godesberg had a separate township identity, but had become a suburb of Bonn. A small city itself, Bonn had the status of a former capital from when it was the political seat of West Germany during the Cold War and, of course, it was the birthplace of Beethoven.

In the underground station, the reflection of Stella and Costa's bodies on the startling yellow walls distorted and re-connected, curving across high-gloss panels. Costa stood out from everybody at the conference as if her eyes were primed to pinpoint him. She watched him oscillate between cheeses which by now must have melted to sludge between his fingers.

Stella kept back from the bully. In the banality of the canary-yellow platform, she inverted the age-old, controlling masculine look. Looking was a legitimate feminist project, a counter-look to the male gaze. Now a woman gazed at a man, not in lust—she had not sunk that low!—but in outrage and power, asserting equality. That was it—she looked at him in the cause of equality.

She found a seat at the intersection of hot and cool air and flapped her damp jacket. At the beginning of the conference, chilled platform air enticed her down the station steps, but the cool shrank as the heat above ground encroached, hour by hour, metre by metre. Costa huddled with a cluster of people in the cool platform middle. World Heritage pamphlets littered the few available seats and red-faced, formally dressed conference-goers squeezed around a ticket dispenser.

A mother with a stroller and a screeching toddler searched for a seat. Stella kept a sharp eye on Costa as she vacated hers. The grateful mother nodded weary thanks as the stink of melting bitumen burnt the air in a rush of dirt ahead of the northbound train to central Bonn and Cologne. Stella held the little boy, with his tender, milky smell, while the mother collapsed the stroller.

Costa pushed to the front as passengers crammed into air-conditioned carriages, elbowing his way on board, grabbing a seat ahead of a pregnant woman.

There was so much to learn from looking. Stella was inside the gaze for the first time, the appraising gaze that men used habitually as a weapon against women. Wild and domestic animals used their eyes to communicate, to lure, to threaten. If she ever encountered a big cat in the wilderness, she would lock eyes. Fleeing would inflame the cat; it would snap its jaws on her neck, but in Bonn she was in control.

On board she braced against a chrome pole and studied her photographs. What trophies! That smirk, those wily eyes…she had caught them perfectly. She scrolled through photographs dripping with his disingenuous smiles and vaudevillian gestures. Food, always lashings of free food, and grinning sycophants who saw only his celebrity and lost their wits. They could not cheer loud enough or long enough to satisfy him. None saw him for who he was.

She enlarged the second-last photo and caught her breath. Costa looked directly at the lens. Tossed back her audacious, new gaze? Asserted his primeval, phallic prerogative? Cold perspiration sprang in her hair in a shock of panic. Bumpily in the packed train, grateful that the fractious toddler had settled into a low-level whine, she slowly enlarged the photo to maximum, deeper and deeper into his essence: nose, wet mouth, stray hair, skin, pores. Her throat contracted. His unnerving, scheming eyes seemed to bore directly into the camera. A trick of the light? The correct focal length apparent in his eyes? He looked bitter and resolved. He had not finished with her.

The screen was too small to allow her to be certain. No? Yes? She slashed the size of the image. No need to worry without cause. She would confirm later on her laptop. Her hands shook as she put the phone into her bag. She risked a glance down the packed carriage and caught the sight of the back of his head with its unmistakeable thick hair topped by green wisps. His head had lolled to the side as if he were dozing. A few minutes later, the train slid into the gloom of Bonn Central Station.

Costa was first at the exit and the first off. At the train steps, Stella helped another mother with a cumbersome, old-fashioned pram which scraped through the carriage door. The world was not made for mothers. The station smelt of cloying human flesh and of a public toilet. Stella needed water and air, but how had she lost the bully and fraud? She climbed on a bench and checked up and down the platform as it drained of arriving passengers. Laughter trumped panic as her energy surged with red-raw life. Ah, the thrill of the hunt!

Dozens of people lined up for bottled water, overwhelming a small kiosk, while Costa had disappeared among advertisement posters. In high heels, Stella raced up freshly washed steps to the street. No Costa. The electricity of her gaze burned; she was on fire. What would she do with her rage if she lost him? Crash in frustration? Women had endured that slump for millennia.

Perhaps he was still in the station? Back underground, she joined the water throng. After olives and cannoli, he'd be parched.

'Wait your turn!' A young man in a smart suit knocked Stella. Men fought her for a seat and even water!

She gave up and followed the stench of urine mixed with disinfectant—that unforgettable odour—to the men's toilets and half hid behind an iron pillar studded with rivets. Men moved in and out of the door, and she saw them see her. She should have wiped off her lipstick and ditched the high heels. The men checked her up and down, crawling their eyes over her clammy, clinging clothes. A salacious whistle! And another, and some vehement German that she did not understand. From long habit, she began to lower her eyes, blind with anger, but, in a fizzle of fury, glared back for the first time in her life, and kept on glaring as men sauntered by. She stood her ground. One by one, they dropped their eyes. Victory! Years of academic theory in practice at last.

Her head throbbed a headache warning; victory came at a price. She struggled with pinched feet back to street level, where she panted in trapped car exhaust. No Costa. Had he stayed on the train and gone to Cologne Cathedral? It was the biggest heritage attraction in the district, but a visit in a heatwave would be a tough duty call. In the street, the crowd had thinned. Costa was nowhere.

Stella trudged into the cauldron of the town; heat shimmered off cobbles and light pinged from stone to stone. A banner for *Der Spiegel* withered outside a tobacconist, its edges contracting and the glossy paper crackling. Another magazine showed a photo of a woman with bruising so bad that her right eye was puffed and closed.

The sun stalled, a smouldering oculus that refused to set. Stella pulled a folded cloth hat from her backpack as her headache took hold. In Munsterplatz, a municipal water caravan offered free drinks in the heat emergency, but the three staff frowned when she asked for two bottles. She drank one whole bottle, rolling back the headache. The other bottle she emptied into her flask. She changed into low sandals and headed down to the Rhine.

What would she have done if she had found Costa? Get that apology? Perhaps the time had passed for such civilities; the fawning Italian party-goers confirmed that expecting sincerity from Costa would be a waste of time. Probably, he didn't remember trying to force her out of 'the seat', *her* seat. She should have confronted him with a rousing feminist gaze.

At entrances to North American wilderness, she and Peter had read that the key was to have a stare so hypnotic that a cougar was disempowered. She must have achieved that stare today in front of the men's toilets. If she ever chanced upon a wild cat, she planned to draw herself up to her full height and lift her arms.

On holidays in the US, she and Peter had lifted their rain jackets above their heads to add height and presence. They'd meowed and giggled, 'I will look after you'.

Peter was heroic against a wilderness of claws, but useless in everyday life. He would be aghast to know that she had taken surreptitious photos, enlarged them, hunted a colleague. He would be horrified, stunned, not recognise her. If he were here, maybe she would not have met Costa. Met? Was that what happened?

A rare wind roared up from North Africa; sand cracked between her teeth. The day was too hot and blustery for returning to the airless hotel. A bakery door tinkled as a toddler bit into a giant pretzel that exploded in desiccated crumbs. A rush of memory. David, a toddler, unbearably cute in a striped jumpsuit, standing by the fridge, pointing to the freezer, demanding ice-cream. Last night—David's email—Stella remembered that she had not opened it. She assumed that it was a typical unloading about an ordinary school day. She would get to it later.

The near-empty road wound to the river, and the dank, mouldy odour of the shallows pervaded the air. In a duty halt, she stepped into a shallow doorway near Beethoven's House, his birthplace besieged by a few red-faced tourists sheltering beneath a merry field of hats. This was the very street, the very spot, where Ludwig had played with his friends. Genius would have to wait for another day. Bloody Costa, she was stuck in the heat and had missed the Board meeting.

🐦

A clump of chestnut trees drooped, heavy with white flowers; a lone bench sat in their deepest shadow. Fifty metres away, a dozen benches dotted the burning shoreline of the River Rhine while sleepy bodies sunbathed on bright towels.

Stella eased her bare legs between splinters and green peeling paint. Here was the place to write an apology to Justine. She should have attended the garden meeting, even if only to help control Michael. She test-ran apologies. 'Dear Justine, I'm so sorry…' Lame. She should not have missed the meeting. She should have stayed to explain the legal technicalities and then shared drinks with the Board. She should be in a bar with everyone right now, not alone in a strange German park where bikes whizzed over desiccated leaves that could not hang on to branches until autumn. She kicked off her sandals and wriggled her toes in the spare, dry grass. Three near-naked toddlers chased a ball, then ran in a heap towards a young woman in a pink sundress who held out ice-creams.

Costa made Stella ill at ease; something was creepy about him. She took out her phone and re-examined that photo. How forbidding. She enlarged the image; he seemed to be looking directly at her, but it was hard to say. She tested her own focal length on tanning bodies beyond the chestnut shade; they were about the same distance that she had been from the glutton. Her eyes adjusted for close, discarded pizza boxes and further away for Frisbees, dogs and kids.

Back to the draft. 'Sincere apologies…' A new member of the Board missing from a meeting, no warning, simply 'no show'. Not a good start. If she were the Editor… She did not deserve to be on the Board unless she acted professionally, but she needed to be on it to protect her professorial status. In academia, enough was never enough; you needed to work your way up to university management. This was the only way—more writing, more Boards, more meetings.

Stella flopped back. Her eyes smarted after the grit and glare of the town. 'Sorry.' An appropriate opening for Justine, but then what? 'Tracking Costa.' Joking! 'I had to check out a jerk.' No! 'Ran into a colleague?' A distinct possibility and half-true. Technically, Costa was a colleague during the time of the conference. Liking someone was not the point; you needed only to be in the same field to say 'colleague'. But then Justine might say, 'Ask him to join us for dinner'. Perhaps not give an excuse; that way she could not be caught in a lie. She did not want to fib to her loyal friend.

She pulled out a tattered conference napkin wrapped around a shattered biscuit salvaged from morning tea and pressed and squeezed the crumbs into an edible lump as her eyes settled on a hazy middle distance which glimmered in and out of a mirage. If she narrowed her eyes, running toddlers turned into stick silhouettes against shining water.

A silhouette in a floaty dress wove through sunbathing families. Two yachts drew perilously close to each other, sails furled. Was that beer being tossed from one to the other? The dress was blue, on a thin woman. Stella yawned and stretched. The woman wended her way up from the Rhine through sprawling picknickers. A new mirage shimmered on the other bank, once a wilderness beyond the Roman world. It was here that ancient Roman civilisation had stopped. Stella dabbed water on her neck as the woman stepped slowly out of the sun's blaze and into the margin of the tree shadow, prodding the grass with a cane. A dog darted out of the way; a child whooped.

Stella nibbled and planned. 'Hi, everyone, hope you had a good meeting, so sorry...' The woman laboured through the purple shade. Her path never drifted off course from Stella and the bench, even when cyclists raced by. Then she deviated for a few seconds around a Frisbee and a golden retriever, and then was back on track. Stella wanted the bench for herself; the river was the only place to be alone and to grab every zephyr.

She saw bony arms and a dress that was buttoned up the middle with an unfitted waist. Now the woman was close enough for Stella to see small, loose folds of creamy face skin. Stella's head tingled— the woman was going to sit. The brightest blue eyes studied Stella, who growled a greeting and shuffled aside, creating a free strip on the bench. Stella resumed drafting: 'I know that was a bad start. Apologies. Something came up from my university department.' She rephrased: 'Something extremely urgent came up...'

Stella planted her small, grey backpack in the middle of the seat and angled her legs away. Stay on your side, old lady. What did you do in the war?

'*Guten Tag.*' A gentle voice.

The woman sank onto the bench and arranged her dress over her knees. Sprays of blue flowers and yellow-green foliage fanned across the cloth. Stella wanted to be alone; strangers had exhausted her.

She made a flicker of contact with the blue eyes. '*Guten Tag.*'

The woman wore her silvery hair in a classic bun; frightening, blood-red lipstick slashed like a wound across her face. Stella needed solitude. She tried to relax, but a prickle pierced her instep. She rubbed the cut as cyclists avoided scattered sunbathers by detouring too closely in front of the bench.

She yelled, 'Slow down!'

'They mean no harm,' calmed the woman. 'We're so happy to see the end of winter and to feel our bodies free in the sun.'

'Yes, but I'm fed up with selfish behaviour.'

'They're joyful.'

She had over-reacted. The cyclists bumped away over yellow, bristly grass, churning up puffs of dust. Festering with anger and yelling at strangers was not like her. But then neither was shadowing a strange man and accusing an old woman of genocide via crude body language. Her jet lag was nearly resolved, but two nights of waking at 2.00 AM caused grumpiness. That's why she was not herself. Yes, must be it. That was why she sat glumly on rough, flaky paint in the heat rather than savouring chilled Riesling with colleagues.

Was that elusive feeling impotent rage? The world would not be a happy place if all feminists took up gazing. She dashed her forearm across the sweat in her hairline as a novel sensation rippled up her neck: tripping, falling and not landing. She rocked on the bench; her focus had to be on her career and a good night's sleep.

The young woman with the ice-creams ran up the park slope and snatched a wrapper from a seagull's beak. She marched the paper to a bin. Stella ceased rocking. Silence between two strangers on a bench felt awkward. She pointed.

'Such an eco-German thing to do, such a green country, a model for other nations.'

The pause that followed was so long that she thought the woman had fallen asleep, but a mumble of words seeped from the shade.

'Not always a good model.'

Stella had never heard such raw grief. The woman's blue eyes narrowed as she met hers, not challenging, but steadfast.

'No, not always.' Stella paused before venturing further. 'Old places have layers of history.'

'Some are more defining than others. We are not all lederhosen and Beethoven. Even Bonn cannot speak only of ravishing music.'

Stella glimpsed again the bright eyes in the weathered face. They were red-rimmed and moist but hinted at energy. Stella nudged her backpack along the bench, staking out more space for herself.

The woman turned sharply. 'I won't bite!' She pulled a handkerchief from a deep pocket and rubbed her eyes.

Stella blushed. 'I... I... I didn't mean to be rude; I'm sorry. I'm not thinking clearly in this extraordinary heat. I... I didn't know that Germany could get this hot.'

She nodded towards the sunbathers and drummed her feet. To be discovered separating herself from another human being, especially one so elderly and friendly... The old lady had done her no harm. Stella had been quick to judge Costa's character, but that did not excuse her re-run of the Nuremburg Trials. She made a show of pulling her pack along the seat, opening more space.

'I think I know what you're thinking,' said the voice at the end of the bench. 'Yes, I confirm that I was born before 1929.'

Stella knew that Israel divided its German visitors into those born after 1929 and those blemished by prior birth and, therefore, sufficiently adult to have committed World War II atrocities.

'I was born in 1921,' said the woman.

'So was my father,' Stella rushed to reduce the strain. 'Um—I was not trying to guess when you were born.'

'Visitors usually do.'

How appalling to face constant judgement for the barbarity of decades past. Stella pulled her pack off the bench and pushed it beneath. The indelible stain of history never quite faded; it branded unborn generations. For the old, it was a stigma that would never dissolve in their lifetimes.

'What terrible things must have happened here.'

'They did. Horrifying things that today seem like a faraway, evil illusion.'

With her thin, white arm, the woman gestured. 'If you wander along the river path, you will come to a small memorial to the deportations.'

Stella looked beyond frolicking bodies, through streaks of sunlight that fell like planks, and towards a memory place. The woman followed Stella's view.

'Yes, down there, along the path. It's not a grand statement, but it's good to remember in daily life.' She spoke softly, as if to herself. 'Even if memory hurts.'

A seagull landed nearby with a chocolate wrapper. Beyond, a few more bickered over a pizza scrap. The woman appeared sad, preoccupied, but still wanted to talk.

'It's hard to imagine what occurred in those days when you see all of this pleasure and beauty.'

Stella tried, 'Bonn is rich in monuments.'

'There are many histories in Bonn.'

Stella took in the long strip of green by the river, as far as she could see in both directions, full of cyclists and families, but twentieth-century history oppressed the park. Ghost soldiers with fixed bayonets marched among heedless picnickers who were drowsy and safe in the twenty-first century.

'There…not far…' The woman pointed south. 'Bonn has also the Siebengebirge, the seven iconic hills that inspired some of the great myths of German heroes. It is one of our special landscapes, romantic and historic.'

Stella looked across the Rhine and tried to move away from German memory. 'You speak wonderful English.'

'My dear visitor, you forget essential history. We are sitting on this glorious summer evening by the River Rhine, once the home of Romans, in what was the British sector of the occupying forces from 1945. You must speak the language of the conqueror.'

Stella spoke the language of the victors; she had never thought of that German perspective. The park thickened with the burden of memory. More soldiers rose along the river; a lost child wailed.

A buzz from Justine cut in. 'Ok? The Board could not go through the agenda without you. I've found another room for tomorrow. We'll start with you presenting on legal issues.'

Career protection. That was why she was here. Stella keyed in: 'Hi, Justine, the craziest thing. V sorry, could not make it, found I was double-booked (in such hot demand!) and forgot to contact you. My apologies. Sx'

FIVE

Again, Stella examined the close-up of Costa. Enlarged on her laptop, there was no doubt. At the cocktail party, the bully had intercepted her gaze and hurled it back flaming. Her chest tightened; she swallowed hard and wiped sweaty palms across her dress in her suffocating sliver of a room at the Bonn Concerto Hotel.

She flipped between the photos. What mean, scheming eyes. From habit, she edged away from a belligerent man, lowered her gaze, looked modestly to a middle distance, checked that her top button was secured, smoothed her skirt, smiled and smiled and smiled, and, above all, pretended that the man had not been pugnacious—'Of course not, who would think such a neurotic thought'. If only she had challenged Costa, then and there, in the Observers' Gallery, she would not still be thinking about the creep and spoiling her time at the conference. She should not have been so preoccupied with decorum. Women needed to make a fuss. Maybe she should rattle Costa. No harm in a bit of unnerving. No harm at all.

When Nigel stole her point, she had quietly left the faculty room, but she had sensed deep in herself an immense, increasing pressure, like a delicate membrane stretching too far, and so fragile that only a rip would release the tension. She should have stayed and fought. Explaining the dynamics of that insulting faculty meeting to Peter had been useless. He had muttered from behind a newspaper, 'Your voice is too soft'.

She needed to finish work on her conference presentation— she had only two nights left—but the meagre hotel window admitted no breeze, only cloying whiffs of jasmine like sickly invading tendrils. As an Australian, she should have been used to heat, but the scourge of high summer struck differently at home with lower humidity, bigger windows and frigid air-conditioning. There, she could escape.

Justine would have to wait for an apologetic phone call. Stella opened a long email from David, full of complaints about school and with three attachments of hockey results. His matches were always mid-week when she could not attend. A sore point for him, she knew that. On her return, she would commit to attending at least one of his matches per month. She dashed off a reply: 'Busy prepping for my presentation. Will answer soon. Love to you and Dad. Mum'.

She enlarged the photo again until Costa's eyes filled her computer screen, huge, black, malevolent pools. He found her camera intolerable, but no lowering of his eyes—oh no—he asserted his right to look at a woman with ancient male control. She clicked to the university library and perused hundreds of feminist titles that critiqued the male gaze: *The Gaze in Everyday Life*, *Pornography and the Male Gaze*, *The Appraising Gaze: Advice for Young Women*, *The Violent Gendered Gaze and Survival...* She was soaked in theory but had had no experience of reversing the gaze. Until today.

She pushed back from the narrow desk, tipping over her water glass. It splashed on a small, silvery frame that contained a photograph of her with Peter and David exploring the vast, flat rocks of Nanarup Beach in the south-west of Australia, a special holiday five years ago when the universe was benevolent. The photo travelled with her everywhere. She wiped dry the frame, bumping her fingers over the shallow embossing as if it were Braille and could enlighten her, but there were no new messages in something so familiar.

She stemmed the trickles, dabbing at Costa's business card as water seeped into his command: 'KEEP OUT! MY SEAT'. The letters blurred in his fattening red ink, while the edges of the card dripped, soft, pulpy, disintegrating. Her notebook lay open, her handwriting broken off as Costa attacked: 'Contested heritage, even among avowed enemies…' The 's' of 'enemies' had ripped like a lightning bolt as he struck and was the physical evidence of his assault. Contested heritage was vital to understanding the world. She thought of lively university tutorials and reminding her students that the Nazis and ISIS had grasped that the foundations of collective identity were in cultural heritage and that was the reason they had routinely destroyed it.

She could not remember where her ruptured and waterlogged sentence had been headed. She blotted the pages again. Too hot to sleep, too hot to work. Appalling to have lied to Justine. This was not how Stella treated people. Everyone thought her dutiful, punctual, empathic.

Pointless calling Peter to complain about Costa. He would be busy at his medical clinic and—like last time—would have nothing comforting to say. The phone call from Melbourne had been a dagger in their marriage.

'We punched above our weight.'

Stella brandished a triumphal fist. She found herself remembering that happy moment, one minute before what came next eight months earlier.

'That calls for a night cap,' said Alexander.

Her university colleague was too close. Uncomfortable. He leered; a flush crept from nascent jowls into his receding hair. Stella stepped back, away from his breath, heavy with red wine.

'No thanks. Early morning flight.'

Stella had travelled with Alexander from Perth to a two-day seminar in Melbourne on university leadership. She was not yet a professor, but deliciously close. She day-dreamed of being a Vice-Chancellor. Nobody would be able to touch her in that exalted position; she would be safe with power in her own hands, a parking spot mere metres from her office, surveillance cameras and a hot line to university security.

After a group dinner, she and Alexander sauntered to the hotel lift. He was already ripping off his silk tie and slinging it over his shoulder. He hummed as he then loosened his button-down collar. His breath surrounded her in the mirrored lift and his inane, tuneless croon resonated painfully in her fatigue. This was not the familiar, sober Alexander who revelled in spreading bureaucracy—more forms, more committees, more reports—until academic staff lost agility and felt trapped. She glanced at the camera above the control panel.

The doors opened silently onto a gilt mirror, a black marble credenza and a long corridor. Stella paused to admire a crystal vase of white lilies, pollen spilling from speckled, red throats—any tactic to normalise the awkwardness in the hope that he would walk on, but he purred.

'Beautiful, like you.'

A sickly smell of pollen, his heat on her neck, the vinous cloud of his breath—lift doors slid shut; work protocols faded. He was too close to her ear. Too close everywhere. His hands—too close! She slipped automatically into pretending that his vulgar pass had not occurred, a lifetime's default. She rummaged for her room key as she scooted down the dimly lit, beige corridor.

He grabbed her shoulder and fumbled a kiss, a repulsive, wet smear. She punched his chest, propelling him across the corridor.

'Stop! Go away!'

He soft-shoed back and clenched a fistful of her black business jacket. 'Aw, come on, Stella, it's been a mighty long two days.'

Unable to see from her trapped angle, she stabbed sideways at the lock with her key. He twisted her lapels, forcing her breasts to swell beyond her clothes. There was a long moment. She should save his dignity. After all, they worked together.

Enough! She dashed his hand away. 'Stop!'

In faculty meetings in the following months, Alexander sat smugly, and those moments would rush into Stella's mind, her nostrils full of the whiff of lily pollen and her jacket bunched in his elegant fingers.

'Ok, not tonight, sexy Stella.'

Humming, he released her jacket and stared too closely into her eyes. 'Sweet dreams.'

Sobs tore at her throat as she phoned Peter with shaking hands. 'He attacked me. I wish you were here.'

Silence.

'Peter?' she asked into the long silence. 'Peter?'

He coughed. 'What are you wearing?'

Stella sat in underwear, fanning herself with tourist brochures. The chatter of garden conversation had dried up. 11.00 PM, 32° Celsius outside and worse inside. A whiff of rotting vegetation. She fetched water from the bathroom and mopped her forehead.

If she proceeded with rattling Costa, she would need to know more about him. That made sense and, besides, Googling was irresistible. She keyed-in 'Giovanni Costa' and found six males on Facebook. Two lived in Canada: a menacing teen in Halifax—appalling acne—and a young man in Toronto cuddling two black lab pups, but he was too cute for the Bonn Costa. A third Giovanni worked on an oil rig in the North Sea. Possible, but highly improbable. She could not imagine a beefy oil-rigger in Bonn, but he seemed to be around the same age, so she enlarged the photo of that Giovanni. He flexed his biceps, demanding that the viewer admire him. Yuck—anyway, Costa wouldn't have biceps worthy of her gaze.

She closed her laptop. Browsing the lives of strangers was not what she did, nor who she was. She felt as if she were strolling a village at dusk, peering into lit rooms. 'Close your curtains!' She dabbed at fresh perspiration on her back. She should write an email apology to the Board and prepare for her presentation. Justine would be expecting to hear from her… right thing to do…

Social media browsing was less powerful than the electrifying, skewering rod of real-life—putting aside revenge porn, but there was no harm in a little exploration. What raw power there was in looking. Those men at the station toilets had succumbed to her eyes, one by one, lowering their heads, slinking off.

She craved knowing how Costa tricked so many Italians and ached to know more about him without feeling like a sneak. The solution rushed into her mind. 'Participant observation'—that was it!—a key method of anthropological inquiry. That's what she was doing, inserting herself into the field of gendered looking, observing from the inside with a legitimate tool of inquiry.

Back to the Giovannis. A fourth had no photo and was connected to Fiat. She clicked open the next Giovanni, a physics schoolteacher in Brennero, in the Italian Alps. About 40, he presented himself in a baggy, black and white snowsuit, a snowboard across his shoulder. She idled through the details of the unknown Brennero Giovanni, perusing his photographs, enlarging to reveal clothing, expressions, teeth. With extreme enlargements she studied super-white smiles, braces and the glint of saliva, but there was no purpose in looking at teeth. Stella wondered whether this was what David did every night, alone in his bedroom, checking on school friends, seduced and lulled into looking at strangers, with no excuse of anthropology.

What would she do with extra Costa information? The answer was obvious: knowledge was power. She did not need to do anything, not even 'rattle', just wait. Knowledge was an end in itself; you could enrich your world with it or use it to achieve a goal.

She wet the end of a towel, squeezed water on her arms and stood by the window hoping that the evening air would force cooling evaporation. Flowers below languorously exuded perfumes—mysterious, riverine, Germanic. 11.48 PM, 31.6° Celsius. She was snooping; she admitted it. She promised herself only one more Giovanni, then a cold shower and sleep. She clicked on the sixth, an architect in Los Angeles. A slim, tuxedo-wearing man cut a red ribbon in front of a huge hotel. His tie was askew, maybe a Windsor knot that he had yet to master.

That was the sixth…a few more…a series of Costa Giovannis and a Giovanni Ludovico-Costa. Facebook was a dead end. The Roman-Bonn Costa did not exist there. It was too hot and brain-sapping to do anything other than amble through more versions of her attacker. Rome…Rio…Naples…Cape Town…Buenos Aires. The world spun in permutations of 'Giovanni' and 'Costa'.

And there he was, lifting a crystal tumbler of whisky. Stella stuck two fingers in the middle of his face and enlarged the image of meaty lips, grey, unshaven cheeks, ruddy pouches beneath spiteful eyes. He toasted the camera while behind him gaming tables filled a saloon.

And there he was in Venice with a full head of lime-green hair, and grinning from the central balcony of the Hotel Danieli. Then a thick hand waved from a window in Positano, a gold ring flashing.

The serial killer peeped through her window when the Mickey Mouse curtains shifted in the Indian Ocean night breeze. Mummy and Daddy whispered and read newspapers at the too-far-away other end of the house, beyond her brother's room and down the hallway where a strip of yellow light from a half-open door cut the darkness in two. Two darknesses!

Yesterday, Daddy hid the newspaper beneath cushions. When he left the room, curious six-year-old Stella got it and read each syllable: 'AN-OTH-ER MUR-DER'. She stumbled over the name of the latest victim, Jill McGuire. She had never seen a 'Guire'. She said it softly: 'Mac—geer'. Jill was added to names she often heard Mummy say to her friends: Natalia Camaro, Alice Montgomery, Maria Russo, Denise Bronsworth. Mummy always looked frightened and spoke softly and said them in that order when she spoke to Daddy and her friends about the devil; she was strict about that list. It made it easy for Stella to remember the names. She added Jill McGuire to her own list and waited to hear Mummy add it to hers.

Black shadows and dazzling sunlight in Positano. Costa's gut oozed from skimpy bathing trunks as he winked at the camera, a cigar clenched between his teeth. Behind him stretched rows of orange and yellow-striped beach umbrellas and the multi-coloured jumble of the hill town that had jumped from poverty to riches through tourism. Costa's hands rested on the shoulders of two teenaged girls, splayed fingers between their skin and bikini straps. Stella enlarged the image, her heart speeding. The girls stared beyond the lens with blank faces, but *he* acknowledged the beach camera, wanting to be admired—by a male photographer? —as he caressed blissful skin. She enlarged his hands. His fingers were active, a slight curving of the knuckles, the bikini straps lifting as he pawed young flesh.

What was she doing? Looking with naked voyeurism, late at night, sitting in the bleaching light of the screen, darkness behind her, silence in the garden. She alone with the images, enlarging and scrolling, scrolling.

She took a sip of water and bit her lower lip. 'Participant observation' made her scrolling ethical...for a brief time. She moused slowly to the next image, Costa surrounded by people, probably an archaeology group. Everyone held identical conference satchels as they gathered around an ancient marble athlete on a grey stone plinth. A junket, without doubt. In another photo, Costa crouched in a trench on a dig, presenting to the camera a delicate Roman wine glass, opalised after centuries in the Italian earth. Did he nick it?

Now he stood at attention, holding a Bible, his face composed and reverent, his hand on the shoulder of a tiny girl at her First Communion, her veil like a halo around her dark curls. A medieval Italian church rose behind them, its bare, crusty stone waiting a thousand years for green and pink marble cladding.

'Bravo, Giovanni,' wrote a visitor to his page. '*Bello,*' wrote another. '*Magnifico!*' '*Stupendo!*' And on and on. Stella rubbed her forehead. Such a mishmash in a person's life: giving and taking, honesty and pretence, a Rubik's Cube of being lived within one body. Each friend, acquaintance or colleague given glimpses of only one or two masterfully crafted façades, the others hidden and contrary.

She devoured each Costa vignette: church, beach, casino, archaeology, flesh. She went back to Positano and enlarged again. His lips were moist, sensuous around his cigar. The young women were disconcerting, barely seventeen, if that. She squirmed; they had pale, vacant faces.

She minimised Facebook and found Costa's Rome office website. It featured piles of high-saturation photographs, scattered randomly, as if about to be sorted for a family album. Hot, blue Italian skies and crumbly brown rocks contrasted to the pure white of Carrara marble. A spade, slicing the ground, filled the signature photograph. Spades ripped and slashed the flesh of the earth; that's what archaeologists did: reveal and destroy. No one else could ever again find what they had dug up, the site ruined forever. She turned to the 'Our Team' section, finding it much easier to follow written Italian than a slangy speech at a noisy cocktail party. Professor Giovanni Costa was 'lead consultant'. He wore a tailored Italian suit and an obviously designer tie, its soft sheen evident. His website face was rigid, professional, no hint of the boor.

She clicked back to Facebook and its Costa varieties, like Venetian masks. Snippets of a resumé followed the photos of the Roman-heritage Costa. He had at least two dozen published papers, all with multiple, shared authorship; he was never lead or sole author. She opened one on an Umbrian site near the Etruscan town of Todi with its laboured descriptions of channels, pipes, oil lamps and jewellery, but no theoretical inquiry. Lists and lists of objects, but so what? There was no suggestion of the meaning of his finds or the queries that prompted the digs. He had headed heritage committees for the past twenty-five years and had advised the Italian government and the Vatican. An archbishop had written a sugary note: 'Our prayers go to you, my dear Professor Costa, for your magnificent and treasured advice'. Two comments, however, cut across the adulation: 'write your own papers, stop sponging' and 'it's my dig, get out of my research'.

Stella whistled. These were the first criticisms; everything else was nauseating sycophancy. He stole intellectual property. That was an effortless way to get ahead in scholarship—tap brains for ideas, get a post-grad student to draft a paper, give it to another post-grad to edit; they'd all be pathetically grateful for the chance to work with the great Professor Costa. When the paper was finished, he would insist that it bore his name first or solo. That was his MO, theft in plain sight.

Costa had replied, 'Esteemed visitors to my Facebook page, I do not edit here. Please disregard malicious and mendacious comments. The history of my work in heritage is witness to my professionalism and integrity.' Stella leaned away from the computer, suddenly afraid, fast thudding in her chest. Even attacks via Facebook he turned to his advantage. Sly.

When would he retire? She went back to the first photographs. His face was flushed with alcohol, the eyes rheumy, lines criss-crossing the lower lids, but he was not close to retirement. And besides, long after official retirement, heritage people packed conferences and expected preferential treatment at tourist sites. If Costa had fifteen more years' work, plus a cushy retirement, it could be decades before everyone would be free of him. Who else had he bullied? Hundreds probably, mostly women.

Absently, she made hand shadows on the low ceiling in the hot, bright oval cast up by the desk lamp. Costa was a stranger and she was a stranger. How sickening that he had got under her skin. She tried to understand the sensations—a mix of trembling, chronic rage, pressure building, an inability to sit still—and his nauseating connection to her childhood.

He was Nigel; he was Alexander; he was the killer.

She picked up her glass, but nearly dropped it as a scream broke the silence. Another frightened woman. Enough was enough! She would have the last word thanks to dear Cleo.

She keyed in 'Cleo Wonder Dog' on Facebook and up rushed several sites. The name was not so original, after all. Five dogs had their own Facebook pages, including her family's own Cleo Wonder Dog in Perth. At least the name had been original in the southern hemisphere.

She entered the password, '*chien*', and time-travelled to David's childhood and standard Facebook photo fare: a poodle lost in a spray of beach sand, a curled ball of puppy sleeping with a cherubic boy on the family sofa. Stella teared up, remembering adored Cleo and the heart-rending loss of her a year ago. Despite the arrival of Bertie, the jet-black poodle puppy, David had not emerged from grief and sometimes followed Stella around the house holding a photograph of himself hugging Cleo. Deep in the cocoon of teenage privacy, his love of Cleo was the only emotion he admitted to his parents. He had created Cleo's Facebook page when he created his own. Stella saw that there had been nothing posted since Cleo died and David had written, 'RIP dear furry friend'.

She scrolled to the top of Cleo Wonder Dog's Facebook page and read every word of every entry for identifying information. Witty comments from David's school friends followed screen after screen of dog fun. There were her own sandy feet and orange-painted toenails and an unidentifiable Peter upside down, silhouetted in a sunset at Cottesloe Beach.

A ramshackle sandcastle half-hid David. The family had compacted sand for an hour to construct the fortress while Cleo snuffled in their elbows. From the Facebook page, Cleo appeared to have transcended earth and become an invisible, untraceable web presence.

Stella wrote in the name of Cleo and posted on Costa's page. 'You scum of the earth; how dare you show your face in Bonn.'

SIX

'DANCING ON THE furniture—partying hard last night!'
Georgette, another new professor, sidled up with her signature spiky, bleached hair and nose stud. Stella picked up a serving spoon and pretended to peruse large white bowls of apricot, coconut and almond varieties of muesli. So, professional fallout had already started from 'the seat'. That hadn't taken long.

Costa could be reading the words of Cleo Wonder Dog right now. She, Stella Amanda Jean Robinson, had threatened someone, she, who bore the names of her decent, honourable grandmothers. In bed, half an hour earlier, she had re-read her words with self-loathing. She was not the sort of person who attacked anyone, and to do so anonymously, like a coward... She had draped a wet cloth over her flushed, puffy face, breathing like a victim of waterboarding, her nose and mouth sucking in the textile with gasps, the cloth delineating her features like a death mask.

Stella forced an amused grin. 'I stood on the chair to look for a colleague.'

Georgette raised her eyebrows. 'Who?'

'No one you know.'

'I'm keen to network.'

Cornered. Stella clenched her fist on the spoon mid-way towards the apricot bowl. Georgette's eyebrows zoomed higher as she slid three Danish pastries onto her plate.

'Introduce me!'

Not a request, but a command; Stella heard it. The situation would only get worse. Georgette would pump her for university faculty information and then whisper it to her buddy, the Dean. Four years earlier, Stella had seen Georgette and the Dean lost in conversation in a corner of a university café, far from their home in Humanities. They had started when she approached with a gormless 'hi'. The Dean had been cold and demanding since that day, and what a battle they'd had over the new professorship. He had blocked her promotion for three years.

Georgette poured two orange juices and slid one to Stella. 'I'm all ears.'

Stella calculated; she would rather go hungry and thirsty. 'It's a long story. Gotta dash.'

The raisin *schnecken*, snail-shaped pastries, were always delicious; she grabbed one.

The Heussallee conference station filled up as passengers disembarked in front of its canary-yellow, glossy walls. Stella spied Costa in a group of sweating delegates bracing themselves for the slog to the conference centre. She had travelled three stops from the Bonn Concerto Hotel and now realised that Costa had already been on the train when she boarded. He had not been at her station, so where had he come from? Part of her—the old honourable part—wanted to run to him and explain away the bizarre Facebook comment. An error. Delete! What a difference a night's sleep made. She was a pendulum, swinging wildly, madly erratic, from righteous rage to red-hot with ignominy. Forget Costa, Facebook and the stupid seat; focus on the conference.

On the platform, Costa walked a few metres ahead of Stella, listening to a young woman who tottered beside him in turquoise stilettos and, from time to time, took a few jogging steps to keep up. Stella joined the surge towards the exit steps. She could see Costa's head if she looked left to his reflection on the glossy walls or right towards the tracks where he strode on the unprotected platform edge.

Perhaps he had not checked his Facebook page today; she crossed her fingers. She would shrivel in embarrassment if anyone knew what she had done. Professors had been stripped of their titles for far less. No professor from Great South Land University forgot that three years earlier a new professor boasted on Twitter about his elevation to Business-Class air travel after years travelling to conferences in Economy. Stupidly, he had posted a photo of himself sipping champagne in the exclusive lounge with the caption, 'At 30,000 feet, courtesy the taxpayer'. He was demoted on the grounds that he brought Great South Land University into disrepute.

Passengers flowed towards the exit as one sticky, sweaty mass. A rubbery wheeze announced the arrival of the otherwise silent train from Bonn on the opposite platform. Costa and the woman—a girl, so fragile in those heels—slowed down near the end of the platform. Absorbed, Costa swung his right leg wide over the space of the track—as if his belly pushed it out— tempting fate. The pugnacious tilt of his head revealed that he commanded the conversation. He highlighted a point in loud, rapid Italian, too fast for Stella, but something about shared publication and deadlines.

On the opposite platform, passengers arriving from central Bonn flapped fans, intent on getting along the road and into the relative cool of the conference centre. The young woman tried to say something, but Costa held up his hand like a stop sign, hovering it close to her nose. Then he threw his arms in the air as if in exasperation and tapped his foot. She attempted to speak, raised her hands, pleaded. Suddenly he pushed his face towards hers and jabbed her shoulder. She lifted her arms as a barrier and stepped away from him. And back further again in stilettos so slender they could snap. Only twenty centimetres from the edge and the drop to the track.

Costa did not see the track—or did he? He must have seen how perilously close she was. Stella's impulse was to drag her to safety, but a stronger passion prevailed. She took three photographs—ashamed that she did not intervene—as the delicate heels balanced mere centimetres from the drop. The woman tried to speak, but Costa persisted with hunched shoulders and thrusting head. In close-up, heart slamming, Stella photographed his furious face in profile as he hectored the woman. Gone was the self-satisfied mask he wore at the cocktail party; this was the same bored, everyday aggression that she had first seen in the auditorium.

Another rush-hour train approached from Bad Godesberg, propelling cool tunnel air. People closed their eyes and lifted their faces into the grimy wind. Costa's open hand slithered across the woman's breasts. Stella could not drag her eyes from the scene, another crime against another woman in plain view.

The train slid behind the turquoise heels as the woman shrieked and fell forward into Costa's arms. She gaped at the carriage—only centimetres away—rammed Costa and wobbled towards the exit. Costa chased her up the steps. Stella dogged them, light perspiration coating her suddenly chilled body. No one saw? Her dishonourable Facebook comments paled beside Costa's violence. Why had she fussed last night about the ethics of looking? Ethics were a waste of time with this low-life.

'Stel-lah! There you are, at last.'

What now? Justine climbed the station steps and reached to pat Stella's shoulder.

'Thank goodness for your polka-dot jacket or you'd be missing in action.'

Justine materialised with two fat briefcases, and wearing a white, floaty dress and silver sandals. Stella panted. She'd witnessed violence with impunity, but here was innocent Justine, over-loaded with Board documents, plugging on at the conference, safe in her naïveté. She took Justine's bigger bag as they emerged in the heat of the street.

'I've seen something...horrible—'

But if she told Justine about Costa, it would put her perilously close to revealing the reason she missed the second part of the Board meeting, failed to explain a journal's legal background, wasted everyone's time and risked her reputation on the new journal's first day. That could lead to Cleo and Facebook and academic humiliation that was far worse than boasting about swilling taxpayer-funded champagne.

'Horrible?' Justine was wide-eyed and sympathetic.

'Oh...nothing, I misunderstood.'

'Something in the station? Now?'

Stella shook her head wildly. 'No, no, no. It was a trick of the eye, those shiny yellow walls...' A colleague. A career. Pay attention.

Justine smiled at her, forgiving and good-hearted, while Costa, slightly ahead, turned into the street at the top of the steps.

Stella plunged in. 'I'm terribly sorry about yesterday. I hope you went ahead with most of the agenda.'

Justine donned her enormous straw hat, taking care not to scratch other walkers. 'Not the same without you.'

'You know how it is at big conferences, you get double-booked. Servile apologies.'

'No need to grovel.'

Stella had not burnt her bridges and the dreaded apology was over, short and sweet. They zig-zagged in and out of patches of shade on the Heussallee road. Costa was close, talking vehemently to the young woman's back a few metres in front of him.

'Hey, cute sunglasses, where'd you find them?' asked Justine.

From attempted murder to sunglasses…chatting was agony.

'A gift from Peter for this trip.'

Stella handed her glasses to Justine. They had nearly caught up to Costa.

'Red stars on a glitter frame. Fun and vintage.' Justine put them on and adopted a self-absorbed super-model pose. 'Fabulous, I love them, but it's too cloudy in Vancouver to over-indulge in sunglasses.'

She offered the glasses back. Stella measured the distance on the footpath to Costa. She was closing in, almost level with him.

'Earth to Stella!'

'Sorry, dreaming. The sunglasses? Peter paid a lot. We've been having a tense time; it was a romantic gift.'

Stella knew that Justine saw a different world when she looked through the lenses, a world of honesty and goodwill and opportunities that friends gave each other, not one of fear, suspicion and hunting.

Justine squeezed Stella's shoulder. 'Are you ok?'

Stella repositioned her starry sunglasses as Costa reached the woman who hurried barefoot on the scalding pavement. He grabbed her arm, then the crowd obscured them both.

'Yeah…fine.'

Still aghast at the scene in the station, she tried to focus on Justine and the elegant nineteenth-century houses that lined the road. Justine looked penetratingly.

'I'm well, really.' Stella forced a short laugh. 'Where are we up to with the new Board?'

Justine brought Stella up to date with the composition of the Board, these strangers that Stella would need to work with via email.

'The journal will work well only if everyone gets to know everyone else, face-to-face, this week. Time is short.'

Ah, yes, the Board. It was still there, demanding Stella's attention that was anywhere but on it. She focused on Costa lumbering beside the girl.

Justine didn't notice. 'I'll provide lots of chances for us to get to know each other in the next few days. I don't want misunderstandings by email; they're awkward, damaging to the Board.'

After the atrocious station event, Stella did not have energy for more strangers. Her body pitched from chilled to hot. Justine sounded half a block away. In the distance, Stella thought she saw exploding leaves.

Tree leaves…not tree leaves? Dizzy and dehydrated, she drank deeply from her water bottle. The exploding leaves resolved into a flock of rose-ringed parakeets diving to the pavement. Someone ahead had scattered seed. Costa? She could not imagine him travelling to a conference with bird seed, but that was the sort of weird thing that he might do. She drank again, but the dizziness persisted and a slight body chill edged out the heat. They approached the feeding parakeets, seed shattering beneath their strappy sandals. Still no Costa.

Stella tried being conversational with professional but intimate gossip. 'Michael—he's overbearing.'

Justine nodded. 'He can be bossy, but he's the best for juggling the politics of archaeology. Tons of experience.'

'And his sexism's the price we have to pay?'

The humiliation of Michael cutting her off had not diminished. Stella squinted at sunlight erupting through leaves. Not only Michael—Nigel, the Dean, Dimitri—they all undermined her. As for Alexander…

'Michael's publication list's impressive,' said Justine.

'He'll derail meetings.'

'But he's a whizz grant-getter.'

Justine would need to be a strict chair; most meetings would be by teleconference. Stella photographed the squabbling birds as beaks probed the slits in the pavement, crossing like swords. The position of Deputy-Editor was good for her career and another powerful step towards safety. She could put up with Michael's rubbish in small doses. No need to rock the boat before it left shore.

Justine took her heavy bag from Stella. 'See you at Breakout Room Two this afternoon. We'll start with you talking about legal frameworks; can't proceed without that.'

From the back row of the Observers' Gallery, Stella studied the auditorium entrances below. No sign of Costa or the young woman in turquoise high heels.

She opened Facebook on her phone. A reply! Costa had posted directly under the words of Cleo Wonder Dog: 'My dear friends, I have discovered these foul words. People are jealous of my success. I prefer honesty and truth. See how good people are targeted by cowards. This is not the way forward for honourable lives.'

Stella's heart raced; her head and back felt blisteringly hot. Regret flamed into rage. Mere hours after she had posted as Cleo, he had checked his repulsive, bragging Facebook page. 'I prefer honesty and truth.' How dare he! Honesty was not what he got from the slimy Archbishop who wrote thanks for 'treasured advice'. She swallowed hard and blinked. The room looked fuzzy, a bit white, a bit silvery-blue. She read the words again—he believed his own nonsense. 'See how good people are targeted by cowards.' What about that terrifying scene in the station? You nearly pushed that poor woman under a train. Sweat prickled in the roots of Stella's freshly washed hair. What a coward he was.

'Not the way forward.' Going where? To your career? To your pocket? Today, Mister Costa, no sycophants commented on your pathetic Facebook page. It was me, Stella Amanda Jean Robinson—but her flush intensified; her clammy hands slipped on her phone.

She tapped in feverishly as Cleo, 'I know who you are and what you are. You cheat and bully.'

Send! That cleared the air.

Or did it? The queasiness she had experienced as she walked from the station returned, washing over in waves sufficiently small that she did not need to run to the bathroom, but dense enough to undercut her focus. She skimmed the programme; she could afford to miss the morning session. She needed fresh air right now. A couple of hours in the park would refresh her for the Board meeting, where she would perform impressively.

❧

The only bench in the shade was occupied. The same old woman appeared to be in a reverie that lasted until Stella was upon her, then she greeted her warmly, her old eyes mournful.

'*Guten Tag.*'

Stella sat down. 'A proper introduction—my name's Stella Robinson. I lecture on Australian cultural history. I'm in Bonn for the World Heritage Committee Meeting.'

The old woman nodded and looked down at her hands with their papery-white skin laced with grey-blue veins like a tropical delta. She scrunched the dress textile in arthritic fingers—tight, loose, tight. She smiled, blood-red lipstick too bright in her waxen face.

'Good to see you again and to share this special bench, my favourite. My name is Hildegard Weber. We are proud that your meeting is in little Bonn which feels forgotten now that Berlin is once again the capital. The most inspiring music is not enough to make a city vibrant, not even Beethoven's *Waldstein Sonata* for all its glory.

57

'Most welcome visitor to Germany, from the faraway, other side of the world, with your curiosity about history. Would you like to know some of mine?'

Suddenly, Stella hungered to hear a story from this person who was born in the same year as her own father and survived the same war, but, shockingly, on the wrong side. Her grandmother, Jean, had told Stella how her only son stumbled home from fighting the Japanese in New Guinea, but was never again the same person who had left home to go to war. He had died ten years ago, still almost silent about combat, except that, somehow, he had surfaced from the jungle and mud and maddening plague on plague of mosquitoes. The near absence of her father's war memories pierced Stella. A firsthand account from the enemy's side, on the other hand, would be an historian's dream.

'Yes, please tell me.'

Her queasiness calmed. She set her phone alarm for the afternoon session and surrendered to the story. Hildegard contemplated the lapping of the Rhine and heat shimmering off the paths and began.

'Even in the darkest of times, in the midst of violence so bestial we can scarcely comprehend, beds need to be made and bathrooms cleaned. And so it was in Bonn in those atrocious days. There's a domestic front as well as a military front. Did you know that?'

'What we call "the home fires".'

'An English-language metaphor. I was on that domestic front. You fight to keep civilisation from being destroyed. For me, it was for crisp, white sheets and a spotless hotel suite. How trivial they sound next to military endeavours, but how abominably linked.'

HILDEGARD'S STORY

In 1941 in Bonn, Hildegard smoothed a white cloth over her grandmother's worn oak table.

'I'm looking for a job.'

Kurt turned from the dresser holding two plates from their new wedding china. Tiny forget-me-nots with electric-blue petals and intense yellow centres swirled around the border.

'You haven't got time.'

'The allowance from my mother is not stretching far enough.'

'Your thesis will suffer.'

Hildegard set down a pot of boiled potatoes. Steam mingled with the aroma of her favourite rye bread and a vinegary cloud from a dish of sauerkraut, heavy with caraway and the tang of fennel.

'But Kurt, be realistic. Soon your Saturday job won't be enough; the rent's going up.'

'We'll manage. Stay focused on architecture.'

'I'd rather have a small job than lose study time worrying about money.'

'You mustn't risk your studies, darling.'

Hildegard leaned across the table in the tiny sitting room, with its one working light, and kissed him on the forehead.

'If I have a job, then I won't need to worry about the rent and will be focused on study.'

Abruptly, they both looked in the direction of the medieval lane beyond their front door as gears grated and a truck inched forward. Kurt paled. Their eyes met.

It was happening.

Grotesque posters had been pasted up overnight in Marktplatz, the market square, smothering the walls of shops and announcing the liberation of the German *volk*. Deportations of Jewish citizens had begun.

A scream pierced the living room. Kurt sat down at the table and leaned heavily on his elbows.

'Damn them.'

Water spilt from a vase of daisies as Hildegard placed it on the table. Another truck started at the end of the lane, barely fitting in the few metres between shops and homes. Engine throbs echoed on old walls and invaded their living room.

Kurt averted his eyes. 'We have all failed in words and actions and now are powerless to help without risking our own lives.'

A truck changed gear as he stood up and held her close. 'If you're at work, then you're not studying architecture.' He kissed her sadly. 'God forbid, but you could be the next Albertina Speer.'

Hildegard searched the job postings at Bonn University. Kurt might be right. They would all bite into her study time. She could do child-minding in the morning or restaurant work in the evening, but she had morning lectures, and the nights were for her new husband. She would check again later in the week.

She waved to her friends, Eva and Marta, who appeared from nowhere, hurrying towards the university library. Eva's tightly braided blonde bun hardly stirred in the sharp draught that slashed the corridor. They did not seen her.

Hildegard shivered as she bent to pick up her father's battered student satchel and then spotted a notice that had been blown off the pin board. 'Sophisticated hotel in Bad Godesberg requires cleaning staff for the afternoons. Must be meticulous, presentable and 100% discreet. Apply to the concierge.'

Hildegard read the card again. Afternoons… Bad Godesberg was conveniently on the Bonn train line. An architect must be meticulous when drawing and planning; she could point out that to the hotel management. She studied her blue cotton dirndl and stout brown shoes. She supposed that they were 'presentable'. They'd have to do; rationing gave her little choice. But why 'discreet'?

The elderly concierge's uniform strained at the seams as he ushered Hildegard into one of the hotel managers' offices. She skirted around stacks of boxes and files. Beyond the window, the Rhine flowed. She had arrived in a world of crystalline space and light as if the river had been designed uniquely to flow past the graceful Jugendstil hotel.

'The Rheinhotel Dreesen seeks a polite, efficient cleaner who will work afternoons only,' said the manager. 'The work will vary, but mostly it will be related to a special suite.'

Hildegard nodded. All would have a bed to be made and a shelf to dust, little difference. The manager stood behind his desk, facing the window, hands clasped behind his back. On her shoulder, the concierge was repulsively close. His breath, heavy with the odour of sausages, settled on her neck, stirring stray hair from her plait.

'We need a person of scrupulous morals and discretion.'

Hildegard scrunched her eyes in the glare of the manager's silhouette. 'I have cleaning experience. From an early age, I assisted my mother. She's fussy.'

'We are concerned with your morals in the first instance. Theft and indiscretion are the scourges of fine establishments.'

'Yes.'

'Yes, what?'

The answer? She had never been grilled before. She focused behind the manager to the blue of the Rhine and a small rowing boat with a swastika fluttering from the prow.

'Sir, I submitted my references to the concierge. I'm a person of good morals.'

'Time will tell.' The manager tapped his fingers in a gothic-shaped arch; the architect in Hildegard observed the line as inspiration struck.

'I would not waste valuable life opportunities like working in this beautiful and famous hotel.'

The manager turned away. Hildegard studied his straight

back and squared shoulders. Beyond him, children ran with a golden cocker spaniel. Family values seemed safe to talk about.

'I often attend church on Sunday,' she said. 'I study hard.'

'Morals are essential to the good name of our hotel,' he said coldly. 'I repeat, morals. Sometimes one might not know that one is being tempted. You would need to be alert to the disguises of temptation.'

He spun back fiercely, looming over his desk. 'Disguises, *Fraulein*, could you see through them?'

Hildegard recoiled into the sausage breath of the concierge, but her gaze on the manager remained cool and level. He scrutinised her reactions, his eyes tight and mean. A cough gathered in her throat; her breath quickened. She would not quaver, nor fumble for words, but a blush bloomed in her neck and travelled into her hair. She would not be intimidated by silly, masculine tactics. She could manage cleaning in a small hotel. She was going to be an architect; by comparison, this would be easy. Composure, remember the message a body sends. She sat taller, neck up straight, sensible shoes together.

The manager slammed his hands on the desk. 'We offer excellent service which has attracted the Fuhrer. He has a permanent suite here and visits often.'

Silence invaded the small, jammed office. Even the children at the river edge stopped shouting. The impossible. Cleaning for Hitler. Hildegard froze. No boats sailed past; the river surged by, empty. Nervous energy tapped up her spine as she grasped the reality: the Rheinhotel Dreesen was the Fuhrer's Bonn residence. She would be connected to him in the most intimate way: his bedsheets, his soiled clothes, his toilet. Her gorge rose. A cleaner would drag his hair and mucus from the basin's plug hole. She swallowed as she covered her throat with her hand and shrank into her only presentable jacket. The men were too close, the room too small. She spotted her skirt hem unravelling; she must have torn it in the train. She fingered the loose thread.

Two blackbirds settled on a hedge beyond the window, fixing Hildegard with their yellow-rimmed eyes. They symbolised adaptability, protection and intuition, what she needed. She refused to think of them as bad luck; that could not be the reason they landed in front of her at this life-changing moment. The plan to keep her head down and out of trouble during the war vanished. She had become truly political. The concierge shifted behind her chair, a slight squeak from his shoe. She would have to touch what Hitler touched. Clean up after him. Bits of his discarded body—his hair and saliva—she would need to touch it all and reveal nothing of her feelings.

'You know of the Fuhrer's celebrated love for nature and beauty.'

The manager swept his hand in a circle to the Rhine, the seven famous hills of the Siebengebirge, and the Godesberg mountain, hidden from view at the hotel but rising abruptly, topped by castle ruins, and dominating the town centre.

'It is here that he can relax in the superb beauty of Germany and have respite from the rigours of his duties for the Fatherland while attending to matters of international importance.'

'Fatherland' echoed in Hildegard's head. The birds blasted their yellow stares through the window. She coughed. Composure... She struggled to keep her eyes blank and her hands still. She itched to twist her dirndl into spirals, anything to let out nervous energy, but that would reveal too much. Should she accept this position? If she walked away from this job, she and Kurt would be marked as anti-Nazi and it would be breathtakingly dangerous, but if she stayed... She ran through her options: not take the job, take it for a short time, feign illness...but the hotel management would check up on her. Already, she knew too much.

'Fatherland'. Once that concept was invoked you were mired in the rhetoric. She sat rigid, perspiration dappling her collar. She and Kurt had hoped that they could survive the war, physically and morally, by continuing with their studies and pleading for a future, voluntary enlistment if Kurt were conscripted.

'Bad Godesberg and our charming hotel can give the Fuhrer what he looks for in Bonn,' said the manager.

She must play along. She would need to act with Nazi enthusiasm from this exact second.

'Yes, sir, our city is beautiful and—' A frightened bleat, her voice cut off.

'Do you love mountains, young woman?'

She was on guard. 'Yes, sir...um, of course! The Fuhrer probably likes to visit the Drachenfels when he's here; it has lovely views of the river and—'

'Do not presume to guess the preferences of the Fuhrer!' The manager's voice rose, shrill, as he loomed across his desk. 'We demand discretion at all times. You will not tell people about this vital war work for Germany. You will maintain the immaculate condition of the *Fuhrersuite*. When you are not attending to his admirably modest needs, you will assist in the kitchen.'

Stella's phone alarm beeped. Time to head back for the afternoon session.

'The kitchen...that was not the job you applied for. They had no right to put you there.'

Hildegard laughed for the first time. 'They had all the rights!'

'Of course, but the kitchen... You can see that I don't like cooking. It bores me; it's messy. When my son was born, I had no choice; I had to learn to cook.'

'Dr Robinson, Stella, do you not see that the kitchen was safer than the *Fuhrersuite*?'

Stella nodded. Yes, it would have been. She dragged her grey backpack from under the bench.

'I need to return to the conference now.'

She was sorry to leave. How generous of Hildegard to share her frightening memories; it had taken her mind away from silly Costa.

'Thank you, Hildegard, I've loved hearing your story.'

'My story is far from over.'

SEVEN

PHOTOGRAPHS OF CHAMPAGNE cellars flashed onto the World Heritage Committee screens in the lower chamber. Costa disrupted the busy upper gallery, barging through people talking in the aisles, claiming his special seat. Stella hunched forward in the back row. His obnoxious behaviour was on display again, but where was the young woman in turquoise stilettos? Journalists and camera equipment overflowed the press gallery for the World Heritage listing of the Champagne region. People made jokey gestures of drinking from imaginary flutes, and Costa kicked aside press cables.

Stella shook her head at the latest commotion. Hildegard's story had calmed her; life could be far more burdensome than the few woes she had encountered. Below on the podium, a spokesperson outlined champagne's poetic qualities: inspiration, celebration, imagination. Stella remembered the cases of champagne at her wedding to Peter; lovely, golden wood boxes filled with fat bottles. Dancing, love and a luminous future for the young scholar and medical doctor.

The presentation began with an outline of ten years of documentation on Champagne's request for World Heritage status. Stella watched a young technician ask Costa to move; he ignored her, and then knocked a tripod. The technician grabbed a leg as the camera swayed, threatening to topple into the lower chamber. She tried again, pointing to an empty seat further along the front row. Costa shook his head and spread jacket, papers and his bag across three seats. Stella exploited the disturbance, moving quickly down from the back row and sliding into the seat immediately behind him. Tingles zapped up her neck; he was too close—but she was close, and he had no idea! The technician shrugged and crouched to gaffer-tape the tripod. Costa pulled a dog-eared business card from his trouser pocket and stuck it on the glass balustrade.

Close-ups of plump grapes, ready for harvest, sprang onto the big screens; shiny blades of secateurs reflected starbursts of sunlight. Stella had a photograph in her office of the family during a Champagne holiday; behind them, barrels in a vast cellar stretched to blackness. Piles of marked, but unclaimed student essays obscured Peter and David.

Stella bent towards Costa's neck, holding herself at an angle that suggested she was reading her phone screen, but she peered up beneath her eyelashes at the back of his head, to his deep tanned and speckled balding crown, embarrassing strands of grown-out lime dye, thick hair brushing his shirt, and the tips of his ears breaking through tufts. Three freckles spotted the back of his right ear.

She shut her eyes. No one had seen him attack her over the seat, so why would anyone notice her today? She did not know why she wanted to inspect the back of his head except that doing so without his knowledge bestowed a sense of power. No one would think that a professor would study the back of a colleague's head because…that would be insanity. But doing so evoked a visceral sense of balance; he had invaded her space and now she invaded his and set the world right.

She held her phone close to her knees, photographing the back of his head and the surprising smoothness of his neck. Her mascara clumped in perspiration. She was close; every pore in his skin was intoxicating. The flesh of him, would-be murderer's flesh—that poor young woman. The reality, the odour of his body. Close. There. Skin. His skin. Touching with her breath—see how *you* like it.

Her writing pad peeped from her backpack. She should pick it up and record her thoughts, expand them into another paper; Champagne would attract publishers and readers. Ought to pick it up—but she had had decades of making notes for academic articles. She had already made a good start in Germany with pages and pages of ideas before 'the seat'. She'd had too many years of being dependable. He was under her skin; she had to act.

She zipped her bag closed and exhaled hotly, a cloud of air ballooning through wide-open lips, almost too faint to be detected. Dark hair draped either side of her face. Her breath enveloped the back of his head; she imagined microscopic droplets grabbing each hair strand, settling, claiming, suffocating. She heard him kick the cables back onto the steps. Absent-mindedly, he ran his hand across the skin of his neck. Stella puffed softly again, wrapping Costa's head in the phantom of her breath, a gratifying, invisible invasion. A single strand of dark hair twitched. He shook and stretched his neck, pressed his hair close to his skull. She had the upper hand now.

More barrels and champagne bottles filled the screens; a vintner crossed her arms in the recesses of an historic cellar. Stella flared her breath like an invisible turban across the width of Costa's head. His hair quivered, revealing a vulnerable, scaly scalp. He started, peered upwards as if expecting to see air ducts. Stella dared rest a hand on the back of his seat as he lifted his shoulders and reached behind, his slim, tapered fingers slowly parting the hair on his collar, exposing a small, inflamed scar.

She stifled a snort. She was as close to the wound as a medical practitioner...or a lover. She invaded *his* body, not yet at the endocrine level, but it was a start. His scar was puckered, the surrounding area crimson. The nail of his right forefinger circled the blistering crater, causing a deepening red ring. He rubbed the erupting flesh into an ooze of blood and pus. The neck skin stretched and crinkled as he irritated the slash, tugging it to a rosy welt and back to bloodless white. As he took his hands from his head, he grazed her knuckles. She tilted headlong into pus.

The gallery exploded in cheers. Stella looked up, disoriented, having missed the announcement that Champagne's hillsides, cellars and houses had entered the World Heritage List. People slapped each other on the back, clapping, whistling, stamping their feet. Everyone congratulated everyone else. A crescendo of cheering. On and on. Men and women embracing and laughing. Louder and louder. Magnums banging on committee desks and the whole world becoming French.

Stella was an outsider, a bewildered witness to celebration. Costa stood, blowing kisses and clapping, first into the joyful tumult of the gallery and then around to the press zone, where journalists and camera operators exchanged high-fives. He directed his clapping in the direction of first this, then that delegate in the chamber below, and mimed a champagne toast before sitting down as a portly late-comer tried to enter the front row. Costa angled his legs, but the space was too narrow for the man to pass. Sighing histrionically, Costa stood and turned towards Stella sitting behind, allowing his seat to flip up so that the man could squeeze by. Costa's eyes flitted dispassionately across her body. She was mere centimetres from him, a flesh-and-blood being, but there was no startle in the sweep of his view, no flicker of his eyes, no infinitesimal rise of his eyebrows. She wore the same polka-dot jacket that she had worn yesterday, but he registered nothing. She dared to catch and hold his eyes, but his focal length did not alter; he looked through her and beyond.

Stella glared. He should be shot through with jitters to see her so close, but he gazed through her, out of the gallery, through the glass walls and decals of raptors, and beyond to the garden. This was the masculine non-gaze, nullifying her being. She was another invisible, older woman, invisible, even when she was a threat. He had no recollection of her. He had a nasty, entitled life shored up by bullying and posturing. She was a mere lump of flesh that had occupied his preferred seat. Her fury connected viscerally to Peter; the anger was sickeningly familiar. Her stomach turned tight and bitter.

'Perfect little black dress?'

Stella pirouetted in the family living room in the new scooped-neck dress that she had bought for the closing party in Bonn. It skimmed her waist and the bias cut flared snugly over her buttocks. Her favourite gold chain nestled between the hint of her breasts as she twirled on gold high heels. Peter rubbed his chin; a crease appeared in the hairy skin between his eyes.

'Yeah…you look lovely, but…'

Stella stopped twirling; he should be her greatest admirer.

'But?'

He neatened a pile of medical and cultural heritage magazines, tapping the ends on the glass coffee table.

'But? Peter?'

'Um…' He cleared his throat and fiddled with the silver candle sticks that held candles that they lit every night of their marriage when they were home. 'Too sexy for work?'

Peter was out of touch. Way out. How long was it since he had been to a medical conference?

'This isn't for work. This is for the final party. Everyone'll be dressed up.'

He took a slow breath. 'It doesn't send the right message for a professional event.'

'It's for the party.'

'I'm uncomfortable.'

'Don't worry; you won't be there.'

Stella ripped off her gold heels and headed to the bedroom. Peter needed to get more into the world; his neighbourhood practice had stifled him and it was none of his business what she wore.

Two days later, their bed was strewn with clothes choices as she undertook a preliminary packing for Bonn. She always over-packed and was determined to avoid a hefty surcharge on excess baggage that the university would not reimburse. Peter sat on the end of the bed, cradling the sleepy, young poodle, Bertie.

'We'll miss you.'

Stella stuffed walking shoes into a bag. 'I hope Bertie doesn't learn new puppy tricks while I'm away.'

She spread the little black dress across the bed and began to fold it with rolls of tissue paper to minimise creasing.

Peter stroked Bertie's puppy fur vigorously. 'Your new black jacket's an excellent choice for your presentation, sends the right message, but…um…not that dress.'

She took an audible breath. She was an adult—a professor, people took notes when she spoke—but he had no respect for her personal clothing choices? Peter flinched as Bertie snapped sleepily; he lowered the pup to the carpet.

Stella smoothed the dress into the case. 'It's perfect.'

'Won't help your career.'

He seized the dress. Stella jerked it back just as Peter let go. She lost balance and crashed into the full-length, antique mirror in the corner of their bedroom, all her weight on her right arm. Blood sprang from deep cuts. She cowered among hundreds of shards of nineteenth-century glass. Bertie yelped and hid beneath the bed.

Stella fought off Peter. 'Get away!'

Glass pierced her thighs; blood spotted the carpet. She had fallen below the window ledge, her head angled oddly against the wall. If she tried to sit upright, the damage intensified with blade-like cuts. Lacerations covered her body in a thousand knife stabs. The curtains heaved and bulged in the night breeze, blocking Peter's face, the bedroom turning into a horror scene. Blood. A headless monster. Get away! The curtains sucked in, then shot up in a gust. Peter's arms snaked towards her, insistent, unrelenting. Eucalyptus leaves rattled and slithered beyond the window. Stella hugged her good arm to her body, shaking her head, kicking at his feet. Stop!

A violent crisis after years of marriage? Over a mere dress? Thank goodness David was sleeping over with a friend. His world would have cracked to see her like this, quivering on the floor, blood seeping over her favourite cream jumper, Peter menacing.

The pink pearl earrings appeared to signal the end of the broken arm event, a lustrous full stop delivered to the hospital with red roses, but Peter made it clear that he did not see the incident as she did.

'I'm sorry, but it was an accident.'

Accident? A convenient re-telling of brute force. 'You grabbed my dress.'

Peter wrung his hands and spoke softly. 'I'm sorry…but it wasn't suitable.'

'It's the twenty-first century and a man tells me what to wear?'

'No…not really, not usually.'

Fiercely, Stella ran her hand over the hospital sheet. 'Sounded like it to me. My arm's broken!'

She slapped the hospital bed with her good arm, making the jewellery box jump and the silver gift wrap tumble to the floor. A week away at a conference was what she needed.

🐦

The two events illuminated each other, a fight over a dress and a fight over a seat. The pink pearl earrings swayed in Stella's dark hair, the perfect choice for a conference, elegant, understated.

A loving gift from Peter—she knew that; she thanked him and loved to wear them—but also a gender transaction. Life was complicated with multiple meanings. Constitutional freedom, yes. Gender equity laws, yes. But the reality of male force persisted. Love and control. In each case she had done nothing wrong but was cast as the guilty party. In Germany, she had retained her seat and, in Australia, simply packed a bag.

Peter said sorry for breaking her arm—again and again. She hugged him, but it was hard to pretend that it had not happened. It had become part of the history of their marriage. He was jolted to see his wife injured and bloodied in their bedroom. In his Nedlands medical practice, his old-fashioned, courtly manners made him a favourite with patients, but he never properly comforted her during those tense weeks while she nursed her broken arm. Her chunk of plaster separated them in bed, as if they were strangers, the injury meaning something different to each of them.

Stella massaged her arm as Costa dragged a finger around the sticky tape, securing his business card to the glass balustrade, marking his territory with no idea of her presence. He picked up his jacket and bag and walked to the exit.

A WhatsApp buzz. Justine: 'Legal discussion, 5 mins. Breakout Room 2.'

Stella had forgotten the meeting. She tapped out a reply. 'CU v soon.'

She walked to the balustrade, tore off his card and tossed it in a bin. Juggling her phone and bag, she tracked Costa as he wended his way to the far side of the main foyer through the exhilarated throng. This way and that, Costa exchanged more air kisses and bowed as if it were the eighteenth century. Was it possible that he knew everyone except her, the person he bashed? She alone had no bodily presence? Two men mimed a champagne toast in his honour. More people fawned. They laughed and slapped each other's backs.

She would force him to behold her. He reached the water fountain; Stella groped in her bag for her reusable conference flask—the environmentally aware Germans had thought of everything. She stood behind Costa and drained the dregs. The reek of sweat and cured meats rolled over her as she set her plan in motion: stand a bit too close, cough too loudly. Exist!

She advanced level to Costa and knocked his arm. Not nudged—'excuse me, so sorry'—but shoved, muscles activated, fist knuckle-white. Knocked him! Where had that come from? Unplanned, not thought out. No response from Costa. He waited his turn at the fountain. Her arm felt disconnected from her body. She was in little, jagged bits, like the leaves that she thought exploded on the avenue. She had no plan; she was out of control. Who cares!

As he bent to fill his water bottle, she rammed hers beneath the spout. A brilliant moment. Now he must see her. He must! In the busy, noisy foyer she was aware of one person only, Costa, as he stood uncannily silent beside her. No clearing of his throat, no remonstration. She was still invisible.

She filled her bottle and, without moving a step and leaving no space for him at the fountain, sipped deliberately slowly, once, twice…ten prolonged, chilled sips and leisurely swallows while her eyes contemplated a vulture decal. She waited for him to ask her to move, but he didn't. With studied, theatrical drama, she wiped condensation from the flask, repeatedly sliding her index finger down from the opening to the base, taking her time. She had not planned anything beyond a vulgar pushing-in, and after the suggestive stroking of her flask…she had no more plans. The game would end. She would remain invisible.

It happened as if an unseen force intervened, grabbed her strong arm and dashed it savagely towards him. One, two, three… She flung her bottle into his chest. She heard a startled intake of his breath as water spurted across his face and sprayed over his jacket. If she had planned to douse Costa, she would not have had the nerve, but now he dripped stupidly in the elegant foyer. From far away, Stella heard people react: 'oh dear', 'poor man', 'clumsy woman'.

Her arm hung by her side, alien, mysterious, a weapon. Water clung to his bushy brows, dripped from his nose, stained his linen jacket. His face remained impassive—what supreme control—but his eyes drifted from her eyes downwards, to the stretch of the silk jacket across her breasts. She gave no apology because she was invisible, except, evidently, for her breasts. He lifted his eyes back to hers as he wiped droplets from his face, flicking them from his hand. The icy droplets landed on her legs, shocking her back into the moment. She stepped aside. His strange, blink-less eyes roved back to her face. She held her gaze; it was all that she could think to do. A direct, powerful gaze back, an inversion of all the patriarchal nonsense that had been flung at her.

Costa swallowed hard; his throat bulged. He too took a step backwards. Then two steps back. And two more. The glorious surprise on his face…his ridiculous retreat. He had finally seen her. Triumph! In the eternal sweep of the universe, it was nothing. The event was minuscule, but so was asking someone to vacate a seat, unless it was Rosa Parks' seat in Alabama, then it could lead to a revolution.

His eyes narrowed. 'Madam! If you please.'

'Madam'? In the conference bathroom mirror, there was Stella's flushed face, strained eyes, lips bitten to a deep red. The Monstrous Feminine incarnate had executed a frivolous, aggressive act and she was still invisible. There was no re-balancing the world if Costa did not register her existence.

She folded both arms tightly across her chest and studied her eyes, dry and itchy from staring, as if she had worked on a computer for hours. But she had not worked; she remembered the unfinished preparation for the next day's presentation, her career highlight of the week. The scholarly demands of the conference bore down. She steadied herself with a hand on the mirror. A sickly white ringed her mouth; she had clenched her jaw too hard and too long. Attempting to start a brawl in an international conference was not what she had planned. Not who she was. But being sexually accosted by a colleague in a hotel corridor was not her either. Nor was finding herself in a bloody heap in her own bedroom.

The door to the breakout room was closed; it should have been ajar, waiting for her. Stella opened the door gently. Ten faces glanced up, but everyone was a stranger. She thought that Justine might have asked extras to join the meeting, to hear what Stella, the new Deputy-Editor, had to say about legal constraints, but there was no Justine, and no one smiled. She apologised and checked the door. 'Room One.'

The numbering of downstairs rooms seemed jumbled. She jogged up and down the narrow, subterranean corridor. Six minutes since the start of the Board meeting. Not too bad, but not good in the light of her previous absence. People clustered around the day's programme pinned to a notice board at right angles to the corridor wall. She pushed past and hurried to the end of the passage and then back through people bustling up and down. No Breakout Room Two. She turned back and spotted the problem. The notice board sliced the corridor in half and effectively hid Room Two. Stella opened the door.

Unsmiling, and without taking her eyes from her notes, Justine pointed to a seat and resumed listening to Michael, who had not paused to welcome the Deputy-Editor. Stella carried a spare chair from the back wall and squeezed in at the end of the table next to Takura. He moved his briefcase, adjusted his chair and slid his pen and notepad away from her. Fatima looked irritated, resting her elbows on the table, blocking Stella's view of Michael.

Stella riffled through notes on legal issues and waited for Justine to ask her to speak. Ready. Now. But her mind fizzed: Costa dripping with water, his steps back and back, the blur of the foyer, bewilderment at her own actions. She had no idea what the Board was discussing and could not catch up without interrupting.

'So sorry. Again!'

Stella hurried to catch Justine, who raced down the corridor at the end of the meeting. Not once had Justine met her eyes.

'Wait!' Stella tapped Justine on the back. 'I'm sorry I was late. I know how bad it looks.'

Justine looked frustrated and sad. 'There's something going on, Stella, I can feel it.'

'It won't happen again.'

'You're not the same person.'

Not the same person? The secret delight of breathing on Costa's head—ok, that had been childish. Staring at his putrid wound…that was not what normal people did…unless pressed. The bottom line was that professors did not have water fights, but Justine had not seen that.

'I know you're preoccupied.' Justine rotated her straw hat back and forth; it swished and scratched as it brushed across her white dress. 'You've been jumpy each day. Edgy. Unsettled. Are you ok? Home problems?'

Home problems—some, yes, not insurmountable. But a massive problem at the conference. She could never tell Justine. Maybe she could have on the first day of 'the seat', but not now that it had burst out of control. She flattened herself against the corridor wall as students shoved past.

Justine winced. 'I need someone who's got time to develop the journal with me. If you have problems, I don't want to burden you with the position of Deputy-Editor—'

'Burden?! No, it's the heat and the crowd and—'

A passing man trod on Stella's foot. She bit back a yelp.

'I thought you were perfect because I like your work and we think similarly and most of all because David's a teenager, he's not clingy and demanding like baby Madeleine.'

Stella shifted her weight to the other foot in the stuffy, dark corridor. This was not the place to talk delicately. 'I got lost, and that notice board—'

She pointed; but the board had been moved flat against the wall, no longer blocking anyone. Her one excuse vaporised.

Justine stared beyond Stella to a wall poster of the Pyramids of Giza at sunset. 'I appreciate how hard it is to make time for a journal on top of daily university demands, but there's something else troubling you. It's not because you're busy. We're all busy; that's academic life. I'm trying to build up the journal. The work can't be around the edges of the life of the Deputy-Editor. I need someone who's focused.'

'I'm still me, but it's been a ghastly few days.'

Georgette swanned by. Stella forced a collegial wave. It was too much; everything was too much.

With her free hand, Justine wound her thick hair into a spiral and then shook it out. 'It's ok. Painful. I understand when life's demands pile up and threaten to bury us.'

She rotated her hat and then stopped. There was a long moment as she frowned at the Pyramids.

'Take the time to deal with whatever's pressing. I'm pleased you're on the Board, trust me on that, but I'm going to ask Michael to be Deputy-Editor.'

Stella shifted her weight and found her body rocking. Imperious, scornful Michael! In her place? The galling indignity. She had already imagined the calculating look in the Dean's eyes when she gave him the news—another success for the target of his bullying. She felt herself pitch towards his malachite paper weight and smash it on his block-cut hair. Justine perused her dazed face. Justine's face was different—cool and pale, but friendship struggled with professionalism. The vertical lines deepened between Justine's fashionable eyebrows. They saw each other's hurt.

Justine's faced softened. 'Let's revisit the position in a couple of years.'

Tenderly, she brushed Stella's shoulder and then strode away, moving gracefully among the rushing and bumping in the confines of the ill-lit corridor. Tears pressed behind Stella's eye lids. She squeezed her eyes shut. All she'd had to do was turn up on time, it was not as if a 3000-word editorial were required by tonight. Stella prayed that Justine would turn back and offer her friend one more chance, but there was relief in the easy set and slope of the Editor's shoulders. And then she was gone.

They should have departed together, shared a coffee, planned the next meeting. She was falling out of the conference and negating all that she had achieved. She could not afford to let her career be destroyed because her imagination was in overdrive. She should take back control and be professional. Of course Costa's stare into her camera lens had been accidental. Of course she had misunderstood the incident on the station platform. Of course he would not murder a young woman. She was crazy, irrational, inventing stuff. She would rescue her career after she calmly and professionally cornered Costa and had the last word, the definitive, last word. The end.

Stella started back up the basement steps to the main foyer. She would chide him for his actions in the gallery, then focus on her tattered career.

But Costa was upon her.

He stood two steps higher, in silhouette, with light blazing through the glass wall on the stair landing behind him. Blood drained from Stella's head. She saw the dark mass of his face, made out his grubby tie and the damp smudges on his jacket. Right up until that moment on the staircase, she believed that she observed Costa, studied him for her own self-protection, made the rules and governed the game, and that she could retreat at any time.

He bent over her. 'We've met before?'

His English was slow and deliberate. She shook her head, eyes narrowed and painful in the glare.

'You're a former student? I'm embarrassed not to remember. My deepest apologies if that is so. I have so many delightful young ladies. They seek me out at conferences; they wish to renew our relationships. So many!' He raised his arms in a gesture of helplessness.

'Nothing…um…like that.'

His gold ring chinked as he rested a hand on the balustrade. 'Why do I see you look for me?'

'I don't.'

Thick-tongued, her words of confrontation did not form. His sheer physical presence.

'I'm climbing the steps, nothing to read into it.'

'Dear Madam, I beg to differ. I see at this conference that you are only ever a few metres from me.'

'That flatters you.'

'Why so rude, Madam?'

The words sounded caustic; his mock politesse slipped. Someone bumped Stella from behind; her sore arm hit the balustrade.

'Ow!' She could not stop her cry. 'I'm not rude. You're rude!'

He stood over her, pudgy fingers stretching towards her body. He turned over her plastic name badge. His hand idled between her breasts.

He cracks open the window, pushes aside the Mickey Mouse

curtains, slinks over the sill. And her parents, too far away at the other end of the house, too much darkness between her and them. She grips the sheet. His horrible hands.

'Why so rude, let me see...Dr Stella Robinson. Let us say "Stella" between us.'

His fingers felt hot and greasy between her breasts. Her flesh shivered. She stepped sideways and pushed her bag in front of her chest. Theatrically, he raised and swung his hand to the railing.

'It's "Doctor" Robinson.' Saying her name loudly, that felt better. 'How dare you touch me.'

'But you touched me, Stella. You stand too close at the cocktail party.'

Stella tried to speak—you touched my breasts!—but he held up his hand as if on police points duty.

'You push ahead of me at the water fountain, knock me, splash water on my clothes, invade my space. Now you say that I should not touch you!'

Arrogant prick. 'Don't dare!'

'There's a dance between men and women: who touches first, who retreats, who flirts with the whisk of a touch.' Costa smirked. 'Is it an answer? An invitation? There are centuries of choreography.'

What rubbish. Now was the moment to speak up for civilisation. 'It's not acceptable to behave as you do, trying to push me out of my seat and—'

'The lady doth protest too much, methinks.'

How weird that sounded in an Italian accent. She would challenge him, haughty, derisive and in control.

'Your behaviour's rude. At a conference, politeness is expected. You dared to try to take my seat. I saw you on the station platform. Aggression to that young woman and—'

'Madam, you're stalking me!'

He pushed past. Stella grabbed the stair rail. 'Stalking!' Madness. That's not what she was doing. Stalking was for nutters. She'd only pretended. To see what it felt like—participant observation. She jabbed her nails into her palms; eight red crescents stung, but they did not distract from her mess. How could she have lost the Deputy-Editorship in a mere day? Her career had unravelled, despite the conference opportunities. Now she was accused of stalking. It was too much.

She could not face the next session, with its jolly, congratulatory atmosphere. She foresaw the long afternoon, the gallery with vile Costa and another ratty business card stuck presumptuously to the balustrade, Michael smirking, and Takura and Fatima avoiding her out of stinging embarrassment. And Justine. Sweet and kind, juggling professional demands and patching up their relationship, trying to pretend over afternoon tea that nothing had happened in the subterranean corridor two hours earlier, showing her more baby pics of Madeleine and asking about David when he was the last thing on Stella's mind.

EIGHT

Beads of blood and dribbling pus, Stella had caught the puce-red wound in her extreme close-up of the back of Costa's head.

Words clanged in her brain. 'Stalking'. Absurd. Justine had sounded worried: 'you're not the same person'.

'*Guten Tag, Fraulein*, Dr Robinson.'

Stella closed her phone camera, shuffled along the park bench and tossed her backpack beneath.

'*Guten Tag*, Hildegard. Excuse me, I was distracted, I've had a professional disappointment today.'

No legal discussion with the Board. No intimate drinks with Justine. No Deputy-Editorship. The conference was a disaster.

'*Jawohl*. Disheartening.'

The old woman's voice was soothing, but sad. She twisted the fabric of her dress, smoothed it out and began again. What was a professional set-back compared to what Hildegard had lived through. Stella wanted to hear more of the story but did not want to appear voyeuristic. They talked politely about the heatwave, global warming and the joy of dogs. It was a relief to be away from the conference with everyone dashing about, pretending to be important. Or avoiding her.

'You're in the park again, Hildegard, I saw you here only a few hours ago.'

'I love the river park and sit always on this same, old bench.' Hildegard patted the weathered slats. 'I see you also come here often, so you must understand the appeal, for a woman of Bonn, of the magnificent Rhine flowing through our town, linking all times.'

Stella had thought little of a place or a river linking different times. For her, places had layers, like the topography of a plate of warm pancakes, each period stacked on the other, with butter and maple syrup—wars, parliamentary reforms, the sweep of change— seeping into the dough. Today, the Rhine park was pure escape from all links in her life, from humiliation, failure, and online posts that seemed feisty when she clicked 'send', but quickly congealed into tacky and vulgar, nothing like the heroism of Hildegard.

Stella shifted closer. 'I would love to hear more of your story. Kurt did not want you to get a job. How did he respond when you told him?'

'He liked to joke, exaggerate—if anything could be said to be exaggerated in those Nazi times.'

'Nauseating,' said Kurt. 'You'll need to burn your clothes when you get home.'

He stood in front of the fireplace, trailing a finger along the gold highlights of a vase depicting a goatherd and his flock.

Hildegard chuckled. 'You've forgotten about rationing. Not patriotic of you!'

'You can find a laugh in this?'

Hildegard slipped her arms around Kurt's waist. 'It's an ordeal, but think of our danger if I'd refused. The manager didn't actually ask me whether I wanted the job; my only task was to qualify morally.'

Kurt rushed in. 'And politically.'

Hildegard flopped onto her grandmother's sofa and stroked the tapestry arm, running her fingertips along the worn, piped edge.

'The manager had a farewell trap. "All young ladies would do anything to share your good fortune. The whole of Germany would want to share it."'

Fear in the manager's office had nearly choked her. There was personal pride in not having run away. She found a hole in the sofa seam and worked her little finger into the feathers. Such comfort to touch the soft, fluffy whiteness, side by side with the steely rachis in the centre. She was soft and also steely, like a goose feather. She could manage that job, but Kurt would need to support her by letting her unwind at home and talk out her fears.

'It sounds odd, but I'm almost glad that Oma has died; how do you tell your grandmother that you clean Hitler's bedroom?'

'She would've been distressed.'

'I'm not allowed to tell anyone, but I don't know if that included my immediate family. Shouldn't the family appear to be proud of me? After all, I work for the mighty Adolf Hitler.'

Hildegard leaped up from the sofa and mocked a Nazi salute. It ripped into the room like a bolt of electricity, shattering their domesticity. Kurt blanched, gaped at his wife. Eyes wide, teeth bared, he rushed across the room and lowered her arm.

He sat down and crossed his legs and, almost immediately, jumped up. He sat again and tossed a cushion at the low ceiling, then prowled around the tiny sitting room, repositioning the lamp to clear space, stretching his arms, wriggling his fingers.

'We need to be deliberate actors in everything we do, little Hildegard. Tell them? Not tell them? They'd hate your work, but your mother not knowing could seem suspicious to the Nazis.'

'But "discreet", it's on the ad.'

Kurt glowed, colour high in his cheeks, alive with unprecedented zest. A silver lining, thought Hildegard, her appalling job could bring her even closer to darling Kurt as they made sense of it together and survived it together.

He looked at his wife. Her right arm—how *could* she, even in jest?—hung rigid by her side where he had left it.

'Oh, we'll be discreet in the barbarous world of war.'

Kurt rubbed his eyes too hard; when he opened them, they were bloodshot, and the surrounding skin wan and stretched. He looked ravenous, running his tongue around his lips and looking slightly above her as he spoke; she remembered that years later.

'The extra money comes at enormous cost.'

Kurt stood in front of the cold grate, his back to her. Hildegard lowered herself to the sofa and hugged a worn cushion with her left arm. Her right she left hanging. Slowly, he slid the goatherd vase back from the lip of the mantelpiece.

He spoke softly, as if to himself: 'In every life moment there's danger and there's opportunity'.

He ran his hand over the open fireplace mantle and contemplated the charred logs from a recent, early spurt of winter. Many moments later, he withdrew his eyes—cunning, elemental—from the cold ash and stared back at her, glimmering with doubt.

Back in 2015, three cyclists zoomed past in the dark purple shade protecting the bench.

'Everything was poisoned,' said Hildegard. 'There was no separate private life and public life. I felt turned inside out and had to focus on being my truest self. Some days I felt that my heart, liver, gut were on view for the whole world, even when I curled up on my grandmother's sofa.'

'You had courage.'

'I did not! I was frightened every hour, but there's a moral imperative to be your best self when the world goes mad. I could no longer hide in the abstract beauty of the architectural line and hope that the war would vanish.'

The skin around her eyes crinkled into two fans as she smiled, her chin in a bed of soft, slackening flesh. 'But each life step reveals another of our strengths and potentials to ourselves.'

Stella turned to the river, disgusted with Costa and wounded by Justine, tapping her feet, heel to toe. She wondered at Hildegard's ability to smile at her memories. Hildegard ran her palm along the withered skin of her arms, bare on a July day, but white from long winters. She stretched out her thin legs.

'We have charitable faces and mean faces. We need the courage to look at them all.'

Stella nodded and patted her own face, feeling the start of soft skin. She folded and unfolded her arms. Her stomach was full of butterflies as she thought of the foyer, thronged with colleagues when she lost control at the water fountain. And then Justine's rejection…she had not anticipated that could ever happen, not after so many years of friendship. It took so little to tumble in academia.

She doubted that she would have survived the job in the Rheinhotel Dreesen; she was at war with herself. She studied her arms, freckled from thousands of Australian summer days in scratchy, white beach sand and the rough, cold Indian Ocean. Under pressure, you discovered new faces of yourself, that's what Hildegard must have meant. In a crisis you became someone else—braver, stronger, more agile—or sneaky. She had not found strength and bravery in herself when she encountered Costa, and now the loss of the Deputy-Editorship stung.

'But it's challenging to study those faces; many of them we refuse to count as our own,' said Hildegard. 'We repudiate the evidence in the mirror. We are not different people, but we understand more of ourselves if we admit those faces exist.'

Stella's damp dress clung to her chest, stomach and thighs;

she waved her hat like a fan. Hildegard's philosophy was too complicated. There was only one Stella who occasionally lost control, a normal human frailty.

'What did Kurt mean by "opportunity"?'

'I didn't know at the time.'

Stella looked closely at the wrinkled face and sad eyes. 'An endless mystery?'

'Maybe. Kurt calmed down and became dreamy. Smiling absently, swinging my plait—an old joke between us—picking up his anatomy book, tossing it down and revealing a gruesome image, a heart sliced open, an ugly magenta, engorged with blood. I could never forget that rawness. He was in and out of the kitchen for several minutes. Around half past seven he said he had a question for another medical student and would be back before curfew.'

To Stella, Kurt sounded like the perfect husband. 'He was back in time?'

'He was always reliable; my mother and I loved him for it. I focused on what to tell her. I knew her disgust with the Nazi regime and was apprehensive that I would change in her eyes, but, of course, a person who worked closely for that evil man, for even one miserable hour, had already changed. History would not let that person forget that terrible life step. '

'Do you mean that person would be marked?'

'You can mark yourself with a uniform or friends, but identity can also be thrust upon you. Think of the millions of Germans who have been born since 1945. They can never escape the war although they saw nothing of it. They are forced to live intimately in that bloody landscape of memory and guilt.'

Stella's eyes roved over the sharp light and shade in the park. Hildegard had endured the war her whole life. She had never escaped the hotel in her own mind, just as the serial killer roamed Stella's brain, slinking into her dreams.

She hoped she used the right words. 'A landscape of inescapable memory.'

Hildegard covered her face with her hands. 'I cannot imagine a time when we will not be marked by that history. Sometimes you have limitations in the identity you desire. Kurt—'

Her voice broke off. Stella saw the burden of memory, and a worn wedding ring, loose on a thin finger. Lovers walked past, arms around each other. A parched chestnut leaf wafted into Stella's lap.

Hildegard uncovered her face. 'It was many weeks later before I thought of what Kurt said. You must understand, every day in that hotel challenged me in the most fearful way, to my very bones. It was as if I had stepped outside time; my days were nerve-racking, and my architecture studies wrecked. I thought that I had lost my career.' A mirthless laugh. 'No more Albertina Speer.'

Stella twirled the chestnut leaf. The brittle, sunburnt edges collapsed and crumbled, faster and faster as she spun the stem, like the torment of being derailed from your career.

NINE

A N EMAIL PINGED in from Peter: 'I'm worried about Davey. You've only been gone a few days, but I think you'd notice a big difference. Extremely mopey, scarcely eating, living off energy drinks. Please contact him ASAP. BTW while you're away, I won't phone unless there's an emergency. I know you're in meetings. Hope all goes well with the WHC. Pete.'

Stella re-read the message in her breathless room in the Bonn Concerto Hotel. She could see Peter at his antique cedar desk, strewn with prescription pads and medical journals. He would have had his mental to-do list: 'important to tell Stella, must tell Stella', but she needed a break from home, and knowing him, he would have over-stated the situation. Peter should have been able to cope with David and be enjoying father-son time. A moody teenager—nothing new. Teens changed from week to week, hormones lifting and dumping them; no kid wanted helicopter parents flying in at every life bump. She scribbled a quick note to David explaining that she would write more soon and sending all her love. First, rescue her career.

Repatriation of stolen artefacts and cultural identity—she needed one more photograph for her PowerPoint presentation. She chose two images of Australia's Burrup Peninsula with its vast industrial infrastructure side by side with the world's greatest petroglyph site, a million Indigenous rock carvings, baking under the sun, a landscape of ancient memory overlaid brutally with the coloniser's industry.

WhatsApp. Justine: 'A chat at morning tea tomorrow?'

From Stella: a thumbs-up emoji. Maybe they could normalise; Justine was trying.

Two hours of conference preparation zipped by. She sent a new book reference to her PhD candidates, then she needed a cold shower and some company. Students in the budget hotel garden laughed in the humid night air that hung like a curtain, heavy with perfume and the whiff of rapid decay. Beneath Stella's window, a fresh crop of flowers had withered, from bud to full-blown in eight hours, the enduring heat accelerating waves of bloom and death. Hildegard's story had been suffused with the portent of death. Stella had been relieved when she stopped talking.

Georgette was not visible in the dank, stifling darkness, but Stella walked quickly around the hotel garden among white tables and flickering tea lights to be sure that she was not listening, ready to rat on her with twisted facts. She heard the Italian accent.

'Do you think he actually packs Scotch tape when he leaves home?'

'Number one, Scotch tape! Socks are a distant second.'

'Wouldn't leave home without tape!'

Giggles rippled around three tables that had been pushed together. Stella tensed. They knew Costa?

She listened from the shadows as Italian students talked with enough other colleagues that English needed to be the shared language. No tatty jeans and shorts for them. Even by candlelight, they looked like fashion models, the men in crisp cotton and the women in pastel linen minis and bejewelled sandals. Two young women in crystal-edged hijabs said nothing, but closely watched the others. Stella sensed their liminal status: with the group, but not quite in the group. She inclined her head in the direction of the only spare seat. The students welcomed her, making space around a table. She sat down, slapping a mosquito.

'We are burning up in our rooms or bitten savagely here,' said a young woman who looked like a Botticelli angel. 'Burnt or bitten, that's our choice.'

The members of the group ran through their names, too many to remember. Stella loved the energy of twenty-somethings. Had they been talking about Costa? A young man leaned forward in the light of a single flame: eyes, nose and a rim of curly, black hair.

'My name's Leo.' He poured Stella a glass of cold white wine without breaking the conversation. 'Did you see the sycophantic way those middle-aged people cosied up to him at the party?'

'Vile,' said the angel.

'Jerk.' A laugh burst from Leo, and the others erupted. Suddenly, they could not stop.

Stella asked over the noise, 'A jerk who loves Scotch tape?'

More laughter, more mosquito whirrs.

'My haughty doctoral supervisor,' said the angel. 'Never available, doesn't understand irony, thinks there's only one aspect worthy of investigation in the whole of Roman history—his putrid sewers! He says civilisation rests on water engineering.'

The students did not hold back. 'The essence of Roman history is "get the muck out and let the art in".'

'The camaraderie of the shared latrines.'

'The Poo Prof!' shouted Leo.

Costa, bull's eye! She could learn something, but a shiver chilled her spine. In talking to the students, Costa felt too close again.

'But let's not forget that he failed my Master's dissertation,' said a woman's voice in the darkness. 'He probably didn't bother to read it. When the university gave permission for another examiner, I received a prize.'

'Stuck up and stuck to his stupid tape.'

Leo leaned forward to explain to Stella, his black curls shining. 'Gio sticks up his tatty business card, with its ludicrous string of post-nominals, anywhere he likes. There's free seating at every conference, but he always chooses the best for himself and shoves away—'

The angel swooped in. 'Indulges in huge conference lunches. He's off in fancy, private clubs with someone else paying. Arrives late, disturbs everyone.'

Leo again, 'We see his games!'

This was the first time that Stella had discussed Costa with anyone. 'You all dislike him that much?'

Crossing a line? Compromising her secrecy? She should have confided in Justine immediately after 'the seat', but it was too late now. She put down her glass. A constricting band fastened around her skull and her fresh, blue-striped dress already clung to her body.

'His Scotch tape is a silly idiosyncrasy,' said Botticelli's young model. 'We laugh about it because we cannot bear other parts of this man that actually harm us. He almost controls heritage and archaeology in Italy, especially in Rome. We dare not cross him.'

The creep had a big reputation; Stella's assessment was accurate. The students could do little against his power over their studies. They suffered personally, whereas she had simply been in Costa's way and there ought to be no long-term consequences like a failed degree.

'He can order you off a dig—like that.' A student in a Versace T-shirt clicked his fingers. 'Even if you've written 60,000 words about it. It nearly happened to me in Ostia Antica. I've seen people in 38° Celsius, leaning on shovels, tears streaking through dirt, research stolen, theses ruined. Three months later we see that Gio has stuck his name on a paper that the poor student drafted.'

A sympathetic murmur flowed around the tables as Leo topped up the glasses. The silent Islamic women students scrutinised every speaker and occasionally turned to each other. They knew something.

The angel shrugged. 'Students lodge complaints every year with the university council, but they go nowhere. Two went as high as the police, but they're his friends. Surprise—a brick wall. Look at his latest strategy; he persuaded powerbrokers to give him a fifty-thousand-euro prize at this conference. Forces himself into shared authorships. And—'

The angel toyed with a tealight, dashing an index finger through the flame. Stella watched the angel's finger miraculously escape injury. The humiliating scene in the Observers' Gallery and Costa's savage insistence that her seat was his, but—Rosa Parks' revolution aside—it was nothing compared to ruining a student's work. The Islamic women exchanged glances.

Stella prodded. 'And?'

The angelic woman drummed her fingers. 'Evidence is being gathered by a feminist collective to try to prove that he sexually abuses foreign students. It's difficult to prove. Young women from North Africa often have no idea what's lawful in Europe. They're reluctant to report; such lifelong shame for them and their families.'

The two silent women in hijabs turned to each other and nodded. One leaned forward into the light, hijab crystals sparkling.

'We're not passive; some of us fight back and protect our honour. We're strong.'

That festering hole in Costa's head.

Stella lay naked on her bed, dragging a damp washcloth around her face, stomach and arms. Grim images piled up in her head: the girl in turquoise stilettos, the perilous drop to the train tracks, young North African women in peril, exploited students. Boorish, vulgar, hairy, green Costa! 'I'm the boss, out of my way.'

Tossing water on him was disgraceful, without precedent, nothing like her normal, demure self, but if he were a sex criminal, that changed everything. A few drops of water were miniscule compared to assault.

He took what he wanted—seats, intellectual property, young bodies—and ingratiated himself with timid Libyan and Tunisian women who were alone in Rome: 'This way, charming young lady, let me show you my etchings. Upstairs, up you go. Beautiful young ladies before gentlemen. I show them only to my special— my extraordinarily special students.'

Overwhelmed by Costa, they shrink. 'Professor, no, please, it's not right. Sir! Sir! No! My mother and father would not allow. Such dishonour. Leave me alone!'

Fighting back with whatever they could grab. Pen? Ashtray? His wound was small, but deep.

TEN

Five quick clicks, closer and closer. Extreme close-up. A drum thudded from a barge on the Rhine. Chatter rose over the beat. Him. Again him. Costa turned sluggishly in the direction of Stella. Maybe he would detect the glint of her lens among the wild summer growth of the conference centre garden.

She photographed Costa and an older man who talked on the terrace by the coffee machine near the end of the lunch break. The older man gestured towards the press gallery, but that was as far as he got. He tried to speak—once, twice—gave up and blotted his brow. Costa put down his coffee and chopped the air with a machete action, knocking the cup. He strode off while a short black dripped down the folds of the white table linen, and the man sagged by cups and saucers. Stella knew the powerful type, someone who had been to twenty consecutive World Heritage Committee Meetings. Young girls might be easy prey for Costa, but what a surprise to see him humiliate a senior male.

For the third time, she stroked her PowerPoint data sticks, snug in her bag. She was proud of her work and ready for her presentation. But what was she doing now? Rattling Costa. Had she actually thought 'rattle'? No, because that would make her a...stalker? With at least twenty-five photos. She checked the latest. She had caught the startled intimidation of the older man in his alarmed tilt back—and the cold anger of Costa and his jabbing finger. It was time that women took on the mantle of voyeur if that was the name of the game, political and necessary stalking that had worked at the station toilets, but no one stalked in plain sight at a conference lunch. That would be ludicrous and criminally close to an 'A for a Lay' that got professors sacked for exchanging high essay marks for sex. She was not some nut who ruined her own life by stalking. Her new professorship and common sense dictated that she leave Costa alone, but that was the old Stella—dipped headfirst in patriarchy at birth—reasoning against herself and intuition. It was obvious that patriarchy would say: 'Don't scrutinise that evil man who abuses women'.

Back to square one. She would talk rationally and civilly to Costa and claim—no, demand—an apology. She was not obsessed with an apology but, logically, it was the only way to restore her equilibrium. He had to take on the shame that enveloped her, the debasement of a fragile, new professor facing censorious colleagues.

Stalking nonsense... She'd talk right back over him if he harangued her again. What pleasure it would be to tell the Italian students that she had confronted him. 'Wow, Stella, we didn't dare. At last, someone defies him.' The Islamic women students had denied their passivity, but it was not enough. Stella had a duty to protest. Their humiliation was hers; feminism was shared. Many of the international women students would be intimidated by his power; she would act on their behalf.

She touched her data sticks—just checking! She darted after Costa, towards the fence in front of the Rhine shore, hugging the shadows, slipping in and out of bursts of burning light. She had twice scoped her presentation room and projection equipment. Fifteen minutes until her time slot; she could afford ten.

Leo—magnificent with his extravagant black curls—called to her, and gestured to a free seat at his table. The Botticelli angel waved; she had turned into a Valentino model, impossibly beautiful and chic despite the humidity. Stella pointed at her watch and waved.

She could not see Costa, but this was the way he had walked yesterday, through the lingering lunch diners, across the sloping lawn and towards the thickest shade where the conference centre and river gardens merged in a muggy gloom, humming with insects. Stella slapped a mosquito on her arm, smearing blood. She zig-zagged half-way up the lawn and fanned her view across the garden, with its wilting, white hydrangea blossoms, sharp-edged blotches of shade and a mix of languages. She surveyed the tables; Leo had found friends. She felt a pang of regret.

A plash sounded of a lone passing boat as Rhine water frilled ashore in a giant, lazy V. Stella scooted back to a rhododendron, heavy with bedraggled flowers which afforded a camouflaged view. She parted the stalks; mosquitoes swarmed from the dank, over-watered roots, biting her limbs, entangling her hair. No Costa. She slapped mosquitoes on her forehead and watched a long stream of delegates forming a loose queue to re-enter the building. She glanced at her watch—nine and a half minutes until the presentation. Time to go.

At the fence's mid-way point, trees thinned, giving her a clear view of the river, but there were no tourist boats on the glassy water, no thumping music. She sensed the sudden increase in mental attention that accompanies the shut down of rackety air-conditioning. Nerves alive, she grabbed the top rail.

'Madam, we meet again.' Costa tipped his Panama.

She arched back against the fence. A roaring pulse dulled her hearing. He's stalking *me*!

'You can't save seats…um, it's all free seating.'

That was pitiful. 'It's about professional manners which—'

'A friendly word, Madam. You have blood on your face.'

She dashed her hand across her nose. He spied on *her*! He was a hundred steps ahead.

His rumpled sleeve snaked out, index finger poised. 'Right there, in the middle of your forehead.'

The same pudgy finger had parted his hair and revealed his suppurating wound in grisly intimacy. Now she knew the probable source of his pus-filled pit: a young Tunisian woman cornered in a lecture room, hoping for extra tuition, but ruined, only an ashtray for defence.

He tapped three times on her forehead. 'Indeed, blood.'

Too astounded to push him off, she tried to arch back further. He pulled an ironed, monogrammed handkerchief from his pocket and smeared her blood onto it from his finger.

'Marked for self-sacrifice.'

'Do you need help?' A woman in the bathroom looked sympathetic.

Dried blood streaked across Stella's forehead and eyebrows like a grotesque 1920s flapper headband.

'Mosquitoes.'

Stella searched for handtowels, but there were only blowers. The woman went to speak again, changed her mind. Stella grabbed a length of toilet paper, leaving the roll unravelling on the cubicle floor.

'Thank you, I'm ok...insect bites.'

She tore off a handful of paper, soaked it and sloshed tissue across her face. Repulsive man. *He* was the stalker! Soggy tissue stuck to her face and matted her hair. She tossed her head. 'Self-sacrifice'?

Back in the basement corridor, Stella crept into her conference room. It was much larger than the breakout room that Justine had booked, but still too small, with several people forced to stand along the back wall. The Dutch chairperson put a finger to her lips, asking for silence because a presenter was in full swing. An audience of about fifty sat beneath a patchwork of World Heritage posters of Great Zimbabwe, the vermilion Shinkyo Bridge in Nikko, Ellis Island, Borobudur Temple, Robben Island and the Great Sphinx of Giza. It was Stella's timeslot, the first after lunch, but it was already ending.

The chairperson called for the next presenter and tip-toed to Stella. 'You're extremely late, but we've got a few minutes to spare at the end of the day.'

'Only a few minutes! Can't I switch with someone?'

'Not possible. Because you weren't here, I let the first presenter take audience questions for longer than usual, so there's no full slot left.'

'Tomorrow? Please!'

'Full. Bad luck, I'm sorry.'

At this precise moment, Stella should have been fielding eager questions from an enthusiastic audience. Justine and Michael sat close to the shallow podium, shoulders touching. Behind them, Georgette scribbled notes. Stella held tightly to her data sticks. How pathetic—a professor begging for a truncated presentation slot. It was Costa's fault, but she was a natural speaker and would shine.

Stella tried not to recoil as someone banged the door. More desperate for coffee than scholarship, half of the audience had slipped out between the last presenter and her tacked-on, curtailed position. She smiled confidently at those who remained and clicked on her first PowerPoint slide. The astonishing red earth of north-western Australia filled the screen, hot, dry, bursting with iron and fringed by a limpid, green ocean. The door to the conference room rasped as two young men departed.

Stella clicked to piles of ancient Indigenous carvings jumbled in artistic abundance.

From the second row, Justine beamed an encouraging smile and Georgette looked focused, but the rest of the audience yawned, whispered and played with phones. Stella saw it all from the podium, only an arm's length from the first row of seats where a middle-aged man's head jerked from a momentary lapse into sleep. Stella ploughed on, determined to win the audience with a fresh twist on cultural identity.

'The Burrup Peninsula has the biggest petroglyph site in the world—more than ten thousand individual carvings, an extraordinary treasure trove. It's the home of the Yaburara people. This pristine environment is under threat.'

The huge rock carving site had enormous significance, but tragically, it had collided with industry. In the resources-based economy of Australia, pleas to protect carvings meant little to many people.

Stella's attention was split between her talk and the audience response. This was her golden moment to win back Justine's faith, but someone giggled; a pen clattered to the floor. Fatima scrolled. No support from that disloyal Board member. Stella pointed with her laser to a carving of a kangaroo side-by-side with industrial detritus. A handful of attendees battled to stop their chins sinking to their chests; an elderly man's faint snore provoked muffled snickers from students in the back row. She had a tough audience, but she'd had worse from undergrads. Being upbeat and showing empathy should help.

'You won't miss coffee—I promise!'

Laughter fluttered around the room and her confidence crept back; a new professor had a lot to say to an international audience. Four more people slipped out; Stella pretended not to notice.

She clicked to the next slide. 'Archaeologists estimate—'

But three more people slunk out, avoiding her eyes. The door creaked and clicked shut.

'Um.' Stella looked at the door. 'Archaeologists advise the Australian government that—'

An elderly woman departed, trailing a blue, gauzy shawl across people's laps. Justine grimaced at Stella, pointing at her watch.

Horror! The entire back row filed out noisily. Ten students tagged along, comically bent double, as if to make themselves invisible. Ringing in Stella's ears. Things couldn't get worse, but then Justine, Michael and Fatima disappeared with toothy, apologetic grins.

Georgette got up. A blush started at the base of Stella's neck. Georgette's defection hurt; at least, a day-to-day, departmental colleague should have offered support, even if they couldn't stand each other. Georgette looked back, expressionless. Stella wanted to shout, 'Go ahead, gloat!' She would hear about this disaster from the Dean next week, but now she would plug on.

'Thank you, colleagues, for attending for this important topic.'

That sounded like pleading when the number of attendees had shrunk from more than fifty to fifteen, of which two were asleep. She clicked to squat, ugly administrative offices dumped on desert beauty, and then straight to her last, best hope. The mysterious, almost mythical Tasmanian Tiger, an extinct marsupial. She clicked to a carving of the thylacine, its thin, haunting image made centuries before Roman legions marched to the Rhine and founded the fortress of Bonna. The burnt orange rock glowed into the grey conference room with the heartbreaking Tasmanian Tiger, whose extinction weighed heavily on the Australian national conscience after two centuries of reckless hunting and land clearances, and with the more optimistic vehemently determined that somewhere—please!—in the vast wilderness of Tasmania, thylacine young still peeked from their mothers' pouches in a paradise that humans had yet to wreck.

And there he was, Costa, with his sleazy grin and fat legs crossed, leaning against the back wall beneath The Sphinx, his head between the giant paws. Stella clicked to the next image, industrial waste beside a car park. A rush of blood was followed by a tinnitus buzz and click. She looked vacantly at twisted, rusting metal, a filing cabinet missing its drawers, a tangle of computer keyboards powdered in red dust, ripped plastic bags stuck to a wire fence. She glanced back to Costa. Intimidation, how dare he. If only the Sphinx would maul him. She clicked again to demountable mining offices in the desert and overflowing bins. Costa sneered; her train of thought was snuffed out.

Stella shuffled her papers and willed her ideas to order, but with no words to make any points, she arrowed forward and back—and forward again—hunting for a clue to pick up her thread. Her notepad, with her final thoughts jotted by hand last night, slipped out of focus and words tumbled on the page. Amnesia, mortifyingly in front of colleagues. Her brain replayed Costa's lunch-time assault: his finger on her blood spots, her squeak in reply. She had no recollection of her lost presentation point. There was only one thing to do. She forced a broad smile.

'Ladies and gentlemen, I won't keep you from coffee any longer. If you have any questions, please catch me in the break.'

She busied herself retrieving her data stick and then called briskly. 'My business cards are by the door. I'm here all week. Let's catch up over coffee.'

Bemused laughter, sympathetic tuts, and the room emptied. Stella gathered her papers and backpack. Only she and Costa remained. Her skull prickled. Why did he wait? He'd already accosted her twice. To exit, she needed to pass him. She could do it. She jumped off the podium, strode to the end of the room and saw that her pile of business cards lay undisturbed.

Costa blocked the door. Stress tightened, like an iron band around Stella's head, as her worst day peaked in the featureless, windowless, subterranean room. If only someone would return for a missing jacket, then she could escape without having physically to dislodge the brute. She focused on the light and dark contrasts of Borobudur Temple with its romantic memory of a long-ago day with Peter.

'As I was saying earlier…'

Costa whistled tunelessly. She had no choice. She charged through the stress like an athlete cracking the pain barrier.

'Your behaviour's unacceptable.'

'Oh really?' Costa folded his arms. 'I need to watch my delegation precisely from that gallery seat. No debate. Everyone knows it, except you, my confused little friend.'

'The chair announced free seating.'

Stella snatched up her business cards with their once-thrilling 'Professor' title. Costa must have sailed through endless variations of their encounter, each making him bolder and providing a rehearsal for the next, culminating in sexual abuse of students with impunity. His wet, fleshy lips whistled too close, breathing moisture on her forehead. She stuffed the cards in her backpack. This was insanity. It was pointless talking about 'the seat'. It had *never* been the point.

'You're uncivilised; you don't belong here.'

He reached to stroke her arm, a hideous caress on bare skin. She leaned away, her shoulders and head hard against the wall. She was back in her bedroom, crashing among shattered glass, a spray of blood seeping down the wall. The pale brown-pink was still there when she returned from hospital with her arm in plaster; no scrubbing obliterated it. Peter moved a chair in front of the stain and draped her grandmother's crocheted blanket over the rail. Neither of them said anything and the blanket was still there when she left for Bonn.

'But do *you* belong?' Costa squeezed hard; she felt his long nails on her shoulder. 'I'm the last of your audience. I'm all ears. I graciously request that you continue your discussion of identity. Let's start with yours.'

She pushed him off and tried to step around him, forcing herself not to shout.

'Out of my way!'

Stella blinked hard to block the inevitable next thought, but there it was, coming to get her. The blob in the garden, huge among the scratching branches outside her childhood bedroom. She tried to edge around Costa the other way, but he flung out his arm, satisfaction in his mean eyes. She had caught that smug, nasty look in the photograph by the antipasto.

His laugh broke the pause. 'You look better without blood on your face.'

Her fingers rushed to her forehead where mosquito stings had swollen into lumps; suddenly, they itched.

He did not blink. 'Impressive presentation, though it—what do you say?—"petered out".'

He knew she was married to Peter!

'Forgive me, Dr Robinson, but anyone would be interested in self-sacrifice, a major cultural moment. A memorable display.'

'You're perverted!'

She shoved him aside—his gold buttons scratched her arm as they had in the auditorium—and wrenched open the door. The corridor had nearly emptied but, at the well-lit end near the stairs, Justine, Michael and Fatima stood close to each other, out of earshot. The shock of Costa receded as Stella looked at her fellow Board members; they had all abandoned her. She hid behind a mobile notice board, peering from a crack between the board and the side frame, and weighed up adopting a pose of bravado, re-joining the group and airily suggesting dinner—'in the restaurant with the statue of the Roman centurion, I hear the sauerkraut lasagne is the perfect fusion dish'—salvaging scraps from calamity. She could perform in that pantomime.

Costa strolled by, humming Verdi, bumping hard on her shoulder. She read his warped mind: 'Such a narrow corridor, Madam, nothing to read into it, don't flatter yourself'.

Justine and Michael leaned against the wall, mirroring each other's posture, listening to Fatima, nodding, adding brief comments. Justine patted Michael on the back. Stella should be conferring with them, but the conference had crumbled, then rotted—from an intimate drink with the Editor by the Rhine, to the new professor cringing behind a notice board.

Costa disappeared as a fluorescent light hummed and flickered, bathing the corridor in sickly yellow pulses. After two minutes, Justine, Michael and Fatima jogged up the stairs to the main foyer.

The new professor walked in the opposite direction.

ELEVEN

Stella jammed her sunglasses with the glittery red stars onto her nose, and headed out, imagining humiliating Board chit-chat: 'OMG, Stella's shipwreck! I'd have died. Lucky she was dumped from the Deputy-Editorship.' She had no plan and no one to talk to in the bitter crisis of being the architect of her own ruin.

A South Korean protest tent dominated the entry to the conference centre. Posters lined the path: 'Wake Up UNESCO! Wake Up World! Wake Up Mankind!' In a rictus of agony, an old woman howled at the blazing German sky demanding that the world wake up to the moral gravity of historical justice. Stella tried to focus but, in her mind, Justine, Michael and Fatima stood in their exclusive circle while she huddled behind the notice board.

Photographs captured the crime of Japanese wartime enslavement of Koreans. Clad only in loin cloths, filthy men stood on rocky ground with painfully bare feet and huge, bony knees in skeletal legs. Beneath clinging coal dust, scars from beatings marked their skin. Sunken eyes turned away from the camera. The images revealed how Stella felt: abused, misunderstood and becoming invisible. She felt ashamed; a failed presentation could not compare to this suffering and injustice.

A young South Korean woman in a blue chima skirt and white jeogori traditional jacket gave her a pamphlet and circled a finger around the front image.

'This is the horror of wartime slavery that the Japanese want to erase from history.'

Stella could hardly follow the explanation which drifted towards her, muffled and ashen, interspersed with the memory of Georgette's emotionless gathering of information from the door of the presentation room.

The woman directed Stella to an aerial photograph of grim Hashima Island, fifteen kilometres from the Japanese coast. She tapped an image of a low seawall which defined a grey, rocky outcrop, only one hundred and fifty metres wide and crammed with derelict concrete buildings stained by salt and moisture and misery. More gaunt, scrawny, starving bodies confronted Stella, but her vestiges of compassion were hard to locate. She wanted to care; she should care, but the skeletal men were far away in place and time, while Costa blocking her exit and the untouched pile of business cards were wounds that dripped fresh blood.

Her anguish deepened as the woman explained the coal-mining island of Hashima was a Korean slave labour site. The Japanese wanted to include it in World Heritage, as one of the first industrial sites outside the West, but they intended to exclude the embarrassing war years from the listing by limiting historical significance to prior to 1910.

Stella knew it was unethical to cut out the war years. She examined herself for remnants of sympathy, but her eyes traced blankly around the battered seawall while Justine's words came back: 'You're not the same person'.

On the train into central Bonn, Stella leaned against the warm window and thought of the family's new poodle puppy and the sad droop of Bertie's shoulders when he was hurt. Like Bertie with an injured paw, she needed to nuzzle away her pain. Passing cars reflected ruthless sunlight. She closed her eyes. What would be the point of complaining that Costa touched her breasts if he routinely got away with sex abuse? He would deny it and call on his powerful friends; it was the way of patriarchy.

She was not the architect of her own ruin. She was Costa's victim, had been from the start. Now her victimhood intensified without him having to do anything. He had unleashed mayhem. Michael and Justine had cut and run, only to gossip outside. Justine had pointed to her watch as if to say, 'I'd rather stay, but I've got to go,' but she too had walked only a few metres from the lecture room. Their relationship was so undermined that Justine no longer cared what her friend thought. Stella had plunged headlong out of a charmed inner circle of World Heritage.

From her handbag cache, she took out a raspberry jam linzer biscuit from the conference morning tea, and ate it in two bites, tasting nothing. Three months' work on the conference paper, too many weekends stolen from Peter and David. Her paper should have consolidated the authority of her professorship, but if the Dean heard about today's fiasco, he would demand an explanation for why she requested thousands of dollars in conference support and failed to perform.

Returning to the hotel ran the risk of having the odiously cheerful Italian students inquire about her presentation. And if she returned to the conference centre…the unbearable buzz of the coffee break…so Stella hid in the gloom of Romanesque arches in the medieval cloister of the great basilica of Bonn Minster, a good place to lick her wounds. She kept her hat low and looked ahead and behind, praying that no other conference participants were visiting. A few tourists whispered as they read basilica history notes.

Leaning on the cloister wall, Stella took in the shiny flagstones. A mantel of hot disgrace enveloped her as she compared past, successful presentations to her woeful performance. In Germany, twice before this debacle, in Berlin and Munich; in Tunis before a big audience; in Paris with immediate publication; in Italy, three times—chaotic, but memorable in Rome and Perugia; in Canada, brilliantly organised in Calgary; in Rio, once—her breakout room not listed on the programme, but found in the nick of time; in New York, a co-presentation, slick and smooth; and in Australia more times than she remembered without consulting her CV. Why had she lost control today and how could Costa be more destabilising than undergraduates with their phones and snickers? She handled them every week.

A rare cloud travelled over the rectangle of striking blue sky above the cloister, cancelling the silhouette of the arches and erasing the glow of the stones. For a few minutes, the scorching day surrendered to shadows. A noisy family piled into the cloister as Stella daydreamed of hundreds of priest-monks, of their rough feet polishing the stones, of their coarse robes swishing the heavy pillars in the exquisite space of one of Germany's oldest cloisters, of their comforting routine, of their expectation that life would go on as it always had, secure that they were being themselves, knowing that another life would not have been a better fit. Stella stroked the black edge of a rough stone pillar. Thousands of hands had passed before wearing down the once-white pillar edge with a greasy, sooty black of hand moisture which lodged in cracks and chips of stone. But Stella knew that the cloister was not so old; beneath the eleventh-century church lay a Roman temple and necropolis and another time.

Water tinkled in the garden. Stella stepped into the heart of the cloister where clouds of lavender rippled around a fountain splashing small waterspouts. She took a photograph of the walkway of arches on the edge of the garden. Near the fountain, a black rock, set flush to the earth, commemorated two saints martyred in ancient Roman times, Cassius and Florentius, soldier saints who inspired the basilica of Bonn Minster. She imagined their lives, so many centuries before her mortifying mess.

~

Two Roman soldiers kicked up dust as they tramped towards the temple in Castra Bonnensia. Sweat ran from beneath their helmets in the unusually hot sun of early October.

Cassius said, 'We will pray with our Christian friends tonight. They wait for our good news.'

'Good news this time,' said Florentius. 'But the Germanic tribes are fierce; this region will not be subjugated easily.'

'Do not query the might of Rome, dear friend, because you, yourself, are Rome.'

Cassius saw that Florentius needed comfort and flung his arm around his shoulders, knowing that a hard campaign should not be undermined by the warriors themselves.

'You do not doubt yourself!'

Florentius nodded thanks. 'It is always a relief to be back in the safety of the fort, to toss off vigilance and the fear of a knife in the night. But there is muttering against Christians.'

'We fight with Christian solders and are no threat to Rome.'

Without warning, twenty Roman soldiers sprinted towards them, all of them friends and brother-warriors of many years.

'Halt!' More soldiers erupted from doorways.

The heathen leader screeched, 'Will you sacrifice to the gods of Rome?'

Cassius and Florentius closed, shoulder to shoulder, in the tight lane, confronting companions of many years. Today they faced their bloody swords, forged in the same furnace.

Spit flew towards them. 'Will you sacrifice to the gods of Rome?'

Their own Roman comrades glared with hatred as if they were the Germanic tribes themselves. The leader gripped his sword and held it high above the head of Florentius, who saw that the leader's nails were still clean from bathing the night before. Florentius had soaked with him in the caldarium; they had planned a shared dinner this very evening.

Florentius beamed strength towards Cassius, evoking—in the last, long five seconds that were granted to them in the dirt lane with the gleam of the white temple in view—the joy and art of swordsmanship, the brotherhood of the battlefield and their faith.

They welcomed their deaths, clasping the symbolic martyr's crown, and crying, 'We worship no other God than the one true and living God of heaven and earth'.

Swords slashed. Ears, arms, hands flew in sprays of blood to the walls, to the foreign earth and across the tunics of fellow soldiers. Within seconds, two Roman soldiers were dismembered, their heads lolling on top of their mangled bodies in a sickening heap in the street, and Rome was delivered of two more troublemakers in the year 235CE.

Almost eighteen centuries later, Stella closed her information pamphlet and pondered monumental, granite versions of the severed, martyrs' heads outside Bonn Minster, a gory distraction from her presentation debacle. The heads were a memorial to the martyrs whose story lay at the heart of the city and basilica. A clean-shaven granite head of a saint looked to the Bonn sky; he had fashionably sensuous lips, but a precise slash cut his neck. On the second sculpture, the shadowed eyes of a bearded saint were cast down to the cobbles.

Stella itched to touch the dense, smooth granite. Its clean-lined perfection highlighted the dread of its opposite, the grisly chaos of murder, and the terror which had pervaded her childhood and bedevilled her adult life. Here it was in grotesque representation in a sunlit city square, surrounded by bustling cafés. The headless trunks of Cassius and Florentius had collapsed near where she stood, close to the Roman temple. Iskender Yediler's sculptures of the heads of Cassius and Florentius had lain since 2002 on the cobbles in Martinsplatz, the small square outside Bonn Minster. Both heads wore Roman soldiers' helmets, but, horrifically, the bodies were missing.

Stella ran her fingers across the fleshy lips of one saint and up and over the tough lines of his helmet. Martyrdom was a puzzle. She walked across to the other decapitated saint and touched the curls of his beard. The carved granite was almost too hot to touch. The day had come when Cassius and Florentius had no longer fitted the Roman military system, which did not hesitate to murder its own soldiers. They had become the threat to Rome themselves, even though they fought in a designated Christian military unit. In the camaraderie, invincibility and spirit of the Roman soldier, the martyrs had retained the essence of themselves and, on the last day of their lives, chose to die as themselves. They had only an instant to decide; but they had not hesitated.

She thought of Costa at the cocktail party, all smarmy and pretence, but in reality a vulgar bully and probably worse. Costa would have slain Cassius and Florentius. What fools—silly fools who willingly lost their lives in a corrupt military machine. They should have fought back sneakily. Confronted by lawlessness and violence, the saints had been absurd. Obviously, they should have faked their sacrifice to Roman gods while practising Christianity in secret. Why be high-minded when there was no one worth impressing?

Stella backed out of the way as three Russian women in extremely high-heeled red sandals minced towards the sculptures. Two performed for a camera, flinging their arms around the martyred heads while tilting their own heads coquettishly. The martyrs' memorial was reduced to a catwalk for stilettos.

The photographer leaned against the bearded head and all three tourists adopted glamour modelling poses, pouting their lips, pushing forward their hips in tight jeans, gazing theatrically to a dreamy middle distance. Yet more empty selfies.

What idiots Cassius and Florentius had been to have stood their ground. They did not have a moral calling to defend their faith before the dishonourable. What a waste of life.

And watching Costa... She had no words for that feeling. Who was she, at her wits' end and with nerve endings atrophying? She left Bonn Minster and walked through the city. Tourists posed for photos in front of the medieval houses, groups of young people quaffed beer beneath striped umbrellas and music strayed out of air-conditioned shops.

Stella turned into Rathausgasse and descended to the Rhine. In the deep shade, Hildegard waited with memories of another time of terror and violence.

TWELVE

'YOUR FIRST TIME in a kitchen, is it?' The woman swished her oily hands over her apron.

'My first commercial kitchen,' said Hildegard.

'No offence, but you're slow.'

Hildegard stopped scrubbing, hurt and surprised. The sous-chefs had not scolded her and she did not waste time gossiping like several others. Today, out of the corner of her eye, she had tracked the woman walking towards her and the unpeeled potatoes which bobbed in a barrel of cold water with crusts of mud and floating loose, black earth.

The woman swept back lank, dark hair escaping her cap. 'You can't be slow in the food-prep line; we're waiting at the stoves.'

'My apologies. The root vegetables are extra muddy today, perhaps from the recent heavy rain. I'll speed up as I become accustomed to the filth.'

When Hitler was not staying at the Rheinhotel Dreesen, Hildegard reported each afternoon to sous-chef Fritz, who directed her to prepare vegetables—'cut 'em dainty, keep the powers that be out'. It was already three weeks since she'd started work and she had not entered the *Fuhrersuite*. She kept to herself, but there were eyes in the dark kitchen with its gloomy recesses and vast cupboards. Some workers observed her from the central tables. Several times in the past weeks, she had caught this young, big-boned woman watching.

Hildegard dug an eye out of a large potato. She would defend her speed; there was the honour of her work ethic to uphold; that would be a normal response from anyone.

'This is not my real work, that's why I'm slow. My main work's upstairs.'

Later, Hildegard would recall two full beats of silence, broken only by the hiss of steam and laboured footsteps as kitchen hands lugged boxes of turnips.

The woman smiled. 'My name is Magdalena. Good luck.'

She tossed an errant potato into the barrel and made her way back to the stoves, where Fritz shouted at her to resume frying brown trout. That was the whole visit. Over in seconds. When the mounds of potatoes came blessedly to an end, Hildegard dried her chapped hands and looked down the frenetic kitchen. Magdalena inspected her.

Two weeks later, Hildegard edged around many more soldiers than usual when she arrived at the hotel. More swastikas flew from the entrance and the manager beckoned.

'Are you ready for the great task?' His eyes roamed her face. 'You are the recipient of an exalted honour.'

Hildegard nodded. She had had weeks of bracing, plenty of time to practise nerve control. No coughing, no blushing this time.

'It is room 106, lucky *Fraulein*. Our proud *Fuhrersuite*! You may not speak to the Fuhrer if you chance to see him. Your main contribution to the Fatherland's war effort commences today. *Heil Hitler!*'

Upstairs, Hildegard trembled as she entered the *Fuhrersuite*.

She felt alive in a base, instinctual way to the horrific intimacy of the rooms—her skin tingling, crawling, rough like goose flesh. She needed air. The balcony doors were heavy with bullet-proof glass and creaked as she opened them. She inhaled as deeply as she could as the Rhine flowed swiftly below and two barges slid by, swastikas taut in the breeze.

'Can you imagine my repulsive work?' said Hildegard. 'So different from the precise lines of architecture and the pure field of imagination.'

She and Stella sat closely, side by side on the park bench. The weekend picnickers and their Frisbees had gone; only mothers and young children played and dozed beneath the trees. Municipal workers departed with full bins while seagulls circled and squawked.

'You had to touch the sheets—*his* sheets—and his dirty towels many, many times,' said Stella.

'There was no escape. He stayed at the Rheinhotel Dreesen more than seventy times. Even Prime Minister Neville Chamberlain met him there in 1938.'

'During the days of appeasement?'

'The gentle Rhine was one of the key scenes for that abysmal policy, leading to unprovoked invasions and to World War II. It was before my time, but everyone knew that Herr Chamberlain had been to the hotel over several days. For what!'

Stella watched a rowboat up-stream; eight oars dipped in synchronous poetry—plash, dip, pull—her body remembered trying to edge around Costa's bulk as he blocked the door. There was a physicality to their mutual hatred.

Hildegard glanced across. 'I didn't know how I could have, as you English speakers say, the "stomach" for the job. My entrails were in turmoil, as if my whole being revolted. My brain knew that to refuse my task carried mortal risk for me and my family; therefore, it commanded my body to act, but it was a case of disciplining myself, a savage discipline that felt as if I were scarring my soul.'

Stella watched the boats. 'My soul'—plash, dip, pull—plash, dip, pull—'my soul'. Almost no one waiting for her paper... the ignominy...Justine... She dragged her attention back to Hildegard. She crossed and uncrossed her legs and said the first thing that came into her mind.

'Why clean in the afternoon?'

Hildegard chuckled. 'That leader of unfortunate Germany rarely rose before two o'clock. I don't know how he managed the war. When he was in the hotel, much of my time was waiting discreetly until he left his rooms.'

As Stella sat with Hildegard in the tranquil early dusk, she tried to soothe herself, but Costa's blinkless, serpent eyes intruded. A tourist boat drifted with its summery cargo of travellers in bright swimsuits, and there was patient Hildegard telling her story, waiting for Stella to catch up.

❧

The smell of sour breath and chocolate hung over Hitler's bedroom as Hildegard's hands hovered over a snarl of sheets and blankets. *Heil Hitler!* A war effort!

She yanked off the blankets. Melted chocolate streaked the sheets and the rucks hid three confectionary wrappers. She scrunched the top sheet. Sudden moist warmth—body to body— to her body—the essential heat of Hitler infused the linen. She dropped the sheet and brushed her hands over her filmy, starched, white apron, then forced herself to seize the multi-coloured chocolate wrappers and toss them in the bin. That left the soiled bottom sheet, as private as underwear, wrinkled the length of the bed and dangling loose from one side of the mattress. She looked at her hands, took a shallow breath and grabbed the sheet, tossing it to the floor, where it fell in a slash of light. She trod gingerly around the cloth folds, taking care not to let the textile brush her ankles. She imagined contamination would slither up her legs and fester in the close heat of her stockings, turning her skin yellow, green, mottled-grey.

Three boxes of papers overflowed on the floor at the foot of the bed. With the toe of her shoe, she pushed them neatly against a wall and looked through the glass balcony doors. From his bed, the dictator could relish the historic river and the Siebengebirge, the landmark hills of German mythology where Siegfried slew the dragon, a landmark deep in the German spirit. In the adjoining workroom, an eraser, a ruler and freshly sharpened pencils were lined up on an occasional table. Positioned precisely parallel to the table edge, they looked like soldiers assembled in descending height, like soldiers standing on the hotel steps.

The door flew open; Hildegard jumped. *Frau* Wagner, in her round spectacles. The eagle-eyed housekeeper prowled around the bedroom and workroom, checking under chairs and small tables. From the alcove hall, the soldier on guard glanced in. Hildegard's heart banged. She waited for the housekeeper to depart, but the sour woman stepped onto the balcony of the Fuhrer's workroom and performed exercises with brisk slaps to her hips. A dozen pins stabbed the meagre, tight bun on the back of her head. It must be true what the other maids said: she had eyes in the back of her head. Did protocol dictate that work should continue during a visit of a housekeeper, or would that show disrespect? Hildegard waited on the oriental rug, her hands by her sides. There were rumours that when Hitler exploded in rage, he bit the rug. It had thick, woven edges. What would a human bite into wool look like? Dry goods stores sold poisons to deal with pests but had nothing for ridding the world of a dictator.

After two minutes of calisthenics on a balcony that could barely fit a chair, the housekeeper marched from the room.

Perspiration oozed under Hildegard's thick, red hair and slicked around her tight collar. Her body sagged as adrenaline rolled back. She would need to get used to the ways of the hotel; surveillance could occur at any time.

She exhaled slowly and touched the mattress with the tip of an index finger. The mattress held body heat and was even warmer than the bottom sheet. Leaving Hitler's bed to cool before she changed the linen, Hildegard went into the bathroom. Boxes and bottles of pills filled a side table—an astonishing cocktail—an extraordinary sight for a man who boasted of extreme good health. How Kurt would have enjoyed perusing the pharmaceutical names! Like the pens and pencils, the drugs were lined up in rows of descending length.

Four towels had been used, folded, and re-hung precisely on the rails, the edges in line with each other, stark against the shiny black wall tiles, consistent with rumours of Hitler's fastidious nature. She could leave them, but a small hand towel lay on the deep ledge behind the basin, folded but used. Hildegard braced for contact with the cloth, steadying herself on the chill lip of the large porcelain basin as she leaned across. She sensed prickling and turned her palm upwards. It was dotted with moustache hair, the corporeal dregs now glued to her own skin. She would never be clean again. She dashed her hand under a stream of hot water, as scalding as she could stand, as the drain sucked away the bristles.

'The one with the slutty hair-do, you must have seen her,' said Magdalena. 'The wife of that general you saw five days ago.'

'Haughty Madam Frida?' asked Hildegard.

When Hitler departed the Cologne-Bonn district, Hildegard resumed washing and peeling potatoes and chopping carrots into julienne strips. Each day, Magdalena abandoned the stoves when the sous-chefs were busy receiving deliveries. She chatted to Hildegard about imprudent guests and lavish hotel menus that exceeded rations.

'She came to breakfast with her buttons undone! The surly cow deserved to be embarrassed. You should have seen her scurry upstairs when she realised. Her lover was at the next table; he spotted the disaster after her husband entered the dining room.'

'Funny!'

'The best laugh in weeks.' Magdalena rushed on, softly, bending close. 'They've given you room 106?'

Hildegard ran her eyes around the kitchen. 'Unfortunately, yes.'

'Unfortunately?'

Hildegard bit her lip. Wrong word. That was all it took. By the door, two sous-chefs argued about the quality of the day's river lamprey; the afternoon sun glistered on the slimy fish. Singing a song from the Great War, the pastry chef rolled out butter.

On guard. Hildegard tucked her words beneath the bawdy ditty, 'I'm not worthy of the honour'.

Magdalena stifled a laugh. Hildegard snatched a small parsnip and scrubbed it too vigorously; chunks of white flesh splashed into the barrel. Heat coursed up her shoulders, neck, cheeks. From the dark doorway of the serving room, the chef scolded the young kitchen hand, Paul, for dragging rather than lifting a box of yellow apples. He grabbed him by the ear and then tossed a sack of onions on top of the fruit.

Hildegard blocked out the bad-tempered chef and focused on Magdalena. 'How do you know about 106?'

'We keep our eyes open around that room.'

'You've been into his suite?'

'You're joking…that's impossible. The concierge and housekeeper choose one person only.'

Hildegard tried not to listen to Paul crying; he was only fourteen. 'But you know all about that room?'

'We do.'

'Who are "we"?' Was that the right question?

A bald and sweating sous-chef plodded back to the central oak table with a dripping basket, packed cruelly with writhing lamprey. Both women glanced at him. Magdalena bent double, swirling the cold, muddy water of the barrel.

'Concerned German citizens.'

She pulled out a large beet which she rubbed furiously with swollen, blotchy hands. She sounded proud and bold.

'Are you with us?'

Hildegard chewed over Magdalena's challenge, murmured only four hours earlier, while her own swollen, grimy hands tackled sludgy clay on beets and parsnips, and questions roiled in her head. Only four hours ago. Waiting for the Concerned German Citizens could stretch into the strain of days and weeks of hyper-vigilance. With her concentration destroyed, it would be the end of architecture studies.

Stiff in Kurt's arms on Oma's tapestry sofa, she turned a page that she had run her eyes over three times without reading. She and Kurt studied by the weak light of the barley-twist lamp, but her pounding head was still in the hotel kitchen. Something would happen. What? Tonight? Next week? The barely perceptible nod that she had given to Magdalena—in that tiny action of a muscle, she had become a Concerned German Citizen.

Her eyes traced blankly over a critique of ancient Greek architecture. Beautiful, grand, exquisitely proportioned, but her thoughts were not in Athens. She was achingly conscious of the Roman-medieval lane beyond the front door. No voices. No trucks. Tonight, not even house beams creaked and settled in the autumn drizzle. The tension in such dead quiet could be undone by a single, faint noise; then she could exhale. Pregnant silence pressed tighter, hemmed in by blackout blinds and in the glow of the single, yellow globe. The war was about to explode in her face, in the tiny sitting room with her new husband.

She eased out of Kurt's arms, walked to the window, lifted the blackout blind and crouched to peek through the slit. Not even a stray dog. It was impossible to tell if anyone was in the house opposite, with no rim of light around the blackout, no door slamming. Their own house must look equally empty. Wartime Bonn was not the lovely city of her childhood.

'Restless?' Kurt did not look up from his anatomy manual.

She dragged her eyes from the dim road. 'Maybe.'

Maybe it would be impossible to sit out the war contemplating the clarity of a line, the sculptural elegance of new architecture. She could not cower beneath the hypocrisy of the hero-architect when the Feuersteins had disappeared from two doors away. Only a few weeks earlier, the Nazis had decreed that Jews must wear a yellow star. When Hildegard waved to *Frau* Feuerstein on the first day that yellow stars speckled Bonn, the anxious woman touched the roughly sewn patch on her jacket. A violent red had leapt up Hildegard's neck. She could not say *'Guten Morgen'* and pretend that nothing had changed, pretend that she was not somehow responsible, however remotely.

Frau Feuerstein had welcomed the newlyweds with a cheesecake. Daniel and Tzipi Feuerstein once played in the lane, but Hildegard came home one day to find their front door swinging in the breeze, the porcelain face of Tzipi's beloved doll smashed on the front step, one leg dismembered and crushed on the cobbles. Hildegard missed their laughter and hoop games and seeing them dodge the few private cars inching through Bonn. Deported? Hiding? Emigrated in the last desperate weeks available to do so? Why hadn't she inquired? She pushed down the blackout curtain as a bicycle squeaked past. Why hadn't she? Why so incurious? Primary school children did not dematerialise. She and Kurt both loathed the German command, but their rare, indiscreet confidences were wary and confined to home. They had never protested in public, even before it was suicide to do so. A despairing silence had clanged between them about what happened in their own street. It was pointless and dangerous to go to the police, but now—after today's conversation—this was the moment to respond. Too late to save Daniel and Tzipi, but she could give something of herself in their names. Magdalena offered her that moral possibility.

She peeped again into the lane. Nobody. When Kurt had returned home an hour ago, Magdalena's words exploded inside her, but Hildegard sealed her lips. Life was too treacherous for unwanted knowledge; she could not burden him.

Kurt looked up, but his head still in anatomy. 'You can't work in that awful hotel all afternoon and then not study at night. You'll fall behind.'

She felt infinitely tender and protective towards Kurt with the shine of lamplight on his fair hair and his pyramid of medical books. Like her, he was no more than a student. They could not call themselves 'concerned citizens', nothing as heroic as that.

'Hmm.'

She patted the curtain closely around the blackout and window frame. What peril was risked in turning over the words in her mind? 'Citizens, concerned...' With an inversion and a comma came a different meaning. She tried 'Citizens, concerned people have reported that the bread has not risen high enough to satisfy Wehrmacht standards'. If only it could be about bread. Or 'concerned citizens have gathered to rebuild Germany'.

Rebuilding the shattered nation? Hazily in the unimaginable future, architects would be needed.

Hildegard opened the front door a crack and breathed the night air. It was certain that Magdalena would ask something of her. Softly, she closed the door. Kurt contemplated her with veiled eyes.

Hildegard curled close to Kurt in bed. 'It's appalling; I hate the job.'

'But you like the money.'

'How can you say that! I'd have gone without if I'd known about Hitler.'

Kurt laughed. 'I warned you: focus on architecture, not potatoes.'

'Potatoes are not the problem.'

'But crisp white sheets are!'

He kissed her in a cave of white linen with embroidered borders, another inheritance from her grandmother, and worlds away from Hitler's tepid, sweaty sheets.

'You know what they say,' said Kurt.

Hildegard snuggled into Kurt's warmth, in a reverie, lost in sun dapples through the weave. 'What?'

Kurt closed his eyes and half-turned away. 'You've made your bed; now lie in it.'

'What did he mean?' asked Stella.

No cyclists had detoured on the grass in front of their bench for five minutes, so she stretched out her legs.

Hildegard sighed. 'I never knew for certain, but I speculated. He was quick, witty and could not resist a joke, even a distasteful one, but I remember that he looked dismayed and was unusually caring for the next few days with more cuddles, and even a small block of real chocolate that he insisted I eat without sharing. And a touching posy of blue forget-me-nots from the edge of the Rhine, the last of the season that he picked himself. I will never forget how he gave me the flowers; he stood so straight and tall, like a noble, ancient statue making a temple offering.'

'A moral ambiguity?' asked Stella.

'A mystery.'

Stella pictured the intrigue of the wartime kitchen: Hildegard frightened, a weeping child, dying fish, dirty potatoes, shrewd eyes, only six kilometres as the crow flew from where now she sat safely under a huge chestnut tree, ruffling her bare feet in the warm, summer grass.

'Did Magdalena work with the Resistance? Maybe she was a White Rose resistant student with a part-time job?'

Hildegard's voice was hoarse. 'I never knew.'

'What about "we"? What concerned German citizens? What concerns?'

'I don't know.'

'Not even after all of this time?'

Hildegard shook her head. 'But they knew me.'

Tree shadows lengthened as families packed up. A squirrel pounced on crumbs flicked from a plaid blanket.

'To protect Kurt, you kept Magdalena's request a secret?'

'I had to protect him. I was on my own, finding my way in a hellish universe.'

THIRTEEN

'DON'T LOSE YOUR Head in Bonn!' Stella winced; a postcard depicted a beer stein hovering over the heads of Cassius and Florentius.

Beethoven keyrings and cheap, plastic busts dominated the souvenirs in Bonn Central Station. Stacks of T-shirts softened the back wall in white, blue, green, red—with team insignia that were a mystery to Stella. A football shirt should appeal to David. Football—oh dear—when David told her about big matches, she didn't know what to say, but she would work on that as soon as she got home. Maybe he liked the Munich team; she studied the red ring logo. Did he have a team photo in his bedroom? She remembered, on the wall behind his bed, a tatty T-Rex, cut from *National Geographic* years ago, and a school commendation with a royal blue border, and a photo of his own football team, but what about the other wall? She eased a middle size from a pile of Munich T-shirts and shook it out. She bit her lip; it was too short. David was no longer small to medium. When had he grown?

She bought a large T-shirt, two giant pretzels and two huge tins of toffees for David and Peter. The tins bore an image in relief of Beethoven; she could feel the waves of his hair flowing to the tins' crimped seams.

The train was not full; she found a seat out of the sun and checked the time—only 7.00 PM, too early to go back to the stifling hotel. She tore off hunks of salty pretzel and consulted the heritage programme. An 8.00 PM session on Australia's Great Barrier Reef; she had to climb back on the conference horse.

Stella recognised nobody. No Georgette. Stella's heart rate was steady, her hands folded in her lap. Her perspiration had dried but left that itchy stickiness.

The Great Barrier Reef was useful when thinking about symbols of identity. What if the world's biggest living thing died? For icons, Australia would then have only Uluru, kangaroos, koalas and the Sydney Opera House. Could an opera house, a giant rock and a couple of marsupials symbolise a whole nation? Why not, if mountains, chocolates, watches and the alpenhorn did the job for Switzerland? She would include the reef in the published version of her presentation and put the afternoon's disaster behind her.

At the end of the session, the speaker invited everyone to take a small, crocheted symbol of reef life. Stella delayed returning to the hotel by sifting through anemone and delicate coral in a raffia basket brimming with frilly, underwater life from the Crochet Coral Reef project. She heard a gentle voice.

'I'm sorry about what happened this afternoon.' Takura also pored over the basket. 'Heard you ran out of time.'

'And then ran out of an audience. Poof!' Stella tossed a crocheted branch of kelp in the air. She felt fiercely ashamed, but she might as well act cavalier.

'The chair should have protected you. After all the work of writing the paper, you should have had a full time slot.'

She was not alone; her neck tension ebbed. 'But no sympathy from the chair.'

Takura held up a blue and yellow nudibranch while Stella ran her fingers over a ghostly, white coral, exquisite in lacy minutia, but its bleaching was the central disaster of the dying reef. The fading coral symbolised the wreck of her presentation. She would keep it as a challenge to get back the Deputy-Editorship.

Takura lingered, hesitant. He squeezed the little nudibranch. 'Not sure about Michael as Deputy-Ed...'

Here was an unexpected confidence. Stella had not realised that there was a gentler, outer circle of the Board; perhaps she could find a home there.

'What do you mean?'

'Abrasive. Couldn't give a damn about anyone's feelings.'

'He doesn't listen.'

Takura pinned the striped nudibranch to his shirt. 'He's bombastic, anti-democratic, rude... I see problems ahead.'

🐦

Stella descended the train station steps to the remaining few metres of subterranean cool in the centre of the platform. She stood on the edge of a conference group; Georgette held forth nearby to another. Stella faced away, exhausted from the appalling day. Everything from bad timing to Hitler. Everyone would be blabbing about the impact of her failure on the credibility of the new journal, burdened so lamentably by one of its own editors, but compassionate Takura had commiserated.

She looked up to check the estimated time of her train's arrival. There he was! Costa eyed her as she coloured from neck to hairline. He jerked his hand in her direction, snared her eyes and glanced down slyly to his middle finger, extended, wobbling and vulgar. She gaped. He was out to get her. Over a seat. He was number-one bad luck.

Heat blitzed through her body. How dare he. Disgusting. Entitled. Greedy. Probably a sex criminal. His insult landed viciously on top of the lingering, paralysing sensation of being blocked by him in the presentation room. He was assaulting her again, was *always* assaulting her.

He forged the victim in her. She was an out-of-control pendulum of rage and regret, unbridled impulse and composure. Too close. Too hot. Too much! Here was the same rush of outrage she had felt against Peter, but there would be no broken arm this time. Oh no! She would not end up on the floor with a man looming over her. Plans for her academic claw-back vanished. Ruddy and furious, she hurtled along the platform. Who cared that Georgette was nearby! Stella would let it all out, right in Costa's face. She would yell: you're revolting, a fraud, a bully, a danger to young women, a disgrace to the conference…

In a volte-face, Costa spun on his heel and faced away, leaving her hanging, pulling up short, delving for insults as he retreated in his rumpled jacket, and people passed between them. Obscenities and accusations roared through her head. Her legs shook, alien, disconnected from her torso. Odd bits of body, sundered here and there like a smashed jigsaw.

One minute until the train arrived. Where the platform had been empty, except for a conference cluster in the last of the cool air, now the station space broke up, became visually complex and difficult to scan as passengers spread out in readiness to board. Stella bit her inner cheeks as Costa wandered along the platform, well away from her, his leg swinging over the edge of the track, no safety rules applying to him, not a care in the world. Naked provocation. He was out to get her. The strap of his over-stuffed bag cut across his flab, weighting his body towards the tracks. An 'unlucky' whack on his back in the crowded station and he would collapse on the track. The tiniest passing nudge from her shoulder—a skim, a bounce, a ricochet—his leg hanging over the edge would do the rest.

The approaching train propelled dirty, warm air. Fifteen seconds until it arrived. The train on the opposite track wheezed off on rubber tyres. Rubber bruised, but it could kill, flattening and crushing vital organs, squishing blood from every orifice. No need to panic, no need to call an ambulance; it would be over.

Stella stormed along the platform towards Costa, hauled by a rope, thick as a wrist—mysteriously of her own clumsy knotting—tight around her waist and squeezing the breath out of her. Tugging. Dragging. All the conference attendees faced the track; she raced behind them. With his constant, swaying gait, it was easy to calculate exactly where Costa would be at the right moment. All she had to do was wait until the last three seconds, weave her way to the front...

The train burst from the tunnel, shooting her dark bob from one side of her head to the other. In a blur of hair, she converged on Costa, sneaking through the crowd, a big cat about to lock jaws on the short, stout neck of her prey. Three seconds till she reached him.

Her gift to the world.

FOURTEEN

Justine caught Stella's reluctant eye. 'Riesling?'

Stella shrank, wedged between Michael and Justine and their clashing colognes as oscillating fans blasted the stink of sweat around the beerhall-style restaurant. She pulled in her chair as another family tramped behind her, each member knocking her shoulder, the same shoulder that Costa had dug his nails into.

Murder…how flabbergastingly close she had come. Her attempt would have resulted in gaol, incredibly in a foreign country. Costa was like a potentate, loathed by everyone, but rarely resisted in a fine balance of autocracy and dread.

Stella nodded and Justine poured wine with a forced smile and a raw mood. Conference rituals persisted, with their long days, dinners and emotions masked by professionalism. Stella pretended to be absorbed in what Michael was saying too loudly.

'Philosophy of interpretation is crucial.'

He gestured recklessly, his hand dominated by a heavy ring, and knocked Justine, who flung out an arm to steady herself. Her straw hat fell from the ear of her chair. Stella spotted Michael's vulgarly big cabochon ruby. He was a night-club MC?

He neither apologised nor paused. 'Tourism authorities are

unaware that best practice is to offer multiple interpretations at a heritage site.'

Stella retrieved the hat, grateful to perform a mundane action and breathtakingly more grateful to be sitting in the tense atmosphere of the restaurant rather than prison. Murder and rage lurked in her sinews. Her hands tingled with the anticipation of the shove that would have hurtled Costa to the tracks, her muscles primed with desire and memory. For once, and only once, thank God for Georgette and her chummy request for a data stick right there and then in the station. Without Georgette's careless shortage, everyone would have witnessed an open-and-shut case and Stella would have committed the unspeakable. Her fury was limitless, but prudence was imperative. If rage dictated her actions, then catastrophe would surely follow.

Justine nodded a terse thanks to Stella but replied effusively to Michael. 'Absolutely agree.'

Stella observed the palsy-walsy interaction; a short time ago she had been the person in that easy relationship with the Editor. Now she sat between the two new scholar friends, ill at the thought of food, even rye bread—a favourite weakness—untouched on her plate. She joined everyone in a toast to the new journal and pretended to sip her Riesling. Surely the others sensed what had nearly happened last night. A would-be murderer sat in their midst, sharing their drinks and their breadbasket, reaching in at the same time, fingers brushing fingers, cosying up with poison in her heart. But no one looked at her; they were too embarrassed by her presentation farce.

Fatima spun her sapphire ring. 'Michael's right. Think of my situation, Islamic in France.'

Fatima appeared unruffled in the humid atmosphere, although everyone else gleamed wetly. She valiantly asserted cultural difference but, beyond doubt, the one who was different was Stella. What a relief not to be calling the Australian Embassy, begging for a lawyer. She did not dare speculate on the reactions of the university and Peter. Oh God, what about David? He would have died when he heard of his mother's bloody actions: 'Mum, I don't know you, anymore. You don't belong with me and Dad'.

Platters of short, fat sausages, sauerkraut and potatoes interrupted the discussion as aromas of dill, ginger and juniper berries drifted over the Board. Stella could not stomach the smell of dill, with its mysterious links to anise; it contributed to her feeling of not belonging. Justine distributed plates and pushed sweet Bavarian mustard and a new basket of rye bread to the end of the table.

Fatima took some bread while she tapped her black hijab. 'Today, I represent a French voice—me—a first-generation immigrant.'

Michael rushed in. 'Interpretation of the clash of voices, that's the key.'

Slowly, Takura rubbed his bald head. 'Interpretation is a problem in tribal Zimbabwe, but not one of our biggest problems. Think about us having Cecil Rhodes' grave in Matobo National Park, the body of the greatest English imperialist in one of *our* great landscapes—now that's an interpretation problem! But we are focused on protection and restitution of art and—'

Michael cut in. 'No surprise that the shrill Zimbabwean position has not changed.'

Justine gasped. Stella gasped. Michael had gone too far; he was plain rude. Stella wanted to jump in and protect Takura, but that was Justine's role. Takura's assessment was right: Michael was bombastic, anti-democratic and, she would add, crass. He was bad news for the Board, but he had already snatched power.

Takura swayed, eyes closed. Michael fidgeted under Justine's glare as he tried mollifying Takura, leaning forward, feigning intimacy and sliding greasy sausages towards him.

'But extremely careful interpretation, that should lead to widespread support for restitution of cultural artefacts—eh, Takura? Eh? Eh?'

Stella observed Michael smile too broadly—a grimacing, scolded monkey—and look from one to the other as if eye contact would erase his rudeness. Ploys and vulgarity, like Costa.

Michael kept grinning. 'Support for restitution would follow.' His grin stretched into a rictus. 'Soon. It would follow…for sure. Soon…'

Takura picked up his beer stein and put it down without drinking. 'But when will I see my great-grandfather's sculptures at home in Harare?'

He studied the silent table of anxious, apologetic faces. Departing diners clogged the entrance; the open door admitted heat, but no ventilation. Michael drained his beer stein.

Justine held up the bottle. 'More wine?'

Fatima served herself sauerkraut and offered the dish to Stella as the silence grew stiffer. Stella pushed the dish away. She took some white bread, cut it into small pieces and made a checkerboard pattern on her plate. She studied the wall posters. Curling grape leaves framed images of Beethoven's House and boats on the Rhine. She nibbled a morsel of bread, but it stuck to the roof of her mouth.

Michael piled his plate high with sausages. 'I appreciate your ethnic feelings, Takura, but I'm the Deputy-Editor.' He drizzled mustard in a thick, yellow zigzag from one side of the plate to the other. 'I've had a private conversation with the Editor. She loves my proposals.'

They'd had a private meeting! Takura's fork clattered to his plate. Stella shoved her shaking hands beneath the table. She was excluded more definitively than she had feared. They'd discussed key issues without the Board. Michael must have exaggerated. Justine busied herself with plates and napkins and pushing around serving dishes. She'd hosted the dinner from her own money and tried to foster new Board solidarity, but an angry crack split wide.

Stella was in pain but tried to help Justine. 'Has anyone seen Beethoven's House?'

Fatima leaped in. 'Justine and I went yesterday, our second time. Speaking of interpretation, the museum claims him for Bonn, although he spent many years in Vienna.'

Justine winked in gratitude. An exclusive, conspiratorial wink! Miserable, erring, excluded, murderous Stella could be her friend again? Eventually? Stella rested her elbows timidly among crumbs… If nothing else happened…if she did not lose control.

Hildegard had grappled with staggering emotions in Hitler's lair, but had not lost control. Stella longed to hear more of her story and to learn how she had survived surveillance, disgust and terror.

Takura left abruptly before dessert and, when Justine asked for coffee orders, Stella excused herself and strolled back to the Rhine, leaving the inner sanctum to get on with it.

An empty bench, mid-evening, but with German summer time, the day never seemed to end. Stella had not anticipated the bare seat slats, desolate with scrappy paint. Hildegard had always been there.

Stella walked slowly towards the bench and sank down, skimming her hands over the weathered wood, having faith that the fragile figure would wend her way over the grass, focused on greeting her, Stella, who waited now in their special place and needed her wisdom. But there was no one walking towards her, and the new Board was already broken. She could not blame herself; Michael had done that and Justine had not stopped him.

Stella sat alone among a handful of families while couples strolled along the riverside promenade. A flautist played Bach's badinerie, the notes skipping through the chestnuts, but the park seemed to have lost its historical layers; it was only a park in a cyclical present of nature's growth, decay, death and derailment by humans.

Stella wandered to the shore, searching for the deportation memorial that Hildegard had told her about at their first meeting. There was no plinth or obelisk, perhaps she had misunderstood, and yet Hildegard had taken care to make sure that she knew it existed. She decided to walk to the bridge. Music thundering from two tourist boats overwhelmed the flute. Exhausted parents with a fractious baby pushed a pram along the uneven path. Stella remembered the long nights when she and Peter struggled with a colicky baby. But the time passed; David now took responsibility for his own life. Well, starting to, at fourteen.

And then she was upon the nondescript memorial. So small, almost miss-able. Not a plinth, not a big, national statement, but the simple memory of local people, small and brown and unremarkable, its inscription blurred and mossy. The memorial stone leaned to one side where summer grasses grew thickly, dark green spears cradling the words. Someone had propped a bunch of silk forget-me-nots on top of the stone; a small deckle-edged card was tied to the ribbon that wound around the blue and yellow flowers. The faded handwriting was spidery and indecipherable. Stella parted the grass and brushed speckles of pollen from the mossy lettering. She made out the German for 'honour' and 'forgiveness' and 'memory'. Behind the memorial lay older bunches of silk forget-me-nots, their cards blotted and swollen, the blue flowers bleached by the sun, half-hidden in the summer grass. Someone came here repeatedly and had made it a private memorial.

Stella meandered back through the mingling picnic aromas of pizza cheese, oregano, cloves and the crusty bread fragrance of German beer. The heroism that Hildegard had witnessed in a single kitchen compared starkly with the grotesque posturing and criminality of Costa. People like him were worthless, but they wrecked lives and caused wars. Someone should have stopped Hitler before 1941.

FIFTEEN

As the park stilled, a few families lit hurricane lamps. Parents tried to settle near-naked toddlers on picnic rugs because the temperature remained too high for people to return to poorly ventilated homes. A dog chewed a bone, a Frisbee trapped under her front paws. The lemony smell of mosquito coils pricked Stella's nose.

'*Guten Abend.*'

Stella had missed the languorous, poetic walk of Hildegard over the grass to their bench, the river, glinting and silvery in the dusk, and the edges of the park already dark. The walk that signalled a royal road back to terror, so like, and yet unlike, her own childhood's of one unknown man coming out of the night. Hildegard's terror blasted out of an entire regime.

Magdalena ambled the length of the kitchen; Hildegard watched her approach from the distant stoves, past bloody fish, mounds of minced onions and steaming bread. The young woman paused for a joke with Fritz. Hildegard stirred the vegetable barrel. Not today, Magdalena. Pass by. But she stopped.

'Checking on the potato speed. You dropped some.'

Magdalena retrieved the lost potatoes, lobbing them noisily, one by one, into the muddy water, splashing Hildegard.

Hildegard angled her face onto the sleeve of her maid's uniform and mopped her cheeks.

Magdalena moved closer, her voice barely audible. 'He'll be in the hotel in seventy-two hours; you'll be back in his suite. Anton will tell you what to do.'

She caught Hildegard's eyes. 'Ready?'

Hildegard focused on the swirling, brown water. This was the moment. What about Kurt? She sloshed her hands; earthy froth formed and burst.

Magdalena flung a glance towards Fritz. 'Too late for thinking.'

Hildegard took the last potato from Magdalena. 'How will I know Anton?'

'He knows you.'

'How long did you wait for Anton?'

Stella lifted her legs as a cyclist veered off the path; Hildegard tucked her feet beneath the bench.

'Precisely from the moment Magdalena dropped those dirty little potatoes in my barrel. Then Paul delivered two big sacks of parsnips, their white skins hidden by a viscous mud. The sacks were too heavy for him, and I was far behind in preparation. I let people down. With my muddy face, I peered over my shoulder, wondering if Fritz used another name. Or maybe the chef. Could he be "Anton"? He ignored me most of the time, but maybe that was the plan of the Concerned Citizens. Being watched was no longer my morbid phantasm.'

'You wondered whether you imagined being watched?'

Hildegard smiled ruefully. 'Oh, Stella, dear. Eyes were the danger.'

Stella thought of the wartime picture: surveillance and dread—always dread—a new husband, a secret, a loathsome job. And pressing studies—or financing them, which was the catalyst for the mess.

'Your studies—could you keep up?'

'Forgotten! Gone! Fear and, I will say also, anger at the situation, consumed my life. If only I had chosen babysitting; the jobs I rejected were not so bad. Instead, I struggled to be myself as each day unfolded without my control. There was no one to talk to, least of all darling Kurt. I found myself failing no matter what I did.'

'How? You were brave.'

Hildegard did not have false modesty; Stella would have detected it by now. This was a history of immense personal bravery, but Hildegard would never admit it.

'Not brave, my dear. Trapped. If I didn't take the hotel job, I exposed my whole family to the consequences of my lack of patriotism. But if I didn't take the Resistance challenge, I would miss what was probably the only virtuous, patriotic action that I could take to assist my tragic nation. My true sense of self was at risk if I did not act.'

'Lipstick!' *Frau* Wagner commanded. 'Get it off permanently.'

Hildegard rubbed her face, smearing pinky-red.

'The Fuhrer arrives tomorrow. All your energies must be focused on the *Fuhrersuite*. It should go without saying that you must uphold National Socialist principles of feminine grace and beauty.'

Hildegard nodded. Let that be the only thing that was asked of her; she could give up lipstick to save herself and Kurt.

'A fresh face is your German beauty and is the least that you can offer the Fuhrer if you have the honour to clean his suite. Scrub yourself in the maid's trough.'

Maids and labourers from the grand houses swarmed the above-ground Bad Godesberg station in the autumn drizzle. For the first time on the platform, Hildegard observed young men smoking and wearing slouchy, threadbare cloth caps. One of them could be Anton. She recognised four maids from the Rheinhotel Dreesen wearing voluminous dirndls, damp tendrils of hair limp on their flushed faces. One of them applied lipstick.

Hildegard examined the waiting passengers. The agony of waiting had escalated to worse than anything she might be asked to do. But what and by whom? She climbed aboard her regular 18.13 and, as usual, chose the front of the second carriage because it gave her the fastest access to the exit tunnel on arrival in Bonn. Anton might know that. Other than attending classes and arriving at the hotel for the afternoon shift, choosing the second carriage was her only repeated action of which she was aware.

She sat by the window, forcing her eyes on her Greek architecture book, and exhaled in massive relief when a crying baby distracted passengers. The mother shush-shushed while those around Hildegard grimaced. Hildegard's eyes jumped around a photograph of an Archaic Greek god with its rigid, left-leg-forward position, hands clenched into balls of marble, and its eerie, fixed smile, replicated, unnervingly, hundreds of times in Archaic sculpture, and symbolising who knew what, but—tantalisingly—reminiscent of Kurt. Implacable, resolved, haunting.

The baby cried louder as the train braked abruptly; Hildegard grabbed the seat in front of her. Silence followed, pierced only by the crackle of a newspaper and a mother soothing her child. Hildegard opened a chapter on the idealising role of Graeco-Roman forms in nineteenth-century northern Europe. The book was due back at the university library the next day, but she had barely started. The train moved off. Hildegard flipped backwards through black and white photographs of ruined temples. She ran her eyes up and down white columns, taking in nothing while her hands sweated on the cover. A few people alighted at stations along the route. Hildegard hid her face behind the metal frame of the window and worked on an innocent expression, but her cheek muscles refused commands. She looked frightened—well, she was.

She lined up first at the door as the train approached Bonn Central. Before the brakes stopped squealing, she jumped down the steps and ran, tearing from the platform to the safety of home, the locked door and Kurt. She slowed in the crowded underpass with its dim lighting and cracked tiled walls. Almost home and the wretched day behind her. Unable to think coherently. Wash off the mud and have dinner. Read in Kurt's arms. Blessed sleep.

A shove from behind. The book flew out of her hands, sliding along the bitumen walkway; annoyed passengers stepped around it. A young man darted from behind and seized the splayed book, brushing it down and wiping it back and forth on the seat of his trousers while an ancient temple glowed in white marble. A cloth cap set low cast a shadow half-way down the bridge of his nose, over colourless cheeks, obscuring his eyes, leaving only his tight lips in the light. With a trace of a bow—a courtesy from a dead Germany—he presented it to her and strode on.

Hildegard stared after the young man for frozen seconds, only his bobbing cap was visible in the station's tired, nightly bumping-along of workers. This was it. Anton had tracked her to the underpass. The book turned alien, deathly; she fought an urge to hurl it. On the cover was a temple in Sicily, once of such delight, but now a place of her own self-sacrifice. It was no longer a simple library book that would soon leave her hands, but a coffer with an awesome, buried message commanding action, for her, Hildegard, who knew only how to draw an architectural line and had never been brave in her whole life.

Stella sucked in her cheeks, eyes wide, but this was not a cheap airport thriller.

'Anton? It was him?'

'Perhaps, how can I say? Anyone could have played "Anton". Maybe Anton was one of the maids giving instructions to another person. Grumpy Fritz? Probably not little Paul, who snuffled when he even glimpsed the chef. It felt as if the universe composed a drama for me and I was forced to take a leading role without knowing the trajectory of my character.'

Stella thought of being trapped in a drama written by someone else, like a puppet, taken out of a box, dangled theatrically, and then slammed back under a lid, voiceless. She wrote her own drama with Costa, and although he often had the upper hand, rage had not deprived her of reason. She could still exit gracefully from their collision.

'Did the man—Anton—turn back?'

'My dear, that could be fatal. Anything out of the ordinary stood out. Who else might have been watching? If he had turned, it would have been like inviting a bullet into his own brain.

'I remember the back of Anton's head, the way his brown, cloth cap was low, but also set at a rakish angle with blond, bristly tufts jutting out. People rushing and eyes, eyes everywhere. It was mere seconds, but I knew that I had been given the challenge of my life. I clasped that library book to my chest as if it were my child and ran.'

SIXTEEN

A SQUEAKY, OVERLADEN BUILDER'S wagon spilt into the Bonn lane, blocking a truck piled high with camouflage webbing. In the wet autumn twilight, honks and beeps sounded as people rushed by, careless of chipped bricks and nails scattered in the gutter.

Shoppers shouted insults as Hildegard ran through rainy streets. She skirted around prams, ladders, carts, and buckets filled with sand, ready for the fires of enemy bombing. She tore into the maze of squares and lanes of medieval Bonn, panting, winding, shoving. The way home was infinite. Run! She sloshed through puddles and whirled around street traders. Workers, friends, all were mortal threats. Run! The city of her childhood metamorphosised from worn cobbles and simple stone houses to a snare.

'What's the hurry?'

Two student friends waved from across the street. Everyday Bonn flipped as if a film strip lost its sprockets. Her life with friends flickered anarchically. Before rationing, silly chatter about clothes and parties. Marta, in baby-blue silk, sobbing in Hildegard's arms when a handsome army cadet abandoned her at a church dance. Hildegard's one and only skiing trip, with rich Eva to Garmisch-

Partenkirchen, giggling and gossiping over cakes, only three years ago. Eva ordering five cakes for herself: Bee Sting, Black Forest, Cheese, Gugelhupf, Stollen. Hildegard remembered the list only because of the astonishing sight of Eva eating them all. Picnics, lectures, helping each other.

Hildegard kept walking. 'Hello. Sorry, got to keep going. My Greek temple essay's due.'

The friends exchanged a shrug.

'But nothing's due for three weeks,' called Marta.

Hildegard strode faster, cold with anxiety, and yet fascinated by Marta's blood-red pout, detectable even in the early dusk. The film strip spun off the last sprocket, flapping wildly, frames from her life before the Rheinhotel Dreesen bunching and creasing. She needed a plausible reply immediately. Eva would persist, gnawing at the issue.

'Three weeks will fly by. I've got a part-time job and I need to plan. Besides, it's raining.'

'Hey, you!' yelled Eva. 'Remember us, we're in your class.'

Blonde plaits piled on her head and a scrubbed face, Eva hurried in parallel to Hildegard, her coat pulled to her chin. She began to cross the road, hands clawing for the book—half joking, half deadly serious—but three black limousines cruised between them with bedraggled swastikas, and curtains over the rear seat windows. Of all the people of Bonn, Hildegard knew that Hitler had not yet arrived, so who were these big wigs taking over the lane with their pretentious drapes? A hand bearing an SS ring gestured beyond the hem of the curtain. The driver slowed and a guard in the front seat looked at her.

'I can see it!' Eva was still after the book, even as the street thickened with SS.

Hildegard was not the only watchful pedestrian. A handful of mothers tugged children by the hand and disappeared into a vegetable shop. A few young men ran and—oh, God!—a drunk soldier mocked a *Heil Hitler* salute. Hildegard's heart cartwheeled.

She gripped the book, hands like vices, and huddled against a wall as the cars crawled by.

Eva shouted louder. 'Hey, you! I'm talking to you, Hildegard Weber. I've recalled that book.'

'It's still out in my name. It's not late.'

So, Eva had become the library stool pigeon. There were only two copies in the library; Hildegard knew she should have returned hers, and she would have, if not for the vortex of the hotel. That glamorous and rich Eva, proud and stiff in her family's gleaming white motor car, should be interested in her, had once been flattering; now it was a mortal hazard.

Eva yelled, 'Why not give it to me now?'

Hildegard crossed her arms over the book and curled her fingers over the spine. 'Bye!'

'You'll only be smooching with Kurt all night.'

Hildegard turned the corner, assaulted by the sounds of the city: the squeak and tinkle of the bakery door, tramping of soldiers, whimpering of children, a distant gunshot, an overloaded truck grinding its gears, and, 'Mean bitch!'

Safe in a side street, she did not slow. What a stupid detail about an assignment, a dreadful error when Eva and Marta had the same architecture work. Her first, appalling mistake and she hadn't even started. Magdalena should never have trusted her.

She sprinted the last metres and bashed the door open. Kurt wasn't there, thank God. She locked the door, fastened the chain, and drew the curtains with such force that she pulled the heading away from several hooks. The curtain dangled, revealing a strip of bare window. Outside, families and students jostled in a promenade, as if it were peacetime and the SS did not cruise the ancient lanes. Hildegard jumped; a man in uniform squinted at the window. She tugged the curtains to cover the gap, and piled up heavy medical and architecture library books to stand on to reach the hooks.

She slumped against the front door. Private at last. No. Secret. This was now a secret place. She waited to be sure that

Eva and Marta were not about to rap on the door, then she whipped through the book to a tiny note lodged in the binding stitches opposite a black and white photograph; she scarcely took in that it was the Doric temple of Segesta. Rough student paper with faint lines—grubby, twisted, worm-like—formed a bulge. Hildegard shivered as she unwound the spiral. Faint pencil handwriting covered the note, the first sentence in a backward, sloping, cursive hand and the next two printed with one of the words in block capitals. The paper was furred from winding and unwinding countless times.

'Boxes of maps of bridges. Take Cologne-Bonn district with the HAND-written annotations. Leave the others.'

Hildegard grabbed the lamp base and sank onto the sofa, but she felt as if she floated above the furniture as she read and re-read Anton's words. They were simple words, but they had no meaning. Bridges, why? They were no mystery; everyone could see them and use them. Whose annotations?

Boxes of maps… She remembered the boxes in the *Fuhrersuite*, several of them at the foot of Hitler's bed by the balcony doors; papers had stuck out of them as if packed away hastily. She would need to sift and make lightning-quick decisions. She was an actress in a horror film. She ran her hand around the barley twist lamp base, knowing the silkiness of the oak grain that she had stroked since childhood. What consequences might there be? Would she cause the deaths of people? Of Kurt? Her mother?

She twisted the paper back into a worm shape. But, if she did not act, would she be responsible for other deaths? She would probably never know, but it would not change the fact. Her implication in death—always knowing that you had harmed someone—a stranger, friend or foe—knowing and not knowing was an awesome life burden.

She crushed the worm between her fingers and checked her watch; Kurt was almost home. She scrambled to find a candle and a match in the kitchen dresser. The drawer jammed as she mentally tracked Kurt trudging along the narrow street, hungry for dinner and a newly-marrieds' night of study and passion. She wriggled a butter knife between the box and the dresser frame. She jabbed too hard; the drawer flew open with a spray of pine-wood shavings that dotted the linoleum. She felt for a candle among the scissors and rolls of string, lit it and fed the message into the flame.

The Fuhrer returned.

Hildegard gathered her cleaning items and climbed the stairs, moving a little slower with each tread, desperate for the day to be over. She struggled with a mop, soap, a scrubbing brush, a box filled with dusters and, under her arm, fresh sheets in brown paper. Beyond the alcove entry hall that gave access to the *Fuhrersuite*, she found a chair set in front of a Bavarian mountain landscape with a climber, a heroic Germanic speck, on a high ridge. Two soldiers eyed her from positions by the door. One she recognised from thousands of newspaper photographs—Sergeant Rochus Misch, a name she would learn after the war, Hitler's long-term, faithful bodyguard.

The grandfather clock in the foyer struck 12.30 PM. Silence from 106. Hildegard pushed the box beneath the hall seat and sat straight, with her knees making a right angle beneath her starched white apron, and her polished shoes together, toes aligned…and considered escape. If she stashed her apron and maid's headband into the box, ran down the stairs, across the driveway and back to the train station, the ordeal would be over. Would the manager and concierge bother to track her? She was the lowest of the low in a rigid hierarchy; she could be expected to be unreliable and replaceable.

An under-manager bustled by in a suit with sharp trouser creases. He ignored her, turned into the alcove and stooped at the door of 106. Shoulders rigid, hips angled, he bent his head, ear near the lock. After half a minute, he walked back through the alcove doors and disappeared. Hildegard squirmed under Sergeant Misch's frown and stayed put.

Perhaps she heard a sound in the *Fuhrersuite*? She strained to hear, but the silence extended, so intense that it seemed to buzz and expand. The grandfather clock struck one. Nothing from 106. Every second that she sat in the corridor, she was deeper in treason. 'Treason'…a word for the worst of the worst, not for her, a mere student architect. Traitors were shot, hanged, guillotined. With every tick of the clock, turning back became more complex. She should have told Kurt; at least, he could have prepared for the worst. He would be alarmed at her rashness. Not proud, but appalled.

Two maids walked past, wordless, scrutinising *her*—someone outside 106. Hildegard had not seen them before. A tread on the stairs, *Frau* Wagner glowering.

'Wait,' she whispered down the corridor.

The clock chimed half past one. Hildegard should have been hungry. There was a hard cheese sandwich in her basket in the basement. An hour ago, kitchen staff would have taken turns to sit on the back steps in the weak autumn sun and eat lunch. If Fritz were feeling generous and had baked too many cakes for afternoon tea, there might have been a plate of pastries. She would never eat again.

The under-manager, this time with two SS officers, walked softly the length of the corridor, brushing past the crunch of starch across her knees and pausing by the alcove. She had done nothing wrong up to this moment, but now she teetered on the blood-spattered knife-edge of treason. Execution could follow within hours of the mockery of a trial. Bravery should be quick, an electric spur to action, not this excruciating stretch of time under gilt-framed paintings. She could still abandon the chair, the corridor, the *Fuhrersuite*, Bad Godesberg, and Anton—whoever he was.

Maybe this was fear, not courage. She thought of heroism that happened in an instant, where the person must have been innately brave. She had seen that bravery long ago when she had been safe and protected, even when surrounded by danger.

Hildegard, five years old, huddled in an oversized jumper, in a winter so hard that the Rhine froze white from shore to shore, and her father's cough hacked through their small house. On the first Sunday afternoon of the new year, he took her for a walk, her tiny gloved hand snug in his, while the shore of the Rhine creaked with wild chunks of ice. Hildegard ran to icicles shining from tree branches, glittering like tassels of diamond in Fairyland.

Papa coughed. 'Too close! Come back.'

She reached for an ice diamond, but plunged to her waist through the ice crust and frigid water bordering the path, her coat floating out like a daisy.

The sick man jumped in after her. His big hands fitted around her waist and hauled her up and out. Blessed Papa to save her, so strong and gallant, but he struggled to save himself. The bitter river trapped her hero; he spat bloody mucus, and scraped at frozen mud and weeds. Frantic passers-by dragged him out. Someone appeared with a wagon and horse; helpers pushed the father and daughter onto the plank flooring, clothes crackling into ice in the freezing air.

The day had broken into ebony-framed memories for Hildegard: holding Papa's hand in the peaceful stroll; the ice beautiful, then painful like fire; poor Papa floundering; blinding sunlight through the rolling steam from the horse's nostrils; thin plaits striking her cheeks, spiky with ice and mud; and Mama screaming and screaming, stripping off Hildegard's clothes, chiselled frozen. Papa on the floor, immobile.

'Terrible,' said Stella. 'Did he recover?'

Hildegard took a long time to answer while the river reflected the rosy sky and flowed beyond the jumble of semi-naked picnickers, sleeping infants and dogs.

'No. Rescuing me was the last meaningful act of his life and the first big lesson of mine. For Papa, it was a day of selfless bravery, of being the truest father, but tragedy for us all. His cough worsened with tuberculosis and he disappeared into a sanitorium.'

Another father silenced, like Stella's. After the war, when the army disappeared from his everyday life, the war became a vast No Man's Land on which she had dared not trespass.

'An awful loss, especially when you were so young.' Stella wiped sweat from her neck. 'You said the Rhine froze? That's hard to imagine.'

'Oh, yes, it would freeze, but with global warming there's been no river freeze for more than fifty years.'

A luxury yacht skimmed by, ghostly in the dying light; careless laughter floated into the scorched and withered park.

'Another loss for you,' said Stella. 'You have told me so much and I am grateful. How could your work in the hotel change your life so quickly? You said your home felt different.'

'My dear, you do not see the word "total" in totalitarian? Assisting Magdalena and the Concerned German Citizens changed my place in the world, so even the walls and windows of my home had to change. The curtain was ripped from its hooks…'

'Did time change too? Did you have time to think?'

'None. All I could think was I didn't want Eva and Marta to knock; I was dreadfully worried. Eva would never let go of a mystery. Friends were not welcome in my home for the first time in my life because it contained a battered library book. If they arrived, I would need to perform like an actress, inventing a story about why I needed the book and chattering about their hero,

Herr Albert Speer, over a diluted cup of our prized, rationed tea—only ten grams a month. I didn't want to share it. My beloved home was lost.'

Stella thought about the idea of an estranged home. When the serial killer roamed Perth, there was nowhere safe in the summer darkness, not even in Stella's bedroom, with its basket of toys in the corner and a spray of familiar beach sand making her sheets scratchy. The menace beyond the window had thrust her everlastingly off course.

'But you did not know the Concerned German Citizens,' said Stella. 'You were astonishingly brave.'

'I was not brave, but awesomely foolish. I had forgotten the assignment submission date. Me, with the prodigious memory! I knew my actions could bleed out into the world. My student self was no longer enough. I had to demand more and more of myself to keep going.'

'What about Kurt, did you need to pretend with him? It would be painful to have a secret in a marriage.'

'That was the worst. Kurt and I had promised always to be honest with each other. He loved me so. When I showed him the place where I nearly died in the river, he said that he could not bear to think that he might have lost me before ever finding me.'

She buried her face in her hands. 'I stop now, too much emotion. I need to be alone. I live close by; don't worry about me.'

Stella climbed uphill to the station, thinking about Hildegard's father. He was as brave as his daughter, with the sort of bravery that does not hesitate. Hildegard's courage was different; it meant that she needed to keep a secret from Kurt.

Secrets... Not telling Peter about Costa would alter their relationship, but only Stella would know it had changed.

Openness, even with arguments, was healthier than hoarding secrets, but she could not tell Peter. The drama in Bonn had gone too far. She would tell him only fragments, a few crumbs to explain her rapid demotion on the Board, but that would be the same as having a secret. But for the divine intervention of Georgette, she would be labelled 'criminal'.

She crossed through the little Martinsplatz square to the heads of Cassius and Florentius behind the basilica apse. Tonight no tourists joked around the site of the atrocity, although the *al fresco* cafés were full and rowdy with holiday-makers. She imagined the obscenity of the headless bodies near the temple, and Roman soldiers horrified to see their friends dead, but too intimidated to show it.

The sculptures of the martyrs had changed, their shadows ballooned out to enormous egg shapes on the cobbles in the pale yellow of lamplight. In daylight, the heads resembled left-overs, something fallen, incomplete, but, augmented by twilight shadows, they dominated the square as light bumped along the cobble edges making a fantasy chess board of distorted waving lines.

At last the blazing blue sky had yielded fully to dusk in wisps of high, thin, pink and saffron clouds. An old couple paused in the square, hand in hand, admiring the apse. Stella walked up to the clean-shaven martyr, looked into his eyes and up to his vision. The saint had not changed, although the world had changed around him. He had stood his moral ground in hell on earth. She thought of the ultimate bravery that provoked death, with death the better option than lying, even to murderous comrades who carried out the bidding of a despot. And of Hildegard, challenged to help the Resistance and thinking always of Kurt, never of herself. She walked to the other head; the bearded saint's view ran along the cobbles. He was earth-bound, but faithful to himself. She trod carefully around the memorial heads, tracing a protective loop.

Costa had demanded her gallery seat, and her subsequent days of reckless, frenetic responses had caused great professional harm to her, but none to him. She had to stop. No more Costa, no more cutting herself off from the world, pursuing a disastrous course, alone. This was not moral courage. He was not her problem; let the Italians deal with him. The students grasped his duplicity, even if his peers at the cocktail party did not. All she had needed to do was retain 'the seat', that was enough of a feminist position. She had already made a mess of her presentation, next would be her moral being.

A teen boy tossed a crust to a waiting dove. Immediately, seagulls attacked, ripping at the bread. The dove flew to the sanctuary of the basilica roof. There was no point organising her life according to her childhood, no point in understanding every brusque encounter as framed by old fears. Not every man, not even every aggressive man, was a lurking serial killer. She could live her life without petrified memories—the flap of curtains, the scrape of a branch—but she was not sure who she would be without them. Perhaps Hildegard had arrived to lead her away from a memory prison. That wise old woman.

The granite heads darkened as the last light faded; now they appeared identical. She had been mistaken to see Cassius and Florentius as foolish. They had been strong and brave, certain of themselves. A horde of spineless murderers could not change that. That was what Hildegard might say. She would counsel against the obsession with Costa, although Stella would never humiliate herself by telling Hildegard the stupid things that she had done. Hildegard would say, 'Focus on your family and career. This man's not worth your time'.

He was not Stella's responsibility. Let Costa's colleagues deal with him. His students, including the young Islamic women, were strong and perceptive. 'Stop,' Hildegard would say.

'Stop,' Stella said.

SEVENTEEN

THAT SIREN FACEBOOK, it lured her again, singing a sweet song of voyeurism and revenge. In under a second, Stella could key in and click. Yes? No? Once more! She keyed in 'Giovanni Costa'...browsed the headings of men from the Alps to Buenos Aires...tapped her fingers up and down the Formica desk and thought of valour, self-control, and her decision an hour ago at the memorial to the martyrs.

She clicked off. That wasn't so hard.

Email: 'My Darling David

How are you? How is sport going? I should be able to attend some mid-week matches in the future. I know I've said that before, but I can juggle my timetable better now that I'm a prof. It's awfully hot here, but the WHC is super interesting. I spoke to a German woman yesterday who fell into the River Rhine during a freeze when she was a child. Her father pulled her out, but the rescue ended up killing him. (I know you don't like sentimentality, but I would risk all for YOU.)

Love

Mum'

Email: 'Pete, teenagers change quickly. TALK TO HIM!! PS please ask the builder for a timeline for the bathroom renovation.

We deserve this long-awaited improvement.'

◆

She arrived early for the Board meeting. Steady, dependable Stella was back; she would work on being both reliable and creative. She had felt unhinged since Costa's attack on Monday, but now, Friday, she was back on track. The breakout room looked bigger and more comfortable with the faulty light globe replaced. She secured a peeling corner of a Kyoto temple poster, poured water into paper cups for each person and distributed half-size pencils. She'd show commitment, salvage her reputation and dazzle everyone. She leaned across the table and set each pencil in the same position relative to its paper cup, pointing at six o'clock. She squared her own papers to the table edge and waited.

Michael and Justine arrived, terse and scowling. Justine's big straw hat spun and scratched, faster than ever. Takura followed a few seconds later with a big, knowing grin for Stella. Michael tightened the knot of his tie and fiddled with gold cufflinks. The room filled up with bodies, satchels and note pads. Justine tapped on the table, calling the meeting to order, but Takura spoke first.

'Our first editorial should analyse the Korean-Japanese dispute.'

Stella regretted her inattention when she learned about the trauma of Hashima Island. Yet another Costa legacy; he had closed her down to other people's suffering. You could not enter the conference centre without being exposed to the heartrending Korean protest photos of starving, enslaved men, their skin ingrained with coal dust from undersea mining. The dust had lodged deep, like a whole-body tattoo, as if it could never be scrubbed off, and ribs stuck out through the dirt. How could she not have been deeply moved when she first encountered this harrowing history? She worried the World Heritage Committee would make a decision that would please Japan while erasing Korean slavery from recognition in the actual places where it had occurred.

Stella nodded and smiled at Takura. 'That's an essential idea for us. Korean suffering has been the horror at the heart of this conference.'

She would recover the week. There was clear energy in thinking of something other than Costa.

Michael rocked back on his metal chair and leered with mock incredulity. 'Horror? That's an over-statement in Nazi territory.'

Stella shook her head. Typical jaundiced comment.

Fatima spoke angrily for the first time. 'There's no competition for suffering and—'

Michael cut in. 'We've voted to focus on interpretation.'

Fatima rolled her eyes. Stella observed unexpected strain in the once-chummy inner circle; a lot had happened since her ousting. She would not fire from the hip. She studied a new poster of German World Heritage showing Neuschwanstein Castle in the snow, the fairy-tale prototype which straddled history and fantasy. Then she turned to Justine.

'We have a long agenda, but would you agree to us first discussing the Korean-Japanese dispute?'

Everyone agreed, except Michael. During twenty minutes of brain-storming, Justine collated the main editorial points on a whiteboard, then Takura spoke.

'I vote Stella for lead editorial author.'

'Yes!'

'Absolutely.'

'Great idea.'

They all smiled, even Michael. She had been right to give up Costa.

Stella and Justine stretched their legs in the deepest shade of the linden tree, eyes dreamy on the fast-flowing Rhine. Eventually, Justine poured two glasses of Riesling.

'Michael's sulking…I complained to him last night that he was being abrasive.'

'He's difficult.'

'Sure is…the new journal needs to make friends, not enemies.'

Stella bit her tongue before she revealed Takura's grim opinion. She knew she would be more collegial than Michael ever could, but it was too much to hope that Justine would re-consider the Deputy-Editorship. It was sour and hard when the prize had already been hers. Damn Costa, but it was good to sit with her old friend again, just the two of them. She pondered asking Justine to change her mind, but the Editor's straw hat obscured her eyes. It was tricky discerning whether she wanted a conversation or not.

The conference centre tomcat ambled by—back smooth, tail curved gently—paused and glanced up the linden. Delicately, he took a morsel from a delegate and curled around her legs.

From beneath her hat, Justine changed topic. 'You seem more like old yourself, calmer and happier.' She sipped her Riesling. 'Don't forget to visit Beethoven's House. Fatima and I would enjoy analysing it with you.'

Stella got it. She was sufficiently on the inside of the Board for friendly chats about historic sites, but the Deputy-Editorship boat had sailed.

🐦

Stella sought out the young South Korean who had given her a pamphlet on wartime slavery and found her in the same blue chima skirt and white jeogori jacket finishing a bowl of barley rice. She was the only person in national dress; others wore shorts and T-shirts. Stella thought how tough it would be to dress in such a tight-fitting jacket.

The woman bowed her head. 'My name is Min.'

'My name's Stella; I want to understand.'

She started work in sickening heat in front of the old Bundeshaus.

She would be her most productive and write a superb editorial for the journal's first issue. What elation in starting a new project…the Board would welcome her back. She wiped perspiration from her eyes and pointed to the posters of emaciated bodies.

Min put down her rice bowl and tapped a pile of Korean history books on a folding table outside the tent. 'There were Chinese prisoners and Allies and 700,000 Koreans. The wartime slaves lived in hell; some were as young as fourteen.'

Young, like David, too awful to grasp. 'The Koreans were prisoners?'

'Yes and no, there was a Japanese fiction that the Koreans were actually Japanese because of the 1910 annexation of the Korean Peninsula.'

Min pointed to the welcome shelter of the tent with its friendly disarray of laptops, gas burners, bowls and chop sticks. The metres of fabric in Min's blue chima seemed to inflate in the small tent, rustling from trestle table to tent flap.

Stella stood back for Min. 'Conquered?'

'Beaten, starved and officially paid wages and pensions, but the workers could never access their money.'

Min pulled out stools and offered Stella water and a sesame snack, and then pushed towards her a thick cream manila folder that had been handled so many times that the edges were curled and grubby. Stella turned over photographs of hollow-eyed, defeated people.

The pursuit of historical justice. This was where she belonged. It was good, important work and she was back in her own skin.

'But paid after the war?'

'Of course not!' Min laughed bitterly. 'The Japanese Treasury absorbed the funds.'

Stella scrutinised photographs of stained concrete buildings, like hulks on a rocky shore. White horses flecked the Prussian blue sea that had become a prison wall. Decades of injustice were compounded by the World Heritage bid that would result in tourists visiting Hashima Island, but not being informed about Korean suffering because interpretation would stop at 1910, long before wartime slavery. She took her pen and notepad from her backpack and opened herself to Korean history, asking question after question.

~

The hotel room had no chance to cool at night even with the window open. Stella's hand slipped on the computer mouse as she finished reading a student's thesis draft. She signed off: 'Well done, I look forward to further discussion'.

She got up from her desk and took another cold shower before checking the conference schedule for the next day. An email alert blinked.

'Hi Stella

I've been rethinking the Board dynamics. Would you consider coming back on as Deputy-Editor? Unfortunately, we've run out of meeting time, but you could cover the legal details of a journal by email. Ok?

Cheers

Justine'

She read it again. A miracle. She was back! The weird week was stabilising. She deserved it. She'd do a fantastic job. They'd be a powerful team and she would take over as Editor when Justine had a second baby. She hit reply with vigour, ready to send an enthusiastic acceptance and invite Justine to lunch, but a dark corner of her mind scraped open. Lead weights in her childhood bedroom curtains chinked dully on the windowsill and beyond lurked a moonless night. The Korean slaves hewing coal, brutalised, terrified in tunnels beneath the sea. Children like David. Perpetually hungry and afraid.

~

In the darkest shade of the linden tree, Stella developed a draft editorial plan with Justine: a journal issue for Michael's interpretation theme and another for Takura's heartfelt need for restitution.

Justine flapped her ponytail like a fan. 'So good to work closely with you again. We almost read each other's mind.'

But for Stella, overhead leaves stirred, shifting, shuffling. Linden leaves merged with eucalyptus.

Back in the auditorium, Stella congratulated herself for sitting nowhere near Costa, nor deliberately far from him, nor even looking at him as the conference afternoon session started. People had spread themselves throughout the upper gallery, many draping their arms over armrests to enable maximum air circulation. A spokeswoman explained a possible approach to the disagreement between the South Koreans and Japanese.

Abruptly, Costa stood. He bumped his bag along the balustrading and talked loudly on his phone as he walked up and out of the gallery and then descended the stairs to the foyer. Stella focused on her notes; she had no time to waste on him, but around the gallery, angry murmurs buzzed.

At the end of the session, Stella walked to the train station to travel to Bonn. Justine caught up to her, out of breath and red-faced.

'There's something I need to say.'

A clutch at Stella's heart. Her new position to be revoked? Limited? Sharing with Michael might be the miserable price she would have to pay; that would be the way that sweet, considerate Justine would try to keep everyone happy.

Justine flinched. 'I was far too quick to switch Deputy-Editors. I made a mistake and I'm sorry.'

'Sorry'…a lovely word; Stella needed it. Typically gracious of Justine.

'Thank you. I was distracted earlier in the week, but a tough situation is now behind me. I'm sorry that I let you down.'

Justine hugged her with a long, warm, pulling-close embrace. 'So glad.'

Stella could feel Justine's heart pumping. 'You Canadians are great huggers.'

'We are.'

Her dear friend was back. 'You even sign your emails with "hugs".'

Justine clasped tighter. 'We don't hug unless we mean it, and we do it tightly, with conviction. Hugs are for real.'

For half a minute they walked silently over scorched leaves, then Justine patted Stella's shoulder with the lightest touch.

'Is everything ok? You seemed unhappy a couple of days ago, even frantic.'

Uh-oh! Stay on guard. Stella concentrated on walking calmly, conscious of Justine's fingertips signalling who knew what. Justine must not be permitted to see the mess she'd fallen into. If she knew what disgraceful nonsense had been going on...

'Sure, everything's fine.'

They waited as two fast-turning cars spun grit across their sandalled feet, then crossed the Heussallee road and veered back to the shade. Justine turned sideways sharply, peering through the lenses of Stella's sunglasses.

'Sorry to press the issue, but you didn't seem like yourself.'

'Yep! All good. Some hard days. They're over.'

Who else had detected Stella's madness? If the Dean found out via Georgette that would be the end of her career, and if Peter found out...

Justine hugged Stella again. 'It's challenging to live out all the clashing parts of our lives: conference, work, families.'

Stella breathed out slowly, alert to the urgency of diverting Justine. Distract, distract with feminist stuff.

'I've asked Peter to manage at home for these few days, but

he still wants input from me, can't manage a single teenager who hides in his room—since when is that a problem?'

'No wonder women are tired.'

Stella felt slightly sick. Poor Peter, she had not meant to disparage him; it had slipped out. Patching up her relationship with Justine should not need little half-truths. This was not who she wanted to be. She felt wretched; she wanted to resume their close relationship, but Costa still got in the way.

They stepped down into the canary-yellow station and Justine took the stairs to the Bad Godesberg platform. Stella waved as she headed to the Bonn platform, labouring through the stifling air, pacing herself to Justine on the other side of the tracks. She had never exploited Peter before. She was being unfair, not herself. She reached the middle of the platform and found the last four or five metres of tepid air; chilled air had been extinguished. She waved farewell with relief to be away from her perceptive friend and checked the current temperature. 36° Celsius.

Costa! Right in front of her. He too was heading to Bonn, but he had not seen her. She edged away from him into the sweaty, noisy crowd, conscious of a pick-pocket warning on the wall and two teenagers laughing at it. A train approached the other platform. Costa pulled off his bag and pushed it between his legs, pressing his calves against the sides. His name tag dangled from a black plastic ring on the bag handle: 'Professor Giovanni Costa, Rheinhotel Dreesen'.

That hotel! Hitler's. Impossible, but inevitable. *Of course* that was where he would stay. It was not convenient to the conference centre, so he must have chosen it specifically, lured by its Nazi association.

The train slid into the station. Delegates pushed forward; the momentum of the surge rammed Stella into Costa's carriage. Irony noted, she sank into the apparent absence of moral choice; she was forced to travel with Costa. She sat down.

But...the Deputy-Editorship...she couldn't risk it. If she followed Costa again, she did not know what she would be likely to do or say. She stood, tried to push away from her seat, but a wall of passengers—insisted—commanded—decreed!—that she travel with Costa. She had no choice. It was a short journey; nothing could happen in mere minutes. She resumed her seat; she was no more than another traveller ignoring a dubious archaeologist.

The Deputy-Editorship! With three seconds to spare, she smashed out sideways through the crowd and clambered onto the next carriage, finding the last empty seat, striped with perspiration from someone's thighs.

EIGHTEEN

A T TEN TO two on a rainy autumn afternoon, the door to the *Fuhrersuite* burst open. The military figure of Adolf Hitler walked down the corridor, precisely in the middle, with knife-edged trouser creases, polished shoes, slicked hair. His left hand trembled before he hooked it over his belt buckle. A portly figure in a white coat accompanied him; Hildegard guessed it was his doctor. Two bodyguards marched with Hitler, including the rigid figure of the bodyguard Sergeant Rochus Misch, ever Hitler's protective shadow. The hotel corridor took on the air of a repetitive newsreel. Hildegard had seen it all before she and Kurt abandoned cinemas. They refused to pay for the privilege of watching propaganda.

Hitler beamed at Hildegard—she had seen that forced, sinister grin in newsreels. With his right hand, he reached into his pocket and tossed her a praline. With sharp reflexes she caught it without thinking. Eat a sweet from Hitler? She'd find a bin at the station.

When he reached the stairs, she pulled the housekeeper's cleaning box from under her hall chair, entered the alcove and waited by door 106. The manager appeared and unlocked the *Fuhrersuite*. As usual, there was the military arrangement of pens, pencils and ruler, parallel to the desk edge. Three bars of chocolate were stacked at right angles to the ruler. Boxes of papers were lined up next to the doors leading to the balconies. Beyond—the Rhine, the sky and the hills of the Siebengebirge merged in watery grey.

The manager shook his finger close to her nose. 'Do not dally.'

Hildegard closed the door, her heart beating so fast and loud that it seemed to thump through the walls and bang down the corridor, echoing 'traitor'. She pushed the cleaning box against the door and propped the mop under the handle, then commenced her hunt in Hitler's workroom, officially room 107. She shoved aside her crackling, starched apron and knelt beside three pine boxes of papers. Feverishly, she leafed through, seeing immediately that most papers were maps and marked clearly in black type: 'munitions factories, military bases, airfields, schools'. It seemed odd to list schools with the first two; perhaps they were holding depots.

Schools… Hildegard sat back on her heels, a clutch at her heart. Perhaps Tzipi and Daniel had been imprisoned in their own school when the mass deportations began, surrounded by familiar drawings, books and old desks which turned alien overnight from a single decree in faraway Berlin. Two young children. She could not grasp their world turning upside down, but this was not the time to be paralysed by the horror of the new world. She listened for sounds beyond the door—a creak, a distant voice, music.

She struggled to maintain order because when stored vertically, the varying paper sizes created a messy, uneven top to the boxes. She pressed the map creases in line with the right edge of the box and read on. 'Roads for heavy equipment. Emergency landing fields'… It was impossible to detect a logical arrangement. 'Sports fields with no perimeter trees', and Hitler's famous autobahns. Autobahns as landing fields…ominous long-range planning. Hildegard and Kurt had never travelled on an autobahn and could never imagine owning a car, despite the Nazi rhetoric of a car for the people.

She worked her way through the maps, clumsy fingers scrabbling at the thick, folded sheets. Each heading was either typed or hand-written in lead pencil. Some maps were new, while others disintegrated along the folds from over-use; they might have been survivors from the Great War. Two more on schools. Eleven rural sports fields. Still nothing on bridges. Still quiet in the corridor.

She moved from the workroom back to the bedroom, where more boxes where stacked to the side of the balcony doors. Movement outside caught her eye; two children in warm, brown overcoats and blue scarves leapt from rock to rock on the river edge, about the same ages as Daniel and Tzipi, maybe from the same school. Other children were tumbling on the shore as if the world had not gone mad.

The bedroom boxes contained maps of Polish landing fields and sports fields as far as Warsaw, with ink squiggles in the margins. Two more maps covered the Dutch border and included notations on heights above sea level. Factory plans and nothing else in the next box. No bridges. She could not afford much more time; *Frau* Wagner knew how long the work should take and would be suspicious if she were delayed. Nevertheless, she had gone too fast to read carefully for Anton's specific request.

She tucked loose wisps of red hair back into her maid's headband and listened. Soft voices strayed in from the corridor. She sprang from the boxes and grabbed a duster so roughly that the cleaning box upended, spilling cloths and soap onto the oriental rug. Her heart knocked as she gathered up the mess. Low voices lingered in the alcove. A voice soft, louder, then soft again. Now distant. Footsteps fainter outside.

She organised the cleaning box, crept to the door and held her breath. Silence in the alcove. She returned to the first box in the workroom, reading each title as thoroughly as panic permitted. With no alphabetical order, perhaps she had flipped over 'bridges'.

Creaking outside. She pushed the box against the wall and pulled back Hitler's bedsheets so that if anyone barged in the housework could be seen to have begun. She should have done this first. Focus! She put her ear to the door. A heartbeat on the other side? She checked her watch—almost ten minutes since the manager unlocked the *Fuhrersuite*. She tossed the top sheet into the corner of the bedroom, grateful for routine, no matter how repugnant. Anton's note had authority; there ought to be maps of bridges, but his error might let her off the hook...for today. What a perfect irony that she should be obscenely relieved to be bundling up Hitler's soiled sheets.

With the bed stripped, Hildegard riffled through the papers twice more. There were no maps of bridges; Anton had made a mistake. She slid the document boxes neatly by the doors to the balcony, side by side, as she had found them, and considered how she might alert Magdalena, who, this minute, would be once again frying river lamprey. Perhaps Hildegard was already in a chain of disaster, linking all the way to her and Kurt.

She unwrapped the parcel of fresh linen and made the Fuhrer's bed, smoothing and re-smoothing the coverlet, plumping the pillows. As she dusted the bed lamps, the door handle squeaked above the mop pole. Hildegard hurried to open the door. *Frau* Wagner, red in the face, half-fell from pushing on the handle.

'You barricaded the door?' The housekeeper snapped her hand in the direction of the mop.

Hildegard smelt bleach and rough soap in what could be a fatal moment. Wagner would holler for the guard...the pretence of a trial...a few hours until the guillotine. Grovel brazenly, that was the only way out. Wagner thrived on the squirming of others.

'An accident. I apologise—sincerely, *Frau* Wagner.'

The older woman and the younger regarded each other. Hildegard's heart beat out 'traitor, traitor, traitor'. Wagner must surely hear it. Hildegard lowered her eyes; Wagner loved lowered eyes. Hildegard dared not look up, but knew that a leer would slink across Wagner's vicious face. A small price to pay for saving her own life and returning to Kurt.

'Not finished yet? Are you sleeping in here?' *Frau* Wagner marched from the room.

She ran her index finger across the hall table, inspected it and disappeared. Hildegard closed the door and ran to the bathroom. She threw cold water on her face and held her breath as she flushed away moustache hair. She took the only unused hand towel and buried her face, gouging her eyes, before she tackled the confronting reality of the bath tub. She inspected soap scum, several rings indicating that there had been excessive bathing in the last twenty-four hours. Such a macabre joy to scrub scum after the map boxes. She had tried and failed. She could not invent maps. There was nothing on bridges, so she could go home, cook dinner with Kurt, return to the grace of ancient temples.

She worked efficiently, making up lost time, dusting and polishing chair arms, tables and lamps, and cleaning the glass balcony doors in the bedroom and adjacent workroom. She memorised the positions of the stationery and bars of chocolates, lifted them, buffed the table and laboured to reposition each item precisely as 'He' had left it. As she leaned to dust the bed's headboard, a hairclip fell, leaving her headband dangling. She knelt on the oriental rug and patted in a circle under the bed.

A box! Her stomach heaved. Sweat spotted under her hair. She glanced at the door and dragged out a brown cardboard box. Papers were tucked neatly, end to end, far more orderly than the papers in the other boxes, but so jammed that the box flaps could not fold. Returning to the door, she eased down the handle and surveyed the alcove from a crack, finding only the stern guard, and stillness in the corridor. The traitor had a few minutes. She forced the mop pole back under the handle and prayed Wagner was bullying someone else.

This box was half-full of stiff, grubby maps. Evidently, they had been handled many times. Sweat blurred the paper. Whose? In the hotel? In a battle? The maps contained information on rail lines and parachute factories, in hundreds of villages that she had never heard of, studded across the whole country and into Poland and the Soviet Union. At the end of this box were maps without titles. She pulled out yellowed papers from the middle and recognised immediately the familiar bridges of the Cologne-Bonn district, friends of many years that she had lingered on a thousand times. Friends that could now condemn her and Kurt. Bold, red pencil writing filled the margins.

❧

'It's always an issue of trust,' said Hildegard. 'What could I do with the maps?'

'Take them?' said Stella.

Online searches were so much easier. Voyeurism was now a casual way of life; Facebook snooping was done billions of times a day. But not by her, she'd given it up. Today she would have photographed the hotel maps with her phone, efficiently and furtively.

'Of course, but in a world devoid of trust, there are no pockets. A simple piece of cloth sewn to a garment, common throughout the world, was not permitted to a maid.'

Hildegard patted the two large pockets in her plaid dress. 'I always insist on pockets in my clothes ever since those agonising days, but there were no pockets in my black maid's dress or in my frilly apron. Stolen items could not be hidden easily.'

'There was a type of surveillance through clothing?'

'This was not peculiar to the Nazis. Your own democracy, Stella, would have done it once upon a time, but it posed me a frightening dilemma. I had not thought of the problem of removing the maps. I could not put them into the cleaning box because I needed to return it. Any quick manoeuvre below stairs would be spotted by that eagle-eyed housekeeper.'

Stella touched her own pockets. She was naïve. Of course, pockets could have a political dimension. Hildegard had survived, second by second, in hell.

'I had a waistband,' said Hildegard. 'I listened at the door, then pushed the maps far down the front of my dress and tied the strings of my apron as tight as I could bear so that the maps would not slip. Breathing was painful, like panting. The maps stayed in place, but I did not know how I could extract them for Anton, or where or even when I would see him. That problem would have to wait. I felt light-headed and so afraid that I felt nauseous.'

Hildegard smelt the dictator—sweat, sugar and chocolate—in the bundled, soiled sheets that she hugged to her body, securing the maps. She delivered the linen to the laundry, crossed her arms over her diaphragm and collected her personal basket of clothes. In the maids' room, she pretended to examine her freckles in the small wall mirror, enduring the whispering of the last two kitchen maids as they ran their eyes over her—they'd never been friendly. When they slammed the door, she tugged off her uniform and pulled on street clothes. She tucked the maps into her underwear and clasped her umbrella and father's old satchel across her waist.

The thick paper snapped and crunched at every move, but she forced herself to walk normally—focused, brisk, the model employee—but not in a hurry. She grinned in a rictus at Fritz, breathing the aroma of his secret honey glaze; he cocked his head and scowled. She waved flirtatiously as she skirted around soldiers in the strip of garden along the driveway. A couple made lunging, groping gestures.

When she reached Bad Godesberg station, she looked for

the man with the slouchy, brown hat and blond hair. Maids and labourers climbed onto the train, but Anton was not among them. She was the last to board, looking back along the platform, maps digging into her stomach. When she sat down, she thought the crunch would be heard all the way to the Reich Chancellery in Berlin. Hildegard surveyed her fellow passengers; some dozed, some read, others seemed to dream, but probably observed her. And reported to whom?

A young mother quietened a newborn and a toddler, their yelling the only sound beyond the chug of wheels. Hildegard sat upright and as still as she could. Two soldiers lounged against the doors; she smelt beer and cigarette smoke. Minutes passed. Eyes everywhere. The few kilometres from Bad Godesberg to Bonn stretched like rubber, out and out, to infinity. Trees, houses, military vehicles flashed by. She twisted to see a group of about twenty people guarded by three soldiers. One of the soldiers bashed a child in the head with his rifle butt. No one on the train seemed to notice. The bald man next to her had also been looking out of the window; now he hummed as he turned to the sports pages of his newspaper. Perhaps he did not dare to show revulsion. She didn't. The announcement of a new law forbidding emigration of Jews had been announced. People wearing yellow stars were trapped.

The train squealed into Bonn. Hildegard forced herself to step slowly. She moved warily through the exit underpass, lingering to give Anton an opportunity—please find me, Anton—stopping to fumble in the satchel as if there were something she had forgotten. Her back ran with sweat; her ears jangled. Travellers bumped past, their eyes fixed ahead. A smartly dressed couple elbowed her aside; the lucky woman wore sheer stockings. Lucky—or a moral price exacted? They both turned back—to spy? I have nothing; I'm a lowly maid, smiling inanely, returning home after cleaning up *his* muck.

She gave Anton two more minutes. She checked all the faces

and all the heads, but saw no familiar brown cap. She trudged back the way she had come, all the way back to the platform. It was filling up as passengers waited for the next train to Cologne. She strode up and down, clamping the scratched and worn satchel to her chest, but still no Anton. She had no plan beyond meeting him, no plan if he did not come, no future beyond this moment. She had to force a future as she left the station and trod warily through the slippery cobbled streets of Bonn, keeping close to stone walls, not calling attention to herself as the stiff, folded paper rasped and pinched at every step, echoing in the narrow lanes and far, far beyond. She was a foreigner creeping through a city that was no longer hers.

Horror! Not again. Marta and Eva giggled near a cobbler's workshop.

Ice crazing in Hildegard's veins.

'Hey!'

Tinkling, splintering ice and a steel trap.

'Yes, you, Hildegard Weber.'

Eva and Marta darted across the road in front of a car; the horn sounded, but they didn't care. They pounced, pinioning Hildegard in front of her own bakery, Eva terrifyingly resplendent in the heavy, full, blue skirt and white blouse of the Band of German Maidens, the girl's group of Hitler Youth. A mother with three school-aged children frowned as Eva and Marta blocked the entry. Others looked away; no help came from anywhere.

'Not in such a hurry tonight?' hissed Eva.

'Tired from work.'

The crackle of maps overlaid the clutch of Hildegard's heart. She resorted to the secretive, Archaic mode—'nothing odd here, you've seen this smile hundreds of times'—a slash of parted lips that she had inflicted on herself for sulky Fritz.

Let the slash be enough. Eva had always been pushy, prying into other lives. Gossip and her endless, probing questions had seemed part of their friendship, but now the spite of that gossip was evident. Hildegard had not participated eagerly in nasty conversations, but that did not make her innocent. Eva rapped her umbrella on Hildegard's arms then slid it beneath Hildegard's own umbrella, levering painfully upwards.

'That's not correct deportment. Arms folded over your chest. What're you hiding?'

Hildegard shook off Eva, but it was too late; her umbrella was slipping and ugly deportment had let her down.

'Nothing. I'm a bit cold.'

Eva loomed over her in the heavy, marching shoes of the Band of German Maidens.

'You're hiding the book!'

Eva's blonde plaits were more perfect than ever. Thick and shining like metal, they marched twice across her skull, forming a helmet. Hildegard had never thought of meaning in Eva's hair, but now the plaits were menacing, hard and bright, conforming to Nazi ideals.

Eva's hands dived towards Hildegard's jacket buttons. Hildegard bent her chest over the falling umbrella and maps, slightly hunching herself. The tiniest incorrect detail...a flicker of eyes in the wrong direction...this was how it was going to end, like this, right here, with a senseless dispute over a library book.

'I haven't got the book, but I'll return it tomorrow. Sorry about the delay, I've been busy with my new job.'

The smile for Fritz had not been wasted; it had given her practice at performing in a hostile, ancient arena. Eva might be a young student, but in the street she seemed to command imperial power. The exhaust from a passing black limousine made Hildegard cough and gave her the opportunity to duck away, but Eva did not give up.

'Not the book? Then what?'

All the certainties of Hildegard's life unwound in a street where men and women hurried past, where she had played as a ten-year-old, outside the beloved bakery where she had bought bread every second day for the past three years, in the once-comforting aroma of rye bread. The bricks in the bakery wall scratched the back of Hildegard's grey jacket; she could not move. Eva crept her fingers across Hildegard's stomach and dug under the satchel.

'You can share with me; we're old friends. Didn't I take you skiing? You'd never have gone without me. Where's your gratitude?'

Hildegard could no longer be certain of a friend, of any friend. She looked beyond Eva's metallic plaits to Marta's anxious face with its shocking red lips. Ah…so the threat was only Eva. Only one of them to deal with.

Marta smiled smugly. Or was it two, after all? They were always together, sniggering and whispering. Hildegard had felt excluded for a long time, but only now realised it.

'Let's meet here on Saturday.'

With her ancient arena smile forced into a toothy grin, Hildegard nudged Eva away and stood up straight.

'Today I'm tired from work, even too tired for cake.'

She opened the tinkling bakery door and gestured for them to enter. The aroma of rye bread mingled with the fragrance of vanilla sugar and billowed into the street. She would never eat rye bread again.

'Your important task is to choose the cakes. I'll pay for all of us with money from my new job. I have enough ration coupons too, no need to use yours. Friends share! See you at three o'clock.'

Eva slapped her hands on her hips, on her blue German Maidens' skirt, her eyes straying to the bakery window with its trays of fresh Gugelhupf. Hildegard pretended to sniff the aroma. The offer of ration coupons should have been irresistible to greedy Eva.

'Yummy,' Hildegard squeaked as if the world were not collapsing.

She heard a gunshot volley; no shoppers halted. Eva

calculated and put one foot on the bakery's oak step. Marta, rattled and worried, met Hildegard's eyes. Apology? Warning? But Marta followed Eva inside. The bakery door closed with a chime. Hildegard forced her feet to slow through the meandering streets. In a lather of sweat, she tramped painfully as cold rain set in for the night.

Home, at last. She slammed shut the weathered front door. Ten minutes until Kurt arrived. She dragged the maps from under her dirndl; they seared like hot coals. She ran her eyes around the small room, hunting for the perfect spot. Too risky between books, especially as Kurt loved her study books, dreaming of romantic travel to Italy and Greece after the war. Anywhere in the kitchen was crazy; Kurt was perpetually ravenous. The chest of drawers?

Three minutes till Kurt arrived.

Oma's vase on the mantle shelf! She grabbed the scene of shepherds with a flock of goats in front of an alpine lake. Rolling the maps into tight cylinders, she wriggled them into the deep, green, porcelain base with its lake reflecting the gold rays of a tranquil sunset.

'Petrifying,' breathed Stella. 'What if *Frau* Wagner had jumped on you a few minutes earlier?'

Hildegard covered her mouth, smudging lolly-pink lipstick.

'I would have been caught. I needed a word beyond "petrifying". Does any language have a word for a body that wails silently for days? My poor heart was young, of course, but it was jumping. I could say over-pumped. "Petrifying" is too weak; there are sensations beyond language.'

Stella wiped hot, damp hands on her skirt. Faint stains bloomed on the silk, but she didn't care. Almost seventy-five years later, she felt emotionally sapped hearing of Hildegard's ordeal, even with the chamber maid alive and well beside her in a majestic sunset.

'The body can be horribly alone when language runs out,' said Stella. 'It's almost impossible to make sense of some life experiences without words.'

There were no adequate words for how she felt with her hotel discovery. Of course, Costa had to be in the Rheinhotel Dreesen. She now had more information than she wanted, or wanted to risk knowing. The knowledge had seeped into her on the station platform before she could mentally grasp it, nudging the weakest, thinnest part of what felt like a protective membrane, deep in her being. Of course Costa knew it was Hitler's hotel. The hotel was nowhere near the conference centre, but he luxuriated in history porn, gorging on depravity and death in the depressing, dark heritage of thana-tourism. He would run his hands along the same balustrading as Hitler, melding their DNA.

Stella clenched her fists; Costa was *not* her problem. It was bliss to be back in her own skin, in a beautiful park, sitting beside Hildegard. A small flock of blackbirds glided overhead, cruising on the warm air. The mighty river swept before them; a lone yacht drifted in the current, the same Rhine that flowed past the Rheinhotel Dreesen in 1941.

In the last of the blazing sunset, the humid hotel garden secreted the sluggish fragrance of jasmine and the stench of over-watering, steaming mulch and rot. Stella waved to the Italian students as she skirted around tables and tea lights.

'Hey, Stella! Join us,' called Leo.

He looked like a young man from a Caravaggio painting, with his ivory-pale face, dark curls and a fleeting, poetic hint of imminent tragedy.

'Too tired, but thanks. I hope to see you all soon.'

Sobered by Hildegard's story, Stella returned to her room. Leo's face was arresting, but she needed to be alone. She took a cold shower and, in her mind, pictured each of Caravaggio's haunting youths; she had seen one tonight in the garden. A trick of the light or a sign of her tiredness? Despite Kurt's blond hair, maybe she was unconsciously thinking of him in that tragic, heroic, vulnerable way. On her laptop, she sleepily added a final comment to a student's thesis draft and browsed work and personal emails.

Peter had written. 'Davey is still acting strangely, cagey and taciturn, stays in his room. Last night he insisted on eating dinner at his desk with the bedroom door closed and said that he wouldn't go to school for the rest of the week. Please contact him. Pete.'

She grabbed her phone and speed-dialled, but he did not answer. She left a voice message.

'Darling, hi! Hoping to catch up and hear your voice. I am sorry to have missed you. Um…I hope that school and sports are all good. I will see you very soon. Um…um…*Auf Wiedersehen!*'

David was another moody teen, but not a haunted Caravaggio youth. She loved him with her whole being, but she was too tired for more than a short email. 'Hi, Darling, too busy to contact you as often as I should. Thinking of you, see you soon, lots of love, Mum.'

She would be home soon; Peter would have to cope.

NINETEEN

'F**UCK YOU!**' COSTA spat towards the transparent security barrier.

Stella stared at his moustache as in a single, smooth movement he hoisted his bag off the X-ray scanner, spun and bellowed a greeting to a colleague. What an idiot she was to have dallied. Danger, danger. Get out!

How had this situation arisen? Ten minutes ago, she was Stella, the scholar, watching herons and egrets wade side by side in a Ramsar Wetland,.an idyllic scene of ecological balance. Ideas raced into her mind for another paper. She jotted down headings and noted three references for her doctoral students.

Five minutes ago, the chair apologised for further disruption to the agenda as the Japanese bid for World Heritage status for sites of the Meiji Industrial Revolution was challenged by the Korean protest. Hashima Island was one of the sites.

Three minutes ago, delegates commenced morning tea in the foyer. Stella tuned into conversation fragments. Her sympathy expanded; there had been decades of Korean pleading with a deaf and callous world. Brave little Min, hour after sweltering hour, protesting the perversion of history and heritage.

Two minutes ago, Stella walked to the security exit,

determined to flee historical friction and become a carefree tourist at Beethoven's House, but Costa slouched through the light that bounced off the paving, a corpulent silhouette against the dazzling July glare. They faced opposite directions in parallel security queues for ingress and egress, but he did not see her; in a conservative, grey dress, she blended in. Stella allowed several people to pass as she slowed, watching. For once, he did not look dishevelled, although his face shone with perspiration and his hair was oily. He had skipped the entire first session of the day, but no doubt expected the balcony seat to be his. It's all yours, buster, of no interest to me.

He looked away, oblivious of her presence. She could gawk in safety—a residue of the fascination that she had resolutely abandoned—and then walk away. His lewd gesture on the station platform still rankled. No, it infuriated. In front of everyone, he'd humiliated her. She had been furious when he had not recognised her at the water fountain but, with bitter hindsight, she should have counted her anonymity a blessing.

She stepped behind an Iranian group, peeping around colourful hijabs as Costa exchanged a grumpy greeting with the X-ray officer and tossed his bag onto the conveyor belt. It travelled towards her with the dog-eared tag facing out. Through the acrylic panel she could read the entire orange label, 'Roman-German Deluxe Historical Tours, Professor Giovanni Costa, Rheinhotel Dreesen', and its hurriedly scribbled pencil number '106', ringed roughly in red by a desk clerk.

Stella bent to read the label. 106! The *Fuhrersuite*…foul, but no accident. She gaped at the tag and then back up at Costa. Still, he had not seen her. He waited impatiently at the X-ray machine, his lips sharp and straight, eyes narrowed and mean. He scratched his inner thigh and shrugged as if to dismiss incompetent German security.

Stella let more people pass. Costa had crawled under her skin and lodged there, an itchy, festering lump of slime. Grudgingly, she admitted it. By now, she should be on the Heussallee road, heading lightheartedly to the station like a normal person. Her Costa obsession was like the apocryphal lump on the back of a foreigner in Bali. Spiders deposited their eggs under the skin of sleeping sunbathers; the eggs matured and hundreds of new-born spiders bit and crawled their way out of living, screaming, tourist flesh. That was her Costa.

He paced in front of the X-ray machine and yelled at the guard. Now he swaggered; now his bottom lip jutted out; now a hand was flung autocratically on his hip. He looked around quickly—no one behind, no one close in front, the X-ray officer preoccupied—he squinted close to the clear acrylic barrier.

'Fuck you, Dr Robinson.'

She staggered. He turned away, slapped a man on the back and guffawed. Departing delegates pushed impatiently past Stella. They must be laughing at her; some must have seen his obscene gesture at the station. He was always a step ahead with his pathetic, childish games. Creep, creep, creep! Not content to have demanded his preferred seat—she had never sat there again—he insisted she knew he was the boss—again and again and again. The water encounter—the fool dripping, his outraged disbelief. That was her big mistake. He would not tolerate or forget it. The bully was out to crush her, but she would be home soon. She picked up her bag and burst into the fiery glare.

Min looked flushed in a tight green jeogori jacket. Today she could not hide the physical challenge of wearing national dress in the heatwave, but she smiled and bowed as Stella ducked under the tent flap. The gentle Koreans could help Stella put Costa behind her. Historical justice was her real work. The world needed it. Min bowed as she introduced her to a friend.

'Ho-jin can tell you what he knows directly from Korean slave survivors.'

A middle-aged man gestured to a stool for Stella. He nestled his half-finished rice bowl in a cooking pot on the trestle and leaned forward, elbows on knees, his face solemn and fatigued.

'Imagine working nearly two hundred metres beneath the sea in horrible tunnels, chipping for coal, rocks falling on your head, beatings, hunger, death, no end in sight.'

'Horrendous,' whispered Stella.

'Crawling in half darkness, fighting claustrophobia every day.'

Ho-jin offered Stella a mug of water. 'And young women tricked into working in aviation construction in brutal conditions.'

Stella sipped the tepid water. The world seemed to judder as she tried to listen to Ho-jin among the cooking odours, car exhaust and Costa gnawing her brain.

Min joined Ho-jin, fanning herself so fast that leaflets stirred on the trestle.

'You're so hungry that you cannot sleep for the pain. You grow weaker and weaker. Suicide is your only escape.'

'You must continue to tell the world,' said Stella. Her editorial would help; that must be her priority.

Ho-jin nodded, his eyes soft and earnest. 'The world wants to forget our suffering, but we are a foundation stone of modern Japan. The Japanese want to cut us out of history.'

A spurt of rage burnt Stella's stomach; she was surprised and relieved to feel deep emotion for people other than Costa. 'But sites have histories across many periods, triumphant, traumatic, tragic…'

Ho-jin's voice rose angrily in the telling of a story too many times without people listening.

'The Japanese say, "stop the World Heritage listing at 1910, chop out the war years", a neat, surgical, lying way to remove history that is internationally embarrassing.'

Stella thought of the impossibility of cutting away your life history. It stuck like superglue. You carried it wherever you went;

she saw sympathy for herself reflected in Korean suffering. She carried her childhood ordeal to Bonn and seemingly everywhere; she never put it down. The national trauma could not be further from her own, but she had tapped into something universal with Min and Ho-jin. Her own frustration and loneliness receded.

Ho-jin watched her. 'Think of my poor father, ruined by Hashima Island. At the end of the war, he was overjoyed to go home to Seoul, but found that he could not live with his family. He was too afraid to have other people near him, afraid of the memories of beatings and claustrophobia. He moved into a single room with a huge window and, although he saw his family, he could not bear anyone to be close.'

Stella sucked in her breath. Fear so great that nobody could get close to you, fear that led to suicide, a ghost formed by history.

Ho-jin shuffled his stool closer, never lifting his eyes from hers. 'It's easier for the world to say, "Let's move on, put the past behind you," than to acknowledge our suffering. "That would challenge national identity, that's too hard," say the Japanese. But for we Koreans, wartime suffering is part of our identity. With a World Heritage listing, tourists would trample around Hashima Island, eat ice-cream, take group photographs and make stupid V signs. Instagram nonsense undermines our history.'

Ho-jin's eyes were teary as Stella thanked him and said goodbye. She wove from tree shade to tree shade on the walk to the station thinking of the despair of not having the hardest part of your life remembered, of people wanting to acknowledge only the transparent, uncomplicated bit.

🐦

Stella escaped the sizzling cobbles of Bonngasse, her face burnt and throbbing after the slog from the central station to the blissful cool of Beethoven's House. Her mind churned over the Koreans, room 106 and Costa's assault—brazenly in public, like 'the seat'.

His colossal scorn meant he was out to destroy her. 'Fuck you!' Hateful words that no one had ever said to her, not even an irate stranger over a parking dispute. She wanted the conference to be over, and to go home to Peter and David and dear Bertie, who loved everyone.

From the ticket booth of the ochre-coloured house museum, she could see a small garden courtyard centred on an ivy-covered plinth bearing the bust of Beethoven with his signature wild hair. Families queued for an opportunity to pose with the composer. She bought a ticket and climbed the stairs to the manuscript room, where faded sheet music filled glass cabinets. She touched the glass; she was mere millimetres from Beethoven's original notation, brilliance that inspired the world, the exhilarating best of the human spirit—but 106 intruded. What a lazy idiot Costa was; he didn't do his own travel booking but joined a pampered tour group. The conference would be a junket to Hitler's hotel. She imagined him calling room service for champagne and caviar and billing the Italian taxpayer. Pest!

Jostled and sweaty, Stella had no idea what she lined up for after the initial thrill of the manuscripts. Visitors thronged three deep around each cabinet in what had once been a tight domestic space. A young piano student called to her parents, 'This is the bit that I can play!' Far too loudly, an elderly couple hummed a melody from *Eroica*. A primary-school boy pretended to conduct an orchestra, waving his arms and striking a toddler, who yelled back. The room was too crowded for an encounter with Beethoven, but she wanted to be able to talk about the house with Fatima and Justine, to show that she had returned, heart and soul, to the inner sanctum.

And then there it was. *Moonlight Sonata*. Stella bent over the glass case which protected the brittle manuscript bearing the beloved 1801 piano music. Quick, slightly slanted bar lines segmented the staves, with quavers and crotchets reduced to hurried dots with tapered tails. Some pages were covered in lacy tracks, a light pressure of composition coming without effort, the romantic ideal of a glorious outpouring of spirit. She had listened to the sonata in countless sad and happy times, and here was its genesis.

A voice behind. 'What a lovely surprise to see you, my dear.'

Stella jumped. Takura? She was not sure in the conservation-darkness of the museum, but then she saw Hildegard, smiling in pink lipstick.

Hildegard circled a man's waist with her thin arm. 'Neo, I introduce Dr Robinson—Stella—my new friend and a visitor to my Bonn.'

Hildegard beamed. 'Neo is my son.'

Neo clasped Stella's hand. She hid her bewilderment at the family relationship between the small white German woman in her green summer dress with patch pockets, and the towering black African man in elegant dark trousers and a business shirt. In his fifties, perhaps. Stella knew a lot about Hildegard's life, but not all; she must have gone on living richly after the war, but her eyes revealed that today she had been weeping.

Eagerly, Hildegard took Stella's hand. 'Neo lives most of the time in Gaborone, but we are mother and son for many years.'

Stella tried to smooth her matted hair. 'You're a tourist today?'

Neo shook his head. 'I'm a classical pianist. When I visit my mother, I always come to this house; it's a touchstone for me.'

Hildegard guided Stella back to *Moonlight Sonata* and beckoned to Neo.

'A moment to share, dear ones.'

Stella let her new friend show her a treasure of Bonn—what an honour to be included with Neo. Costa's insults diminished; inspirational music trumped his bullying. The hand of Beethoven blazed across this paper more than two hundred years ago. The yellowed pages rested on tiny props, imminent with music, islands of calm amid the museum horde. This was where Stella belonged.

'Such intoxicating sound from these squiggles and dots!'

'But it's more,' said Hildegard. 'The sonata is part of the soul of Germany.'

'Even more, Mama,' said Neo. His elegant fingers hovered towards the sonata in a caress. 'Of the world!' His fingers dashed through an arpeggio. 'From the third movement.'

Stella blurted, 'You're from Africa'.

Bemused, Neo nodded. 'Yeah, Botswana.'

Stella flushed hotly. Neo and Hildegard had not realised that she had made a simple statement; she had not asked a question. Of course, an African could be a classical pianist. She knew that; she had not meant to suggest otherwise, how mortifying. And, of course, Gaborone was in Africa. She knew that it was in Botswana and even wanted to go on safari there one day, but they didn't know that. She looked red and sweaty, and now she appeared ignorant of geography, another patronising Westerner who knew nothing of Africa. She would rescue the situation, show them how much she knew and cared about the issues Neo must juggle.

'You don't worry about Western hegemony and an oppressive musical canon?'

'What a mouthful!' laughed Neo. 'No, I don't worry.' He shook a fist at the manuscript. 'What a lot of chaos wrought by a sheet of old paper!'

Hildegard covered her lower face, but Stella saw that she too laughed.

'We Batswana take what we want and leave the rest,' said Neo kindly. 'No one tells us what to do.'

Stella could not meet Neo's eyes. There was no way to make this right. She had performed like one of those Westerners who were anxious to protect non-Westerners from the West itself, as if non-Western identities lay eternally in colonial tatters. And the Koreans...they asked only that the world acknowledge their wartime history and anguish, asked day after day in the endless heatwave. She acted the fool; she knew it. The crush of the room, the shame of insulting Neo… She felt a wave of cold, then heat. She steadied herself on the edge of the cabinet.

'Shall we?' Hildegard pointed to the door.

Neo took her walking cane. She linked arms with him and Stella, and walked gracefully between them through the international tourists to the back of the museum and into the bare room where Beethoven was born. Stella prayed that the awkward moment had passed. She grabbed the frame of the low door, ducked and passed dizzily into the attic, with its scrubbed, wooden floor and small windows tucked under the narrow eaves, the shatteringly inauspicious birthplace of a genius.

Tourists dropped their voices. Stella hunched her shoulders, making herself small in the tight space. It was here that Beethoven first breathed, a little before Christmas in 1770, with ice clinging to the wavy, misting windowpanes and his parents still mourning the death of their first-born. The new infant, Ludwig, was born into grief. So many identities criss-crossed in the impoverished space and somehow found a home as each place and time and culture and person discovered Beethoven's music.

Tourists tried to separate themselves from others, each family group seeking to photograph itself in the lowly chamber as if it were occupied by a single family alone. Hot and cold waves accelerated across Stella's head and body. Her bottled water was finished and headache throbs converged behind her eyes.

Hildegard turned to Stella. Her eyes were penetrating and compassionate; how concerned she was to see her friend's distress. Horrified by the misunderstanding with Neo, Stella pulled out her camera to give herself something to do. Hildegard probably thought her a racist. To steady herself, Stella copied the tourists who crammed into the bare room trying to photograph the interior, but it was impossible. Everywhere—floor, window, wall, door—sunburnt, twenty-first-century tourists cooled themselves with museum brochures. The famous dark, furrowed brow and waves of romantic Beethoven hair flashed around the room as flapping pamphlets turned into fans.

Bonn was fixated on Beethoven, but the fate of Tzipi and Daniel was erased from daily memory. Stella panted in the claustrophobic birth chamber, sensing the children's tragedy slipping into the casual violence of present-day Costa. Her body tingled, fiery then icy. Costa…she itched to slap him hard. Leave a bruise on his cheek. And then what dreadful consequences? An assault charge? Sacked from the university? She had always been self-disciplined, denying herself, forcing herself to do what she did not want to do. She had missed out on the joy of impulse her whole life. Creativity emerged from impulse, and she'd killed it. She was at war with herself. Stella blinked; Neo and Hildegard swayed. The short space across the plank floor to mother and son expanded and contracted. She wiped her eyes and tried to focus. They watched her, muttering. Their eyes met and travelled back to her.

Voices sighed, hummed, murmured in the tiny birth space under the old eaves. A foul sibilance sprayed. Saliva from every language spat, stripping out oxygen, coating the room in a repulsive slick. The walls glistened in a foul coating of hissed worship. The stifling birthplace shrank, reeking with sweat, as the walls tilted. She could scarcely see the wooden floor around her own feet. Through her lens, she tried to line up the tiny window with the dark grey bust on the garden plinth, but the image blurred, the window frame in sharp focus, and the bust, no more than a blotch. Stella grabbed the frame and shut her eyes.

Hildegard grasped Stella's elbow and spoke muffled words. When Stella opened her eyes Neo had appeared on her other side; tentatively, he touched her shoulder. She babbled an excuse— 'hot, tired, conference'—and teetered downstairs, knocking into visitors, blundering from step to step. Staircase too narrow. Walls swinging. Manuscripts jumbling.

Hildegard called, 'Stel-lah! Stel-lah!'

But Stella did not look back from the door nor the scorching street beyond.

TWENTY

Next time Stella saw Hildegard, before she sat down, before either said '*Guten Tag*', admired romping dogs or commented on the appalling heatwave, she would say, 'I never meant to suggest, and would never suggest, and would never even think that Neo could not play the piano because he is African'.

Beethoven's House had not been a highlight of her Bonn visit. Every hopelessly maladroit encounter seemed mixed up with other excruciating, embarrassing moments. Stella thought of the possibility she was having a nervous breakdown as she travelled back to the conference centre to escape her shame in the city, ironically, the place she had gone to flee foul-mouthed Costa. She ricocheted up and down the train line: hotel, conference centre, city, running away each time. A bundle of scrunched, cancelled tickets bulged in the outer flap of her backpack. She would explain to Hildegard and beg her to apologise to Neo. He would be gracious. 'I understand…any friend of yours, dear Mother…' but he would be offended.

Stella splashed her face with cold water in the bathroom and then slowly climbed the stairs to the Observers' Gallery. The conference continued even on Saturday afternoon and people were slow to return from lunch. Some would not come back; for others, working lunches would stretch into pre-dinner drinks. By contrast, focused young doctoral students rushed into the auditorium. And there was Michael, looking daggers in an absurd Hawaiian shirt.

'Pleased with yourself?' he jeered. 'How dare you take my role on the Board!'

Stella strained to hear as a group of French climbed past. 'It's not what happened.'

Michael glowered, furious and implacable. 'Justine swings around, can't make up her mind.' He rammed his index finger too close to her eyes. 'You got to her!'

My crap quota is full! 'Justine thinks for herself.'

'Oh, really! You slink off sulking, I slave over a plan for the Board and then—'

'I didn't "slink off". I stood down.'

Instantly, she hated herself for lying. She tried to cover her shame by standing aside for a group of Americans. Their formal dark suits challenged Michael's splashy outfit.

'It was a sacking!' Michael's upper lip curled. 'How the narrative changes when it suits you.'

Caught out lying… she wished she'd said nothing. Menacingly, he stood two steps higher. Costa had weakened her for tense encounters. The conference was a bad dream; her career raced backwards. Michael stepped sideways, boxing her in on the stair rail. On his shirt, yellow hibiscus stamens were a phallic attack at her eye level.

'You feminists are all the same, plotting to undermine men.'

'For God's sake, it's not the 1980s!'

'The job's mine.'

'This isn't about gender politics. Where's your respect for Board members?'

Michael looked baffled by the word 'respect'. Observers brushed past as Stella gripped the rail with both hands and ran through a quick debate in her mind over whether she should enlighten him, but it was too hard; her head hurt. Michael's abrasive behaviour had lost him the job. She thought of the boundaries of her role; it was Justine who should tell him why he lost the position and she might choose not to.

Stella groped for a nimble exit. 'You're fantastic at writing grant applications; the Board needs you to do that.'

Disbelief, disappointment and finally, rage, flitted across Michael's face. 'Fuck you! I'm not a hack.'

'Fuck you!' Twice within a few hours. Stella sat in the nearly empty row at the back of the upper gallery watching tired, but dedicated observers straggle in. Silly, vengeful Michael and his preposterous shirt.

She checked the rows of blue seats; Costa was not in his special place. She perused the remainder of the day's programme. Two natural heritage sites were listed for debate. It would be an afternoon of scientific evidence on diminishing habitat and endangered species. She stifled a yawn; Michael had destroyed her focus. The other lone observer in the back row bent over a laptop. The buzz of a conversation drifted irritatingly from the corridor as the big screens lit up with depressing images of dead hatchlings in a clear-felled forest; hacked tree stumps and fires stretched behind.

Hours until sunset and sweltry in the airless hotel. A museum would be cool, but too demanding when she needed space and time to calm down. That left the river park. Hildegard would not be there; she was busy with Neo. A solitary afternoon nap in the deep shade…the plash of boats on the Rhine…the twinkle of light through chestnut and linden leaves…that was what she needed.

Stella plodded through the conference centre courtyard for the fourth time that day. Light attacked like razor blades, slicing into her head and shoulders. The South Korean protest spilt further than usual into the road but was hard to see with light blasting off glass walls and a mirage shimmering at the top of the driveway.

Min, in a fresh mint-green jeogori, called to Stella. 'Hello. Please sign our petition.'

Stella took one of Min's three clipboards and pens, and shaded the words on the glary paper as she read a summary of the plea to the World Heritage Committee. South Korea requested that the listing process of the Meiji Industrial Sites be stopped until the Japanese had agreed to include the history of forced labour in interpretation. Several other people also examined the wording while a stream of observers, sun hats and parasols clogged the road.

Min ran a finger over the petition. 'Ho-jin told you of suicide attempts, starvation, beatings. Why is this history not enough to stop the listing? Many slave survivors are still alive to tell us precisely what happened.'

Stella felt tears welling. Min endured the misery of slavery's legacy, but the World Heritage machine threatened to crush her work and unwittingly deliver thousands of tourists looking for fun and the souvenir shop, with no idea that they were in a slavery site on Hashima Island.

Min pointed at the poster of the old woman screaming at the sky. 'The survivors suffer from trauma. Respectfully, please study their faces.'

The face of the screaming woman dominated a poster, one of millions of unheard people burdened by the torture of memory. This was the extraordinary, emotional field Stella worked in, the intersection of politics and memory. She felt proud to be writing the editorial for the journal. Beyond student lectures, academic papers and ambitious career publications were real people howling to be included in history. Stella counted the pages of signatures collected by the Koreans.

'Well done, Min.'

Min brandished two clipboards. 'Sir!'

Costa again. The last person Stella wanted to see. He sauntered up the driveway, smoking a cigar and wearing his Positano beach outfit of Panama hat and dark glasses, minus young female flesh to fondle. Stella braced for sharing a clipboard, ready to thrust it at him and head for the station, but he didn't stop.

He didn't stop!

Min pleaded. 'Sir, please. Help us.'

Costa waved his hand in curt dismissal. He did not bother to look at Min, not even that basic courtesy. He brushed her off as if she were a mosquito.

'Sir!' A sob in Min's voice. 'Sir, please!'

Costa called back over his shoulder. 'Can't dally, got a date with Ludwig van Beethoven, most important man in town.'

Stella raised her hands, palm upwards. Beethoven? Absurd, infuriating. That's the reason for ignoring anguish?

She yelled after him, 'How dare you! A simple signature… that's all… The devil can cite heritage!'

Costa strolled into the mirage, skirting municipal workers who squirted purple herbicide into cracks by the road; the spray spilt onto the pavement in scalloped smudges.

'Outrageous!' Stella shouted to his back.

Without turning, he gave her the finger.

'Three seconds for a signature. You won't give even that!'

The clipboard dropped to her side. Min's pen rolled down the slope. Drifts of purple poison speckled the length of the entrance road.

Delegates looked askance; she didn't care. Here was his clear moral failing in public. Disgusting. Despicable. The Korean protest was the central event of the Bonn meeting, a protest against an historical injustice so grave that it had disrupted the conference agenda for days, but Costa and his cigar waltzed past. Everyone talked about it; everyone decent supported the Koreans. But oh no, it was nothing to him and his egotistical life.

Something precious snapped. A cracking, a gash in her body. Maddened energy.

She screeched into the mirage. 'Jerk!'

His smoke hung in the air; she exhaled hard to rid her lungs of it, but coughed, great hacking explosions that tore at her chest. Grey-blue, acrid drifts curled around protest signs. He'd tried to rip-off her seat; he'd pawed her breasts, invaded her lungs. Looted her very air! If he had no empathy for Korean war history, then there was nothing worthwhile in the barbarian.

'People don't listen, they don't care,' wailed Min. 'Even though they are at the World Heritage Committee Meeting. They are paid lots of money to think about historical justice, but they drink champagne. If these people, of all people, will not listen to our suffering, who will?'

Min went back into the tent and sat with her head in her hands. Stella stood back as Ho-jin spoke softly.

'Her father's health was destroyed on Hashima Island. She's lived in the shadow of the island all her life. Her father had cruel scars on his back and arms.'

Ho-jin edged Stella away from Min. 'As a young child, Min could not bear the scars; she ran away from her father at the beach, calling him "monster". She heard him weep in his sleep. She would yell at him to stop, night after night. She lives with the guilt of making her father even sadder.'

Stella knew too well that childhood memories could poison a life.

'She wears a jeogori and chima,' said Ho-jin, 'even though it is dangerously hot. For her, this protest is directly for her father. She honours him by being here and wearing these clothes that highlight that this is personal and national suffering.'

Min huddled on a stool, her face hidden in a voluminous blue chima. She did not look up when Stella patted her shoulder and signed the petition. Stella squatted in front of Min.

'That man was dreadful. I'll come back. I'll get my colleagues to sign your petition. The most important thing at the World Heritage meeting is *here*.'

Stella raced after Costa, bursting through the mirage as the ripping in her body accelerated. She'd changed, slashed by rage. She did not know what she was going to do or say, but she had to act. A moral duty. Demanded of her. She would not endanger her Deputy-Editorship or repeat her stupidity. This issue with Costa had nothing to do with stalking, water, 'the seat' or tatty business cards.

Costa dawdled fifty metres ahead on Heussallee, meandering to the station from one patch of shade to another. Gardeners straggled back to let him pass. Stella closed in, running through poison, borne on a current of frenzy. Heat, toxins, beauty, killing, death, re-growth. An eddy dissipated a wisp. A fallen, dried leaf fell open like a dappled fan…and another and another as purple-speckled leaves wafted among walkers' legs. Costa sailed away among purple, cloudy puffs, never looking back.

He halted by a tree trunk and appeared to tap it with his cigar. Stella could not see what he was doing, but when he did it a second time, she noted the tree and inspected it when she drew level. At shoulder height, rolled cigar ash smeared the trunk, a silvery-grey mess across the dappled bark, ending with a deep scorch wound. This was the ugly way that he rid himself of ash.

A deeper rupture racked her body. She clasped her arms across her chest and slowed as she thought of the physical reality of looking him in the face. She had quailed before—the dreadful moment in the garden when he touched her breasts, his cool appraisal of her in the presentation room—but not this time. Madness coursed through her veins; she could withstand his evil. She would utter the truth: 'You're a bully, a vandal, a pervert…'

He'd hardly quake…she'd have to do better. Where could she speak to him? Under a tree while he was throwing around ash? He would flick it on her. On the train platform? He'd hail a colleague and vanish.

The hotel? Bull's eye! She'd trail him back to the Rheinhotel Dreesen, quietly and sneakily, let him get inside, and then hammer on door 106. She would have the upper hand and, while he was surprised, she would push into his ghastly room and let loose with the truth: 'You're vile, hateful, abhorrent'. It would be a miniscule, global rebalancing for victims—Koreans, foreign students, colonised peoples. Crucially, she would hint that she—and many, many, many others—knew about the persistent rumours of his sexual abuse of international women students. Police somewhere would listen. He would be stunned and humiliated and, at last, afraid of her. His fear would be her maximum revenge.

An intervention calling attention to a disastrous aspect of someone's life had grown in popularity as people shared responsibility for each other. Not to intervene was to turn away from human need. It was mid-afternoon, plenty of time. After, she would find Justine, work on the journal. A drink followed by dinner…she would have fulfilled her moral obligations and protected her career.

Her rage simmered, nicely under control now, giving composure for thinking. Stella let more conference people move in between herself and Costa. His swinging trousered leg arced out. More people passed, including a bored toddler in a stroller, his mouth ringed by melted chocolate. A mangled bar oozed through his chubby fingers. He daubed thick blobs of chocolate onto the stroller's safety bar and licked them off.

When she reached the station, she watched Costa wander to the Bonn platform. Wrong way! That was not in her plan. He should be returning to his hotel in Bad Godesberg. She had forgotten that he had said that he would go to Beethoven's House in central Bonn. She would never make a scene there. Fascinated by the messy child, and in an intoxicating chocolate miasma, Stella stood in a sliver of shade and considered her options.

Revenge was a dish best served cold, although it would need to remain theoretical as even tepid air had gone from the train platform. Stella pulled her sunhat low. Frosty revenge filled her with resolve and tranquillity. From the corner of her eye, she watched Costa on the opposite platform. Passengers edged away as cigar smoke shot from his nostrils. A young man pointed helplessly at a 'no smoking' sign. The Bonn train arrived and Costa departed. Shortly after, Stella removed her phone battery, helped the mother board with her stroller and chocolate-smeared child, and travelled in the opposite direction.

Stella forced herself to blend in with sweaty shoppers as she identified specialist merchants, and studied corners and ledges to locate security cameras. Six kilometres from Bonn, the red-brick outdoor mall in the centre of Bad Godesberg had everything she needed. A tree obscured most of the front door of her first destination, a fashion boutique. The interior was small, dark, and cooled by a single oscillating fan that every few seconds ruffled a wad of red wrapping tissue.

The young sales assistant nodded an absent greeting and resumed tapping on her phone. Hiking outfits, swimsuits and sequined camisoles crammed the racks. Beneath the clothes, cheap, wedge-heeled sandals studded with rhinestones formed a colourful line from the door to the dark rear. Stella left on her sunglasses and hat as she riffled through hundreds of filmy, summer outfits. Too much stock; it clogged her brain. She glanced at the assistant, but she seemed indifferent to her customer.

A row of sundresses offered every type of print and pattern, plus backless, buttoned, tied and zipped. Stella held up a white, broderie anglaise shift; it was interesting enough not to call attention to itself, but simple enough to be unremarkable. The price was higher than she wanted to pay, but she had little time and much to do. It was out of character for her to choose white; it did not suit her freckled face. She remembered trying on a stark, white gown for her wedding and her immediate decision to opt for ivory. In white broderie anglaise she could be anyone, or no one, but not herself. She would morph into an avenger, glowing in white.

Stella carried the dress to the assistant. 'I can't keep up with the laundry. I'm headed for a cold shower and a change of clothes.'

The young woman folded the dress, one eye on her phone. 'Yeah…one of our best summers, but I'm stuck in here.'

'Hats?'

Without lifting her eyes, the assistant pointed to a stack by the window. A large navy-blue straw hat would cast a shadow on Stella's face; it balanced the white of the dress and made for a perfect, humdrum outfit. She counted out 78 euros in cash and requested a big bag. The assistant folded the dress into a large paper bag and rested the hat on top.

Beyond the mall, Stella looked for a way up the forested hillside that dominated the centre of town.

TWENTY-ONE

CHATTER IN THE mall faded as Stella headed across a short pedestrian bridge and onto a path that spiralled to the early thirteenth-century ruins of the castle keep of Godesberg. The fortified tower rose from the castle ruins atop the hill and could be seen for kilometres in every direction, its flag hanging slack and damp from the battlements. Stella breathed out long and steady, grateful to be alone in the dank shade of heavy trees. She took off her sunglasses and hat, letting the breeze dry the perspiration coating her hair. Close trees and overgrown understory thrived in the soil mix of lava and ash. Every shade of green wound around the exceptionally steep hill, an eroded volcanic plug or lava neck. Stella grasped the curled-up edge of her paper bag and climbed, looking left and right for an in-road from the main path to the forest that clung to the sides.

Blackbirds whirled high in the updraft, barely visible ahead through the canopy. They were symbols of many attributes, positive and negative, friend and foe, but today she could not help but think of them as bad omens, potent signals of death. One bird flew higher with a simple flap of wings. The others wheeled to follow, soon mere specks in the sultry sky. She was too emotional, reading signs that were not there. They were mere birds in an updraft, the only sensible, cool creatures on the Rhine.

The background buzz of town and vehicles dropped away; distant voices drifted through the whirr of insects in the moist, scented air. Stella put on her hat and sunglasses, but the glasses slid down the bridge of her nose. She blotted perspiration and waited. The trail obscured orientation, but the sharp, narrow lava neck afforded unfolding views of the river plain and the township leading to the Rhine. Stella checked behind and ahead; the path was empty. Her arm ached in its old, familiar way, a pain that had become strangely comforting. For the first time since Peter caused her crash into the antique mirror, her body felt like it belonged to her—albeit an avenging body.

She sipped water and breathed in and out slowly. One, two, three... A squirrel scampered around the corner, studied her flushed face and leapt up a tree. It was far too hot for most people to climb to the tower; she should be alone.

She turned a corner overhung with branches and nearly collided with two running women, their Lycra outfits dark with sweat. Stella made herself small on the side of the path, backing into blue-green hostas and waist-high ferns that clung to the precipitous trail. If she stepped off the track, she would need to cling to trees or else risk falling down the hill. The young women dashed past, black ponytails swinging from baseball caps and white sneakers flashing bright. In breathy bursts, they conversed in Spanish.

The track led to an open area around the Burgfriedhof Bad Godesberg cemetery, and the eight-hundred-year-old Chapel of St Michael carved out of an unexpected widening of the flank of the hill. It was a relief to be off the alarmingly steep sides of the lava neck. Stella soon found what she was looking for as the formal cemetery perimeter tapered off into wire fencing. She checked that she was alone and crashed through shoulder-high burgundy oleanders. Mercifully, she brushed no stinging nettles, but a cloud of mosquitoes rose in a resentful hum.

After five metres, the understory gave way to a clearing in front of the wire fence, an abandoned camp of a person without a home. Stella rubbed her arms, soothing the new stings that added to the dozen bites from the conference garden, as she took in cigarette butts, squashed fast-food boxes, rusty cans with jagged lids. A grey army blanket dissolved into the black soil next to the scattered remains of a fire…a sodden T-shirt…a plastic spoon…a mouldy quilt. Stella kicked charred chicken bones in the ash. Dismal but safe, no one had visited for months.

She was a new and whole person in an unfamiliar environment, complete and energised after decades of cringing. She hummed the opening of Beethoven's Fifth as quietly as her exuberance permitted while she changed into the broderie anglaise dress. Goodbye, timid Stella. Hello, moral warrior and actor on creative impulse.

She put on the navy hat and white dress, then folded her grey conference dress and original sunhat into the shop bag and tucked it deep inside a bush on the edge of the clearing. She examined the bush from several angles, but nothing was visible from the camp site or through the wire fence from the cemetery. Besides, cemetery visitors would be focused on graves, not her bag. Checklist: change of dress, change of hat, phone battery removed. No one could connect her to Bad Godesberg today.

Back in the mall, she found a convenience store and bought two metres of gold ribbon with wire stiffening along the edge that could be curled and moulded into a flamboyant bow around the most expensive Belgian chocolates that she could find, two kilos in a wooden box, topped with a royal-blue, quilted, velvet lid. At the checkout, she picked up a chocolate bar, but grimaced; her cash ran low. There was always an ATM, but not here; she'd get cash in Bonn station. As an afterthought, she dashed back into the store to find plastic catering gloves.

Next visit, a felicitously empty pharmacy. A middle-aged assistant focused on Stella as soon as the front door jingled.

He leaned close; she could see the beginning of his five o'clock shadow. She angled her hat low and spoke slowly in English.

'I need a syringe to measure medicine for my baby.'

The assistant looked baffled. 'A measuring device should have been provided with the medicine.'

The plan was not working. 'I don't have one. Not in my package.'

'It's customary, a worldwide standard of pharmaceutical delivery. What's the medicine?'

She was making mistakes. She should have had a brand name for her lie. Of course she made mistakes. She was new to this. This? What was 'this'?

'Something for croup.'

The assistant's puzzle deepened. 'But what is it? It would be best if I sold you the exact medicine and the proper device. It can be fatal if the dose is incorrect. Croup is serious in babies. You need a doctor.'

Danger. Out of her depth. 'I'll get the medicine from the hotel and bring it to you.'

The new self was hard to inhabit, so peculiar when she had yearned her whole life to act with brash poise. The man looked too closely at her. She saw every one of his fair, nearly invisible eyelashes. Her peripheral vision blurred.

He spoke carefully. 'Yes, bring the medicine here; that would be safest.'

An horrendous transaction. In the mall, fresh perspiration slicked around her neck and trickled down her back. Her new body no longer fitted easily, with skin too tight and eyes huge and watery with suppressed trepidation. A prying pharmacy assistant...she had not rehearsed the rest of the drama; she had nothing to offer him. The drama had not been written beyond 'my baby has croup'. Act one should have sufficed.

She found a different pharmacy chain, on the corner of the mall, out of eyeshot of the first, but in view of a surveillance camera. She scurried fifty metres in both directions, up and down the mall and huddled under the slit of shade in front of the southern shops. No choice. Not much time. She considered a new narrative and persona, pretending that she took recreational drugs and was undertaking her own needle-exchange programme, but for all she knew, German pharmacies had registers. She might need to produce identification. Why was an Australian scholar doing a needle swap in Germany? That'd be weird. The story was bound to get so complicated that it would escape any tale she could spin.

Already 75 minutes since she had left the conference station and 78 since Costa headed for Bonn. If he were lingering in town for dinner, then she had several hours, but if he were not… if he were simply visiting Beethoven's House, then he could be returning to Bad Godesberg any time. She thought fast, applied orange-red lipstick and fastened the moonstone drop earrings that she had carried all week in case she unexpectedly attended an evening event.

'I'm a visiting artist,' she told the next pharmacy assistant. 'I need syringes for an artwork about the debate over vaccines. It's a massive problem when people refuse vaccinations; they endanger us all. Polio, measles! God forbid they should roar back.'

Her breathing was shallow. Would he buy it?

'Your art sounds essential,' said the young man behind the counter. 'I hope that it changes the minds of those who don't support public-health initiatives.'

'Wow! That'd be artistic success.' She flinched at her squeaks.

The man's lab coat gaped, revealing the sports logo of FC Bayern Munchen. Red and blue, the same as the T-shirt that she had bought David. How had she missed David shooting up from small-medium to large? She had not heard back from him.

The young man picked up four bags of syringes. 'Enough?'

She had dwindling funds and no safe access to an ATM. 'One bag is enough, thank you.'

'Only one?' He put the syringes in a paper bag. 'I'm in my fifth year of medicine and have studied vaccine scepticism. It'll kill us all in the end unless we can turn it around.'

She smiled. 'Doing my best.'

'Good luck with your art. Where can I see it?'

He bought the story and then threatened to blow it up! She thought quickly. 'It's still in the early stages. I'll put up posters to announce the exhibition.'

Stella took the bag of syringes and marched to the door. She'd nearly made it, fingers on the handle, only three steps to the mall and safety among the shoppers, but the young man hurried out from behind the counter.

'*Fraulein*, let me give you four bags. My father owns this pharmacy. I'm sure that he'd want to support you. The business could be listed as an art patron. Ok?'

The script did not extend this far, not all the way to act five with a curtain, and thorny roses pelting the stage. She stood still, slowly turning the handle, while she dreamed up a reply.

'Generous, thank you.' Brava, Stella, keep it simple.

She slipped the extra bags of syringes in with the chocolates.

'What's your name?'

Stella's mouth dropped open. Sustained, impromptu lying was arduous. 'Roxanne's my working name.'

Back in the mall, Stella passed three packed cafés jangling with vying music. She contemplated pots of petunias outside a hardware store—red, white and blue—ready to transform outdoor spaces in the torrid summer. Inside, dust-coated shelves reached to the ceiling. A jumble of carpentry and gardening tools cluttered the narrow spaces, making room for boxes of summer fairy lights, barbecue starters and cooking utensils.

In a side aisle, Stella found a vast array of poison. Every animal seemed imperilled; the suffering of animals swept over her. She had never purchased poison for anything, not even for the most tenacious weeds, the sort with rhizomatic roots that were the curse of her lawn. This was not her, perusing dusty metal shelves for poison. She leaned against a shelf and closed her eyes. How did she come to be looking at poison in Germany? The caustic encounters of the week paraded before her. Costa, and now Hawaiian-shirted Michael, even Justine dumping her. Much easier to fight a mobster with a machine gun and a scar slashed from ear to ear, but a champagne-sipping, back-slapping archaeologist—now, that was tricky.

Revenge—how far? She did not kill unless it became necessary. Necessary... Here was a selection of possible deaths for purchase in the heart of the fashionable mall, within metres of people sipping complicated mixed drinks in a civilised tradition of music, laughter, conversation. Necessary because no one challenged evil at the heart of polite society. Or no one did effectively. Complaints about routine sex abuse were only now being investigated—'shocking, how could we not have known'— the victim humiliated by the judicial process—'I wish I'd said nothing'. Centuries of crime unexplored. Bullying was even lower on the list of crimes that roused society.

She had to act, but she didn't kill! That'd be insane. She studied the colourful boxes of poison with their silhouettes of aphids clinging innocently to rose buds, ants burrowing industriously under chic garden paving, and rats with long whiskers and impossibly long, stringy tails who simply lived rat lives and, for doing so, were judged offensive. What other choice did they have for living than as rats? Rows of boxes promised an easy life on the planet Earth for what would be the sole remaining species, *Homo Sapiens*.

She had survived the pharmacy near-death experience. She was getting better at this. There it was again. 'This.' This...this? What dread to imagine Justine, Peter and David having even an inkling of her crusade. It would kill her if they knew that she was shopping with evil intent. It would be impossible to explain. They'd not seen what she had seen, nor experienced days of bullying and verbal abuse. It was not the role of individuals to exact vengeance; that was the role of the state. But what if the state did not see the problem, blinded by the criminal's prestige? If the state failed, the huge problem persisted, a problem that harmed people: a man who injured people with impunity, year in and year out. Someone had to act.

On garden teak furniture, rows of plastic wine goblets and opened striped umbrellas promised summer fun, but she was not having any because of her project…'this'. This obligation! Her resolve crystallised into a diamond. Adamantine, brilliant, reflective. That's what 'this' was, an obligation. Talking to him would never work. A moral exit. Relief! She'd scare him, follow up with a Cleo Facebook message; that would be enough.

She hunted for rat poison, quickly discarding pellets. They were no good, too visible, although they did the job quickly, in a day or less. A colourless, odourless liquid was less merciful with several slow, agonising days of dying. 'Days' plural. Always, multiple days of dying for rats, but not for Costa. What gross suffering humans inflicted on unwanted creatures, but there would be plenty of time for a human to seek medical aid. No need to doubt hideous Professor Costa's ability to yell for help. Stella chose a small commercial bottle of diphacinone and its comparative promise—to the more charitable pellets—of an excruciatingly slow death, delightfully flavoured with the lure of peanut butter.

'Got a pest problem on holiday?' asked the elderly manager.

He rested his elbows on the counter, his body language announcing an ominous chat.

Too much lipstick? Earrings too come hither? 'Yeah, on our boat.'

She was not prepared for another interrogation.

'That's tough. Rats and even more, mice, are coming inside

207

to get out of this toasty week.' He greeted more shoppers by name and wiped dust from the poison box on his leather apron. 'Perhaps you need solid bait? The Greens are rumoured to be fighting this liquid any day. Inhumane, they say.'

'Then I'm just in time.'

'Not a Green?'

This was his idea of flirting? Poor sod, he was rusty. 'Not today.'

'You look the type.'

The rehearsed shopping story and her new identity slipped from her grasp, disappearing beneath the loneliness of a balding, hardware attendant. Where did the political discussion burst from during a simple transaction? The man would be bewildered if he knew that she had a Greens' membership card in her wallet, but he had not finished. He stepped his elbows closer.

'I'd like to help; where's your boat?'

'Thanks, but this'll fix it.' She had to escape before a *deus ex machina* blew up her plot.

'Would you like a bag?'

She smiled, shamefaced. 'Too green for a bag.'

Back in the forest camp, a squirrel's fluffy tail waved from a rusty can. Stella stood in the mess of the detritus of human life and its intersection with wild animals as serrated metal encircled a now-rigid squirrel. She held her breath. The tiny animal wriggled out backwards and dashed into the lush ferns and mosses. How could she be holding diphacinone in her hands while overwhelmed with compassion for squirrels and rats? A painful dilemma she could scarcely grasp.

Two hours and seven minutes since she left the station. She used her foot to sweep aside dried leaves and twigs, and then laid out the poison and bags of syringes, four hundred individual syringes. She worked loose the cellophane on one end of the box of chocolates. The box slid out easily while the wrapping maintained its rectangular shape, sitting transparently in the dirt, waving in a faint leaf stir. Like a chocolate box ghost. Another bad omen, perhaps.

The velvet lid she placed upside down on her new sunhat, away from the chicken bones. Her mouth watered at the sight of dozens of fine Belgian chocolates; the aroma of cocoa and sugar and fruity fondant drifted deliciously in the sultry afternoon. She bit off a chunk of her cheap chocolate bar and opened a bag of syringes, the first she had ever acquired. After turning away resolutely from recreational drugs as an undergraduate, here she was.

No time to waste. She pulled on the caterers' gloves, glad of the afterthought; in the humid day, it would have been impossible to avoid fingerprints on the glossy chocolates. Silver- and gold-foiled chocolates filled the centre of the box. Hard to re-wrap, she decided to leave those alone. She studied the chocolate guide on the inside of the lid as she took another bite of chocolate. Let's be logical. Top left, first choc, almond swirl. Second choc, strawberry praline.

She dipped a needle into the poison and gently pulled out the plunger. The liquid oozed into the barrel. So, this was the life of a junkie: an ashy, rubbish-strewn clearing and poetry in the viscous swirl of the nectar.

TWENTY-TWO

THE GREEN PORCELAIN vase with its tender pastoral scene mutated into a tyrant in the once-cosy living room; shepherds and kid goats bulged and shrank as the vase pulsed malignantly on the mantelpiece. Whenever Hildegard passed through the room, wherever she stood or sat, the vase and its traitorous cache of maps commanded her attention, compelling her to tear her eyes from books, dinner and even darling Kurt. On the first night that the vase hid the maps, Hildegard went to bed early rather than spend another moment in its presence.

Kurt appeared mystified. 'You're not well? I missed something?'

'A long day.'

He seemed to look through her and beyond. Hildegard feigned a yawn. The ideal had been no secrets in this marriage.

The next afternoon, at ten past two, the manager unlocked the *Fuhrersuite*. Beneath the bed, the hidden box held sway over the room; its palpable absence of bridge maps eclipsing the splash of the Rhine and the honoured presence of the mighty Fuhrer. Weak autumn light glimmered through the balcony doors as if yesterday the world had not stopped. The rumpled, just-abandoned bed awaited Hildegard, and the map boxes were lined up neatly near the glass doors, precisely as she had left them.

When there was silence in the outside alcove, Hildegard scrabbled under the bed, seized the box and leafed frantically through the maps. No markers had been inserted since yesterday. Their absence not detected or not marked? There was time to put them back. There was time!

She risked the threat of *Frau* Wagner bursting in, but she could not stop shuffling the thick folded papers, gaping at the places where the maps had been. New scarlet blotches fanned out from her wrist. The spots were not there yesterday—but they reflected in the mirror that morning while she brushed her teeth—disfiguring crimson spots, thickening in the webs between her fingers. She hid them from Kurt, clasping her hands behind his neck when she kissed him good-bye. God forbid a medical student should diagnose her state of mind.

Still no contact from Anton; there could have been an error with the Concerned German Citizens. Perhaps she mistook her task. Maybe she should have simply verified that the maps existed. No need to nick them. Tomorrow she could put them back, but tomorrow was hideously distant.

Two hours earlier, when she arrived for the afternoon shift, maids crowded the change room, whispering to each other after *Frau* Wagner departed. At the end of the room, Magdalena changed into her kitchen uniform with its heavy apron. Hildegard fastened her own flimsy white apron and tried to catch her eye, but Magdalena seemed fascinated by the green linoleum.

Hildegard scratched at the itch between her fingers. Perhaps Anton would knock on her front door, but what if Kurt answered? Then what? What would Anton say to Kurt? She tore at the skin with her nails until beads of blood broke through. What would Kurt say to Anton? What would Kurt say to her? What happened to complete honesty in their new marriage?

In the forest, Stella batted the belly of the mosquito swarm that had buzzed around her from the cemetery fence to the clearing. The afternoon heat spurred hordes of insects, so she took her grey dress from the paper bag and draped it over her shoulders. The evening before, Hildegard had told her about young, frightened Hildegard driven to live on the razor edge of morality and courage, neither moving forward nor back, stuck in escalating peril. She described the acute tension that invaded her body after the message from Magdalena and the strain that did not cease when she took the maps. It got worse, invading her whole body.

Stella tried to smooth out her own thick, strained muscles. She rubbed back and forth, gouging into her neck, but the growing ache commanded her entire being. So, this, now, here in the forest clearing was what it felt like to step out of your skin and wholly into another. But whose? Just when she thought that she had reclaimed her body… She chuckled as she thought of common adolescent growing pains arriving late in life, the skewed fit of young adult skin, settling awkwardly over worn-out, middle-aged flesh. Her laugh swelled into a full-body collapse. She put down the needle and roared up to the tree canopy, to a droning mosquito, to cemetery visitors on their hands and knees clearing pine needles off a grave. The belly laugh gave her a simultaneous sense of wholeness and a raw, unique, un-nameable sensation.

She re-positioned each chocolate in the velvet-lidded box, exactly where it had been, horizontal for Brazil nut oblongs, vertical for mint crisps, circles for strawberry pralines. She wiped tears of laughter and injected according to the symmetry of the box, working from top to bottom. Her new skin settled around her more satisfyingly with each bonbon.

She had almost enough ambrosia to inject the last five chocolates if she reduced the dose, but a cramp built at the base of her right thumb. She stretched her injecting hand, looking around the clearing, taking in a handful of discarded syringes and throw-away coffee cups caught in a blackberry thicket. She refilled the barrel of the syringe and started on the honey creams, the easiest to inject, with the unctuous filling easily absorbing rat poison. The first of the crème de menthes made a mess when, under pressure, the green liqueur squirted, spraying across a blueberry praline. Stella wiped off the droplets with the hem of her grey dress, consulted the guide, worked out the positions of all the liqueur chocolates and gave up on them. It would be ok. The foils and liqueurs were no more than a tenth of the box; he'd eat further than that. Costa didn't know self-discipline. He did what he wanted, when he wanted, where he wanted and to whom he wished.

She rested her hand. He might die. It was not in the plan, but he might. After all, he was much larger than a rat; the poison would disperse and dilute through millions more cells in a human. Maybe he would not wake up. A missed breakfast, his hotel door still closed mid-morning; no one would guess anything was amiss. He would be ill, but the plan was not to kill. The plan was to make him temporarily ill—a tad—reveal her anonymous, secret power, and threaten more attacks if he did not change.

But if he did die...she had already stepped over a line that she had never imagined facing. Murder was not a crime that a person like her would commit, but Costa got away with anything. No one stopped him; he was a criminal at large in the international community. She thought of the silent Islamic women in the garden and the gouge in his head. Many people would owe her a debt, especially future students, but they would never know it. It had come down to her obligation.

She finished injecting when the dregs of the poison settled around a chocolate-covered Brazil nut and the symmetry of the re-filled box was faultless. She examined the chocolates, looking for signs of intrusion. A smear from the plastic gloves? Tacky residue from the crème de menthe? A whisper of a breeze ruffled ferns and cooled Stella's neck. She would never be able to tell anyone, not even Peter; she would need to be silent forever. The frightening life burden of carrying the memory of this day in Bad Godesberg bore down hard. It would never lighten. She would need to keep this a permanent, absolute secret.

She struggled to refit the cellophane on the chocolate box; it was slippery in the enervating humidity and the wooden box seemed to have swelled, and the mosquitoes made everything laborious. She would rehearse what to reveal to Peter. Check: the day was spent in Bonn, nowhere else. Check: she had not sat in the auditorium with any Board members. She would close up any gaps, disingenuously offer unrequested information, quirky, invented details—a cone of lemon and coconut ice-cream, twice! —all the while looking steadily into his eyes. She unrolled the expensive gold ribbon as she wrangled with a mixture of shame and moral resolve. It was obvious that her visit to Bad Godesberg was knowledge that Peter would not want, far better to protect him.

Finally, the stiff ribbon was tweaked to hold the cellophane in place, and the luxurious gold bow masked any oddities. Stella thought of abandoning all the new syringes in the clearing, but she hated to contribute to addiction and chaotic lives especially when she felt more tranquil than she had in weeks. This was the calmness of resolve: focus, commitment, control, no detail escaping. Even Justine had noticed the new, calm Stella. Corded neck muscles had subsided, the ache almost gone. Stella's body flowed languidly and gracefully, sinew to muscle. Brain, bone, muscle in harmony with heightened senses. Action at last, following days of Costa's aggression.

Despite rubbish and evidence of wrecked lives, there was great beauty in the high summer forest. Stella breathed in the dank, musty air and listened for walkers and cemetery visitors. Leaves quivered in a zephyr. A puff of ash in the fire ring lifted and settled. She put the syringes and empty poison bottle into the shopping bag and hid the bag behind the big tree with her grey dress. Two hours and forty-nine minutes since she left the station; two hours and fifty-two since he left. Brava, Stella.

She headed down the hill, Hildegard on her mind. She too had faced a challenge and had been forced to step over a line that she had never imagined.

'I was boiling in terror,' Hildegard said, 'looking around with dread all the time. I felt as if I had a tight metal band around my head with my forehead bulging on the sharp edges.'

Stella shuffled closer to Hildegard on the shady park bench and offered her a paper cone of strawberries from the famous Bonn Market.

'Taking the maps didn't diminish the stress? Didn't you feel relief because you had done it?'

Hildegard chose two small strawberries and hulled them expertly.

'You never stop thinking and making the right decisions. Life rarely offers moments that finish in an instant. I had to think of my family, at so much risk! Always the thought of what could happen to Kurt and Mama and cousins.'

Hildegard nudged a tennis ball from under the river park bench and kicked it gently to an eager beagle pup.

'It's more than seventy years since these events… Life moments can take minutes and even days, although we might remember them years later as being like lightning. Their power stretches on into your life. I changed. My hands were wet for hours at a time, then suddenly dry. The red spots spread up my arms and within hours across my chest and neck.'

'That sounds like hives from stress. Kurt must have noticed.'

'How could he not! I bought calamine lotion for the scratching; I looked like a two-legged leopard.'

Stella up-ended the cone and shared the last of the strawberries. 'Did he ask?'

'I should have realised that his silence was eloquent, but I did not at the time.'

'Eloquent? That's peculiar.'

Stella's hands too were wet as she contemplated a life in close quarters to the dictator. How enigmatic and even dangerous Kurt sometimes seemed in Hildegard's memories, but his wife never criticised him; she remembered his words, and his seeing and not seeing, and wove them into her narrative.

Hildegard waited a long time to reply. 'Eloquent? It only seemed so, weeks after, when I had long, lonely winter nights to remember each minute of those horrifying days. At the time, my heart would race and then quieten; I remained constantly on edge. I learned years later that the body runs out of adrenaline; you think calmly when depleted, but soon, the body makes more, and the brief respite from terror is over.'

Frau Wagner tapped her foot. 'What a dreadful sight.'

The housekeeper waited by the door of the *Fuhrersuite*, hands on hips over her black twill dress. Hildegard stood by the map boxes. A boat puttered on the Rhine. A spear of light struck Hitler's bed.

She had not heard the approach of the thin, bony woman, not even the slight scritch of the twisting handle. Haltingly, Hildegard crossed the room, eyes lowered, shoulders drooping demurely. Surely, the map box had crawled from under the bed, glued itself to her maid's uniform and now stuck out of her back with giant black cards marking the empty spaces with white chalk and announcing: 'Stolen by the traitor, Hildegard Weber'. She smelt the chalk and sensed its squeaky itch through her uniform.

The housekeeper pulled Hildegard's hands from beneath the

maid's apron and turned them over in her own veiny hands. She rapped on the spots.

'As I was told! You're too delicate for honest German soap? You shy away from scrubbing the Fuhrer's bath?'

'No, *Frau* Wagner. I clean the Fuhrer's bath. My apologies for the state of my skin.'

'The spots are joining up, you ugly lobster. If the managers see these hands, they'll ask me to put you out of sight in the kitchen and we will not easily find a replacement this week. You must stay decent for our revered guest.

'Here!' The housekeeper tossed a pair of rough, white, cotton gloves. 'Do not discredit the Rheinhotel Dreesen with your moral and physical weakness. Germany needs only the strong. Remember the honour of working here.'

Hildegard put on the gloves and nodded. 'The honour.'

When *Frau* Wagner departed, Hildegard jammed the door with the mop handle and stripped the bed. She piled the sheets near the pine map boxes along the wall and dragged the cardboard box from under the bed. Maybe she had missed a sign that someone had been there after her. The yowling gaps in the box had been in the same room as Hitler for the entire night. Surely, the map absences yelled 'treason'. Things, spaces, absences, all could be articulate. But she found no sign.

She aligned the top folds of the maps and slid the box back under the bed. She could sneak back the maps she had taken tomorrow, in the same way she had smuggled them out. Or she could rush back this afternoon and return them today. Get access to 106 by saying she had dropped a hair clip. 'I would feel such remorse to have sullied the Fuhrer's room.' What a blessing it would be to be finished with the terrible task. Free to go back to Kurt with a full heart. And a secret.

Cold rain drizzled on the river; from inside the glass doors, she traced a finger down a long trickle. This was the view that the Fuhrer enjoyed from the comfort of his bed.

She did not want to have a secret from Kurt. She could put the maps back…but then Anton might come for them. She would have let everyone down. He had already risked his life in contacting her and it would be for nothing. She thought of boyish Anton with his stiff blond hair, the bounce of his gait as he hurried away. She thought of him, handcuffed, in the basement of the Bonn central police station, his screams banging off the walls. Of him abandoned to the Gestapo, tortured and imprisoned for something that had never happened. She thought of herself in prison. She thought of her family knowing nothing. Of Kurt. Waiting.

'But you couldn't turn back; you couldn't return the maps,' said Stella. 'You were on the Resistance path. You were committed.'

'Nothing was absolute until the maps were found to be missing,' said Hildegard.

Stella saw that she clung to the truth she had invented more than seventy years ago to survive the crawling wartime hours. No one knew that the maps were missing except her; Kurt was still safe.

'But someone might already have discovered the maps were gone,' said Stella. 'No one would have told the maid about the theft.'

'"Theft". That word terrified me. The hotel management emphasised honour and honesty. The Nazis might kill millions of people, but if the petty cash did not balance, there would be trouble.'

Hildegard peered across the Rhine as if someone waited for her, close by, but on the other side, out of reach, across the stretch of glassy water and bobbing seagulls. Stella sensed that Hildegard had looked across the river countless times since those excruciating days.

'Management was oh-so-flattered to have the Fuhrer choose

the little riverside hotel when he could have stayed much more conveniently in Bonn. The bosses would have called the police on even the longest-serving maid if something were missing.'

'Missing? But you'd stolen maps.'

Hildegard looked challengingly at Stella. 'Strictly true, but I did not see a thief in myself. I never stole, not even one of Hitler's famous sweets. If you take something for the Resistance, have you been a common thief? If you act for the common good when only you can act—is that a crime?'

'Yes, technically, but in good, helpful, moral ways.'

Hildegard rushed on. 'Some things look bad on the surface, even extremely bad, but they might save lives. We have obligations to act for others when no one else will or can.'

Stella thought about doing something bad that could be good, something even cowardly like threatening someone online, doing a wrong thing but for a good reason. The little beagle joined them in the shade, panting with her tongue stretching nearly to her jewelled collar. Hildegard reached out with gnarled, arthritic hands; the purple veins fanned from finger to wrist as she patted Stella's hand and the dog's head.

A wrong action could become right.

—

The climb up the Godesberg volcanic plug had been easier than scrambling down. Stella braced her knees and spat out a midge. Dust coated the leaves to shoulder height and rose around her feet, settling like a crusty, powdery skin on her sandals, feet and calves. She tramped down the perilous track, slithering on pebbles loosened by too many parched weeks, slipping in and out of thousands of tiny insects and high-pitched whirring. She prayed that the chocolates would not melt. Not long before they cooled off in hotel air-conditioning. She gripped her bag and curved her new hat closely around her face.

'Hello!'

Stella's heart skittered; David's football T-shirt with its red ring and blue and white diamonds materialised in the lush foliage. Why had David not replied after she wrote describing the conference? She had not written to him since, but she would tonight when her mind would be clear.

The voice was faintly familiar. 'Seeking artistic inspiration?'

She gaped at the Munich T-shirt. Peter had not written back either.

'You forget who I am? You don't recognise me without my lab coat. We met this afternoon in the pharmacy.'

It took all Stella's nerves not to thrust the bag of chocolates behind her back. 'My apologies.'

The young man who'd gifted her hundreds of syringes now trapped her on a path so narrow, and on a hill so steep, that to step off the path was to be certain of falling. She attempted to walk by, but he looked with such friendliness that she halted.

'We were not introduced. I'm Rudi.'

'Sabrina.'

'But you said Roxanne.'

That name! How preposterous it all was; her plot had unfurled with only slight hitches, and now she was slipping up at the eleventh hour. Criminals got caught over ludicrous details, like parking over the line of a parking stall, when the issue was the dead body in the boot.

'I use both. Different media. Roxanne for collage.'

She avoided blushing at the expansion of her lie, but he looked quizzical.

She grinned. 'It's all about segmentation and branding. Isn't it always these days!'

'We Germans like to stick to one identity.'

Stella did not want to talk about identity. She wanted to get down the hazardous hill, through the town and into Hitler and Costa's hotel, and then back to her own hotel and shed Roxanne,

Sabrina and Costa forever. She could fight the urge no longer; she slid the chocolates behind her back.

'Um…has work finished early, Rudi?'

'No such luck. Godesberg hill is super steep; it gives me a healthy break from work in the town. This or a cold beer!'

Now she had to chat about work-life balance! She fought back an expletive. The pharmacy assistant stepped closer, concentration on his earnest, sunburnt face.

'I told my father about your vaccination art project. He's seen some ghastly outbreaks of disease and is a great supporter of vaccination.'

'Vaccination. Hmm…extraordinarily important.'

'It's encouraging to see art and medical science together. My father wants to sponsor you and meet you. He said that if I saw you around town, I should invite you to dinner.'

You're joking! 'Very friendly…thank you. I'll bring some literature about the project to the pharmacy.'

'Your art is a step forward in solving this debate once and for all. You're doing something good for humankind.'

Rudi wanted a thesis on art and public health? No tutorials! She had to escape. 'Excuse me, I have lots to do. Enjoy your climb.'

She skidded on the steep descent and grabbed a branch. 'Something good for humankind.' Was her decision 'good'? Rudi's words highlighted the way she had talked herself into believing it. Costa wined, dined and raced around the world destroying young lives… and here she was. She ran her hand over the outline of the chocolate box and tapped on the velvet lid, soft and yielding through the dirty bag.

In the mall she walked slower and slower through the radiant heat of brick paving, envious of carefree people sipping cold drinks beneath striped umbrellas. Her moment of decision was not finished. She tried to hold on to her calm resolve, but it wavered before Rudi's words. She could still return to Justine for a long, intimate dinner. She could, but why?

She lumbered in the mire of a long moment in which she had a choice. Leave Costa alone; he was someone else's problem. A stellar career, that's what she wanted. Wasn't it? It seemed buried in the chaos of her time in Bonn. It was what she had worked towards for years and sacrificed so much for, especially time with Peter and David. She felt sad about missing David's sports fixtures, but the time was never right; there was always a committee meeting or a postgraduate in crisis. But chronic, everyday bullying and the years of Costa's abuse of students were somebody's problem. If not hers, whose?

At the end of the mall, two yellow charity collection boxes stood a few metres away from a large, general-purpose bin. She peered in, finding it pleasantly without odour; perhaps Germans perfumed their bins. It had recently been emptied; only one ice-cream wrapper leaked sugary white and pink across the base. If she dropped in the bag of chocolates, it might sit there for days with the poison and ridiculous quantity of syringes. She could toss the chocolates and take the next train back to Bonn, but no one else stopped Costa.

TWENTY-THREE

T WO POLICE CARS slowed on Rheinstrasse, cameras scanning the dignified nineteenth-century houses on the avenue leading to the Rheinhotel Dreesen. After the long walk from the mall, Stella's hand sweated on her shopping bag. She changed sides, tightening her grip with the arm that had not broken when Peter policed her luggage. In the overhang of trees at the sleepy intersection in front of the hotel, she wavered. The intense cobalt blue of the Rhine lay before her; behind, luxurious white and pink houses climbed high for the view. Three hours and thirty-seven minutes since she had seen Costa, who, if fate were on her side, lingered in a chilled Bonn café. She could not see anybody at the hotel so she stepped into the street, but the police cars turned past her and into the hotel driveway, past a romantic, curved tower.

No way! No. She stepped back again, further into the tree shade. It was inconceivable that anyone knew that she was coming; it was a surprise to her. Yet, here were the police. She ought to appear innocent, an historian visiting the famous Jugendstil hotel with its celebrity guest list...the Kaiser, Charlie Chaplin, Greta Garbo, Eisenhower, Gorbachev, Kissinger... Adolf Hitler.

Two police officers stood on the entrance steps talking to a hotel employee. UK Prime Minister Neville Chamberlain had climbed these same steps in 1938, greeted by Hitler smirking two steps higher, Chamberlain's cause lost before he departed London. Hildegard had climbed the same steps on a day that swastikas flew and choice was gone.

The avenger tied her hair into a ponytail and walked briskly down the driveway.

'Key 106, please.'

Stella's voice rang in the hotel foyer. She was perfecting the art of impromptu lying. How fortunate that the shop keepers had given her practice.

The receptionist beamed a smile fit for advertising. 'You're staying with us, Madam?'

'Yes, of course.'

Blonde hair wound into a tight bun, discreet pearl studs, tasteful eyeliner; the receptionist was new and trying hard. With a hunter's knife-sharp instinct, Stella had detected that the woman was on probation and eager to please. The woman could not know that Stella had targeted her, lingering at the rear of the entrance hall until the senior, middle-aged receptionist disappeared into an office.

Stella pretended to explore the old foyer with its metre-high brass candlesticks and the incongruity of a contemporary reception desk. And Beethoven yet again, this time on a brown marble plinth. She ambled over to examine the bust, her heart thundering, but her body poised, whole.

'In room 106?' confirmed the receptionist.

Feigning nonchalance, Stella took a photograph of the intense face of the great composer. Everyone claimed him, although he could not have stayed in a hotel constructed in 1893.

'Um...yes.'

She strolled back to the desk and gave her English a slight Italian inflection. 'I don't have a lot of time.'

The receptionist pouted and glanced behind to the manager's office. 'I need to check.'

'Surely, you recognise me by now.' Stella tapped her knuckles on the edge of the desk. Roman aristocrats would do that.

The receptionist ran an index finger down the computer screen. 'I have one person only in 106.'

'Ridiculous. I'm in 106 with my husband, Professor Giovanni Costa. You've seen us at breakfast.'

She leaned forward as intimately as possible in a large hat. 'He's the one who eats too much.'

Every lie needed a grain of truth. She was perfecting this... this obligation.

A wan smile from the receptionist. 'One person only in the computer records.'

'We're here for the World Heritage conference. Maybe there were too many of us checking in at the same time for hotel accuracy?'

The young woman bit her lip. She was cracking. Almost there. Stella shook her conference lanyard; with luck the receptionist would be too flustered to check it. This was the pointy bit of the venture, but she had the next story ready if needed. 'Oh, the name "Robinson"? Yes, not Italian, I was my husband's graduate student...'

Stella winked. 'Don't worry. A hotel error. I won't tell!'

The receptionist bit her lip. 'We take security and privacy seriously, our reputation—'

A man behind Stella cleared his throat and pushed his suitcase closer to the desk. The couple behind him, edged forward. The whole queue shuffled up. More semi-polite throat clearing. The universe was on Stella's side.

'I'm in a hurry, no need for an interrogation.'

'I should wait...' The woman looked around for the senior receptionist, scowled at the queue and handed over the key.

Stella tip-toed into an effluvium of blue cheese. A fast, shallow in-rush of breath. With the balcony doors closed and no air-conditioning, bacteria bloomed. Of course, the Costasuite-*Fuhrersuite* would be repugnant at a visceral, instinctual level, but it also pulsated with an aura, resonating through history, beyond the sensations of her own body, to another part of her being of deep, collective revulsion.

In this very room, Hitler had connived to humiliate Chamberlain and wreck the appeasement process, the last chance to avoid the abomination of World War II. He had lain in bed, luxuriating in his personal view of the Rhine and the Siebengebirge, intoxicated by the medieval epic, *The Song of the Nibelungs*, some of it set there on the other side of the river—a dragon, a knight called Siegfried, German greatness—munching sweets and scheming the incineration of cities, the obliteration of villages, murder on murder. Such a banal place—stinking of a stolen hunk of cheese—for the emanation of carnage, despair, ruin.

In and out quickly, that was Stella's plan; but Costa now blurred with Hitler and was curiously naked, in a place trite and terrifying, disgusting and fascinating. She held herself small and tight as she surveyed the comfortable two-room riverside suite, and was lured by the source of the salty-blue stench. On a side table sat five paper napkins, side by side, translucent with oil that fanned out to the scalloped edges, and bearing two over-ripe cheeses, Bavaria Blu and Edelpilz. Next to them, a generous handful of cashews spilt onto the table with six thin slices of rye bread, three quark balls smothered in cinnamon sugar and two raisin *schnecken*, the patisserie snails that she loved from her own hotel breakfast when she was able to evade Georgette, but now impossible to contemplate eating. On the floor was an open jar of sauerkraut emitting the odour of anise and dragging her back to the awkward Board dinner. No wonder the door sign said 'do not disturb'—half the buffet was here.

She covered her nose and put the lid on the sticky sauerkraut. Four hours and two minutes since she left the station. If Costa had planned a quick trip to Bonn, then he would have returned already but, obviously, he was dining out, freeloading off taxpayers. The time pressure lifted as she perused the minimalist elegance that undercut the bloody reality of Hitler and Costa...brown linen upholstery, a black and white abstract print. How should an interior designer have responded to the history of this place? It ought to be impossible to romanticise, with its gruesome history trumping its mesmerising view and nostalgic mythology. Perhaps minimalism had been used to drain history from the rooms, creating an empty stage.

The river slung back the late afternoon glare as it swept by the historic balconies. No one sailed, and no one walked on the shore. She looked, as if with Hitler's eyes, through the glass doors to the beloved Siebengebirge, soft, rounded, green hills, the inspiration for romantic art and music. She sensed the ruinous weight of a disastrous war, and the devil at the absolute centre of it.

She held her breath at a noise from the alcove. Soft footfalls and two murmuring voices, a young man and an older woman. Now they retreated. A third voice. Metal rattling. Another frightened chamber maid with a bucket and mop. A hotel resident opened his door and bellowed, 'Fritz!' She ought to leave, but the space was hypnotic.

No one moved beyond the window. The humid afternoon was soundless behind the glass. Hitler and Costa had looked out to the same timeless, glinting river. The weight of history pressed on the empty hills. This must be what Hildegard had meant by a place linking different eras. The extraordinary multiple Germanic pasts tumesced and clotted into a hideous festering of mythology, Costa and mass murder.

A blackbird landed on the promenade between the hotel and river, plucked a worm from the rocks beside the path and glanced around jerkily with yellow-rimmed eyes. The war and Hitler closed in. Eyes, eyes everywhere. Eyes in Hildegard's station tunnel. Hitler breathing on Stella's neck. Costa's hand on the glass balcony doors. Her fingers gliding along the window frame. Windows. Who sees through them? Who sees me? Alone. Here.

Five-year-old Stella watched the curtains balloon; two giant skirts strained from the rod.

No!

For the last half hour, the curtain had been still, not even a wobble. She knew because she watched. The only way to go to sleep was to be sure that there was nothing. Nothing in the garden. Nothing anywhere.

The curtain sighed and settled, brushing below the sill, where she kept plastic toy dog gifts from cereal boxes. Now she had eight dogs. Each fortnight when Mummy bought a new box, Stella washed off the wheat dust and rolled a new dog dry with a tissue. Tiny legs poked through wet, soggy clumps. She started to count the clean dogs, but something rustled. The curtain couldn't move all by itself. Mostly, it hung still and straight, like a sheet on a wall. Sheets and curtains should stay where you put them. Two dogs had fallen over, maybe the terrier and the golden retriever. Her little brother sometimes stole the dogs. He must have knocked them over when he sneaked in.

The curtain lifted and the tree branch filled the pane. During the day she liked to climb the tree; now it was the devil flashing at the glass.

Be still, devil.

Eucalyptus leaves were long and skinny like bookmarks; they flapped together, making a slithery, plastic sound.

Leaves, please don't move.

Twigs scraped along the glass and lifted off in a screech.

Be still.

Dark blobs bloated and withered on the ceiling.

Can't bear it.

Stella pulled the sheet up to her nose.

Don't!

A black plastic poodle toppled from the sill. It was blue when she shook it from the box. The curtain rushed back. The door banged shut.

On the promenade below, the blackbird flew off, the agonised worm thrashing in its beak. Stella turned away, resolved to fulfil her obligation to the young women. She could not afford to weaken at the moment of action because of the brutality inherent in a bird's meal. Young Hildegard had had nothing but a common mop to protect herself from *Frau* Wagner and Nazi tyranny.

Stella froze. Grotesque familiarity…a photograph frame on Costa's bedside table. Small, faux silver, embossed, exactly the same type of cheap frame that she travelled with—the family on Nanarup Beach, Peter with his arms around her and David. Costa had selected the *same* frame. It defied credulity that with a whole world of tacky choices, they would choose identically. But they had. Odious coincidence of taste! A shocking overlap. She shivered as she picked up the frame and ran her finger over the embossing that was an everyday part of her life. There was Costa with the First Communion girl that she had seen on Facebook, but his face seemed softer, lacking its usual sneer. Perhaps he had another life. She trembled as she thought of herself and Costa perusing a variety of frames, choosing the same and both tucking it into their luggage. In making the choice, they had looked through the same eyes, made the same commercial, aesthetic and emotional judgements.

She jumped, observing herself in a mirror across the *Fuhrersuite*. Confusion, alienation from herself, like concussion, but she rammed down self-doubt. She and Costa were polar opposites!

Another frame held a photo of an African family, perhaps cut from a charity newsletter. A skeletally thin mother avoided the camera lens, reticently lowering her eyes. Behind her stretched a lane that doubled as a communal drain. Squalor and deprivation sat side by side with Costa's abundant, filched breakfast. Stella smelt cinnamon underneath the blue cheese aroma and the persistent odour of anise, while in the slum, grey and white plastic bags, rusty corrugated iron sheets and poorly tethered, green tarpaulins framed human heads, leaving the stench to be imagined. The mother clutched two naked infants with bulging stomachs and huge eyes, a horrifying sight in the luxury of the room.

Stella checked the time. She ought to go, but a charity voucher book tempted her from the top of a pile of heritage brochures. Time was alarmingly short, Costa could be returning now, but she needed to understand this other side of him. She loathed her sneakiness, but flipped through the donation chits. He gave regularly, three hundred euros a month. The African woman was scarcely older than Costa's students. Could there be a decent side to the monster reflected in the mother's beautiful and sensitive face?

Pah! The donations would be a tax deduction, calculated shrewdly to the last eurocent. Even if he made a genuine gift, motivated by a desire to help, it was not enough, not nearly enough to expunge his crimes. No heart-tearing poverty would stop her. No last, urchin-eyed hurdles for her project. She'd come too far.

Her eyes drifted from the donation vouchers to the messy bed. Her hand hovered towards Costa's bottom sheet, but she dared not touch the turmoil, with its abandoned underwear and stains. The dregs of the man. He didn't care that he exposed himself to staff after he scoffed stolen food. He bragged to them about his goodness by leaving on view his charity vouchers. The measure of obscene power was not to need privacy.

She pulled the chocolate box from the plastic bag and fiddled with the extravagant gold bow, using the wire edge to stiffen and shape the ribbon. She had the gold-edged card ready and slipped it underneath the ribbon.

'RANEOC
Roman Archaeology Northern Europe Organising Committee
To our dear Prof. Giovanni Costa, with our greetings and admiration. It would be our honour to have you join us for cocktails on the last day of the World Heritage Committee Meeting. 6.00 PM, Room 2:13.
We remain sincerely yours, dear Sir,
RANEOC'

Stella cast about for a place to display the chocolate box, somewhere to catch his greedy eye the second he entered, but there was more to see. She gave herself one more minute.

Dim, cooler than the bedroom, the bathroom was comfortable and practical but a mess. Stella switched on the light over the mirror. Towels—none on the rails, but scrunched in the tub, and a tripping hazard on the floor—were tangled with hotel soap wrappers and leaking shampoo bottles. The toilet stank, stained and unflushed, and too horrible to contemplate. Blobs of soiled tissues had landed here and there, and nauseating moustache clippings speckled the floor and basin lip and clumped in the plug hole.

Foetid air. Blue cheese and hair, plumbing and raisin *schnecken*. A vortex dragged her into Hildegard's ordeal, her gorge rising. Got to leave. Staying too, too long. She splashed her face and threw herself into the brown armchair.

Air, she needed air, but if she opened the window, a security camera… She focused on the middle distance of the empty Rhine. Frenetic action was a distraction from retching. She ran her hands through her dirty hair and over the hollows of her temples. She cupped her knees, rubbing at residual dirt and forest soil. She slid her hands over the arm rests and down the fine linen to where the cushion met the side of the seat, back and forth, up and down, until her hand encountered something crinkly, wedged partly beneath the seat padding.

She pulled out a smeared and dog-eared A4 photograph, obviously from a home printer. A young Islamic woman walked in front of the Pantheon. Behind her, a cellist played in the great portico; to her side, a family of tourists strolled with ice-creams. In black felt pen, the woman's genitals and breasts were outlined. With a red pen, a gag had been drawn across her mouth; chains crossed her chest and wound around her neck.

Stella jumped up and hurled the seat cushion to the floor revealing a tattered sheaf of gruesome A4 photos of young women. She recognised one of them, a student from the hotel garden. The quiet and knowing one, the one who peered from the garden darkness. In red ink, the monster had spattered the student's clothes with blood. It was too horrible. Blindfolds, handcuffs, knives twisting in flesh. Stella leafed through the pile, each image more searing than the last. A scream funnelled up her throat, but she bit it back as methodical Stella commanded impulsive Stella, and she neatened the papers into a precise A4 pile and hid them under the cushion.

She propped the chocolate box behind the stolen breakfast and fled.

TWENTY-FOUR

No swastikas, no soldiers. The hotel foyer was almost empty. A middle-aged man appeared to catnap. A white rose bud had popped up in front of Beethoven. With her hat low, Stella slid the 106 key to the senior receptionist, blinking tears as she thought of the horror of the despoilation of the young women. She closed her eyes and forced herself to focus. Thirteen minutes since she crossed the hotel perimeter. Four hours and fifteen minutes since she left Bonn. Little nerve jabs raced up her neck and down her spine; she was jumpy, jittery, electrified by the confirmation of her dread in the hand-drawn gags and crude genitals.

The police car was still in the driveway; the driver and a young woman held hands through the open window. Stella strode by in the intense, late afternoon light. At the end of the short driveway…Costa! Red-faced, in a sweat-stained business shirt, lugging two magnums of champagne.

Stella clamped her hand over her mouth. He was nearly on her with his arrogance and criminality. Cigar smoke and sausage fumes announced his foul presence. The driveway was frighteningly narrow and she could not escape back to the foyer without him seeing her. If she ran to the Rhine side of the hotel, he'd spot her in an instant and accuse her of stalking.

She slipped sideways into the meagre garden at the street entrance, where her white dress was horribly bright among the foliage. Make herself small, small.

Costa shouted into his phone. 'Police involved? Fuck!'

She clasped the dress around unsteady legs and crouched among thin, vertical, poplar branches, awaiting his screech of discovery. The chocolates…the police will test them and they'll reveal…me.

Costa halted as Stella peered through the poplars. The coarse tooth of a leaf slashed her eye. She pressed on the eye socket while she ran through possible traps that she had inadvertently set for herself. DNA…on the chocolates? On the ribbon? If he spotted her, he'd know that something was awry. Why else would she hide? Be small, small.

He yelled, 'Moving antiquities? Not my instructions!'

She foresaw a shameful future of interrogation and humiliation. She tried to watch him, but with her watery eye, he blurred. She spread her grey backpack across her shoulders to hide some of the appalling whiteness of the stupid dress.

Costa stamped his foot. 'Fool! You'll give me a heart attack.'

Trapped like Hildegard. Costa was dangerously close. A right forearm clamped his magnums. He spat into the poplars; a gob landed on her instep. She dared not move.

He yelled, 'Supposed to be covert.'

He spat again. Struck her cheek. Skin. Rip it off. 'Marked for self-sacrifice.' That's what he said. This was it. Career, reputation, family. The end.

He clutched the bottles and hitched his trousers. 'Fuck off!'

Stella's heart churned in her chest, her head, her arms, her legs, everywhere. The crooks of her knees sloshed. Why had she lingered? At a snail's pace, Costa moved away. His saliva coursed down her cheek.

Stalking, impersonation, burglary, poisoning…prison. There would be no way she could talk herself free of the chocolates. He would grasp immediately and have proof that she had been in his room like a common criminal. There could be no other plausible reason why she would skulk in his hotel garden, six kilometres from the conference centre. Normal people didn't do such things.

Costa laboured up the steps and disappeared into the foyer. Stella tore off handfuls of poplar leaves, scraped her cheek and instep, and darted out of the driveway.

He is sliding his hand under the cushion.

In the Bad Godesberg mall, Stella purchased hand sanitiser from a small supermarket and scrubbed her face, neck and instep. It didn't matter if her skin burnt and shrivelled, strip by polluted strip. Her hands shook as adrenalin slopped around her body. Victory! Spectacular! A near-fatal squeak in the driveway but she'd done it. She was Queen Boudica defying the Romans. She was Marie Curie with two Nobel Prizes. She was Amy Johnson flying from England to Australia, the tropical northern coast in view at last. Nothing was impossible. Hallelujah!

Her skin still stung ten minutes later when she reached the forest clearing on the abrupt lava neck. Escape from Costa by the skin of her teeth, but a glorious victory. She could live with herself in the harming of this abhorrent man. She shook out her pony tail and doused water on her foot and face before changing back into her grey dress. She'd done it, come horrifically close to disaster and skated away. She rolled and scrunched the white dress into the crown of the new hat. No trace of her in the *Fuhrersuite*, not even a hair. Triumph was hers.

Returning to the mall charity bins, Stella held back the injecting needles, but stuffed in the dress and hat, jumping as the lid grated. She tasted metal. Victory and hyper-awareness created a toxic mash, gumming up her brain. She whooped at the sky. A near-collision with Costa, but the laurels were hers.

Sweat dripped, slippery against her zip as she marched back to the station, taking a long route via back streets. The criminals of 106 convulsed into brain fever. Hitler and his demonic barbarity. Costa swooping on the huge velvet box, ripping off the bow, his gluttonous awe on seeing rows and rows of chocolates, gulping them down, smiling at the smarmy RANEOC invitation, groping for his loathsome images. The sleepy summer mood of the mall bounced off her; she was jubilant, levitating, untouchable.

In the street leading to the station, she looked around for security cameras. None. The project was magnificent, but not finished until she escaped the sweltering town. And what did the evening hold for Costa? A handful of RANEOC chocolates followed by dinner in the hotel's famous dining room—'yes, yes… the SS table'—a fine wine, blood-dripping steak, massive, creamy dessert. More chocolates. The jolt of the pinch. The first vicious cramp would startle him awake with a slicing and tightening of his stomach as he haemorrhaged, his vitamin K blocked by her anticoagulant, delivered oh-so-sweetly in quilted velvet and a gold ribbon. He would think, 'I've eaten too much, no need to call a doctor'. Within half an hour he would blame food poisoning and brace for the inevitable, certain that he would be well by morning but, like a rat, he would be bleeding internally.

Thinking like a rat, she left behind cars and broad streets, and turned into a cramped, shaded lane. The lane was dank; she wrinkled her nose. Moss, still vivid green in July, splotched stone and brick. Food wrappings stirred in the gutter and a seagull pecked at a pile of squashed fries stuck to the bitumen by the impression of a tire.

So hilarious to see a gull and squashed fries! She laughed at the strip of sky.

At the end of the lane, sunlight slanted, bouncing off a white wall. Her slashed eye smarted. She waited while her eyes grew accustomed to the low light around the old buildings. In a disused doorway, a man sat on a faded blue quilt, his gold, curly hair flopping on his knees. Torn jeans signified nothing; fashion and poverty rolled into one in the current fashion scene, but his dirty, bare feet had precise meaning. Next to the man was a yellow fast-food carton and a filthy calico bag. He looked up, struggling to focus.

She saw that he was not much older than David, a schoolboy. His face was thin, pale, unlined. A young person in mortal danger. Something about the way he held himself hinted at a privileged childhood, an inculcated confidence in the bearing of his head, despite the bent knees and peeling brown paint of the doorway. She wondered, as she had so many times, whether David had ever been tempted to experiment with drugs. God knows she preached against it, but his eyes glazed when she reported another tragedy. What family misfortune had cast this boy in the only unsanitary street in the whole of dignified, lovely Bad Godesberg?

What if David were tempted? She would want to reduce his danger. 'Harm minimisation', that was the bureaucratic expression. That meant clean needles. She could have dumped them in the bin back in the mall, but then they would have been incriminatingly close to her hat and dress. The young man's head settled back on his knees. It would be bizarre to toss needles to a stranger, but they would be welcome. Junkies needed clean needles by the bucketful. Hepatitis and tetanus were only the beginning. She might save him from fungal infections, HIV, wound botulism, even necrotising fasciitis. She remembered the grim list from her attempts to frighten David. She stood close to the wall, so that she appeared in profile, and took out the bags of syringes and needles. She walked towards the boy, tugging her hat lower, and placed the bags gently on the squalid quilt.

'Young man, look after yourself.'

He looked sideways; his shirt moved. A thin wrist poked out, the bones knobbly against the frayed, plaid cuff. She held back money for two train fares and piled the rest of her notes and coins next to him.

'Go home to your parents; that's where you belong.'

Stella added an apple from her backpack, and walked away quickly. Did Costa's students live in dodgy hostels, unanchored in vast, predatory Rome? She looked back. The boy had not moved, and her ten-euro note might have been blown into the street.

A municipal bin stood at the end of the road. She dumped the plastic bag from the dress shop. There—she had avoided waste and contributed to harm minimisation. No one knew that she had visited Bad Godesberg. Costa's accusations—God forbid that he made them—would be without evidence. The strain lifted; the job was done and spectacularly so. Only one more threatening post on Facebook and it would be over.

And so, to the future. Peter would have talked to David by now. She would write to him tonight, send some photos, cheer him up. But first, draft notes for Takura, get that done, and then David. She turned out of the lane, into the sunlight, thinking of her son.

🐦

Young workers returning to Bonn thronged the Bad Godesberg station. Stella stood in the middle of the sweaty crowd fighting a ferocious urge to laugh, raw and crude, like an eighteenth-century depiction of lunatics. She swallowed laughs and yelps; they turned into hiccoughs. She had done it!

'Roxanne-Sabrina!'

A gleeful bay died in her throat. Rudi, from the pharmacy and every other damned place in Bad Godesberg.

'We keep bumping into each other. Crazed from the heat.'

She struggled to rein in a crazed grin. 'Yep, the heat…'

The weather was safe; she launched into a circuitous conversation about the heat dome, climate change, rising seas, what can we do, blah, blah, blah…

Rudi interrupted. 'You're wearing a different dress? I'm sure you were wearing white. I've a good memory for colour. I want to be a doctor and an artist. I read colour theory.'

Rudi was the ultimate hurdle. Stella looked down at her stained, grey dress.

'Hmm. You're still wearing your Munich T-shirt.'

'Yes, but I remember your dress because I thought it was the same shade of bleached white as my lab coat.'

Stella stared down at her dirty dress. What now…another script?

The train arrived. She called over her shoulder.

'Excuse me, Rudi, I need to work. Notes on vaccinations, of course.'

Sabrina-Roxanne-Dr Stella Robinson, scholar, and installation and collage artist, stepped to the platform edge, narratives and shifting identities exhausted.

TWENTY-FIVE

S UNSET BURNED AS the river park emptied and seagulls begged
from the few remaining families. Stella settled on the old
bench and opened a mangy conference napkin wrapped around
a stale currant bun. She laughed aloud and hurled crumbs in a
manic arc. A nearby family looked at her and then turned away
politely; the park was for everyone, even misfits.

Stella took ten deep breaths, almost hyper-ventilating, as she
watched a toddler on a picnic rug sucking on a bottle of orange
juice. She had won. Thank the fates that Costa had been busy on
his phone abusing someone else. He had spat on her but, if she'd
been visible, he would have dragged her to the police. He did not.
She was the victor. The heat felt tolerable, the warm grass silky
on her ankles, the sky magnificent, streaking into ribbons of red,
blue and pink. The moon hovered, fuzzy in the high humidity.

She imagined Costa stuffing chocolates into his mouth, any
pretence of manners abandoned in the lurid privacy of his room.
In that same room, unthinkable crimes had been dreamed. Her
laughs disintegrated into snorts, vulgar grunts that caused more
people to look up. She could not stop giggling and snorting while
she pitched and hurled crumbs in every direction. Birds flew in
from throughout the park. When she ran out, seagulls screeched,

jabbing each other with orange beaks, dislodging scraps from their mouths.

Stella stretched out her legs and observed red, swollen feet squeezed into sandals which once had seemed both practical and sexy. The straps cut into her heel. A slump settled on her shoulders. She could not make a report to the police about Costa's violent pornography on the bodies of his students without revealing herself.

Victory and stalemate.

Primeval laughs, gathering in her throat, failed to burst. Energy dwindled. She tried to force a chuckle. Vitality drained to a full stop. There was nothing to laugh about after finding the cache of vicious images. And her? What descriptions were there beyond 'avenger'? She might as well be honest and try new ones—stalker, liar, murderer—as long as no one knew. Not Peter or David or Justine or Takura. No one would understand, no matter what she said. It had to be done and she'd done it.

'Murderer'…that was a tough word, not one for a scholar of historical justice. Executioner…but where was the jury? Now she dealt with the perplexing twin curiosities of victory and stalemate; there was nothing she could do with the disgusting information under the cushion. Victory cut off at the knees.

'Hello, my dear.'

Stella jumped. Hildegard had taken another route, approaching the bench from the vast tree behind.

'Good evening, Hildegard, I'm happy to see you.'

'And dear Neo was pleased to meet you. I told him I had met a sympathetic young historian. So rare in these days of revisionism.'

'I need to forget today.'

Costa would be in the *Fuhrersuite*, carelessly re-reading the card from RANEOC, ripping open the chocolates, guzzling mindlessly. He would not have made a courtesy call of thanks to RANEOC, not his style, but he would feel the first twinges of a low, dull ache; his forehead would bead with cold sweat. She knew that it would be horrible for him and for rats, but at least he deserved it.

Inventing identities, wearing a stark white dress, injecting chocolates in an abandoned camp—it was all alien. Jubilance had vanished, but she still felt calm and whole. So be it that she had achieved victory and stalemate; the point was that she had stopped him.

Hildegard frowned. 'But I said Neo was charmed to meet you.'

'Only a few hours ago…it feels like last year. I'm sorry I was gauche, I did not mean to offend Neo.'

'No offence, but you seemed unwell. And now your eye looks sore; you need drops. Deal with today; tomorrow is the future where you can always be your better self.'

Hildegard pulled a slim photo book from one of her huge pockets and flipped through the pages.

'Look—Neo at five when I first met him.'

In front of a vast yellow hibiscus, the child, Neo, grinned at the camera. Hildegard, wearing orange lipstick, had her arms around both him and a woman, perhaps Neo's biological mother.

Stella leaned in, not daring to touch the precious image. 'What a beautiful child, and how the grown man loves you.'

'I am blessed.'

In another photo, Neo as a young man and Hildegard in middle age stood in a safari jeep; a herd of elephants grazed behind.

'Those exceptional animals…zebras, rhinos…I love them all, but now I am too old for the long flight to Botswana.'

Hildegard put the book back in her pocket. 'In the past I have visited many times. You observed correctly; I receive great love from darling Neo. There was Kurt, then Anton and the bloody mess of the war but, after, dear Neo and his beloved family waited for me.'

'You finally heard from Anton?'

'I never saw him again.'

'But someone came to collect the maps?'

Feathers swirled like perverse snowflakes in the once-cosy sitting room. The stout SS officer thrashed Oma's blue velvet cushion against the sofa and smirked at his thin, red-haired partner.

'Snow! Quite out of season.'

Hildegard grabbed the back of the sofa. The dreaded moment hurtled into her young life. The room reeked of boot polish.

Only two days since she had taken the maps, but endless as she waited for Anton, and sickening as she kept a secret from Kurt. He would love her to the end of time, he would never endanger her, but her secret menaced him. She hauled her eyes from the goatherd vase and glanced at him. He knew nothing about Wehrmacht maps; he was innocent and she was right not to have told him.

With a barely perceptible shake of his head, Kurt counselled restraint. She saw an animal cunning flit across his face as he bit hard on his lower lip. The red-haired officer casually picked up Hildegard's umbrella from its soggy lean by the front door and plucked Kurt's books from the shelves—crash, crash, crash. Hildegard thought of all the households being torn apart in Bonn that very day. Jammed vehicles on narrow roads, despair behind bolted truck doors.

Beyond the house and street, the trilling of blackbirds heralded the autumn migration. Only last year, she and Kurt had held hands in front of the basilica, marvelling at the enormous flock lifting in a portent of immense change. She had found a feather for good luck, a portent of their pending marriage. It glistened black on the narrow mantelpiece, brushing the edge of Oma's dismally fragile vase.

Kurt spoke with gutsy confidence, but Hildegard detected his higher pitch. 'Nothing here to concern you, sir.'

Dust ballooned from the top bookshelf where Kurt stacked lecture notes.

'Poor cleaning. Ironic in the circumstances,' laughed the officer. 'Don't you agree, you treacherous maid?'

That was her, Hildegard, 'treacherous maid'. The person who had failed everyone. No! That was not her; she was a terrified young architect. The red-haired officer fanned away dust with his peak cap and then swept his hair aside as he put the cap back on. As if from habit, he ran a finger across the metal skull and cross bones in the centre of the band. He had not finished. He swiped along the middle shelves. Ripped books thumped to the floor, mounting up around his over-polished boots. The brute flipped through pages and wrenched off leather spines. Kurt jumped as the other officer, squat and balding, kicked over the tapestry sofa and raced his dagger along the hessian underlay. Wads of horsehair plopped out and lint floated in the weak lamplight.

Hildegard leaned in, curious and trepidatious. Something shone in the wadding, but she had hidden nothing in the sofa. Had the officer planted false evidence? His fingers gouged into the grey, matted clumps and held up a gold barrette. She was flung back fifteen years, sliding seed pearls and gold into her hair, pirouetting in front of her grandmother's gilt mirror in the old house. She remembered the smoothness of the pearls and the sharpness of the gold catch, and Oma admiring her beloved only grandchild. That world was gone. No more rummaging in a box of jewellery; no more story times and split pea soup warming on the wooden stove. That world was being destroyed by soldiers from her own nation.

The squat officer's hand closed around the barrette, concealing it in his thick palm. He glanced at the back of his SS partner and shoved the barrette into his pocket. Hildegard felt the violation as if he had torn it from Oma's silver hair.

Kurt stood tall. 'These are my study books; I hope to contribute to a greater Germany when I graduate from the University of Bonn.'

Hildegard took his cue. 'We've done nothing to endanger Bonn or our dear Fatherland.'

The tall officer did not look at them as he smacked more volumes from the oak bookcases and ripped faded gold lettering. He brushed goose feathers from the length of his knife, his manicured hand caressing the blade and its motto. Hildegard read the familiar words upside down. Everyone knew them; *Meine Ehre Heist Treue*, my honour is loyalty. A few years ago, the motto had made sense; now it was impossible to remember that time.

Her heart beat so furiously, it must surely burst out of her rib cage and hit the wall. For an instant, she fantasised her heart propelling from her chest and smashing the vase. Kurt snarled as more of his books bashed on the floor—and now Hildegard's architecture books with their yellowing strips of newspaper markers.

Thousands of blackbirds flew in a vast black mass over the rooftops of old Bonn. Some would lose their way. One year, Hildegard found a waif.

Stella clenched her hands. 'A terrifying event—and in your newly-weds' home! Did Kurt know why?'

Hildegard patted Stella's knee and, at that moment, Stella's stomach shrivelled and her throat contracted. Why had she thought she had victory? Brave, brave Hildegard, but Stella had turned into a poisoner. The grass became spiky. She swished and irritated her ankles. The orange sky dimmed, but the heat did not lessen. Peeling paint scratched her legs.

Hildegard looked infinitely sad. 'I must tell the story in sequence. I can survive my own history only if I keep it in order.

I became a different person that night, saying the first words that came into my mind—safe, prudent Nazi slogans. Using the murderers' own propaganda seemed the only way to survive. I knew I must use their poisonous words.'

It was not hard to tap into Nazi rhetoric; *Frau* Wagner had given Hildegard daily practice. Now in her own home; she drew on it.

'You respect your family history, and you respect your grandparents. Family and Fatherland, we are all as one.' Hildegard clasped her head in her hands. 'Um—our history is our nation's backbone—and um—our glorious future.'

The squat, balding officer punched Hildegard on the mouth. The force surged through her teeth; blood spurted on her tongue. She staggered and flung out her arms, striking the oak shelf over the fire, dislodging the tall vase. It toppled to the stone hearth, the crash deafening over the thud of books. Folded maps and green and blue porcelain sherds burst among feathers. Hildegard collapsed in a tangle of sofa legs and cushions, long red hair slapping her face. It was over. She had fatally endangered Kurt. She had failed Anton and Magdalena.

Kurt sprang to Hildegard. He crouched low, cradling her with one arm and sweeping paper and sherds towards him with the other. Hildegard struggled to sit up inside his right arm, pain flaming in her hip. Poor, poor Kurt. Look what she'd done. Not even a year together. No baby, no future.

She shifted her weight accidentally onto the knife-edged fragments; jagged porcelain pierced her dirndl with a dozen stabs that she barely perceived. Fearless Anton? Lost already. He was never going to collect the maps. She gripped Kurt's shoulder, thinking, 'Run away, dear Kurt, our world is gone'. Kurt swept the sherds closer to their bodies. The maps crunched and creased beneath her thigh. The thin officer knocked Kurt back and kicked Hildegard in the stomach. She doubled over, exposing four thick, creamy sheets of folded paper scattered between the vase shepherd and his tiny broken goats.

The stout, thieving officer sneered. 'When snow melts, all filth is exposed.'

Hildegard watched her torment play out. It was over. Resistance was suicide. The officer opened the first thick map. A deadly lull invaded the room beneath the roaring trill of blackbirds and broken, tumbling memories as Hildegard caught glimpses of family photographs on the walls behind the officers. Kurt and Hildegard in their wedding splendour. A muscle memory on her cheek of the wispy tremor of the family veil. Her grandmother gathering wild forget-me-nots, never guessing that they would become a symbol of Masonic Resistance to Nazism, the tiny blue and yellow flowers and thick summer foliage once filling the same vase on Oma's hall table.

The officer studied the map before shaking a detailed drawing of bridges towards Hildegard. Pain rattled up through shock and terror; maybe she would never be able to talk to Kurt again. These SS soldiers would arrest her tonight, right now, just as Daniel and Tzipi had disappeared in an instant. The thin, red-haired officer perched on the back of the sofa, taking his time. She cowered with Kurt by the hearth while a twitch beneath his right eye flickered in the weak gold of the single globe.

Kurt scrambled to stand, but the balding officer shoved him back. Hildegard was on her elbows, looking straight up at the lout's chin where he'd nicked himself shaving.

The barbarian screeched. 'You and your hypocritical prattle have betrayed the trust of the noble German people and profaned the sanctity of the *Fuhrersuite*.'

Kurt grabbed Hildegard's hand. Their last seconds together were to be crouching before Nazi trash!

'You were a trusted maid who was given a great honour. How

247

many young women would have given anything for that trust that you betrayed so brazenly? Stinking traitor!'

Hildegard braced to be cufflinked or shot on the spot. She would never see Kurt again and she would never be able to explain; they would arrest her tonight. It was over. Kurt huddled beside her on the floor of their first and only home. She felt the last of the warmth of his body and saw pale skin flicker wildly in the lower right eyelid of his honourable face. She had never before seen the tremor.

He stood and took a vast, audible breath. 'My wife knows nothing! I tell her nothing. She's innocent.'

Hildegard gulped. Kurt stared beyond the sherds to the ash in the fire grate.

'I exploited her access to the rooms of the Fuhrer.'

'Stop!' Hildegard squeezed hard on Kurt's calf.

The thin officer picked off a last goose feather from his jacket and placed it with scrupulous attention on an upturned sofa leg.

Kurt did not look at Hildegard. 'I sneaked in while she was working in the *Fuhrersuite*. She was cleaning the bathroom; water covered all sounds.'

'No! Not like that. Stop!'

This was not the story. She'd tell the proper story. Only one story. Anton would tell them.

She got to her feet. 'The maps. I took them. Me! Not my husband.'

Hildegard would always remember that the thin officer acted so matter-of-factly as he knocked her aside and yanked Kurt across the sofa.

'Pah! Young love.'

Kurt's feet snagged on the cushions and he fell facedown on the floor. They only needed one body to satisfy orders: a male, preferably. Her mind flashed to the *Fuhrersuite* and relying on the distended pressure of her body to hold the maps. She had tried so hard. Who betrayed her? *Frau* Wagner? Eva? Too late for those questions.

'Me! I took the maps. Kurt—my husband—a medical student. Doesn't work in the hotel. Never been there. I took them.'

Kurt should not sacrifice himself for something of which he was ignorant and innocent. Trilling overhead. Deafening. Too hard to think. She'd lose Kurt, in ten minutes…in five…in one… Can't think.

Kurt stood resolutely in profile, stony, cutting himself off from her. Or…did he too have a secret life? What about when he was late home? When he said he was going to the library to study but left home without his satchel? He had a parcel, tight with string, held low against his thigh. He wore his heavy jacket, but it was a mild night. Now Kurt would not look at her. He rose in the poky living room like an Archaic Greek god, legs parted, fists like balls of carved marble, his stature exceeding the room. He clenched his jaw and set his mouth in a gash, in a face she had never seen.

She tugged his arm. 'Kurt! Look one last time. Kurt…turn. To me. Last time. See me.'

'To the car.' The thin officer ordered Kurt, his tone vapid, understated, in a deadly routine.

The officer thrust him through the narrow door of the sitting room, headlong into the gloom of the medieval street and into a car.

The squat officer yelled over his shoulder, 'Your husband duped you'.

Kurt turned, at last seeking her from the back window of the car where he sat wedged between the two officers. The shadow in his eyes—so enigmatic, she bled.

'I'm desperately sorry,' breathed Stella. 'You never saw Kurt again and you never saw Anton?'

'Nobody.'

The tragic story settled like a battered memorial stone on Hildegard's frail face; her lips and forehead were tight. She did not seem her usual self, with spare energy to consider the impact on her listener. She looked towards the deportation monument, as she had so often. Stella held Hildegard's hand and let time pass as dusk crept out from the tree shade and darkened the whole park. Only the path glimmered, leading directly to moon sparkle on the Rhine.

'How do you cope with your history?'

'I tell it again and again, to myself, to special people. Bits of it. All of it. You need to understand yourself in your own story and keep it in order.'

TWENTY-SIX

A RUSH OF STALE, hot air rolled into the corridor of the Bonn
Concerto Hotel as Stella opened her door. She re-inserted
her phone battery and scrolled for Peter's number. A crackle of
satellite static as the connection was made and there was Pete, as
clear as if they were in the same city.

'Stella? Is that you? Oh! Oh...'

Peter's voice sounded high-pitched, strangled. She could see
him pacing the living room; he could never be still while on the
phone. With his spare hand he would re-arrange books on shelves
or inscribe in household dust, 'Help me.' She would reply: 'The
dust or you?'

'The hotel desk clerk said to ring you urgently.'

'Where've you been? I've been calling for hours.'

She looked longingly at the bathroom; she should have had
a shower before making the call. After Hildegard's tragedy and
the photo discovery in 106, Peter's domestic histrionics would be
taxing. Besides, she was almost home and did not want his sulky
treatment over long distance.

'Sorry. Phone's been off.'

Peter shouted from fourteen thousand kilometres away, 'For
pity's sake, why?'

Stella dropped into the desk chair and pushed aside a mound of notes and brochures. 'I needed some peace. It was not aimed at you.'

She switched her phone to her left hand and re-directed the heat of the desk lamp. She opened her laptop to browse emails while Peter made a mountain out of a molehill.

'When you're this far away from your family, you should be in contact at all times.'

His voice was squeaky, scratchy; she hardly recognised it. This was the first time that she had spoken to him since she took the pivotal step of poisoning someone. She had vaulted over a moral line; she had done it perfectly, but the brilliance shone less brightly as the hours slipped by. She imagined Costa with two kilos of toxic chox. The defeated fool. A faint, stray laugh slipped through her lips as if she grudgingly acknowledged a weak joke. She fiddled with the family beach photo, everyone smiling and hugging inside the hideous coincidence of Costa's bargain-basement frame—she must replace it, unless it became a symbol of her secret revenge.

'Give me a break; it's a busy conference. I've been talking to an old German woman. I'll tell you her terrible story.'

Anything other than tell him what she *had* done. 'Oh yes, scoffed two lemon and coconut ice-creams.' A detailed enough decoy, but she would have to work hard to sound normal. Peter could be intuitive when she least expected it. Years of general medical practice had honed his antennae, giving him powers to detect depths beneath words and silence.

Revenge had its gutting come-down. No more laughs. A slump hollowed her out. Not a single chuckle gathered in her throat, not even a cough. She had committed a serious crime. Exhausted from the day—Neo, Costa, rat poison, the SS—she hardly trusted herself to speak. Peter would know that his wife had changed.

'So…great to talk to you, Pete.'

The sight of the young women in Costa's room had pierced her, but the African mother...the charity vouchers...Costa was complex. She hated to think that he had a decent side; it would make life too complicated. If he had caught her and the police were called, Peter would have been aghast that his wife could turn into a criminal. And David? She saw his pale, pimply face, the shock of betrayal. Even worse than Peter's would have been David's reaction. His crooked mother. He would have withdrawn further and she would have caused it, but there was no reason on earth for anyone to find out. It was hard to convince herself.

'Pete?'

Silence.

'What's happening at home? Are you there?'

Silence. Not for the first time, he insisted on a sour, moody pause. She scrolled through emails. One from the Dean that she would need to answer immediately. It was late; she'd forgotten the time while Hildegard talked. Before bed, she wanted to write to David and spend a few minutes in the garden with the Italian students and put out feelers about Costa and pornography. Maybe she could let the police know without revealing herself. That was the right thing to do. That would annihilate her morally dubious revenge and turn the poisoning into a social good. A bad act could have a good outcome; history was full of it.

She tried to focus on the phone call, but Peter's silence was disturbing. She felt off-balance, tilting somewhere unknown.

'I can't be everywhere. I'm sorry. I know that it would be frustrating not to be able to reach someone.'

Her voice echoed back. She thought that she heard a sob. Peter's silence inflated to an eerie dead calm.

Peter crackled and faded. 'It's David.'

'You said "David"?' she whispered. 'He's...ok?'

She was about to write to him. Peter's silence rammed her back into the silence of 106. The past, the stench, the wretched, desperate worm in the bird's beak. Silence grew ominous, linking parts of her life that must remain separate.

'Whatever that means,' he said.

'What?'

'Sit down.'

'I am.'

'He has…he's…he's…self-harmed.'

The screen of emails blurred.

'Tried to…kill himself.'

A breeze hit a corner of the Mickey Mouse curtains. Mummy's lead weights in the hem knocked on the sill. Leaves scratched the windowpane. Sweat spotted her forehead. The door swayed on oiled hinges. It slammed, plunging the room into hot darkness. She screamed down the decades to her childhood bedroom and back across the world to blazing Germany and a tiny phone in her sweaty hand.

'What happened? Is he all right?' She jumped up. The chair crashed.

'Calm down! He's alive.'

'Self-harm! Means what?'

'Ambulance, hospital, the works. Trauma Room in Emergency. That's where I'm calling from.'

'Trauma.' No lazy squiggle in the homey layers of dust. No comfy little marital game. No sulking, only grief.

'It's not true!'

Glary lights. Acres of white. People running with clipboards.

'What happened?' she yelled.

'I'm trying to tell you. Davey wasn't here when I got home, but he should've been.'

Stella tugged at her hair as her tiny son filled her memory. Sleepless nights with an adored baby.

'I can hear a baby crying.'

'Paediatric Emergency.'

'Oh…' Seriously ill babies. He was among them. Even bare

foot, he was taller than she was when in high heels, but still a child in medical terms.

'Chaos here. David should've been home.'

'He's allowed to be a bit late; he's fourteen.'

'Very late.'

She could hear anger in his voice. Anger and fear, they went together. She was angry with herself; why hadn't she re-inserted the phone battery the minute she got to Bonn? She'd lost so much time. She'd let Peter down. Let everyone down. She was the one who was different, not Peter.

'His phone defaulted continuously to messages. When he hadn't come home after forty-five minutes, I tried to reach you to see if there were plans I knew nothing about.'

'That's not so late.'

'It was too late. That was my first call. You'll find a lot.'

Stella clicked open the missed call log. Eighteen from home. All from Peter's phone, except three from David, one after another, only two minutes between them. All missed while she prowled around Bad Godesberg.

'Did you call him?' asked Peter. 'He was waiting to hear from you.'

'I left a phone message and sent an email.'

'As if he's no more than one of your colleagues!'

Peter accused her! 'I told him that I'd call soon.'

'That's the best you could do for our son?'

'You were the parent picking up the pieces. I'm away for only a few days.'

She felt ashamed. There was no need to be angry with Peter; she loved him. He was alone in a terrible moment.

'I'm sorry, Pete…what happened when—'

She heard him talking to someone in emergency. 'He's usually placid. Can't understand any of this.' A pause. 'I've already given you the name of his usual clinic.'

'Pete?'

'I told you this, only a few minutes ago.'

Peter became edgy, impatient; he was no longer a compassionate and tolerant GP.

And she…she was half a planet away from their child.

Bang. A clipboard fell?

'I'm sorry, I thought you were the other person,' he said too quickly and too loudly to an utter stranger who was caring for David.

'I heated up dinner,' said Peter. 'But forty-five minutes of nothing from him, I began calling around. Occasionally, he goes home with a friend.'

'That's ok, but I always say to let me know.'

'But he didn't.'

What was Peter not saying?

'I left a recorded message on the school phone.'

'Not monitored at night.'

'I know, but maybe there was a late choir practice.'

'You're right. Someone might've known.'

There were hundreds of kids at school. Massive, gangly, hairy, young men who were still boys. David would be only one of them when the teachers heard the news. Every school expected at least one annual disaster, a paralysing fall in the rugby scrum, an overdose, a car accident. But never for her child.

'I rang you again and again. I rang the other parents. Bertie was whimpering without ceasing. He's only a puppy, but he picked up on my panic.'

'What happened?'

Stella forced out the two words, remembering last year when sixteen-year-olds exploded Coca-Cola bottles, causing the loss of an eye for a curious little primary-school boy. It had seemed overwhelming at the time, but now, please God, let it be only an eye.

She heard tears in Peter's voice. 'I must tell it from the beginning; there's no other way. Got to keep it in order. I must tell it like this to cope or I'll fall apart. Damn, I have fallen apart.'

'Go fast. Can't bear it.'

'Bertie kept running everywhere, bumping into my legs. When no one knew where Davey was, I looked throughout the house and garden again and again.'

'Did you call his name?'

'Of course.'

'You kept calling "David, David"?'

She had to say his name. It made him alive. They had both agreed on it fourteen years ago. Biblical King David for inspiration. Why not?

'Until my throat hurt.'

'Where was he?'

But she didn't want to know. She wanted to be home, everyone safely around the dining table, eating David's favourite super-cheesy macaroni, with her asking him to turn off his phone during dinner, as she did every night. Him sighing and rolling his eyes and blaming her. 'But, Mum, you say, "I've got to take this call", and you jump up from the table and you take ages. Often! You do'. And her leaning across the table and squeezing his hand and saying, 'I'm sorry, darling, I'll try not to'. And it happening again the next night when the Dean rang.

Peter struggled on. 'I saw a strip of light under the small garage door that leads to the garden.'

'You didn't see it before?'

'Only a tiny strip of yellow.'

There was a rim of yellow top and bottom if someone were inside the garage or forgot to turn off the light. She always double-checked it to save on electricity.

'But you'd already looked in the garden.'

'I hadn't seen it; Bertie was fussing and crying.'

She had planted jasmine to climb up the garage wall, white sprays nodding over the door which had never fitted snugly, always at an angle, sagging on its hinges. In her fingertips, she could feel warm brick and cool, taut jasmine stems. She could open the door to the garage; it was that close in muscle memory. Her to-do list had said for the past year: 'get carpenter to fix hinges'.

'I heard a bang,' said Peter.

'What sort of bang?'

'He was at home all the time.' Peter breathed hard. A long sniff. 'You know the rafters in the garage?'

'With our three kayaks?' Something cold slithered into her mind. Her wet hand slipped on the phone.

'Yeah.' His tight, high voice that she had not heard before. 'Remember how we argued with the builder, said that he had over-engineered the garage?'

Tears flooded her face, racing down her cheeks for the first time since she called.

'Massive jarrah beams.' She leaned her forehead against the wall. 'The most contentious part of the house project.'

She could hear Peter sniffing. 'We said that the timber was too strong and expensive for a light iron roof.'

She almost shouted, 'Don't tell me!'

'David. I found Davey.'

She tapped her forehead rhythmically on the brick wall of the hotel room.

'Davey,' wept Peter. 'Hanging from the rafters. Sweetheart, I found him.'

TWENTY-SEVEN

FROM A MILLION miles away, a door banging. Callous laughter. A bell ringing. The desk light, bright and hot. Perspiration running cold on her back and forehead. Sickening jasmine sweetness bore a miasma of rot and cigarette smoke.

'Alive?' Stella bashed her forehead on the rough brick of the hotel wall. 'Tell me!'

Peter sobbed in a shock of cut-off breath like a hiccough.

'He'll be all right?' she yelled.

He must have held in weeping until he reached her. Now he let go. 'It seems so.'

'What does that mean?'

His voice wet, muffled. 'Doctors need time...to assess.'

She had never heard Peter cry, not even when his mother died and he stood at her grave with her favourite tulips, but she had wept for a mother-in-law she loved as deeply as her own mother.

'You're crying, Peter. *What* do doctors need to assess?'

She could not picture the real hospital scene; hospital trauma she knew only from films. She struck the brick wall with her free hand. Someone in the adjoining room pounded an annoyed reply. She talked into a visual hospital void. Where? Day? Night? Noisy? Peter, standing in a corridor? Sitting on David's bed?

'Doctors are with him now. I'm waiting outside.'

'He's alone!'

'Stop, Stella!'

She smashed her forehead on the wall, feeling the cut of mortar line in the bricks, but no pain.

'What hospital are you at?'

'I told you, the children's. Call you back. Doctors want me.'

Click. Peter gone. Alone in a foreign hotel. Stella pressed her head on the wall; her weight thrusting down her neck. The edge of the brick bit above her eyebrows. David had disintegrated. She hadn't seen it. Seen nothing. Ascribed his morose behaviour to unremarkable hormone flux. Missed his battle. He'd seen her miss it. He had phoned her three times today, giving her three last chances.

What do you do when you're torn inside out? She bore down harder on the brick edge. Her world distilled into her forehead skin and the rough wall. She was all brick and skin—brain, bone and memory gone. She stood for five minutes leaning on the wall. No call from Peter.

Something to do. She threw herself into the desk chair and began keying in flight requests. Her sweaty fingers sloshed across the keys. She made mistake after mistake. Date? Time? Route? High season prices blinked on the screen, but nothing was available in economy on Emirates or Qatar. She considered other routes. A short rail back-track to Amsterdam and fly with KLM. She could be there quickly and take any seat, but there was nothing. Hop to London and take British Airways? She flashed through Qantas's London and Frankfurt departures. All gone.

Rome? A long rail trip through the Alps, but she would save time by arriving adjacent to the Fiumicino train platform. Scroll. Peruse. No seat.

Rome…? Costa… Stella glanced at her grubby dress. Maybe he would go home to recuperate. He could not stay at the conference—assuming that he was alive. Stomach pumping? At the Rheinhotel Dreesen? It seemed years since she was there… once upon a time when she was another person. Forget stupid Costa. He probably travelled first-class with someone else paying, but business class in a crisis would do for her, cost irrelevant. She checked in her wallet for her spare credit card, the emergency family fall-back that she shared with Peter and David. Here was the catastrophe that they had prepared for.

She skimmed Qantas, faster and faster. No seats. The Qatar site had crashed: 'Apologies for the Disruption'. Nothing in Emirates. KLM full. The whole world was on the move. Winter in Australia and summer in Europe were both high season. She was stuck.

Ring. Stella grabbed her phone. 'What did the doctors say?'

'To be patient,' said Peter.

'Patient? How? It's routine for them, but not for us.' She drove her head into the rough mortar lines. 'They see kids top themselves daily; we don't. Doctors are heartless. I must speak to David now.'

'Not possible,' said Peter with his high, tight voice.

'Give him the phone!'

'He's intubated. Machines everywhere. Good news is that his spine's ok. I was in time.'

'In time?'

'I had that—er—Swiss Army Knife; the one you—er—gave me years ago.'

It couldn't be true; that was for cinema. 'You cut down your own son?'

'Held him with my left arm, cut with my right hand. The rope…'

'The thick rope…with that little knife?'

'Ah-ha…Bertie went berserk,' Peter sobbed.

'What rope?'

'Does it matter? We're waiting to see if he develops pulmonary oedema. It can be delayed by a few hours. No quick answer. They're calling me.'

'Don't go. Pete!'

Click, silence.

A rope and a knife. Unbearable. She could not see the actual hospital, but the messy garage was achingly clear. Skipping ropes? One of those? The thin one with yellow winding through the white cord? Broken yellow plastic handles and a jumble of sports bits and pieces, once nostalgic reminders of David's childhood. It did matter which rope. Every bit of David's suffering mattered… his clothes, his last words to Peter, his last friends, last teacher, last meal. She needed to know it all.

This was the end point of her obsession with Costa, the moment of apocalyptic reckoning. She had been heading to this, bashing her head on a wall for days, but not knowing it, had thought—if she had paused to think—that she could separate family from her reckless actions on the other side of the world. It was never going to be the police who came for her; it was always going to be infinitely worse with immediate revenge exacted by the universe. Only slamming her forehead into the bricks made her feel alive. Barely three triumphant hours since she left 106.

She resumed the hunt for a flight. No cancellations on any airlines in the past ten minutes. She would fly first-class and give up the bathroom renovation. Thank goodness that they had not yet signed the contract. She could live forever with 1980s avocado tiles if she could get home quickly.

She keyed in flight requests for early the next day. She thought of twenty-four hours in the air in the silent privilege of a first-class air room. No one to distract her, not even a welcome crying baby. She would have offered to give the parents a break, jiggled the little one for a few minutes while they ate dinner. She knew how to soothe a baby at high altitude, but there would be no baby for her in first-class, only isolation in four blank walls for thousands of kilometres, a whole night and a day. But there was nothing available, not even for twenty-five thousand dollars.

Thoughts like torture; time was her enemy. From the small, square hotel window, she saw students having fun at four tables pushed together. Their laughter must have glided over the family catastrophe the whole time she spoke to Peter. Italian laughter was different, more musical, but could still be callous. If she sat with the students, time might pass.

In the bathroom mirror she saw blood on her forehead, specks and drips from the sharp brick edges, just as she had appeared in front of Costa in the mosquito-infested garden. She had felt nothing then and felt nothing now. She went back to the wall and tilted up the desk lamp, making an elongated oval of white light. Four splotches of her blood marred the edge of a bare brick; they had already penetrated and turned dull brown. 'Marked for self-sacrifice.' She was the victim, but she had not chosen to sacrifice herself. To whom? For what?

The slightly less hot garden was a mishmash of cloying night perfumes. The aroma of *al fresco* dining combined with adrenaline to make her feel queasy in the odours of sharp, vinegary sauerkraut, herbed sausage and yeasty beer. The students welcomed Stella warmly. Leo stood, an ivory Caravaggio youth who had already seen too much; his pale face wounded her. The students had taken tea lights from unoccupied tables and created a circle of little flames which made their faces lambent and rosy. They sat at three small garden tables covered in beer cans, and with two empty red wine bottles and two fresh bottles of prosecco. Stella picked up an empty crisp packet and placed it on a table. Such a carefree life. Was she ever like this? Happy with friends, whiling away a summer night?

Leo, unsmiling, poured prosecco, more intensely a

Caravaggio youth than ever before. His face emerged ashen from the darkness, timelessly vulnerable and Baroque like the *Young Sick Bacchus*. Slowly and carefully, he handed her the cold glass. She touched his damp fingertips as she took the prosecco and caught the glint of candlelight on his wild black curls.

Stella put her phone on the table next to the glass and sank into the jokes and gossip, letting vivacious student talk wrap around her, as if she were miraculously still intact in the thin, transparent plastic of their babble. The plastic pinioned her arms and legs, and flattened hair onto her lacerated forehead. It bound her body and held together its pulpy mess. Each sheet stuck to the next as it spiralled around her, soaked in perspiration, just holding her shape. She no longer had a whole body; it had spun to fragments. Pinging voices, echoes of talk. Voices bouncing off the plastic. The shadow of Leo's eyes, the pallor of his skin. Mould and dark beyond the glow of tealights. The white tabletop blurred into sterile hospital trauma.

The Botticelli angel was talking. The beautiful, earnest face floated towards Stella—lips moving, honey-coloured tendrils of hair, candlelight in her enormous eyes. Stella clasped her phone and leaned forward but could not make out the words.

'Sorry, noisy,' she mumbled.

The angel understood, floated closer, with tiny, tea-light flames like pinpoints of corrosive yellow in her pupils. Stella shuffled back in the garden seat, shrinking gratefully in the plastic wrap of student talk, tugging her ears beneath the shiny, stretchy sheet. She swirled perspiration on her phone screen. Peter, ring!

The angel repeated, 'Have you seen Professor Giovanni Costa?'

The first silence in the garden; Stella tried to lift her arms to block the angel. Vaguely, she was aware that the students observed her. She took her first sip of prosecco and shook her head. The Costa part of her life was dead and buried.

'Ok, Stella?' asked Leo. 'Are you well, Dr Robinson?'

The angel drifted back into the dark. 'Gio said he would meet us here tonight to discuss a compulsory excursion to the Roman ruins in Cologne.'

Voices skated over Stella.

'Late as usual.'

'Nothing should be compulsory at doctoral level except the thesis.'

'…swastika mosaics in the heart of Cologne, right next to the cathedral. A two thousand-year-old Roman joke.'

'Those prophetic Romans.'

Too much talk. Too fast.

The angel explained, 'Gio will distract us with embarrassing ceramic swastikas while he's pinching someone's bum'.

'And more of his sewer anecdotes and scatological puns.'

Groans, laughter and more jokes. Stella watched the two women students in Islamic headscarves. The quiet one had walked innocently in front of the Pantheon and been skewered by Costa's abominations. The universe was hideously swift to punish Stella, but had it forgotten Costa's rabid photos? The two students did not laugh, but wriggled out of range of candlelight.

Leo looked at her across the table, a faint question forming on his wan face with a raw, painful imminence that she could not bear. She nodded goodnight. Her hand trembled as she placed the barely touched prosecco on the table. She moved slowly in the viscid plastic wrap, spinning to mush.

No Peter.

In the dark hotel room, Stella pulled off her dress, fell onto the narrow bed and traced faint shadows on the ceiling with half-closed eyes—laughter outside, her phone silent, and the unbearable present. She knelt on her pillow and pushed her forehead down on the bricks above her bed. She had to feel alive;

only pain could do it. Stupid, stupid, stupid to spend the day in Bad Godesberg without a working phone.

She pulled up all the emails that she and David had exchanged in the last month and scrutinised them, topic by topic, line by line, word by word, for lost meaning and tragically missed opportunities. She had been abrupt in the last three weeks while she was getting ready for the conference. Why had David emailed her from his bedroom when she lived in the same house and, as usual, was going to have dinner with him? How long had he been asking for his mother? Her emails from Germany were terse. There were long gaps between David writing and her replies, but she was gone only a few days and Peter was home with him... Not enough! He had wanted to talk to his mother.

Someone shouted, 'Gio!' Raucous laughter from the garden.

She started a new email. 'My Darling David...' Perhaps he would not be able to read it, too injured, too angry. 'I love you so much and am devastated...'

Perhaps he would never read it. Rescued suicide victims died even after revival. If he lived, David might be months in rehabilitation and years in therapy. She tried again, 'Peter... Dad... told me that he found you. What can I say...'

She checked her phone; she might have missed Peter's call under the froth of student laughter.

She wrote, 'I was desperate to talk to you in hospital today. I tried, but understand it was impossible. Darling David, please know that I tried.'

A gust of wind. Curtains flapping up to the ceiling, metal rings scraping along the rod. Daddy locking the window and pulling the curtains tight, putting three safety pins in the middle. Mummy giving her a night-light in the shape of a blue flower that glowed until she woke in the morning.

Stella switched on the desk light and opened the Qantas website. An email from the Dean asked her to reply 'ASAP!' Still no seat in any airline class. Terrifying lung diagrams illustrated online articles about pulmonary oedema. David's pallid, ivory face. A tube jutted from his bloodless lips. His eyes were closed, fair lashes deathly still. Distracted medical staff. Peter somewhere. The Dean emailed again, this time with a red exclamation mark.

She snapped the laptop shut and pushed it to the back of the desk. She longed for a shower but could not risk missing Peter's call. She brushed her teeth and patted herself with a damp washcloth, then washed her filthy, grey dress and hung it to drip in the cubicle.

Buzz. Peter. 'Stella Darling. Davey will probably be ok, too early to say definitively. Pulmonary oedema is worrying. He's not left the trauma unit but soon he'll go to intensive care.'

Peter sounded more in command. She would not let him down.

'That's good, isn't?'

'No.'

'But leaving trauma's good!'

'An accident case came in. Broken spine. David had to move out. Space.'

'Oh.' Stella's tears started. 'But you rescued him from the rafters.'

'Not instantly.'

They were both silent. The satellite relayed Peter's jerky breath. It hit her ear, wordless, beyond words. Around their two cars, the garage was piled high: the ten-year-old Christmas tree stored in end-to-end hessian bags, unsorted primary-school books, David's cricket gear and on and on, all the bits of a child which were out of season. Horrendously, David in the middle between the family kayaks.

'I can't get home early. There are no seats.'

'Go first class, forget the bathroom.'

'Tried that.'

'Then you'll have to stay. Go back to World Heritage. I'll do my best without you.'

There was a hanging-up finality in Peter's voice, but she needed to talk. When he clicked 'off', she would be alone in the room with David's short life jumbling before her.

'I love you and David so much. I'm desperately sorry that this is happening to us all.'

Peter cleared his throat. 'I love you both too. We'll be ok.'

Stella composed an email to David during the interminable grief-night. He must know that she would never forget the marvel of his birth, the joy of watching him grow, her despair at his despair. She wrote and re-wrote until 4am and then checked the airlines again. No seats. She would have to wait for her original, planned flight. The university provost wrote.

'Please answer immediately!

Great South Land University

Dear Dr Robinson

The Dean of Humanities has been trying to reach you. We have checked through Humanities travel records; you are the closest senior staff member to Rome. Would you mind swinging by on the way home? Only half a day. The meeting is impromptu and urgent. You will be work-loaded to attend. Details will follow your acceptance. Quite a feather in your cap. Let me know ASAP and I'll have the travel department do the necessary. Remember that you have a professional duty to keep up to date with emails.

Cheers

Prof. Vinh Trinh'

A tatty feather and a considerable saving in airfares and staff costs for the university. Stella jiggled the delicate white crochet coral that she had found with Takura, her symbol of renewed academic fervour. She would not reply tonight.

She took a sleeping pill and slept until her phone alarm beeped three hours later. She sat in bed with a pillow supporting her back and her laptop flattening sweaty sheets. She did not want to face the day, but Peter had written two hours ago.

'Darling, David's still intubated, but stable. He sometimes cries for you. I know, surprising at 14. I told him that you wanted to talk to him and would be home soon. He understood. He's injured, but I could see glimpses of our Davey, even a smile when he looked at all the hospital machinery. Go to the World Heritage sessions and we'll talk soon. I hope your arm is feeling stronger. I love you. We'll be ok. P.'

It was the first time all week that Peter had mentioned her broken arm.

TWENTY-EIGHT

THE KOREAN PROTEST tent had collapsed, as if a vandal had kicked a pole and the tent had imploded, right there, in an unseemly tangle in front of the old Bundeshaus. It lay in a yellow nylon heap in dwindling shade while South Koreans gleamed with sweat, tramping back and forth with boxes and poles.

The tent had been part of Stella's everyday coming and going. Like a dazed survivor of an air raid who stumbles into a bomb crater, she stood before the tent pile, blinded by dust, ears ringing, nothing making sense as she hungered to hold David's hand.

Over breakfast, she had scrolled again through every airline and pounced on an over-priced business seat for the next day to Sydney. Her circuitous route went north before it went south, had two long lay-overs making the journey thirty-two hours and would land her almost four thousand kilometres from Perth, but it was a start.

She pictured herself at the hospital, roiling in numbness and anguish. She remembered the breathtaking first moments of cradling David, 2.94 kilos, his delicate neck, perfect little face, just born, but she could not go deeply enough into tactile memory to evoke the feel of his new-born skin. That memory was buried beneath inconsequential moments: 'pick up your lunch box; dentist after school'. She had not realised until that moment that the memory was lost. Still wrapped in shrink wrap from her time with the students—a slithery, sticky, winding sheet—she was only vaguely aware of conference voices.

Min trod slowly up the driveway lugging empty cardboard boxes and wearing a grubby white jeogori and blue chima. She dumped the boxes by the tent. Stella offered to help. Min's eyes flitted over the dried blood on her forehead.

'The Japanese will make a lot of money from tourism in their new World Heritage site.'

After anticipating it all week, Stella had missed the crucial session on South Korea and Japan. Another loss. University colleagues at home would want to discuss it and she would have little to say except 'missed it', with a goofy grin.

Stella helped Min to wedge a portable gas stove into a box buffered by protest slave brochures.

'I'm sorry, Min. You worked hard to make everyone aware of slavery, but the listing was inevitable. Countries want those listings because tourism money and World Heritage go together.'

Min slammed the box lid and taped it. 'Korean slaves will be forgotten…once again. The irony is that the dispute over memory and history will not cause people to remember our suffering, but it will result in more people visiting Hashima Island. The Japanese will win again.'

The turbulence of two passing police cars dragged blank petition pages towards the conference-centre entrance. Stella ran after them, grateful for the chance to feel alive. No! The cars parked behind two other police vehicles, making four carloads of police. She shielded the lower part of her face; David needed her.

She handed the pages to Min. 'How did the Japanese get the listing?'

'They agreed to erect signs acknowledging forced labour.'

271

Stella prolonged the interaction, anything to help her endure the visions of a coil of old rope and David intubated.

'Harmonious agreement?'

Min shook her head. 'The interpretation signs will be tiny; they'll fall down and not be replaced. We Koreans know there is little good faith when a nation wants to forget a disgraceful past. Our suffering will be forgotten, marched over by the Japanese industrial miracle.'

The Japanese delegation bowed, accepting congratulations on a hard-won success. Stella manoeuvred past a group of twenty lining up for a photograph in front of the World Heritage Committee banner. Baleful bird decals darted up the glass walls and sharp raptor beaks framed the door. Beyond the entrance, police swarmed over the foyer. Stella found Justine in the security queue, someone else to help her annihilate time.

Stella pointed at uniforms and peaked visor caps weaving in and out of startled delegates.

'Are the police here because of the Japanese listing? Are history and memory now policed?'

She was back on the familiar terrain of the politics of memory, the Deputy-Editor with her Editor. Maybe, she would survive her maelstrom.

'That's yesterday's scandal,' said Justine.

Stella had metamorphosised into criminal and mother-victim in the same day, oscillating between guilt and grief, life and half-life. It was too hard. Three policewomen pushed behind them; Justine pulled Stella beside her.

'You must be the last person to hear.' Justine raised her voice over the commotion. 'Someone was poisoned. It was the only topic at breakfast.'

Poisoned! If only Justine had said 'drunk and hauled from

the Rhine...wounded by gunshot...fell off a bike'. Stella had not escaped, not yet safe at 30,000 feet. Her heart sped up. How should she appear? She'd appear light-hearted.

'Not on my toast.'

Such a silly joke when she was cauterised by the image of Peter, screaming, and sawing back and forth with his short, blunt knife.

Justine laughed. 'What a hard heart!'

Not a hard heart. A wounded, grief-struck, terrified heart. The joke was wrong...she'd play it neutral.

'Poison sounds medieval. In safe little Bonn?'

'Medieval' sounded like another stupid joke. She was not on top of this; she had never imagined talking to Justine about Costa. Danger!

Justine stood back to allow a policewoman to pass into the foyer turbulence. 'Not in central Bonn, but deep in Nazi territory, in Bad Godesberg, in that famous Jugendstil hotel, the one that Rudolf Hess introduced Hitler to.'

Hess too!

Coffee from three hundred cups permeated the humid air of a labouring air-conditioner. Jostling and knocking and gossiping. Police crawling over the conference centre, seeking Dr Stella Robinson, who only wanted to go home to her injured child.

Stella ran through the risky day: she had removed the phone battery, worn different clothes, and then ditched them, but Justine knew her too well; she'd spot nerves. Stella wiped sweaty palms up and down the side of her grey dress; it was still faintly damp from dripping in the humid bathroom. She faced away from the police. She had to get to David; Justine had become the new challenge.

'Poison? Who?' A shrill, piping voice that she did not recognise.

Justine looked quizzical. 'That pompous sewer-archaeologist from Rome. You must have heard of Giovanni Costa; he knows everyone. Vulgar and powerful.'

Stella frowned. 'Not sure…lots of people here. Why him?'

'No one knows.'

They should know. He's a sex criminal, a bully, a thief. 'Why are the police here?'

Justine shrugged. 'You look ill. Your forehead—awful.'

Stella caressed thick scabs. A howl funnelled in her throat. Change the topic!

'Is there a Board meeting today?'

Justine shook her head slowly and narrowed her eyes. She had detected something awry. She was always going to be dangerous, but Stella could not believe it fully until that moment. Justine's threat derived from her honesty. The world tilted perilously through the intuition of a good friend. I am the poisoner, dear friend. It is I.

'I've had bad news from home. Can't talk about it.' A falsetto, not her normal voice.

Justine started to smile, reached for Stella's shoulder and then stopped.

'I can see you've had little sleep. Let me know if I can help. It's been a long week.'

Only a few days before, Stella had browsed books with Justine in the foyer; now she skirted behind three police officers who had set up a trestle. Today, no one flipped through glossy heritage magazines. Delegates buzzed, picking up second and third cups of coffee, delaying entry to the auditorium.

Stella plotted her course, weaving around police and—oh God!—two dogs. She fished a perfume vial sample from her bag and splashed her wrists, elbow joints, neck and ankles. She raced up the stairs two at a time as the busy, familiar foyer waxed ominous. Officers stopped women and tapped notes into iPads. Oblivious of the hubbub, the Japanese continued to assemble for photographs.

Stella climbed shakily to the last row of the mezzanine gallery with its easy escape to the stairs and exit. She could just make out Costa's business card, still taped to the balustrade from the day before. Her legs trembled so violently that she could not still them. She heard, 'Poison? Poison!' as noisy observers trailed back into the gallery. A student laughed, 'Un-effing believable!'

To distract herself, Stella re-read the email from the university provost; it was curiously chatty given that she had hardly ever spoken to Professor Trinh. A couple of days in Rome keeping tabs on Costa would have been appealing, even yesterday morning. She copied the email to Peter. He would be pleased that something positive came out of the week, even though she was forced to decline.

He wrote back immediately. 'Darling, I'm at the hospital, stayed all night and day. I grabbed a shower and fresh clothes at home, back in fifty minutes, not bad for someone who's notorious for singing in the bathroom! David's asleep. Intubation out tomorrow. He looks much better. His head doctor is Priscilla Ho, 40-ish, athletic-looking, focused. I feel confident with her looking after Davey. Tragically, she has dealt with this type of injury multiple times. Fantastic news about the Rome meeting. Why not go? It would do you good and only delay your return by 24 hours. We're coping. I'm proud of you. Kiss, P.'

If Peter could look after David, would it matter if she went to Rome for a few hours? An elegant escape from Bonn...a boost for her faltering career... Hollowed-out emotion coursed sluggishly through her body; Costa might be there.

A crazy thought. Of course she couldn't go. Her faint stirring of excitement was no more than an habitual response. She'd tried being impulsively creative and look where she ended up. As the chair of the morning session arrived, Stella wrote back, 'My place is at home now'.

She emailed Professor Trinh that she had a family emergency and could not detour to Rome. What relief to be free, finally and completely, of Costa. She would never see him again or lurk outside his Rome office, or—shameful thought—connive to go inside.

The big screens on the lower floor lit up with *Welcome to the World Heritage Committee Meeting Bonn Germany 2015*, as if it were business-as-usual and the worst day of her life had not dawned yesterday and delivered her desolate child to the garage. She could never park there again.

'Excuse me.'

A voice cracked into her image of David dying among the kayaks; it was Michael, Hawaiian shirt replaced by a white business shirt.

He stood, his head slightly bowed. 'I need to apologise. I should not have said what I said yesterday.'

Now what after the contemptible tirade on the stairs? 'Ok, thanks.'

'I know you didn't take the decision about the Deputy-Editorship.'

Who cared, she'd all but forgotten. 'Right.'

'And I realise that if you had, it would not excuse my behaviour.'

Textbook apology, he'd consulted a therapist. Below, the session started; tardy students crept along the back row. Stella gave a polite smile of dismissal, but Michael wedged into the seat beside her.

'It's going to be a great Board.'

She saw him assess the blood on her forehead and decide to say nothing; her forehead led to a can of worms it was best not for him to open.

'Hey, nice cologne.' He rubbed his hands in a business-like manner. 'We're going to work well together.'

Make him go away.

'Inspiring leadership from you and Justine.'

'Inspiring'—mawkish! She and Michael could not go back to the happy, hopeful beginning of the week, but he kept trying.

Fortunately, in the main forum below, a thin, middle-aged spokeswoman tapped the microphone.

'Good morning, ladies and gentlemen.'

She sighed into the microphone like a desiccating gust of wind scorching a withered paddock, sending ankle-high flames leaping towards Stella.

'World Heritage is a global initiative that unites us in our common humanity. It is, therefore, with shock and personal disbelief, that I have the melancholy duty of announcing that one of our most valued members, Professor Giovanni Costa of Rome, has been the victim of an unprovoked attack. He is well known to many of you and loved by his students; several are here with us in Bonn. Professor Costa is a specialist in Roman sanitation.'

Whispers tore around the Observers' Gallery. Stella strained to hear. The announcement could not be happening; it was a fantasy. All she wanted was to go home to David, but news of her crime inflamed the auditorium. Speculation and brazen gossip erupted. The poisoner cowered.

Michael leaned over. 'I heard that prof's a dumbass; too many years with his head in stinking pipes.'

The spokeswoman continued, 'Professor Costa travels widely to many of our spectacular heritage sites, freely offering his advice and assisting with research papers. Felicitously, he is expected to make a recovery, but only time will tell.'

Michael laughed. 'He probably deserved all he got.'

'Bonn police ask for anyone who knows anything about an incident in nearby Bad Godesberg to contact them immediately.'

Stella and her broderie anglaise dress sprang onto the screens. The floppy hat. Her nose. Her neck. Incredibly her—in an indistinct still taken from one security camera at the Rheinhotel Dreesen.

Terror. Choking terror. Not true. Imagining. Michael suffocatingly close. She—the embodiment of the serial killer of her childhood. Creeping, creeping...

From below, words spiralled in a giddy vortex. 'The police are with us talking to anyone who visited Bad Godesberg yesterday afternoon. They are especially interested in an excessive quantity of medical needles that were dumped on an unhoused person.'

They'd made the connection? Impossible.

'Most tragically for the reputation of World Heritage professionals, the perpetrator appears to be one of us because she carried the lanyard of the World Heritage Committee Meeting. That such a person is among us fractures our global identity and integrity. Please look closely at the police photo and offer assistance if you can.'

An extreme close-up of Stella's face and hat burst into the auditorium, wide-angled, blurred. She reeled, clutched the seat arms. Hunted. A criminal. A poisoner. But Costa wouldn't die, he couldn't; he was too fat to absorb minuscule squirts of poison. Far too fat. He was safe; she was safe. Bad Godesberg was ancient history; David was the present. She no longer had those clothes. With the efficiency of German rubbish collection, they would have gone to landfill hours ago. The huge photo was from an unsettling angle, her lips pursed, chin jutting, a swath of cheek. Not her, never. Justine might recognise her, but unlikely; the angle distorted her nose and chin, unbalanced her face. She would not be expecting to recognise Stella. So she wouldn't. She wouldn't!

Where was Justine? Stella spotted her a few rows ahead, bent over her laptop. The indigo of her dress highlighted her shoulders, pasty from years sitting in libraries, the dutiful scholar who was also creative and kind. Justine keyed in vigorously, oblivious to the unravelling of her friend's life.

The boy with the lab coat—so inquisitive. Wretched Rudi. She'd met him three times; he'd remember. When the photo appeared—in newspapers—and where else? On posters? Online? TV? Stella pushed her fingers hard into her brow; it was painful, crisp with dried blood. Rudi would go to the police; it would be his nosy style. Of course he knew about the miserable needles;

he'd foisted them on her. Chunks of words flew at Stella; a police officer droned on.

'...the respected conference lanyard...devious person...evil attack...premeditated...bullying of inexperienced hotel staff... meticulous criminal planning...a master poisoner...'

How ludicrous that Rudi's father wanted to be her art patron. She should never have let that narrative escape. If she had reined it in and stayed on track, this would not be happening. There'd be no end to the trouble from Rudi. He'd seen her all over town. He was probably with the police now. The incriminating photo. Rip it down! My child needs me.

'The alleged perpetrator spoke native English to an unhoused man and a medical student. Both are assisting the police.'

Her huge face dominated the old Bundeshaus, of all unlikely places on the planet.

'The police are grateful to these civic-minded young men who had the time to look closely at the alleged perpetrator and confirm that this photograph is a good likeness.'

Horrible chin and nose in wide angle. The slanting hat brim, her hidden eyes—

Eyes, eyes everywhere. Sunglasses! She'd forgotten to change them! There they were. Red stars speckled on glitter frames. Rudi had seen them three times. Justine had admired them. Lusted after them. Worn them! One hundred per cent incriminating.

Justine straightened up, rigid. Sick with fright, Stella watched her head jolt; her white shoulders had set so squarely that the back of her dress gaped. Justine closed her laptop, looked left and right, and then half-stood to see the lower seats. Stella shrank, drawing her neck down into her shoulders. That woman. Her. Enormous on the screen. Criminal. Poisoner. Never her. Not me. But...me.

Michael laughed. 'Uncanny, she looks like you.'

He mocked a quick identity check, looking rapidly from screen to Stella. 'Yep, spooky resemblance.'

People scanned the auditorium, a sea of sweaty faces swivelling. Head bent, face blazing, Stella pretended to scribble notes, her hands so wet her pen slipped.

Michael elbowed her playfully. 'A secret life, Stella? Eh? Eh?'

That person on the screen was her before, ever so briefly. Before…before David hurt himself. Before she spoke to Peter. Before David was intubated. Before David's despair.

David… David… Slowly, she became conscious of the only scrap of flotsam she could clutch. His near-death…her understandable grief and trauma… They'd mask her crime. A mask, that's what she needed because David needed her. A shattered, desperate mother could never be accused of poisoning an almost unknown colleague.

Appalling hotel security stills. Omni-present Rudi. Damn the needles, damn the sunglasses. New dress, new hat. They were not enough. She was a criminal on the run, wits sharp and on the lookout for every hazard and opportunity. She was every crim who scaled a prison wall, scraping through shards of glass, blood dripping from her knees. On the other side, an escape tunnel yawned wide, perilous, sinister. She entered that dark place.

If the screw tightened, she would play the David card. She had already hinted that she had bad news. She would tell only Justine. Her empathic, high-integrity friend would speak for her. Protect her. Defend her. The last thing that David needed was his mother to fail to come home because she was in a German prison.

Ready to sprint, Stella leaned to pick up her bag, but a stab of hot shame cut. She shook. Sat back. What a disgraceful plan. This was not her. Even her skin was not hers. Adrenaline surged; her legs trembled, studded in goose flesh.

Justine's laptop was packed away, the bag strap over her shoulder. She turned 180°. Stella looked at the ceiling. It was shameful exploitation of David—and Justine—but it was her maternal duty to return. Her duty to do whatever it took. Whatever!

Stella grabbed her bag and let her hair swing over her face. 'I've had some news from home. Excuse me, Michael.'

She dashed out of the auditorium and at the top of the gallery steps came face to face with the Islamic women students. She had failed them; she could not tell the police about the crimes they endured. It was agony to see them. She had come so close to being able to help.

The usually silent student spoke. 'Dr Robinson, please join us tonight. We need your experience as we talk about supporting the Koreans.'

Stella forced a professional smile; of course she would be delighted to help any students. Rational debate and protest were the way to right wrongs. Theoretical investigation, research, testimonials. Blah, blah, blah.

Immediately behind the students, Georgette climbed, red-faced, puffing and primed to unleash mayhem. Stella drove her hands into her hips to check their shaking. Please, let Georgette be too late to see the photos.

'Hi,' said Stella, 'so…so…the Japanese-Korean dispute was settled, the *big* issue this week.' I'm desperately sorry, Min and Ho-jin. I had no choice but to use your trauma.

Georgette tried to push past her to the auditorium. 'Yes…we all saw it.'

Delay, delay. Prolong, prolong. 'Colleagues at home will want to know chapter and verse from us. We were there!'

Georgette tried to manoeuvre past. 'No doubt.'

A Stella brainwave. 'We should run a…um…staff seminar to explain the dispute, issues…emotions…'

'Ok.'

'Let's do it together.'

'Whatever.'

'Um…um…a hard problem…political…'

She had nothing more to say. Fate would have its way. A draining sensation plummeted through her body as Georgette hurried towards the Observers' Gallery. Don't go in…for once, be on my side, Georgette. But she was already at the entrance. A stress stab started at the base of Stella's skull. Don't go in!

A phone rang. Georgette turned away from the entrance and leaned against the glass wall of the corridor. A divine reprieve. Cold sweat spotted Stella's messy, scabby forehead.

A middle-aged police officer approached. '*Guten Tag*, Madame. Speak English?'

'Yes.' Stella looked the policewoman in the eye; the make-up was too heavy on the cracked, weathered face.

The policewoman perused Stella's forehead. 'We're checking everybody. The Italian professor poison case. You know about it?'

'A little, only what the police said.'

'Funny—most people knew before they arrived today.'

Stella's knees nearly gave way. She tried to lock them, but then her whole body trembled.

The police woman raised her eyebrows. 'Confirming, you'd heard nothing before arriving here?'

Stella shrugged.

'Hotel?'

'Bonn Concerto.'

The policewoman tapped into her iPad. 'Were you in Bad Godesberg yesterday?'

'I don't even know where it is. Excuse me.'

Stella ran down the steps and into the glare of the forecourt with its sickly radiant heat. I'm coming home, David. She wrapped her new sunglasses from Peter in morning tea paper napkins, dropped them in a bin, put on spares and raced by the empty space where Min had packed up only a short time ago. The Japanese had finished their photographs and the forecourt was empty. She hurried alone along Heussallee as grit peppered her ankles.

A shout behind. Justine! Stella sped up. She crossed the road and half-turned. Justine crossed too. Stella raced down the avenue, for once not sticking to the patches of shade. Justine closed in with clicking sandals.

'Stel-lah! Stel-lah! Stel-lah!'

Half-way to the station, Stella turned to face her breathless, frightened, stunned friend. Justine bent double, throwing her hands on her knees, panting, wordless. Stella crossed her arms over her chest and leaned back in a domineering pose that she had seen policemen adopt.

'Oh, hi, Justine. I was going to send you an email. I'm flying to Copenhagen tomorrow and then on to Australia.'

Justine's mouth dropped open. Stella braced for interrogation, shame snaking up her chest, encircling her neck.

'It's a backtracking flight… Yeah, longer. You know how it is, postgrad pressure, university committees. I can't afford more days here.' Whatever it takes.

Justine pushed a sweaty clump of hair off her face. She seemed absorbed in the old houses lining the avenue.

'Ok… Going north to go south?' She took a deep breath. 'You've been shopping?'

Stella said nothing.

Justine breathed heavily. 'Um… Are they sexy new sunglasses?'

Stella's heart banged. Perspiration coursed down her back, trickling into her underwear. She edged towards the bleak point of no return with her faithful friend.

'I always travel with a couple of pairs. You know we wear sunglasses all the time in Australia, even in winter. You probably don't in Canada.' Don't push me further.

Justine shook her head. Stella watched her eyes rove about the street as they stood in strained silence for a beat far too long. A car passed, stirring dust. Stella rubbed her right shin with her left calf.

Justine tried. 'You're not attending the closing party? All the board members will be there, even the much-reformed Michael.

283

It's a last chance to get to know each other before we work together online.'

Stella had forgotten about the closing party, even though she had purchased a flashy cocktail dress especially for it, the black dress that had threatened Peter so desperately that she had ended up with a broken arm. Would it be safer to disappear, or to attend the party and appear normal? Risky. Everyone had seen the hotel security photographs; someone would connect her. Ironically, she was not going to wear the 'inappropriate' dress, after all. What a waste of a marriage disaster.

'No. I'm tired; I need to pack. It's been a long week.' I beg you, Justine, no further.

In cutthroat light, they stood alone. Justine did not swing her straw hat but wrung and scrunched it with white knuckles, crackles popping in the bone dry air as the straw snapped into an angular mess.

Stella pointed at the sun. 'Your hat should be on your head.' Don't make me do it. I'm already monstrously ashamed to have used the Koreans to escape Georgette.

With exaggerated slow motion, Justine positioned her broken hat. For the first time, she dragged her gaze from the elegant houses and stared into Stella's eyes.

'The attack on Professor Costa has made the week seem longer.'

Too late to escape. Justine narrowed her eyes and inclined her head slightly to the left. Did she raise her eyebrows? Hard to tell under her thick fringe. She tilted her head to the right. Stella dropped her eyes and looked down at her own feet, speckled with dirt. How could she, Stella, be doing this? But what alternative was there? Stella quivered, her back and head cold, while her legs and arms sweated.

Justine licked her lips in the sweltering air and Stella saw precisely, with zero doubt, that Justine saw through Stella's pitiful ploys and had run out of words. Justine's friendship should not have been the blood price Stella had to pay. But there was no going back. Too, too late. She could not explain that she had discovered pornography and student photographs in Costa's room after she had broken in. It was not the excuse, but a healthy justification after the fact, but not one that she could ever use. She had evidence that she could not take to the police, and she could not salvage the relationship with Justine. But she could try to get home to her family; it was all she had left.

Fiery, clammy dishonour—she was initiated in the open street into a terrifying moral disgrace. After David's tragedy, she did not want to be an unprincipled person who told half-truths and exploited unrelated tragedies—baits, traps, decoys—to wriggle out of her own shame. She wanted to be open and full-hearted. Too late to go back to chattering about the new history journal. Too late to share the protection of chicks from a tomcat. Too, too late for sharing confidences with a wise friend and avoiding the Costa disaster altogether.

Stella clenched her fists behind her back and launched into execution of her depraved plan. She had no choice. She didn't!

'I've… I've had some news…from home.'

Stella wrapped her arms around her own shoulders, shivering. Forgive me, Justine. All the underhand moments of her life knitted together, there in the street, in the face of a good, true friend, moments that made her ashamed—sneaky elisions, hints of bad faith—moments that she had aspired to transcend.

She watched Justine's eyes; she did not blink. Stella told her of the near loss of David. The misery of the intolerable distance from her child. Of the burden on Peter.

'I'm torn inside out.'

Justine was gelid, hat still, lips pursed, eyes locked on Stella.

Stella felt it before she saw it, a chasm, deep, rocky, unclimbable. Justine stepped back on the hot footpath. So much space between them. Stella could see the entirety of the pink house on the other side of Heussallee, a rosy portal to debasement. She watched Justine and wondered how much of Stella herself was intact. She had not stopped Costa from attacking her; she had not saved the chained and gagged students, and she had nearly lost David. She was lost in the abyss of her infernal self-knowledge.

Stella looked down the avenue, empty of cars and people in the enervating morning. Rose-ringed parakeets jabbed at each other as they squabbled over seed in the pavement cracks. She had become the person she loathed, but she pushed on with the pantomime of convincing Justine long, long, long after it was pointless. She spoke louder over the birds squawking, making her words into a stilted declaration rather than the heart-tearing despair of a mother.

'I can't think of anything else; the nightmare of David takes over.'

Justine took off her hat and resumed agitated swinging; massive arcs pumped dust over Stella.

'Sorry. Unimaginable. Frightful.'

Her emotionless words dropped like stones, one by one, in a pure performance as the icy moment stretched between them. Justine moved first; she inched out her arms and stepped haltingly to hug Stella. So loose her arms around her friend.

TWENTY-NINE

O N THE TRAIN into Bonn, Stella scratched her arms until she saw a worried young woman peer over her spectacle frame, a question forming on her sympathetic face. Stella plopped her backpack over her arms. Underneath she squeezed, crushed and pounced, pinching viciously until her hand ached. Crimson ridges flared before she flattened and stretched them; welts streaked from knuckles to elbows.

After her glacial hug at Heussallee Station, Justine had coldly excused herself and pushed through the crowd to a carriage at the end of the platform. Stella choked back an impulse to call out as each step took Justine further from their friendship. What could she have said? *If* Justine had turned back? That she had discovered photographs in Costa's room that justified everything?

Flashes of passing trees hit her retina, blurs without meaning. A tinny music beat escaped a school kid's earphones. Stella imagined Costa in a Bonn hospital, surrounded by magnums and bouquets. He would survive, unnerved, but eager for more coprolite and graffiti. Greed was his undoing. She had spared his students his cruelty and sexual predation for a time, but at massive moral cost: lying her way into Costa's room, neglect of David, barefaced lying to Justine. She'd had many faces this week. From the stunted perspective of less than a day, her visit to Bad Godesberg had switched from feminist triumph to a hideous phantasm, and she, from dedicated scholar and mother to…? In Bonn Central, she helped an old man with a Zimmer frame negotiate the train exit, then hunted in vain for Justine.

In Munsterplatz, café doors were shut against the heat, but signs announced 'Open for COLD BEER!', 'Air-conditioned' and 'Fresh water for DOGS!' Stella trudged over the cobbles; sunlight reflected off shop windows in dazzling attacks. Tourists crowded around Beethoven's House, but Bonn was mostly empty. A final walk through the town centre via slits of shade made a fitting end to her shattering visit. Not long until she flew to David. And a farewell to Hildegard? She had always seemed to intuit when Stella would appear by the Rhine and had never given her address.

In the river park, only a handful of mothers and toddlers played under the trees. A panting dog rolled off a picnic blanket and onto the cooler grass. Stella sat in deep shade, hardly able to bear the sight of happy children with their parents. The snagging paint of the old bench bit her thighs. She twisted the skin on her left forearm, raising welt on welt, then tormented the right.

She sipped water from her flask and studied each stalking photograph of Costa, gradually deleting them from her phone, except one of the first, the image at the cocktail party in which he glowered into her lens. She needed to be able to recall his caustic, masculine gaze and how, in defying it, her image landed on two giant screens before an international audience, she was degraded before her dear friend, hunted by the German police and nearly lost her son. She clicked off the phone and scanned the park, but there was no frail, slender Hildegard.

She stretched out on the bench, covered her face with her hat and dragged an underarm back and forth along the rough plank edge. Splinters caught on her skin with a tearing sensation, but there was no nerve response. What would she tell Peter when he realised that her new sunglasses were missing? Lost? So careless with his gift. Stolen? Odd at the World Heritage meeting. Disgracefully, she'd improvise again, dream up something plausible... Why worry about this when David was injured?

Sunlight glitters pierced the thick weave of her hat. Muffled voices. The late morning heat intensified. No Hildegard. She had spared Costa's students—for a time—but she had become someone else in the process. That could not be the way that good worked. Surely, her better self would be strengthened by a moral act. She pulled in her arm when a lone cyclist peddled dust. Poisoning was not a moral act.

She tore her arm harder on the bench, vaguely aware of a zip and burn as wood punctured skin. Physical pain should have been able to command her whole attention and give back a modicum of life, but pain did not come. The torment of David's despair, she could not create enough injury to dim it. She dragged harder and deeper.

Seagulls fought over picnic scraps as Stella walked up the hill for the last time. She looked back to the shore, but there was no Hildegard. Far away on a yacht, a dog barked lazily, then once again she was back in heat radiating from shuttered houses. She pinched her arms. Without pain, she was lifeless, plodding one foot in front of the other. In the still of the late morning, a few cars raced towards the Rhine. The World Heritage meeting was a wreck. Stella was alone in all the world. Only David mattered.

At a bend in the road, a distraught toddler wailed in navy blue shorts that sagged to mid-thigh; his feet bled as they curved over a cobble. A block away, two adults argued in front of a silver sports car. The child lifted his arms to Stella. They were soft and rounded with creamy skin folds around his wrists, but his shoulders and chest were badly sunburnt. She yearned to pick him up; here was someone who needed her, she who had harmed so many. The baby pleaded, wrapping his arms around Stella's legs, pressing his wet cheeks on her knees. If she picked up the baby to soothe him, she might be accused of attempted kidnap. She was a stranger in a strange land.

'Mama?' Stella pointed up the street.

She considered calling to the adults, but they were too angry and self-absorbed to hear her from this distance, but if she ran to the people to ask whether the infant was theirs, she would be abandoning the baby in the street.

She risked it. She scooped up the child and walked rapidly over the cobbles while he snuffled into her neck. She had forgotten the feel of David's plump little baby body with its silky-doughy skin and innocent milky scent. She spoke soothingly, stroked a dimpled elbow. It could have been David. He could have been alone, desperate for rescue by a good-hearted person.

He *had* been alone. He had called for her. More than once. But she had not answered. She was not good-hearted; she could never again think of herself in that way. She was different from everyone—secretive, lying, acting in bad faith.

The child's crying intensified. Two guilt-stricken people raced towards him. The mother stared at Stella's bleeding arms and yanked the baby from her.

Stella's fingertips burnt on the carved granite memorial to Florentius and Cassius as the martyred heads cast short, intense shadows in the midday sun. She had not stuck with the resolution she made last time she stood here. She had tried—she really had—to walk away from Costa, but he had provoked her, never let up. Now he was ill. Shamefully, she was the cause. By what moral code was she judge and executioner? Why should she step into the jackboots of the SS soldiers who had ruined Hildegard's young life?

She took some last photographs of the monument, the basilica, Martinsplatz and vast, near-empty Munsterplatz with its umbrellas and dozens of café chairs arranged to face the basilica.

A voice called, 'My dear Stella! You view one of Bonn's most challenging monuments.'

Hildegard appeared from around the apse lugging a cane basket of books, which she put down by the bearded saint. She caressed his severed head, her pale coral lips and gauzy dress in fierce contrast to the granite and her own sad face.

At last, something in the world had gone right; Stella could say good-bye properly. 'The heads are confronting.'

'That's why we Germans like them. There is a sculptured head in Cologne, of St Gereon, also by Iskender Yediler. See it when you visit.'

'I can't; I'm leaving tomorrow. I looked for you at the river to say good-bye.'

'Oh...' Hildegard looked even sadder. 'I shall miss our impromptu meetings.'

Without the middle distance of the Rhine to ponder from their shared bench, an awkward pause hovered. Stella glanced in Hildegard's basket; the books were on global warming. It was too hot to talk about that!

'The monument's a puzzle.'

Hildegard glanced up from under her straw hat. Even at their last meeting, she had lessons for Stella.

'What do these tragic heads say to you?'

Florentius and Cassius had first told her to be her truest self and leave Costa alone, despite his bullying and goading. She had tried so hard to do that, but from where she stood today, after the rat poison and harm to David, that was too simple. Hildegard's hands cupped a carved Roman helmet, a probing look visible in her hat shadow. Today the message of the memorial was more elusive, but thinking about it gave Stella respite from agony.

'I think that they say, "Be on guard in the face of moral ambiguity. Sift the evidence in front of you and examine who you are when you confront it. Be your true self."'

'I think so too, dear; we need to look and listen at different times of our lives. There is never one answer only.'

Stella touched the place over her heart. 'Their deaths are hard to accept. They could have pretended to accept the Roman gods, but instead they showed respect to a bloody, criminal system, answered truthfully and were murdered.'

Hildegard gestured to Munsterplatz. 'About here, near the Roman temple.'

'But what did anyone gain by their sacrifice?'

They stood back to let a handful of tourists pose with the heads. When the selfies started, Hildegard smiled the biggest smile that Stella had ever seen, bigger than the one she had given when introducing Neo.

'We're still remembering them—well, some of us—and we're still puzzling over their brave choice. That's enough.'

The moral role of memory—the very controversy that the South Koreans had aroused—but Stella had not connected them to the martyrs. Millennia stretched between the Romans and Koreans and, yet, here was the same challenge.

Hildegard took Stella's hand. 'These sculptures have many messages. When it snows, they are like Christo's wrapped art works, muffled, about to burst out of their bindings, but today they cut and burn.'

'Literally and figuratively.' Stella drifted her hand around a scalding granite eye socket as the tourists drifted off, chatting about drinks.

Hildegard pointed to a café with an air-conditioning sign. 'Let's say goodbye properly over my favourite cake.'

David's tragedy bled out of Stella. It was torture to think of him in despair, hunting for a rope in the weak, fluorescent garage light, and Peter with his rusty Swiss Army Knife.

Two slices of raspberry curd cheesecake arrived with coffee

and icy orange juice. Stella emptied her glass too quickly; her nose throbbed.

'I feel I'm punished for wrong doing. That David's life has been threatened by things that I have done badly.'

'The universe doesn't work like that.'

Hildegard's words were little comfort in Stella's pit. There would be no absolution ever for Stella. She recognised *Kreutzer Sonata*, played on a ridiculously low volume. Any old Beethoven would do for tourists. The only other guests slammed the door as they returned to the square.

Hildegard brushed her hand along Stella's forearms, over scores of criss-crossing welts and beads of blood and embedded splinters. 'Why?'

Stella did not know what to say, but no more lying, especially to Hildegard. She tried to soothe her skin, but the puckering and welts reddened. Except for the rescue of the baby, the day had been a disaster.

'You harm yourself! You would deprive your son of his mother when he most needs her?'

'Fourteen thousand kilometres between us. I feel horrible pain.'

'First, you need to get the splinters out of your arm and look after yourself. Disinfectant before you go to sleep. And eye drops. Secondly, you can't be blamed for attending a conference; you're a young woman making her way in the world. A fine role model for your son.'

Stella shook her head; she could not tell Hildegard about the violent, criminal immaturity of injecting poison into chocolates. She had no words adequate for her self-disgust.

'It doesn't feel like that.' She glanced towards the CD player. The sonata made her restless; it was too impassioned for the small café, muted, but straining to burst out. 'How do you explain why your son would...would...hang himself...without examining how you've cared for him?'

'Everything's entangled,' said Hildegard, 'but he will be a better man for understanding respect for women. That's what you're teaching him simply by doing your job well. You'll be home soon and the family will be complete.'

Talking about the tragedy made it more real, more dreadful, and her guilt crushing. Hildegard passed her a fork and the larger slice of cake. Stella contemplated visitors disembarking from a tourist bus and straggling towards the martyred heads.

'Everyday tourists go there,' said Hildegard. 'I am relieved that they explore beyond Beethoven's House.'

Stella finished her water. 'What happened after the soldiers arrested Kurt?'

THIRTY

LAUGHTER PERMEATED THE café as a family of tourists banged the door, speaking loudly in Dutch. Hildegard took two long sips of coffee. She cut and ate the tip of her cheesecake and gestured to the waiter for more water. *Kreutzer Sonata* snapped off.

'What happened? Panic and a sense of slow motion, of life unravelling,' said Hildegard. 'I staggered after the car with my injured leg, but could not keep up, so I stood still in our little street. Bits of information flew at me. One part of my brain smelt the SS car exhaust and observed—as if utterly detached—that it became fainter as the monsters drove away, but nevertheless lingered. Scientists say that smells are notoriously difficult to remember, but I will remember that acrid, smoky filth until I die.

'I began to move as if in a theatre performance with myself as the audience. I did not know whether I imagined neighbours peeping at me. Did that curtain move? Was that old door ajar? My inner eye held on to the glow of Kurt's hair in the black car, but the screaming part of my brain was like a terrier with a rat, refusing to let go of the mystifying look in his eyes.

'Today I wonder whether the stinking exhaust and Kurt's beautiful hair were conspicuous because I could not take in any more. You'd think that I would be afraid that the SS would return for me, but truly I was not.'

Stella frowned as she tried to understand.

'I limped home,' said Hildegard. 'My leg dripped blood from the broken vase; it felt as if I had been stabbed a thousand times. I checked our blackout blind and tattered curtains and pressed my ear through them to the window and listened for so long to the sound of the soldiers' car that even if it had back-fired, I could not have heard it even though the town was dead quiet. I could not bear being in my head. Screeching cats fighting on a roof would have been a blessing, but nothing moved. The name "Kurt" tolled in my head. I said it to myself without ceasing, as if I could force him back on the sofa with the incantation of one sacred name.

'My mother had a telephone, but Kurt and I didn't. Mama would call us at six o'clock each Sunday. I would wait by the public box in the square, but that night, I could contact nobody.'

'What about your friends?' The loss of Justine stabbed Stella again.

'Who? The person I went to might've been the one who betrayed me.'

Hildegard described Stella's desolation. This was the future that awaited her, never fitting in, pathetic gratitude for a screeching cat, but a key element marked her as different from Hildegard. Stella would live in perpetual shame.

Kreutzer Sonata re-started; they both looked at the CD player, listening to the beginning. After a while, Hildegard resumed.

'The shadow in Kurt's precious eyes; this was penetrating and new to me. I was haunted by him looking back at me from the SS car and in despair at what I had done.'

'But you yourself must have felt desperate.'

'*Jawohl!*' Hildegard nodded. 'Indeed! I took the train to my mother as soon as curfew lifted. Such upheaval for her to see me wild-eyed on the doorstep. No tears from me, never, but sleep-deprived and raving. She put me in my childhood bedroom beneath the roof, with its narrow dormer window and my battered ragdoll sitting on my pine chest. She tucked me into bed to soothe me, mother me, but the reality of being back in that architecture of my childhood home only confirmed that Kurt was gone.'

'Did you tell your mother about taking the maps?'

'Oh, Stella! You *know* that would have been too dangerous.'

Stella hesitated, tapping her fingers. 'I hate to ask…but did you feel guilty?'

Guilt—her own, new, steadfast companion, but Stella had no SS thugs to blame for David's despair and injury; she stood alone, stripped naked, before her child's suffering. *Kreutzer Sonata* arrived at the passage in the first movement with its manic slip from control, its breathtaking sense of possibilities, of living a life of electrifying intensity.

'Guilt—of course!' Hildegard slapped the table. 'I had been insane, what a dunderhead to touch anything in Hitler's suite. I was young, naïve, not a heroine. Who would not feel crushed by remorse? I was drowning in guilt, the sort of guilt that would do anything—anything!—to turn back the clock so that a tiny child would not fall into a frozen river, so that Kurt would not be caught in my rash actions. Sometimes I could scarcely breathe; I didn't want to live with the disgrace. No—the sin! Guilt hounded me for years. I wanted to die, but what then about my widowed mother?'

Who would comfort Stella with her terrible secret? 'But you cannot blame yourself.'

'I had to take responsibility and blame.' Hildegard raced on. 'My stouthearted husband had protected me from the consequences of my actions, and I had to hold on to the vestiges of the life that we'd dreamed. I owed him that. The puzzle was that I also felt proud that I had acted for the Resistance. But oh, the price…'

'You stayed at the hotel?'

'Huh! Only mud and potatoes after that.'

'I'm amazed,' said Stella. 'You were permitted to work there despite your marriage to Kurt?'

'The management was what we now call "sexist", and I knew the ropes, as you say. Easier to keep me than to sack me. *Frau* Wagner said nothing when I made up my face to appear bright, to mask sorrow. My lips looked as if I had chewed them raw. A young woman in paralysing mourning for her traitor husband appeared harmless.'

'Dreadful to work in the same place.'

'I was so depressed that I hardly noticed. The hotel employment still served its purpose; it let me go on with architecture, imagining new forms and new people inhabiting them. While I scrubbed potatoes, I was oblivious of the chef bullying Paul. Here and there was a moment's break when friends were affectionate and I learned to trust again. And one day, I saw Paul fight back, arguing that the watermelon basket was too heavy. The sous-chef backed him up and I never saw the chef being mean again. Some things change.'

'What about Eva?' asked Stella.

'Not Eva! Never! She had no benevolence for me. Self-protection comes first. And silly, weak Marta? In the market square, I courteously acknowledge her, but we never speak, not even today.'

A smile flickered on Hildegard's face. 'Ironies are everywhere. Last year I saw Marta at the Rathaus end of the square. We both glanced down at the new book-burning memorial, right under our wet winter boots, little bronze sculptures of book spines set into the cobbles. It's a reminder of the 1933 Nazi book burning— you must see it before you go. Marta reddened most hotly, like beetroot. She was so flustered that she dropped her fancy gloves in a muddy puddle. She picked them up and strode away, flicking off dirty water while I remembered the SS ripping our books. I saw her deep shame.'

Hildegard nudged a slice of raspberry curd cheesecake closer to Stella, who imagined never being free of her own past, of always hiding the appalling week from Peter. She toyed with her wrapped fork.

'You can't escape history in Bonn, in Germany…anywhere.'

'It's impossible,' said Hildegard. 'Eva left in the late 1950s; I was then glad to walk in my Bonn without the anxiety of seeing an old friend I no longer trusted.'

'And Magdalena?'

'I never saw her; it was as if she had never sweated in that kitchen. Turnip boxes still piled up under the tables; river lamprey squirmed and died, grumpy Fritz sang vulgar Great War ditties and baked a tray of raisin *schnecken* for the workers, if he were in a good mood. All was the same in that daily sense. In those days, people could disappear and no one had the courage to ask where. Silence was the norm.

'Apart from me, nothing else wailed that Kurt had disappeared. A new woman worked at the sooty stoves and picked up the fish. She never made eye contact. Where once I feared that there were eyes everywhere, watching me, now was the opposite. Eyes turned from me.'

Hildegard paused. 'This is my favourite cake. Please eat, it'll sweeten my story.'

Stella unravelled her fork from a tightly wound napkin. She stared at the cheesecake and then set down the fork, wondering whether she had the stamina for her coming times.

Hildegard finished her cheesecake. 'I learned the trick of disappearing into the beauty of the architectural line, dreaming of the time when I would be an architect in a new Germany. The government might have been reformed, but if thousands of ordinary Germans had no roof, then their war continued. The aggressors became the victims. You probably know the photos of rubble in the grand boulevards of Berlin, but we also had 10 million refugees and had lost 2.3 million houses.'

In 1952, Hildegard leafed through Brutalist architectural sketches for housing in the reconstruction of Bonn. She slid one out, angled her desk lamp for maximum light and hunched over the late stages of her design for a hundred and thirty families.

'Working late again,' said Erik Walter.

From behind three rows of high, slanting desks, Hildegard observed one of the managers. The overhead fluorescent lights cast a green light over the architecture studio, rendering him washed-out, flattened, like a man back from the dead. He buttoned his old double-breasted winter coat, then locked the under-manager's office and picked up his hinged leather bag. Every night he interrupted her work, always awkward and curt. Hildegard sharpened her pencil.

'Sir, I have only ten days to complete these housing-estate plans.'

'You'll become ill. You work without ceasing.'

Architecture had grown to become her whole life; she asked for nothing more. Herr Walter lingered after work and found numerous excuses to break her concentration: agendas, a new client, the adequacy of winter light, desks too close, too low… and even the role of Brutalism in an historic German city—'Let us not forget Bonn is the city of mighty Beethoven'. He wasted her time. She avoided speaking boldly to the under-manager of the architecture practice, but after hours, she could loosen formality.

'We are all a little ill, sir, the ruin of war hasn't disappeared.'

'So eloquent.'

A strange response. Ironic? Goading? She would not rise to the bait of 'eloquent'.

'Sir, people need decent housing to re-start their lives.'

'Yes, yes, quite…but don't sacrifice yours for theirs. Go out, meet young people. The watchman reports that every night you work late.'

Hildegard placed her pencil in the desk groove. This was personal; it was far more than he usually said.

'Speaking plainly, Herr Walter, I work. I'm grateful for creative, useful, distracting work. I don't expect to get back my youth. Like so many of us, I have a story.'

She studied his face and began. The loss of Kurt haemorrhaged in the telling, as she almost shouted across the studio. He focused on the green linoleum floor, nodding throughout.

'*Frau* Weber, I confess I knew your story. It's tragic and I've wanted to tell you something for a long time.'

Hildegard's heart raced. Herr Walter had been aware of her before she joined the practice? Sweat sprang under her cropped red hair. She blotted her face, smearing crimson lipstick.

His face was solemn. 'I've wanted to speak to you long before you became our newest star.'

Star? His face seemed ever greener as he continued to stand rigidly beneath the central fluorescent tube, his shoulder drooping from the weight of his bag. The light buzzed over the studio, filling their pauses.

'Remarkable to see a talented young woman in a man's field.'

Flirting or bringing her more sad history?

Herr Walter scraped a stool over the floor and set it behind the back rim of her high pine desk. He curled his manicured fingers over the desk ledge, into her lamplight and, for the first time, she saw that the index and middle fingers of his right hand had been broken and re-set crudely. How could she have missed such a painful injury? How did he hold his pencil?

He pulled the stool closer. 'I'm sure you want answers.'

His ghostly face hovered beyond the rim of light. In the banality of the studio, surrounded by pencils and chipped in-trays, would Hildegard at last find out what happened to Kurt? Was it possible after years of fruitless searching and hoping that she would find him alive in a clinic or remote camp? She fidgeted with an eraser and ran her gaze over the latest sketch of the estate balconies. Only five minutes ago, they had made her tranquil as she calculated space for storing mops and children's bikes, but now...

'Do you want answers?' he asked gently. 'Many do not. Germany's still full of secrets.'

'I've looked everywhere, sir. There are no answers for me.'

'Are you ready now?' Herr Walter leaned closer, his chin jutting into the light. 'We admired you, such bravery.'

Hildegard blurted out, 'We?'

'There were four of us in a Masonic Resistance cell.'

She gasped. 'Kurt. A Mason?'

'You didn't know?'

'What? How?'

She shook her head. How could she not have known? There were secrets beyond the promised honesty of a marriage.

'Kurt was our leader.'

'But his studies filled his days; he insisted that study came first.'

'His studies were an effective mask until they weren't.'

Herr Walter bit his lower lip. 'We applauded you; who else would have had the daring to swipe maps from Hitler's room?'

Hildegard felt light-headed. 'You know what happened to Kurt. You know!'

He nodded, hesitant and sombre. He glanced at the door, perhaps wondering whether he should have departed as usual. Everyone had been exhausted by grief; who could shoulder any more or cause any more?

Looking and waiting had calcified in her body, but now, at last, she stood on the cusp of knowing. Architecture was the only vestige of her old being that she had salvaged from the war. All the rest of her being had been sucked into the void of not knowing. Herr Walter spoke as she grappled with the monumentality of the end of waiting.

'Such courage. He was taken to the Gestapo at the local police station.'

'I guessed! I asked the next day, but the officer in charge said that he had not been there.'

'Local police stations in those days were gateways to a hellish netherworld.'

'I went also to the railway station. People everywhere, but no Kurt. After a while, I asked our friends, most discreetly. He was deported?'

'No, but that might have saved him.'

She gave herself a few more seconds of her eleven years of frail hope built on not knowing. A car moved slowly in the street. She heard herself swallow.

'He was shot?'

There…she'd said it aloud for the first time. She had never even whispered it, not even to her mother or Kurt's grief-struck family. A hundred thousand times her body had lived the slump of Kurt collapsing on the cobbles of an execution yard. Alone? With others? A few moments of consciousness.

Her hands cradled her head. The world upside down, blood spurting from his chest, and then his beautiful young body tossed on a truck and dumped in a communal ditch.

'Immense courage. I was in the next cell, but the SS never connected me to him or, I should say, Kurt never allowed them to. He protected his wolf pack.'

Wolf? Wolf? No, he was a Greek god, Archaic and mysterious. Hildegard wept silently, tears smearing her face in the blast of the lamp.

'He was tortured all night,' said Erik. 'I could hear it. He didn't let them connect anyone to him. Yes, he screamed, but mostly not. He was not in their clutches for long; his fortitude was obvious even to cowards.'

Herr Walter leaned across the desk and touched her elbow. 'Can you bear for me to go on?'

Hildegard nodded, a screech threatening to rip apart the studio.

'He was shot around lunchtime the next day.'

'The time I visited.'

The sketch flapped off Hildegard's desk, a twisted scroll on the floor among drifts of dust. Through tears she watched it roll and be still. Unbearable... Kurt, young and idealistic, bleeding, dying on the cobbles. Unendurable, although she had always known that was how it had ended, that no matter how long she waited or who finally told her, this would be Kurt's end—murdered—a word she would need to use if she were not to continue the false language that had led a nation astray.

'But why was Kurt—murdered? I took the maps. This doesn't make sense. Anton gave me a message; he did not give one to Kurt.'

Herr Walter shrugged. 'His cell was betrayed.'

'But I had the message...and I was not in a Resistance cell.'

'Remember the Concerned German Citizens?'

Herr Walter suddenly leaned his whole face into the brilliant desk light and caught her eyes sympathetically. 'I'm infinitely sorry. It was war...the country had fully mobilised; people were afraid, ripping at each other. A slight advantage for a better life, especially for more ration cards, a *sotto voce* word at the right time, in the right ear— '

'But he was so recently a weak schoolboy,' said Hildegard, 'and then he was fighting Nazi evil. It was too much.'

'All transactions were embedded in reckoning for and against each other. People calculated craftily every day.'

'Kurt did not.'

'Not Kurt. He dedicated his heroism and idealism to protecting people, but he was nearly hysterical when he arrived at the station. Screaming your name.'

She gathered up the fallen draft and brushed off the dust. Her name, 'Hildegard'. That is what he said.

'I heard it from my prison cell. The beautiful, ancient name, "Hildegard", could be heard all over the basement of the police station. Hildegard of Bingen and her music... Hildegard the Valkyrie who guided heroes on their way to Valhalla... Hildegard so brave in the Resistance and now rebuilding Germany, brick by brick.'

Hildegard brushed the dusty draft paper until her pencil marks smudged, her grief pouring into the repetitive arm action.

'His focus was on you, *Frau* Weber. He convinced the Gestapo torturers that you had not taken the maps. He yelled in snatches during the night. "Far too obvious for my wife to have taken them... credit where it is due!...I crept in while she cleaned the Fuhrer's bathroom; you know he likes a powerful waterjet. So noisy..."'

'It was not like that.'

'No. You took the maps; I always knew. Kurt had rehearsed for torture. It was part of his plan for us all.'

'Imagine, planning for torture,' said Hildegard. She took two deep breaths and signalled for more orange juice. 'Planning not to protect yourself, but others, not only me, but his Resistance team, Anton, Erik and Magdalena. Such resolution and valour.'

'Valour?' said Stella. 'He had a Resistance team without telling you, his wife? That's shocking.'

Slowly, Hildegard shook her head. Questions burned Stella's mouth. She curled her fingers into the old woman's dry palm and they sat in silence while a party of teenagers scraped chairs and shouted drinks orders.

She asked as gently as she could over more noise, 'Did you ever discover why Kurt wanted the maps?'

'Erik himself did not know because of the rules of secrecy.'

'If you don't know why Kurt wanted the maps, then you don't know why you lost him?'

She winced asking that cold-blooded question; it was harsh after all these years of Hildegard's fidelity.

'You are strong to ask,' said Hildegard. 'Few have dared, not even Mama. Even Erik was uncertain about the maps, but he suspected that the red pencil writing would have given clues to a code.

'I brooded for eleven years but then discovered that from the beginning, the narrative was not as I had understood it. I had mourned inside a mistaken story. I had cast myself in another role, and Kurt too. So strange that his friends saw him as the leader of a wolf pack...'

'You had to learn a new story and a new kind of mourning.'

'Yes, but I was still married to Kurt, nothing changed. In that fact, I still knew myself. I'm still married to Kurt.'

Stella baulked at saying the bitter words, but they had piled up like scrap lead between them.

'But he used you...betrayed you.'

Hildegard shook her head calmly and deliberately. 'It is difficult for someone imbued with Hollywood romance to grasp another kind of romantic love, one that could encompass others, even as it imperilled the two at the heart of the drama. Can you see that big picture of humanity?'

Hildegard saw Stella's bewilderment; she took her hand and rubbed the biggest welt.

'Kurt was a valiant man. He sacrificed himself for others.'

'A terrible moral ambiguity.' Stella frowned. 'I think I understand; his identity was being a good citizen.'

'Kurt got Magdalena to ask me to take the maps. She was a woman and, therefore, could not be a Mason, but she was connected to Anton. This was Kurt's way of protecting us both.'

Stella ripped her hand away. 'That was not protection!'

She saw the wry look on Hildegard's face as she, Stella, her friend from another nation and another generation, struggled to understand. Hildegard had had seventy years to accustom herself to the story, but only a perverted world would call Kurt's bizarre actions 'protection'. Hildegard had been in peril and ignorance.

She had tried to protect Kurt, ironically, the person who had exposed her to danger.

'Kurt put you in a chain of likely death, in the *Fuhrersuite*, of all accursed places. He should have put you first.'

The old woman shrugged, as if she had shrugged countless times in the same perplexing conversation.

'Should he, Stella? Should he? There were people beyond me.'

Stella considered the cold, rational, utilitarian calculation. Where was love? Love should make life simpler, but if she revealed Costa's violent images to the police David would lose his mother. What duty did she have to the Islamic students if, in trying to protect them, she harmed her son? Emotion needed a place somewhere, but it muddied thinking.

'Does that make a difference in his duty to you? Are there times to abandon a loved one?'

Hildegard fiddled with her wedding ring, worn flat and thin over more than seventy years. 'These were not ordinary times; the stakes were the highest possible.'

'He saw himself and you as husband and wife, but with a greater good to be had beyond your marriage?' Stella had to say it. 'That's hard.'

'Some days it's still hard, but I have accepted it.'

Hildegard drank the last of her coffee and waved for the waitress. 'I have a way to explain. You remember that we saw the manuscript of *Moonlight Sonata* with my dear Neo?'

The inspiration and humiliation of the day flashed through Stella. 'Of course.'

'The name makes me think of how Kurt might have weighed up the different parts of his life. *Mondscheinsonate—Moonlight Sonata* was the German code name for the 1940 bombing of Coventry. Historians are undecided whether Prime Minister Churchill knew in advance. One line of thinking is that he chose not to protect the city, so that his actions would not also reveal that the Allies could decrypt German codes.'

'A famous moral dilemma.'

Like the dilemma that she found herself in, but she could never champion the good of the numerically greater Islamic students over her own child's health and happiness. She understood that now as she sat in the café; there was no debate.

More water arrived; Hildegard pushed a glass to Stella and quickly finished hers. 'It's possible that he let the people of Coventry suffer terribly so that, in the long run, more people would live. If that were the thinking of the British Prime Minister, it would have found an echo in the philosophy of my Kurt. I know he wanted to apply this way of thinking to his future in medicine. It seemed ominous; I see now that he warned me.'

Kurt, so young, and leading his even younger wife into his tough philosophy—the conscientiousness amazed Stella. Did such people exist today in a world of instant gratification?

The door opened and three people entered. A cloud of fresh, cool air rolled into the café's dry chill; Stella breathed in the long-awaited shift in temperature.

Absently, Hildegard resumed stroking the contusions on Stella's inner arm. 'It was painful, but over the years I began to understand how he must have been compelled morally to take the opportunity when I became a maid in that hotel. It only looked like a betrayal if I did not think it through.'

Her kind hand soothed Stella's spirit. Someone cared, but Stella felt like a pariah. Hildegard had waited more than a decade for answers, so long that you would expect never to know. And David? What answers would she find?

'Dear Erik—Herr Walter—became a lifelong friend,' said Hildegard. 'He accompanied me to the police courtyard to see where Kurt died; this was his loss too. Bullet holes had been patched. So many. I could feel the roughness, the sandy spill-over of the new cement beneath my fingertips. The wall was pale yellow, but the cement was dark grey, as if no one cared to do the repair properly. The same cobbles are in the police courtyard today as we have in the streets of my Bonn. I see them everywhere—the same...'

Stella looked at the gentle old hand patting her torn skin. The same fingers had caressed the bullet holes while she wondered, which ones...?

'Erik died one week ago. Forgive me, Stella, I have been talking to you as I would have to him. I need to tell my story again and again to survive it. Knowing that Erik knew my story, and his own part in it, was mostly enough. I am not crazy, trapped in the past, eager, as you say, "for closure and moving on". Forgetting is not an option for me; it would be like severing a limb.'

'I always saw you were sad,' said Stella.

'In the past twenty years, Erik and I met nearly every day by the Rhine and sat on the same bench that you and I shared. I miss him. But then *you* were waiting for me in the park. You and Neo have helped me get through these days. Neo cancelled three concerts and flew from New York.

'Do you see that Erik completed my story? I knew that Kurt had been arrested, but not what happened next for eleven draining years. But now it is as if I have lost Kurt all over again. Erik was my last golden link to him.'

So Erik was a new loss. Hildegard had recounted her history in a heatwave to a stranger and would never have been able to forget, not even for a day. Stella knew memory's trap.

Hildegard spoke in a reverie, dragging herself back to the mid-century architecture studio.

'Erik was an awkward man, talented with a pencil despite his tortured fingers, but halting with words. He had suffered himself, two years in prison. He had not known how to tell me about Kurt. When he did, he told me how Kurt had agonised over involving me without warning. My young husband could find no other way to help the Resistance. It was not a betrayal.'

'Why tell you after all of the years that you searched for Kurt?'

Maybe Hildegard would have been happier to have continued to inhabit her original story; the new truth was too hard.

'Erik had his own tragedies. His wife and twin baby sons died in British bombing of Cologne. Erik was maddened by grief. My story was my story, only on the edge of his.'

Stella and Hildegard got up to leave as the café owner opened the door to catch the first cool breeze in a week. A few fat rain drops sizzled on the cobbles here and there; a child stuck out her tongue. Waiters set out rush chairs on the cobbles under green-and white-striped umbrellas. Hildegard wrapped Stella's uneaten cheesecake in a paper napkin and gave it to her.

'Eat it later; it will make you feel better. And get disinfectant for your arms today.' She pointed to a pharmacy. 'Take care of yourself, David and Peter.'

Hildegard prepared to leave, but Stella was not ready; she held on to Hildegard's thin arm, watching drops splash her wrist.

'Godspeed, dear Stella.'

'Please wait.'

Stella jogged to a nearby flower stall and was confronted by roses, daisies and exuberant white lilies, the same type of lilies with the nauseating pollen from the night of Alexander's attack. She mulled over the choice and then scooped up the largest bouquet of lily blooms with their speckled red throats and dashes of pollen. Quickly, she paid and hurried back.

'For you, dearest Hildegard. Thank you for everything.'

Hildegard smiled and then embraced her in a long, tight hug. She plunged into the crowd emerging in the wonder of a cool evening. Soon the nodding lilies and the tap of the walking stick were lost and the wise woman had vanished.

Stella thought of being halfway through life and not knowing herself. Of having seen herself with lying and murderous faces that would take the rest of her life to come to terms with. Her immediate task was to care for David. Then she must crack her veneer of professor and, at last, confront the malevolent alien. Mother, scholar, criminal… Maybe she had always had the potential to stalk and poison. One bully and one seat, that was all that it took.

Hildegard had not looked back; she was gone. Tourists in Martinsplatz assembled for a group photograph behind the martyrs' heads. The photographer snapped away. The tourists horsed about, sitting on Florentius and Cassius, pretending to kiss the huge granite lips. Many of them made the V sign. Stella did not know what it meant.

She was like the sole survivor of a bombing raid. Stupefied, ears ringing, coated in masonry filth. She dragged herself from the rubble—clothes shredded, shoes missing. She rubbed grime from her eyes and took a bare footstep, only to collapse into a bomb crater beside a young man's body. The worst had happened. No head in the eucalyptus garden. No one reached down to help. The crater sides were precipitous, friable. She stretched up to the lip.

THIRTY-ONE

In 1980, ten-year-old Stella ran across huge granite boulders on Nanarup Beach.

'Hey, Dad, it's my favourite place in the whole world.'

She stretched out her arms, arching into the uplift of the wind. Dad took a photo of the skinny kid in the big sun hat with bare feet on the hot, smooth stone. Mum sun-bathed by the picnic basket. Stella's two younger brothers licked runnels of chocolate ice-cream from their forearms.

'There's no one in the garden,' he shouted. 'Forget your nightmares, have fun.'

Stella giggled and scampered off to the last of the great rocks, twenty metres wide of pale, dappled, orangey-cream stone; beyond was the crescent of the empty white beach and the suck and swell of the Southern Ocean. She lay on her stomach, toes hooked over a crack in the rock, sensing rough warmth through her T-shirt and shorts.

Near the end of winter, boulders on the edge of the Southern Ocean were cold; the chill seeped through Stella's jeans, and wind buffeted the anoraks and thick scarves that muffled her and Peter. The bright sun belied the briskness of late-August. Decades later, Stella remembered that day with her father as she sat holding Peter's hand on a vast slab of rock that ran in flat, contiguous ledges and dropped to the hammering ocean.

In the distance, Bertie sniffed dune grasses while David moved idly across the boulders, stooping to squint into long, shadowed splits that suggested a giant tiled floor. His blue jacket advanced and retreated across the orangey stone. Stella remembered blue and orange as colour wheel opposites, satisfying, complementary. She slid her phone out of the sun.

'He'll be ok,' said Peter.

'What can we do to make sure? I'm due back at work in six weeks.'

'With both of us working part-time, we'll have a good safety net around him and us. We're with him; that's what the psych says is best. Quiet, loving parenting.'

Peter rubbed his thumb gently on the fading, crimson welts on the back of Stella's hand and wrist, and lifted her fingertips to his lips. He had often looked at her scars, but never asked about them. She had neither hidden them nor explained.

The rocks still looked as they had when she was a child, like hunched dinosaurs tumbling down to the giant space of the deserted beach. Discarded seagull nests cartwheeled over the rocks, and tufts of tenacious plants found enough soil, here and there, to flourish in the salt and ceaseless wind. It was weird not to have the chronic pressure of academic work, to have given up ambition beyond a professorship, for a while, at least. Peter had slashed his surgery hours and seemed content. Stella scratched in a deep crack and exposed a tiny plant peeping above the grit of sand and smashed shell.

Abjection and dislocation framed the person she had become

for a few days in Germany, but bad faith to Justine was worse than what she had done to Costa. Emails from Vancouver had shrunk to being merely business-like with not a peek about Justine's baby daughter.

What would be the point of confessing about Costa? Another person goes to prison, a titillating news story for a few days, a disgrace that David and Peter would also suffer. Why more punishment when the worst in her life had happened? She was punished.

'But David was listless at dinner last night.'

'He's missing his friends,' said Peter.

'The psych said to give him a break from them, but he's always texting them, never stops.',

Peter nodded towards David. 'Not now. No phone.'

David crouched near the boulders where the dune grasses whipped about; Bertie snuffled into his elbow. Wind swept David's hair off his forehead and crushed his blue jacket against his chest. He concentrated, his shoulders relaxed. Stella had not seen him so absorbed for a long time.

'Flowers, even here.' Peter pointed to balls of pink petals shaking in the stiff ocean breeze.

David loped further down the rock ledge, laughing as salt spray shot up.

'Hmm,' said Stella. 'We'll always be the people who survived their child's suicide attempt. Life will always be before David was in the garage and after he was in the garage.'

The price of fighting back against a Nigel, an Alexander, a Costa had been her child. And yet, it had felt sensational to have the upper hand—thrilling, here and there. Nigel would never again get away with his petty powerplays. Remnant fiery energy swept through her. What a life-and-death battle it had been to get to this point. She squirmed, remembering her loss of control on the train platform, the day she had not killed the bully—but could have.

Costa was far from dead. That morning she had checked his Facebook page and discovered news of a forthcoming retirement party in a Roman palace. At least he would no longer have predatory access to students. There was something good in her dishonour; she would cling to that. She would never again cower before another Costa. She would stand her ground at the first hint of aggression.

And Peter? Something had changed in him too. His face looked gentler; he listened carefully. His silence was companionable.

David waved to them from the edge of the rocks. Stella waved back and held Peter's hand tighter.

'These days you never park in the garage, no matter the weather,' said Peter. 'You never will again—am I right? We should move house, a fresh start for everybody. In a new place you can be a new person.'

Stella remembered grief-stricken Hildegard setting out to provide housing among millions of lost people.

David stood. 'Mum! Dad! Come and see. Baby birds.'

Ring! Peter's head jerked towards Stella. Stella stared at photo caller ID—the Dean of Humanities.

AUTHOR NOTE

M Y FASCINATION WITH the past in our everyday lives led me to write this novel and a PhD thesis on theories of cultural heritage. In fiction, I write about characters who move through historic landscapes and experience the multiple pasts as force fields emanating from ordinary places in daily life. I am from Western Australia and live in Seattle, USA. My website can be found at jenniferharriswriter.com

I hope you enjoyed this book. Please leave a review.

I am grateful to my writing mentor CM (Craig) Taylor and those who read the manuscript at various stages of the writing, Amanda Saint, Ann Leander and Joel Gilman.

READING GROUP QUESTIONS

DUAL TIMELINES

A 'braided novel' weaves together two or more narratives. *The Devil Comes to Bonn* has dual timelines and dual stories. The 1941 and 2015 stories refract each other. What does each story say about the other?

Do you think that the stories of Hildegard and Stella mirror each other?

What is the significance of the Roman martyr story? What is its relationship to the two main stories?

Does reading a braided novel dilute the reader's attachment to the key characters? Does it make the reading experience richer?

GENDER

The novel was inspired partly by the #MeToo movement and its power to remind us of everyday gendered violence and bullying of women. Discuss #MeToo in relation to the story.

Was it an accident that Peter's actions resulted in Stella's arm breaking?

Does the world of the book appear to lay blame on Stella for David's self-harming?

MORAL AMBIGUITY

Was Kurt fair to his wife?

Was Stella right to act against Costa if no one else did?

Is it sometimes right to take the law into your own hands?

Is there a moral duty to act if doing so will endanger ourselves and / or those close to us?

Is Kurt more like a wolf or a Greek god?

WORLD WAR II

Some of the action takes place in a historic hotel that Hitler visited many times; room 106 exists today. Discuss the blending of fiction with verifiable historical fact.

Most readers are not historians; they experience history through narratives on screen and in novels. What do you think of the role of historical novels as a way of engaging with history?

There have been hundreds of World War II stories. Are the events of the war so significant that more can continue to explain that period and enrich our cultures?

CHARACTERS

Stella stalks Costa and yet is shocked when he accuses her of doing this. Why does she have difficulty comprehending what she is doing?

Does Costa stalk Stella or is he an opportunist?

Have you met bullies like Costa?

Hildegard appears never to put the past behind her. Why?

What is the role of the Italian students?

Why does Stella think often of Caravaggio's paintings?

Eva is depicted as a Nazi in her Band of German Maidens' uniform. How would you characterise Marta?

Africans—Neo from Botswana and Takura from Zimbabwe—appear when Stella is in crisis? What is their role?

African men are contrasted to Caucasian men—what are the effects of this?

MEMORY

What is the role of memory in this novel?

Is there a moral element in memory?

Is there a duty to remember dark pasts?

What is the role of World Heritage listing?

The Korean-Japanese dispute highlights some World Heritage problems. Is there a time to forget the collective past for the sake of harmonious contemporary relationships? Can we do this if issues are not resolved?

How should we respond if memory is an unbearable personal burden?

How does collective memory (e.g. of the Koreans' wartime experience) differ from personal memory (e.g. Hildegard's and Stella's)?

LANDSCAPE AND WEATHER

Hildegard says that the River Rhine links different times. Discuss the narrative role of the Rhine.

What is the role of the heatwave?

Birds appear throughout the novel; how do you interpret them?